THE
RAG & BONE
MAN

About the Author

Lee Morgan is hugely privileged to live on a communal homestead in Kunanyi/Mt Wellington, where he creates a sanctuary for other weirdos, raises books, people, and ideas from the grave. He has had novels, non-fiction, and papers published by Collective Ink Books, Three Hands Press, Witches Almanac, and Rebel Satori, with his most recent books being *People of the Outside: Witchcraft, Cannibalism, and the Elder Folk* and *The Gusty Deep*, a paean to the trickster Robin Goodfellow. Highlights of his career have involved speaking about his books at Watkins Books in London, receiving an Australian Post-Graduate award where he got paid to research, and participating an artwork called The People's Library in Tasmania.

Having survived an enormous tumour, where surgeons warned his intellect might be impacted, and a series of further complications, Lee is currently busy filling the fresh room in his skull with new brains. His time is taken up by research, working on the property, and spawning a writing that cross-pollinates in hybrid, monstrous ways with all other art-forms. He is greatly blessed with an incredible support network, especially in his immediate coven brothers and sisters. And with the presence of a kelpie rescue dog named Clementine, who doesn't perform any of the working dog jobs one might have hoped for, but is loved despite this fact.

LEE MORGAN

THE RAG & BONE MAN

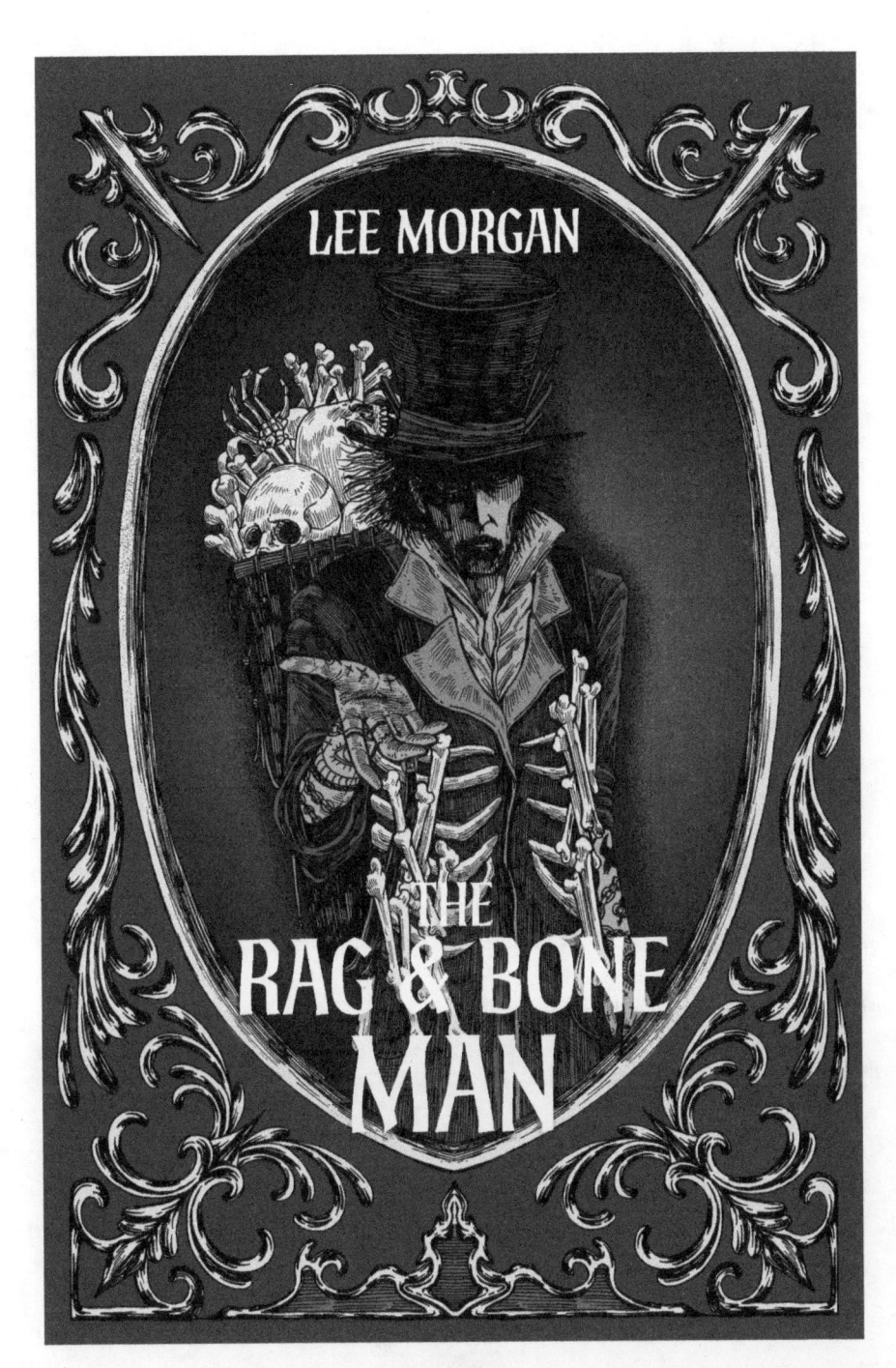

Chicago, IL

The Rag & Bone Man 2025 by Lee Morgan. All rights reserved. No part of this book may be reproduced in any manner whatsoever without written permission from Crossed Crow Books, except in the case of brief quotations embodied in critical articles and reviews.

Paperback ISBN: 978-1-964537-52-8
Hardcover ISBN: 978-1-964537-71-9
E-Book ISBN: 978-1-968185-41-1

Library of Congress Control Number on file.

Disclaimer: Crossed Crow Books, LLC does not participate in, endorse, or have any authority or responsibility concerning private business transactions between our authors and the public. Any internet references contained in this work were found to be valid during the time of publication, however, the publisher cannot guarantee that a specific reference will continue to be maintained. This book's material is not intended to diagnose, treat, cure, or prevent any disease, disorder, ailment, or any physical or psychological condition. The author, publisher, and its associates shall not be held liable for the reader's choices when approaching this book's material. The views and opinions expressed within this book are those of the author alone and do not necessarily reflect the views and opinions of the publisher.

Published by:
Crossed Crow Books, LLC
518 Davis St, Suite 205
Evanston, IL 60201
www.crossedcrowbooks.com

Printed in the United States of America.
IBI

Other Books by Lee Morgan:

A Deed Without a Name:
Unearthing the Legacy of Traditional Witchcraft

Sounds of Infinity:
Traditional Witchcraft and the Faerie Faith

Standing and Not Falling:
A Sorcerous Primer in Thirteen Moons

The Bones Would Do

The Gusty Deep

People of the Outside:
Witchcraft, Cannibalism, and the Elder Folk

Wooing the Echo

An Acknowledgment of Country

This work was written on land that belongs to the Muwinina people. Despite theft, disease, and displacement, they persist. The ancestors and emerging ones always were, and always will be. They pulse away in the rock, throb away in the ferns, breathe whenever the air stirs. Sometimes when it's misty, they are closer, even, than that.

Table of Contents

Preface · XI

Part I - Of the Head · 1

Part II - Of the Heart · 19

Part III - Of the Hands · 263

PREFACE

THE HAUNTOLOGY OF THINGS

*"Old kettles, old bottles, and a broken can,
Old iron, old bones, old rags, that raving slut
Who keeps the till. Now that my ladder's gone
I must lie down where all the ladders start
In the foul rag and bone shop of the heart."*

—W.B Yeats

Welcome to a story that has a head, a heart, and two workable hands. We have come here to become possessed by the word-spell of Victorian Age inspired sorcery with, and for, the dead. First we must understand it, allowing it to reach our conscious mind, then we must feel it exquisitely, letting it burn its way into our heart. Then it will take flesh-root in us, as we experience how our somatic experiences burn their way into us—and ink us like a tattoo. This book is an expression of nineteenth-century witchcraft, mediumship, theory, and praxis (not in any particular order).

In my previous book *Sounds of Infinity: Traditional Witchcraft and the Faerie Faith* we went on a similar journey of three separate interwoven parts. Beyond this similarity, this book won't be anything like that one. Stories are complicated and often a needy, wrangling presence in one's life. They congregate with others of their kind but are always ready to try to show you why they are the best one to ingest. We always need to digest a new story if we are going to bring about lasting sorcerous change in our lives. One can see from examples like the history of the faerie witch Bessie Dunlop that the first sorcerous act a familiar offers to do for the witch is usually one that helps said witch.

Just as one must hold the oxygen mask over one's own face in an airplane emergency in order to be able to help others, it is often the same with magical power. Unless you activate yours first, others will hold no benefit from your sacrifice or the weakness that follows. This is a thing I know from experience.

The book I'm offering you is an artwork, one that I need your help to turn into a reality. Only through engaging your mind, your heart, and finally your hands, can this Work become something real in this world, something visceral, bloody, and manifest. Thus, it is an art, as well as an artwork, that you just became a part of. So, welcome, if you'd like to come in?

Here in my parlour we can sit down together—uncomfortably close at times, during the strongest parts of the story. By red light we will weave through some of the Virtue of a period where a lot of our modern witchcraft ladders get started. Through stealing the Fat from the previous era (one that still exists inside us in the presence of our own great-grandparents), we can nourish ourselves here in this one. As selfish as that act may sound, you will find that all of us feasted on the bodies of our great-great-grandparents just by being born. Mostly, they don't begrudge it. They do like to be remembered though. Even their ladders came from other ladders—ones that all wear the torn rags and gnaw on the bones of earlier times, in the great ongoing sacrifice we call parenthood.

Here, where many of the ladders start, we are able to refresh ourselves at some of the root-systems of modern witchcraft, as if history were the Fat in the butter and the cream we are skimming from the dead with our living hands. We will claim this fat-of-the-land via the crucial witchcraft art of Paying Attention. This skill is important to every pickpocket, every juggler, every practitioner of stage magic, or the kind that a real sorcerer might do to win trust—a kind of necessary cheat. A fox-whiskered gentleman indeed, this power, one that also knows how to teach us to direct and hold the attention of others.

The importance of the hauntology, or the ghostly presence of the previous era in our own, is manifestly crucial to our endeavour. By engaging in this work, with our true feeling-life, as well as our hands, we are also feeding the ghosts of that previous era, ones that are howling in people's aching joints and in our stretched ligaments, haunting particular organs or whole body systems, rising up as a contagious sickness in our midst. They've always been there, and we have no guarantee they will stop. Particularly the Othered and the silenced, and the forgotten among them who have scores to settle. Their screams are louder voices jumping back at us, because they were made quiet in the living world.

Help me to make some new soap and candles from the gatherings of the forgotten, from the sack contents of the Rag and Bone Man, would you? And if you do, you will learn why a necromancer or a medium needs to be a hollowed bone. In an emergency, they should even be able to pass themselves off as one of the dead. You may need this skill one day. You will know something

PREFACE

new about witchcraft as a revolutionary force when you join your awareness to those of the forgotten.

They rise like a rude little push from a ghost, a poltergeist-style assault with a deathly touch. You are dead; you are therefore the fox, the trickster, you will help to bring through more of the Virtue of the previous era's forgotten by going down many a crooked alleyway. I will hold hands with you while we do it. We will both make mistakes that turn out not to be mistakes, but the teaching-intent of something greater than ourselves. Something we might call a "story." Despite the fact the mistakes won't be our fault, we must own up to them anyway to become free of them. A heretical style of confession.

My parlour is lit with red, evocative of the bowers sex workers. It helps to remind you that we are going inside the body. You see red as a foetus sees it through the mother's skin. You are inside yourself. You are one of the forgotten. I climb inside my velvet shroud, séance-red, to bring through the whisperings and slimy ectoplasm of the past. Please, as you take a seat, prepare your mind, prepare your heart, whatever things it has seen before this moment. There is no greater or lesser in this space. Just people here for a wild experience of reverberation. People ready to experience a particular species of Knowing that is what might we call it? A bit different?

PART I

OF THE HEAD

The Mesmerist's Watch

"In those days the dead manifested as muslin, stained and smelly from the psychic's body cavities. The dead were packed within you, so you coughed or vomited them, or drew them out of your generative organs."

—Hilary Mantel[1]

Somewhere in the nineteenth century, a change gestated that caused the modern occult movement to be born. You could explain it like an academic, pick it apart, reference to reasons why it happened. Part of it was more mysterious than this, though; this part you could only explain to another occultist. There was a readiness making something of itself, something brewing beneath the consciousness line in the collective mind. It was in the next generation when someone would first call it the "unconscious mind," and here we are trying to imagine a world without an unconscious…

We could talk about the birth of the term folklore, one that has suckled us moderns with all the material that caused the growth of folkloric witchcraft. The word *folklore* itself was coined in 1846 by William Thoms.[2] The coming-about of the term revealed something, a new kind of self-consciousness, a sense that now fully manifested itself in us with the innocent intent to study ourselves. Oddly, this self-consciousness had a lot to do with science and a weird space that opened up at the beginning of the concept of science. It happened back when the telegraph was seen by some as words appearing from the Otherworld, where séances reigned supreme in the hands of a post-Charles-Darwin's-evolution sort

---

[1] Hilary Mantel, Beyond Black: A Novel (Fourth Estate, 2006).
[2] Martha Sims and Martine Stephens, *Living Folklore* (Utah State University Press, 2011) 23.

of world.[3] In this world, the role of the body changed; it became infiltrated by a story with apes in it, the natural locale of the primal, and the haunted ground of all the ghosts of the past that were suddenly beginning to pour out from the orifices of mediums.

Years ago, in a book called *Hands of Apostasy*, I wrote about how I see the soul of modern witchcraft as first having been kindled in the hearths, imaginations, and hearts of the people.[4] I argued, that the soul of our witchcraft movement is still essentially of the Romantic Age, part of an early nineteenth-century upsurge of beauty, strangeness, and our perception of wild instinct. These forces were trying to match their stride with industry, the enclosure of common land, and the breaking up of traditional communities, when people went to cities to work and lost contact with the places their ancestors had lived and died in for centuries. This mournful soul-song is still part of who we are today, regardless of whether we class ourselves as pagan or find ourselves locked in a dervish with some other form of witchcraft.

Here I want to conjure forth not just the soul but the actual embryo of the body of witchcraft as it developed into the current age. It makes a kind of sense that the embryo should be made up of ectoplasm. To do this, we must explore the Victorian Age. This, I would argue, is where, as W.B. Yeats would put it, all the ladders of the rag and bone shop start. There is a whole way of seeing the world behind the notion of folklore that reflected a change in people's way of seeing, but also in turn began to itself change people's way of seeing the world. It was part of what Ronald Hutton called a "trickle-up effect," where concerns of the poor were romanticised and drifted upward in society—into this relatively new, newspaper- and book-reading middle class.

This later part of the nineteenth century gave us Spiritualism. The spirit medium was usually a woman, but there were plenty of men as well, and it rested upon an unspoken return of the carnal. Tappings and rapping on tables, the movement of objects such as lifted tables, and the excreting of ectoplasm from the flesh; these were all very tangible signs of the presence of ghosts. In his book about the dead, Claude Lecouteux spoke of how the ghosts of the dead were once seen as quite physical.[5] Lecouteux's book famously reminds us that only five hundred years ago there was a world where the bodies of the

---

3 Julia Philips, *Witchcraft and the Fourth Estate in Victorian Britain* (University of Bristol Thesis, 2022) 137.
4 Lee Morgan, "Literary and Folk Cross-Pollination in the Nineteenth Century: Exploring the Romantic Age roots of British Witchcraft," *Hands of Apostasy* (Three Hands Press, 2014).
5 Claude Lacouteux, *The Return of the Dead: Ghosts, Ancestors and the Transparent Veil of the Pagan Mind* (Inner Traditions, 2009).

dead—their ghost bodies—were looked on as far more substantial and chunky than we see ghosts as being today.

It was a spectre of that earlier time that bounced back upon us in the form of Spiritualism. A kind of mass, an unconscious invitation to the body springing up from the Underworld. The carnal life of the dead returned through the bodies of mediums. Even if it was heralded by fake noises produced by the Fox sisters—Maggie, Kate, and Leah—it was the right moment for such an arrival. Fakes of the real became a big part of this era. Take the Cottingley Fairies for example; they were a fake of a real event that the girls weren't able to capture, and the question of truth with the Fox sisters is also complicated.[6]

One of the methods the Fox sisters claimed to use to make fake rapping sounds was the cracking of their own joints. This was enough to please the sceptics who had legally hounded and tested them, but it did not account for a number of other phenomena that went far beyond rapping. Such examples included the relocation of a bell from a locked study where other people were in that room and witnessed nothing, phosphorescent manifestations, and the extensive tests carried out by the scientist William Crookes who said of Kate Fox:

> *Moreover, actual contact is not always necessary; I have had these sounds proceeding from the floor, walls, etc., when the medium's hands and feet were held—when she was standing on a chair—when she was suspended in a swing from the ceiling—when she was enclosed in a wire cage—and when she had fallen fainting on a sofa. I have heard them on a glass harmonicon—I have felt them on my own shoulder and under my own hands. I have heard them on a sheet of paper, held between the fingers by a piece of thread passed through one corner…by a pre-arranged code of signals, questions are answered, and messages given with more or less accuracy.*[7]

All of his tests involved multiple witnesses and attempted to prevent fraud. He recorded one of the mediums bringing through two different messages whilst being in relaxed conversation at the same time. There was unseen writing done in front of witnesses that appeared both back-to-front and written from right-to-left, in the back-to-front way of the dead. None of this is surprising

---

[6] "Fairies, Phantoms, and Fantastic Photographs," *World of Strange Powers,* from Arthur C. Clarke, Anna Ford. 22 May 1985.

[7] William Crookes, "Notes of an Inquiry into the Phenomena called Spiritual" in *Quarterly Journal of Science 4,* 1874, 77–97, https://play.google.com/books/reader?id=Mu1fAAAAcAAJ&pg=GBS.PP4&hl=en.

for a couple of girls who used to address the poltergeist in their home as "Old Splitfoot"!

The movement that spread from the Fox sisters was linked directly to people involved in the movement for the abolition of slavery and equal rights for women. This element of radicalism at the core might explain why Spiritualism was later linked to orgies and sexual license. The fleshiness of magic was rising, with a sudden post-Darwin, primate tang to it. Another thing that makes this era the place where so many witchcraft ladders start is an odd one: "…spiritualism was a remarkable global phenomenon that appeared in Victorian Britain and the Commonwealth following its founding in the USA in 1848. Its popularity was significantly enhanced by extensive coverage in the press."[8]

The huge explosion of print media—in the hands of a large number of people who could suddenly read it—meant that information could range further and crash into new locations. The print press was also responsible for Spiritualism finding its way to popularity here in Australia, leading to the South Australian Registry talking about Spiritualism in the news as early as 1850, only two years after it began.[9] We can witness these far-ranging, Springheel Jack-like stories from things like the popular children's rhyme: "Are you a witch or are you a faerie or are you the wife of Michael Cleary?"[10] This chant was said in Australia, among other places, but it is based on the Victorian Age murder of the Irish woman Bridget Cleary. She was believed to be a changeling whose husband set fire to her in an attempt to drive the faerie possession out.

As a story, the sensationalism had far greater reach in an age of trains and newspapers than it would have done prior to them. Information started moving quicker and more people knew how to read it than ever before. When it comes to the movement of witchcraft and devil-focused narratives like Springheel Jack, we can understand that these local stories were no longer going to stay entirely local for long. Mix mass information with what a lot of people like to call "superstition," and we see examples of jumping stories. Ones where Springheel Jack can appear in London, then in Scotland, Liverpool, Lincolnshire, and eventually Prague!

This story-jumping brought on by the newspapers impacted lore about witches and devils on a large scale. Much of this lore might have been said

---

[8] Julia Phillips, *Witchcraft and the Fourth Estate in Victorian Britain:* submitted to the University of Bristol in accordance with the requirements for award of the degree of Doctor of Philosophy in the Faculty of Arts, School of Humanities, 2022, 162.
[9] Phillips, *Ibid.,* 153.
[10] Springheel Jack was a famous apparition or devilish man who spat blue fire and could leap nine feet in the air. He reportedly appeared in London during this era and was also popularised in newspapers. This story is very typical of the folklore of the Victorian Age, as it mingles faerie lore, witness reports, and perhaps even a touch of mass hysteria.

to be sacredly local—as in, deeply attached through stories and practices to places and sacred sites. It's easy to imagine some local customs mixing between convicts, here in an Australian gaol, where one person might bring knowledge of mummified cats and another a witch bottle. But sometimes there was more than that going on. In reverse witch trials, where it was the person who did harm to the person they accused of witchcraft, we see the drawing of a witch's blood (specifically above the breath) make its way out of a novel.

The idea that drawing a witch's blood could break her spell over you was widely spread. Likely as old as blōdwīte that found its way into Manx law in 1581 from an Anglo-Saxon legal practice. The actual words of "above the breath" found their way into wider tradition when Sir Walter Scott used them in his novel *Waverley*.[11] Whilst it seems likely that Scott would have used something he'd heard in folklore to come up with the idea of being "scored aboon the breath," it seems to begin in fiction. Here we see the old dance between story, fact, fiction, folktale, and science that gives this era its specific vintage home goods scent. Inside that smell, the one you find inside an old fox stole from the time, is the scent of the birth of modern witchcraft, a legend-truth, or a truth-legend, of itself.

A pamphlet inspired by a witchcraft trial in 1593 was also very popular and spread the concept of scratching so far it might have been part of bringing the concept of scratching into the courts. Local lore of the witch moved around further; also, the changeling became far-flung and well known folklore in a similar manner, even important details like how to "cure" a changeling. The press, in looking for salacious storylines to sell newspapers, became a strange actor in this nativity. Some of these figures were seized up by the character of the era and put towards different agendas to previously in history. "To the Victorians, the changelings became an internal enemy—alien beings who gnawed at the insides of an otherwise perfect society, corrupting them from within. In this, the changelings became the scapegoats upon which all of society's flaws were projected."[12]

If "they," the strangers, chose to take away your baby, there were a number of things you needed to be prepared for, and the press made sure people knew. One of them was that your baby might not be replaced with a faerie child at all, but with an animated stock. A stock was a physical object—a piece of wood, a broom, or other item glamoured to resemble the child that was

---

11 Sir Walter Scott, *Waverly Anecdotes* (J.Cochrane and J McCrone, 1833) 308.
12 Michał Różycki, "Outcasts in a Perfect Empire: The Role of Changelings in the Victorian Era," *Acta Philologica*, vol. 37, no. 37, 2010, 99–105, file:///Users/leemorgan/Downloads/99_acta37.pdf.

stolen. This mindset of having become a moving or inert stick was extended sometimes to adults, like Brigid Cleary, as well. This new object that used to be a person was something you could do whatever you felt like with—without sin—as it was no longer a human being.

The removal of the personhood of the changeling in the transformation to object allowed for intense neglect to be excused, and even attempts to send the faerie stock back to where it came from—something usually described as murder. In doing so, you were released from the sensation of having done something to your own family; it was to an enemy of your family. It is interesting to note that the changeling is almost always a woman, a child, or what we would now identify as a person suffering from a disability, or a taboo, wild, or disobedient individual.

As early as the 1600s, Thomas Hobbes implied that parents used changeling children to get away with poor treatment towards the disabled. "The Fairies likewise are said to take young Children out of their Cradles, and to change them into Naturall Fools, which Common people do therefore call Elves, and are apt to mischief."[13] Hobbes' word *mischief* refers to a talkative nature; it doesn't mean anything fun. Mischief was a word Hobbes also used to describe acts of extreme maleficium, or black magic, by witches. So, what he means here by *mischief* is child abuse.

Examples of torture and murder towards changelings are rife. There was being thrown into a river to worry about, being sent up the chimney in fire, or abandoned onto the so-called "Stranger Stone." But stories had begun to jump the county boundary now, as well as the country border. Originally, these stories moved but moved more slowly; they travelled across oceans with convicts and free settlers, allowing boots, witch bottles, and mummified cats to appear, even down in Hobart Town.[14] It took them some time, though, those immense migrations; now information could arrive more rapidly.

During this time, there was a huge Celtic diaspora, including a relocation of people from Ireland after the famine inflicted on them by English policies. What this resulted in were populations of stranded folk who had lost contact with their original homes and brought with them the ideas of their people. According to Doreen Valiente, who received the information via a third party to whom Rosaleen Norton gave hearing permission to Valiente, convicts introduced The Goat Fold into Australia. This involved ritual material Valiente said was a bit

---

13 Thomas Hobbes, "Comparison Of The Papacy With The Kingdome Of Fayries," *Leviathan*, 1651, https://historyofeconomicthought.mcmaster.ca/hobbes/Leviathan.pdf.
14 Ian Evans, *Touching Magic: Deliberately Concealed Objects in Australian Buildings*: submission for Degree of Doctor of Philosophy School of Humanities and Social Science University of Newcastle, NSW, 2010.

OF THE HEAD

like a Welsh-inspired version of Gardnerian Traditional Wicca, with less tools.[15] Norton believed The Goat Fold continued to survive up until her time here in Australia, and there are people alive today who believe the same.[16]

Over the next generation or two, these people must have been hungry for tales of home, gobbling them up with great gusto. Three changeling-related murders happened between 1820 and 1890, and *The Daily Telegraph* made sure everyone in the English-speaking world knew about them. I'm not going to dwell on the details as they contain terrible cruelty to disabled people with physical and mental illness symptoms, one of them being the famous death of Bridget Cleary. These were acts of violence against powerless minorities, but unlike many hundreds of years earlier—such as the ones Hobbes witnessed—these acts were able to be shared with a much wider distance.

During this time, the concept of the changeling and the faerie-other in general became linked to a variety of other enemies, some of them racial. What was important though was that the changeling became established in the Victorian Age as an *enemy from within*, a pathway to persecuting someone as a non-person, an individual who was no longer a human but could with the right story become an object. They were also linked to the class and colonial tensions in the relationships between the English-driven press and people of the so-called "Celtic fringe." The changeling figure to the Victorian Age readership was about prejudice, especially towards the Irish Roman-Catholics.

This prejudice was not alone. John Rhys also aimed at "Welsh aboriginals" who apparently had conspicuously long heads and were dark of colouring, who he claimed were part of the foundation of faerie stock.[17][18] This resulted in a *zeitgeist*, or spirit of the times, that both wanted to *take* knowledge that belonged to the Celtic people who were still living in-situ—people who were guardians of traditions—*but also* assert their inferiority at the same time. One can often see the same mindset playing out today in what is now called "cultural appropriation." Many of the concerns one can see beginning to palpitate in the Victorian Age find their full expression today in the hauntology of our current trials and tribulations.

Ronald Hutton called the combined hatred and seductive quality of the Celtic nations, and most specifically the underclass, a "trickle-up effect." An alien wobble of the faerie, passing its way from local dweller to becoming a

---

15 Doreen Valiente, *The Rebirth of Witchcraft* (Robert Hale, 1989) 156–157.
16 Known to the author.
17 John Rhys, *Celtic Folklore: Welsh and Manx* (HarperCollins, 1983) 240.
18 The idea of the racism behind these perspectives was explored in Peter Narváez's *The Good People: New Fairylore Essays* (University Press of Kentucky, 1997) 240.

literary personage. Passing through the time of our great-grandparents in a collective reflex against factories and industry, a bid was made to bring folklore about the Good Folk, as well as ceremonies for hearing the lost Morse code of the dead, back to life. With this trickle-up effect, we witness the beginning of our first fully recorded generational rebellion, a reaction against the parental example, of the type we just take for granted these days.

On the edge of science and partially in reaction against the age itself, a lot of people tried to prove that the dead, mesmerism, and faeries existed in the way they now understood existence: scientifically, through means like photography. The nature of perceiving reality had shifted somewhat already. A concept I touch on in *A Deed Without a Name* is the idea that people experience of what was "real" was governed by a different set of sensory experiences in the pre-modern age. What we once saw as a werewolf in his transformed state has become a person having a mental breakdown.

Photography was believed to be an art that could capture the invisible and make it visible. We see this in the case of the fake Cottingley Fairies that duped Arthur Conan Doyle. There was something phantasmagoric about photography right from the start—something that immediately made people superstitious. There was a sense that those images, caught in time, could in some way reflect the doings of an Otherworld. Or maybe bridge the gap between here and there in some other way. Many indigenous Australians around the continent believe that images of dead people are dangerous, and I would suggest this idea holds a deeper understanding—both of the dead and of photographs—than most of us have achieved.

The Cottingley Fairy photographs were fake, yet drew on something really experienced. The Fox sisters made all their rapping sounds with their toe knuckles, yet didn't. Springheel Jack was an Irish aristocrat, but couldn't have been... In this we tumble towards a money-making, celebrity-chasing "modern" world. We see people's increasing need for literal, physical, touchable proof of *real* things. Real becomes something more than herself. Real was simply experienced as real through a whole different recourse to our other senses. In modern times, those senses were becoming separated and almost broken apart. This line between what was experienced as real in pre-modern times and things you needed proof of in the Victorian Age was a mile of difference. The real was being stretched to fraying edges. If you couldn't capture it in a photograph, it was disputable whether it could truly be called "real." Did the camera do this to us? Or did we do this to the camera?

Since the beginning of the nineteenth century, in the Romantic Age, when the soul of modern occultism and witchcraft was still forming, people had taken a melancholy look at faeries and the world age. Both Charlotte Bronte and a famous geologist Hugh Miller agreed that the faeries were now leaving Britain.[19] Folklore was the cure for this sadness, for the faeries themselves only lived on through the body of folklore. Nobody was sure why they were leaving; they just were. Not as fast in Ireland, though. It probably had something to do with enclosing land and factories. The Scottish and dreadfully ill Robert Louis Stevenson claimed to have woken from a fever nightmare he termed a "bogey of a dream" and been inspired to write *The Strange Case of Dr. Jekyll and Mr. Hyde*.[20] It was a lot like the work of the Rag and Bone Man, this process of reclaiming the traces of the past rituals of seers and calling them "dreams," or anything you learned embedded in-situ, "folklore."

Folklore reaches beyond a veil that was slowly coming down in our minds between magic and science. There may not have been a veil between the worlds in times past, but it was beginning to form now. It was the Rag and Bone Man's job to take away the refuse that nobody wanted anymore, the bits and pieces of old things that were once sentimental but now had ceased to be so. After sentiment comes the era of resource. Just like half-broken cultures that could now also be pillaged and culturally appropriated by colonialism and greed—and could then be reclaimed and rendered into new soap and candles for the readers of the middle class—we are now in the recycling bin of the Victorian Age.

Whilst we wouldn't have so much glorious information about past practices and beliefs if it wasn't for the gathering of folklore, this practice also had its victims. When Catherine Earnshaw's apparition is sighted in *Wuthering Heights*, one of the characters finds it easy to associate changelings with a poor behaviour: "She must have been a changeling—wicked little soul!"[21] It had become a knee-jerk reaction for people at the time to associate wickedness with being a child who might have been left on The Stranger Stone. The very notion of there being strangers among us was taking on a new resonance. Some of these same kinds of stressors created a new type of witch as well—something we will return to later.

Whilst the notion of the changeling—made popular all over again via the print media—changed the meaning of a human body from person to object, Spiritualism made magic and the dead corporeal and thus potentially "real." It could be said that Spiritualism with its séances tried to drag spirits over into

---

19 Carole Silver. "On the Origin of Fairies: Victorians, Romantics, and Folk Belief" in *Browning Institute Studies*, vol. 14, 1986, www.jstor.org/stable/25057792, 141–156.
20 Lettice Cooper, *Robert Louis Stevenson* (Home and Van Thal, 1886) 53.
21 Emily Bronte, *Wuthering Heights* (Macmillan Education, 1847) 31–33.

this new way of being real. Ectoplasm dripped from the people's noses, ears, and genitals—of those who were skilled at producing it. Fully manifest phantoms emerged from a hidden cabinet (or other enclosed spaces) into which the medium would climb to do their work. The emphasis on red drapery, hidden cupboards, and darkness had womb-like connotations: "Serpentine ropes of the stuff [ectoplasm] would emerge from the medium's ear to rest in fat coils on her shoulder and embryonic limbs and heads would drop like otherworldly stillbirths from the medium's genitals."[22]

This world formed as an upsurge from the Underworld, where witchery of all sorts had long been pushed down, hunted, tortured, and executed into a now very well-hidden realm of human life. It couldn't be extinguished, just as the Jungian shadow-self can never be erased. Spiritualism was a reclaiming of the physicalised, literal nature of the spirit-body that Lecouteux spoke of, as part of the pagan mind. It appeared that the female body in particular was good at creating these substances, and the format of the séance was dark, enclosed, and redolent of her reproductive organs.

What then was the substance of ectoplasm, in the days before it was granted this scientific-sounding name? The French physician Gustav Gelery defined ectoplasm as "being sometimes vaporous, sometimes a plastic paste, sometimes a bundle of fine threads, or a membrane with swellings or fringes, or a fine fabric-like tissue."[23] This draws to mind the many threads that Fate weaves the world from, ones that are visible in certain trance states, to a diviner. They are made up of possibilities, influences, and spirit movers and shakers. Sometimes these are tendrils of influence from things that are sure to occur; other times there are numerous other threads that could still manifest. Sometimes those threads belong to our own bodies and ancestry and can be felt to emerge from our bodies during spirit dance. Ectoplasm is likely originally linked to this feeling of substances passing into and out of bodily orifices.

What is interesting is that many of the photographs of ectoplasm are almost certainly true-fakes or fake-truths. By this I mean, this material speaks to us in the way an artwork should. When you look at the images of ectoplasm appearing from people's noses, mouths, ears, and even between their legs, it gives across a strange sense of overflow, of over-fullness. The early modern nineteenth century world was simply aching to expel its ghosts. As a visual text,

---

[22] Anna Delgado, "Bawdy Technologies and the Birth of Ectoplasm" in *Genders* (Issue 54), 2011, 1, https://www.colorado.edu/gendersarchive1998-2013/2011/09/01/bawdy-technologies-and-birth-ectoplasm.
[23] Guy Christian Barnard, *The Supernormal: A Critical Introduction to Psychic Science* (Rider & Co, 1933) 1.

OF THE HEAD

these phantasmagoric photos tell us a great deal about the era; they are images that speak. They tell us about a feeling of eruption—the idea that a medium had become too full up with voices of the dead, with repressed power, with squashed-in emotion. So much so that the person's cup runs over. Faces erupt from ears; extra hands from the chest; the dead world that is legion converted to muslin and slime, slithering on out of people. Such a notion was so powerful that it survived into the "I've been slimed" world of film in *Ghostbuster*s.

Ectoplasm teaches us two things. One is that since the Spiritualist no longer lived in a faith-based world, now people felt the need to produce a manifest form of proof for their work. The other is that the Underworld had its own way with this movement, producing these artworks of slime, mist, and goo that made up a slimy road for ghosts. Here we see the wet roads that are often used for the feet of the dead in some modern necromancy, and a reaction to the breaking apart—possibly traumatically—of the barrier between the body of the living and that of the dead. The arrival of modernity made a deep psychological impact on people. When something is as powerful as the metaphor of ectoplasm was, it often links to something fundamental in our psyche. In this case, something liquid-feeling, thick, massy, and substantial exists. One example of this in a different poetic form, is the golden, honey-like nectar called "amrita" in yogic tradition. One book on the topic of *kundalini* outrightly refers to ectoplasm as being a slightly less evolved form of amrita.[24]

In our Witch House, we speak of Fat as being the substance that feeds the Fire of our Craft, and of which we have strong somatic experiences. When I say *somatic*, I mean physical but also highly sensory experiences—as normally when people say *physical* or *manifest*, they mean they could *see* it, and maybe they could touch it. Sensory can also mean smell, taste, as well as these other senses. Unrefined Fat can smell like the crackling from pork fat, whereas Fats that have been refined in the body might smell like milk fats in cream or butter, and at their finest, they might smell like honey or even cooking bread.

I wouldn't be sure how to compare it with something like amrita, but the touch-sensation of Fat very much reminds me of ectoplasm. The more refined version of Fat that is purified by certain practices—that I mentioned before as smelling like honey—some of us have naturally gone on to call nectar. Usually in witchcraft, it is more complicated, though, because the terminology for the manifestation of that blessed material depends on where it manifests on the body. We have one term for strange tears that flow

---

24 Alfred Ballabene, *About Kundalini* (BookRix, 2017) 13.

during a trance, and another for liquid that spontaneously leaks from a witch's nipple, which tends to be called "witches' milk."

What then forms the line between Spiritualism and witchcraft? Is there one? Julia Phillips suggested that class was part of what kept the witch out of the medium's parlour, with witchcraft being an underclass phenomenon and Spiritualism being a middle-class one. There is also the fact that one, Spiritualism, is well-publicised in newspapers, and the other, witchcraft, tries to keep its workings and most of its members secret. It is arguable that Spiritualism didn't invoke the Devil, at least it is until we stumble upon the early tales of the Fox sisters and their invocation of Old Mr. Splitfoot. Spiritualists didn't meet for a Grand Sabbat with others of their kind, and yet they were accused of indecency and orgies.

Yet, Richard Noakes tells us the following practices were all united under Spiritualism.[25] He includes "Christian miracles, witchcraft, and sorcery, apparitions of the living and dead, haunted houses, fairies, and second sight." He suggests that these things were all regarded as being under the catch-all description of Spiritualism.[26] So, clearly the line between a Spiritualist and a witch wasn't clear to everyone alive at the time. Witchcraft had come to be very specifically associated with the elderly woman by the Victorian Age,[27] whereas Spiritualism was also available to younger women and men. This fact might suggest a generational crisis where the witch came to be imagined with an aged figure from an old, almost extinct world.

Whilst the old women of *Macbeth* were stereotypes that were hundreds of years old, during The Persecutions it wasn't always so settled. Men were accused of witchcraft in the past, as were younger women and sometimes children—similar groups to those attracted to Spiritualism. There was an increasing power of this *Macbeth* stereotype during our era. It had a bit to do with the press and the popularity of the three witches in lampoons against rival, but also with the popularity of the play in Victorian times. Julie Phillips gives a very clear rundown of how the play was much more popular than usual at the time, how there was music being composed for the witch's dance, and how often it was referenced in popular reports.[28]

---

25 Richard Noakes, "Spiritualism, Science and the Supernatural in Mid-Victorian Britain" in *The Victorian Supernatural,* ed. by Carolyn Burdett Nicola Bown, Pamela Thurschwell, Cambridge University Press, 2004, 26.
26 Phillips, *op cit.*, 154.
27 Phillips, *op cit.*, 18.
28 Phillips, *op cit.*, 85.

OF THE HEAD

Midsummer Night's Dream was also thriving in popularity during this period, and the presence of a Fairy Queen—and a Puck or Robin Goodfellow—can't have been lost in the consciousness of the time. In an age before the television, one must pause and think about the impact of stage plays on the minds of the living. This regular exposure as children to the presence of Robin Goodfellow as a narrative personage likely led to the same children-as-grown-ups, Edwardian creation of the Puckish Peter Pan, as well as Rudyard Kipling's *Puck of Pook's Hill*, where he declares Puck to be "the oldest old thing in England."[29] We meet this figure again during the so-called "golden age of children's books," in the form of the horned god who appears before Mole and Rat while they are searching for Otter's child in *Wind in the Willows*, during "Piper at the Gates of Dawn."[30] He gives both characters the gift of forgetfulness of the ontological stress of having seen Him, and yet still delivers to them the baby otter. An enormous act of wild grace.

Robin Goodfellow was a usually graceful good guy by the time he was handed down to the children of the Victorians, but during this earlier period, he still had more of the trickster up under his skin. Be this so, Spiritualism was still a medium for the expression of the same Underworldly forces in which witchcraft originally rooted itself. Some writers saw this clearly and declared: "Witches were mediaeval 'mediums' without knowing it. They would have called themselves mediums if the word had been invented, and they would have dubbed themselves professors of psychology instead of witches, and then, perhaps, they would have been more cordially received by a world that insisted on drowning them in horse ponds..."[31]

The same source goes as far as to make this connection clear: "On the whole, the cause of witchcraft would seem to be almost as flourishing now as it ever was, and if we do not desire that persons holding themselves out as in communication with another world should be taken to the stake, we may certainly wish that the same fate could overtake the 'medium' wealthy with his spoils that fall on the 'rogues and vagabonds' who are punished for fortune-telling."[32]

This door opens to a parlour. We must go down a laneway first, one that leads us to another door. Beyond the door is red light and the close environs of having to hold hands with strangers. On the other side of a perverse public shudder, in close confines with the bodies of women—women surrendered to their somatic, sensory life—we find slime, thread-woven sluicing, mysterious...

---

29 Rudyard Kipling, *Weyland's Sword* (Puck of Pook's Hill, 1906) 1.
30 Kenneth Grahame, *Wind in the Willows* (The Templar Company, 1908) 104–105.
31 Daily Telegraph & Courier (London) on 22 May 1883, https://research-information.bris.ac.uk/ws/portalfiles/portal/370166320/Julia_Phillips_Doctoral_Thesis.pdf.
32 *Saturday Review;* was republished in the *Nottinghamshire Guardian* on 15 September 1876.

the half-congested remains of the digested underclasses from whom land had been stolen, the millions of Irish and indigenous bodies that the middle class feared it had supped upon the Fat of; they were now slippery with bioplastic slickness and sliding on out of the bodies of mediums.

PART II

OF THE HEART

1

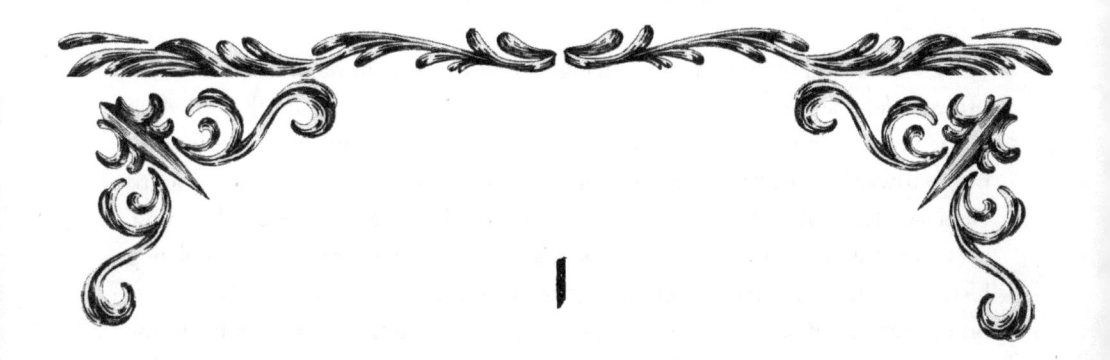

I used to watch him at twilight, the rag and bone man. Coming silently up Macquarie Street, out of the fog-soup at day's edge with his ominous hook. When I was very young, I thought he was Jesus, with his gaunt cheekbones and his dishevelled holy-man hair. Only now do I realise he's me. This might sound strange if you've never felt the winds of the future blow back on you as visions—full of already half-lost potentials—but I'm tired of apologising for being strange.

The first thing that happens when we begin to play the game is the rag and bone man. You'll see him coming up the street when it's barely light, collecting the town's refuse: rags of outmoded thoughts, bones of old loves. Hair and teeth of past lovers that someone has long-slept cuddled up to—but just this very morning, when your voyeur-eye is present with a sudden lightness of being, exposing them to the sun's purifying kiss. That is what he does—or should I say, what I do: feed on the carrion of dreams. Just as cheap candles are bulked up with fat boiled off from the leavings of Hobart Town, so is my voice powered forth. It's how I am still talking, this carrion fuel. I take the dreams that polish up all right for a second go-round; others will need to be melted down for fat to make soap, their sadness pulled out and carded to spin words, their soft regret rubbed into my cello strings as rosin.

I am the Rag and Bone Man, and this is my story. It begins with me seeing future-me from the outside, dressed in ragged clothes. It makes sense I should appear to myself as a beggar, for this truly is nobody's story. And generally, everyone pretends they can't see the rag and bone man, as they do with the entire spectre of poverty that throbs hungrily under and around the cobblestone edges of our world. All except for one or two children who haven't yet learned which people they are meant to find invisible. This story is my rag and bone collection, the flotsam that washes up on my shores when my mind, like beach rubble, is being taken apart and melted down for the knife handles and candlesticks of Hobart Town.

RAG & BONE MAN

I was born in the age of public hangings, and I am skimming the cream from off your latte as we speak. So, be warned: this story won't stay neatly folded up in the bottom drawer of the past. You will follow the sound of my voice and move towards it in the dark and follow where you can hear the floorboard yield to release of pressure. Extend your fingers. I'm speaking. You're listening, yet you're listening in the present, which is ever-skittering forward, accumulating history behind it, so that's where the story plays out—not in my time, but always on the cutting edge of the breathing now. On a retreating horizon, which to my forebears lay to the west, to the west and ever further. The retreating *fata morgana* of The Plain of Delight. That was all before the great discombobulation, where the direction of Forever-away got its axis tilted to the south.

Behind my voice is an enormous silence which is humming, now you think of it. The silence marks out time as having passed between my life and yours. There are eight turf shovels of grave dirt between you and me, five fathoms of Sullivan's Cove full of salt tears between my first breath drawn screaming at the pink-nerve rooted horror of life, and yours, which I imagine began similarly. My voice must filter up through a lot of layers of forgotten to break the air. I don't even exist anymore, you see, (just the way you can see the light of a shooting star long after the death of the star, my consciousness a light still not fully expended and spilling out ever further) until you read these words. In the moment where you give me a voice in your head, that travelling light meets with a barrier that for a moment checks its flight, and so, in the black mirror of your pupil, I am still alive. Maybe you thought you were reading, innocent of the fact you are resurrecting light into voices?

You read these words in the silence a person leaves upon dying, filled with suspension dots and perhaps a question mark or two—if they were lucky, a welter of exclamation marks and some breathless dashes. Stare down into it, the tiny breath-interruptor of punctuation. The immensity of the past compressed to a tiny space by the weight of time. They are my pupils looking back at you from below the sidewalk, in the water of a Hobart laneway or gutter. I am so far away; this is why they look so small. It's the blackness left behind by all the compressed pain and soot of loss that's rendered from the mess and fat of our lives when we're gone, and it's fertile still. You need only look at it and blow upon the coals.

Time bites its own tail in this unique friendship that's about to begin between you and me. Everything is now. So I suppose this is an invitation. Follow my voice through the dark? Everything must happen when the Rag and Bone Man comes back to town. Bring out your bones! Bring out your

OF THE HEART

dead! Bring out your *memento mori's* and your dolls with missing eyes! Bring out the abortions of your life history! The bits that didn't fit together properly. The essential parts of yourself you put up for sale when desperate but have never stopped trying to buy back.

At the bottom of the world, Van Diemen's Land still lurks underneath Tasmania. Underneath Van Diemen's Land there is *lutruwita,* the mystery puzzle, where the creaking bones of stirring giants contort up from the icebergs of the frozen south. When the gas lamps flicker low, an Other god rules here who knows nothing of church bell or steeple. Hobart Town is the Devil's playground, His dark park, His stomping ground. Really, He is beyond Devils, older than Devils. But under the surface of this is a beautiful, dirty place, this secret little town of ours. This infernal paradise, a city teetering on the edge of a mountain of wilderness. When he had opened the second seal, I heard the beast still nattering on, saying: *come and see.*

You will see me as a pale-faced child in the upstairs window of a middle-class, mid-nineteenth-century home. I could mention the silver fob watch making broad arches of monotony before your gaze, but I'm going to give you more credit than that and assume you know how to let the past become present. Where you see my face through the distortion of the glass planes of the period—the type you now know as antique glass—I am watching for the rag and bone man. It's an important moment, as this is the hour my fate is set on course.

Let's go closer, shall we? In through the ear, into the inner chambers of the mind. Do I know this is the hour where my doom is to be fixed in place? Not precisely. But I know *something* of texture is about to happen. I feel it in the hollow cleft at the middle of my ribs. I am watching for a revelation. My eyes are ready for one. I am looking for the rag and bone man. Unlike other passersby, the rag and bone man would nod his head and doff his hat when he caught a child staring. He would admit with his grey eyes that he knew the secrets, that the town coughed up her guts for his ears and eyes as she did for mine, and a child was not a lesser being. What are the secrets? All I will tell you for now is if you knew the secret lives of *all the people* in the town, it would seem quite other than it does.

On this particular evening, for the first time, a human boy responded in the same way as the holy bone-taker to catching me watching him. I smiled wistfully through the glass ripple, which had a few droplets of rain running down it from an earlier shower. I was waiting for the rag and bone man to come out of the treacle-thick mist. I'd stopped seeing him of late. The fact was filling me with my first sense of blue-grey nostalgia and the long ache of ripening adulthood.

Moments earlier there was the sound of the horses and the carriage and adult men greeting each other in the street. There are some of these sounds that you won't be able to conjure as skilfully. Because the Victorian Age is a different animal when it comes to audio and scent echoes, as much as it is visually. There is the smell of our coal fire, burning kerosene from the lamps, the creak of the stiff leather in my shoes, the silence behind it in a house with no hum of refrigerators. It's like the taste of Port of a certain year; it wasn't a great time to be alive for a lot of people, yet its ashes and dust compress down to something that's quite sophisticated on the palette.

Am I trying to put off mentioning him? Well, probably. My death begins ticking away towards me in this moment, a feeling much like a soft embryo spawned to be aborted, so it would be natural enough. I'll let you see it from inside my eyes. I'll let you see how the boy takes off...took off his hat. (Let's swap to past tense shall we, so you can relax away from all this now-ness? I will speak in present tense only when time compresses me down into a knot.) He took off his hat and gave me a quick duck of a bow. In the uncertain light of the gas lamps and the rain on the glass, I couldn't altogether see his face in those first few moments.

When Father told me we would host one of Hobart's better-known barristers and his son, I'd taken little interest. I intended to discharge my responsibility of entertaining his son in the manner of Cordelia, as was my duty. Even when he appeared inside my house, I don't remember paying any heed to his family's greater prestige. I need to fill these details in because I know they must have been present, these differences between he and I. I did not feel them at the time, and from the way he doffed his hat to me, as to another gentleman, we were alike in missing the minor class division between upper and lower middle class.

"Henry!" My Father's voice. "Don't gaze out so at our guests like some ominous gargoyle! They'll take you for simple, and God knows that is the one thing that's never been wrong with you."

"Sorry, Father," I murmured, stepping back out of our guests' visual field whilst Father went downstairs to open the door. I don't want to be a bossy voice in your head, but the best vantage point for this scene is to come down the stairs with me and stand as a ghostly presence in the darkened hall. From here you will best witness a gentleman arriving in his top hat and great coat being welcomed inside with the orangey streetlight illumining them into silhouette. Behind the gentleman, dressed in the identical smaller costume, Master Allport.

"Please come into the front room, Morton; I'll take your coat," Father was saying. "Pleased to meet you, Master Allport. My Henry will show you around.

OF THE HEART

Henry!" Now I realise that the Allport family probably had a servant who would have taken my father's coat, if we were ever entertained at their place. To me, it seemed a perfectly respectable thing for Father to offer. From where your gaze is stationed, you will see how I slipped out into the hall and stood near the wall observing our guests. I was down to my shirtsleeves, and my tie is a little loosened. Can you imagine a world where your child wears a tie every day? Where I'm dressed-down because I have the buttons on the cuffs of my button-up shirt undone?

The adults withdrew. His father was, naturally, too grand to bother interacting with another man's child. In my time, we—us undersized adults of whom much is expected—are the most physically scrutinised and at once emotionally unnoticed of creatures. That's why the rag and bone man and the child are great hiding places for angels and demons, because no one ever sees either. In the home of a widower like my father, children were often neither seen nor heard. I don't recall minding this or feeling lonely. All up until I was suddenly alone with the young Master Allport and able to see our ages matched, and all at once I felt a pang of eager friendship where I was meant to feel a class divide. After all, not allowed to go to school as I was, I endured an isolation from others my age that would these days earn you a visit from child services.

My guest held out his hand to shake mine, and I remembered my manners. "Pleased to meet you; I'm Henry. What's your name?"

He peeled off one glove to shake hands with me. Possibly out of a desire to be personable, but maybe also because he saw I wore no gloves and was trying to be democratic. It was impossible for me not to wonder at his motivations. The less powerful in society are apt to pay close attention to the nuances in the moods of their superiors, for often our fortunes are bound up in their decisions.

Master Allport was pretty at that age, before manhood made him handsome, with a straight nose only ever so slightly upward-turning at the end, full lips, expressive eyes, and dark, wavy hair. Your modern eyes might amaze at his parents entrusting a boy his age with silver cufflinks, and the fact he has a little chain in his waistcoat, and all the fussy details of being an upper middle-class child. I was never one to be taken much with trinkets. It was his nose that first struck a positive impression on me. There are some types of nose that never seem to belong to a cruel boy.

"I've got lots of names," he confided to me as we shook. "Do you want to try and guess one?"

I tried to imagine what a family like his—artistic, well-respected, rabidly anti-transportationist (back when the question of whether to receive more convicts was still a question dividing Hobart)—would name their son? "Arthur?" It seemed to fit the bill because he looked like an Arthur, and the name had poetic connotations I associated with Tennyson. Also, it was the preferred name of George Arthur the Governor around the era of our births.

"Oh, I wish it was!" he replied. "Like Lord Tennyson's Arthur for whom he wrote *In Memoriam*. I read that last summer up at Lake St Clair."

"Yes," I agreed, hiding a flash of my white-hot pleasure. "Arthur Henry Hallam. It's one of the reasons I thought of it."

"He had both of our names? Well, that settles it, I'm keeping it." He smiled. It seemed he knew he was winning me. I was never the sort of child-shaped creature to be fooled with charm alone.

"But what are your real names?"

He kept smiling mysteriously and refusing with his eyes, as if he found it fun to hold in—and later give—this first secret. It is only gradually in a true friendship where one learns the other's rhythms of giving and holding, adapts to them, and watches them adapt in turn, until our in and their out breaths become aligned.

When he took my arm in his, we began to ascend the stairs as if by mutual agreement, with he neither pulling me nor me entirely meaning to invite him. I was struck by his innate genius for overcoming resistance.

"I want to be Arthur with you; I'd like to be an *A* person for a while."

"Well, you look like an Arthur."

"I've heard you're a changeling," he said, leaning in closer to me. "Don't worry, my grandmother is artistic, and artists have an understanding with the faeries. She called her home in Upper Liverpool Street "Fairy Knowe," after a hollow hill in the Orkneys. I also hope to become on the best of terms with the Good Folk." He winked at me. All this time, we had stood on the landing. It was darker up there; to save money, Father didn't keep lamps going in the halls. Kerosene was only for the good rooms. Bedrooms could make do with candles. Beeswax for the rooms where company was expected, paraffin and sometimes stearic acid for the bedrooms.

I must have eyed Master Allport up for a good twenty seconds before answering. "Well, what are *you*?" I asked. "Other than an Allport?"

He smiled and looked down awkwardly at his shoes. "Guess I've never thought about it." It was clear he had no idea yet of the saints, beasts, devils, angels, and hob-men tumbling in and out of focus behind his eyes. "Not about myself at any rate, but I shall be thinking about it now that you've asked…"

Of the Heart

I could tell already he was much more than a surname. He was clever for a start, even when compared with his notoriously talented family. His soul went down deeper, darker byways. Did I know that in this moment where he waited to be invited into a room? Or was this just a conceit on my part as the artist? *Straight down the Devil's Well with a noose around your feet, and you'd still not fathom his soul,* my dead mother said, leaning on the doorframe with her arms folded. She was pretty in an austere sort of way, before the yellow-smelling fog wound its way out of the rivulet to choke out her life and left her with this hue of gaunt-grey death, yellow urine on the floor. Yellow is a death colour. It always reminds me there was the mucous of death up inside her for so long before I found her in the rocking chair that day.

Only I can still see her in the house off and on. When the moon is doing the right thing for my eyes. This is the Celtic-mist-tinged tragedy of the second sight. The past is all messed up for me; the layers of time are all mixed, and I see them out of order. Ghosts are just the fact that the past is still happening. Along with the time-collapse my eyes do, one of the clocks had stopped ticking the day my mother died and was never wound up again. She'd become another face forming in the elder tree at the bottom of the garden. I used to imagine siblings had become trapped there by my faerie magic when I'd squashed them with my growth, like the cuckoo does to his nestmates. Of course, he doesn't know he's going to do that, when his cuckoo mother lays him in a stranger's nest. Like the cuckoo, I became the wooden faerie stock boy who doesn't smile enough, slowly turning others to wood.

"Do you want to see the clock that stopped ticking the day Mother died?"

His eyes immediately piqued with interest, and he nodded. I took his arm in mine and led him to my room. Instead of being behind my eyes, I suggest you emerge from my ear like Venus from her shell and follow us, as if you were another ghostly presence, a future that walks beside us, just as the past does.

"You sleep in the room where your mother died?" he asked, as I pushed open the door and he correctly guessed that it was my bedroom. "That's so forlorn."

I had the feeling this was a new vocabulary word he had been looking to use in a conversation and finally found his moment. To me, this idea was endearing. "There are not that many rooms in our house," I explained with a shrug. "And all of them someone has died in, so… It doesn't matter though, her ghost is tied to the memories of the rocking chair and that is in my sister's room."

"Oh! You have a sister? Is she asleep?" he asked, considerately lowering his voice in an apologetic sort of way.

"Very soundly, and I trust you won't wake her. The wee lass is tucked in tight in her grave."

"Beg your pardon." He cleared his throat awkwardly. "We've been so lucky like that; death hasn't touched my family too heavily, so sometimes I don't think." Immediately he rushed to touch something wooden in line with the old superstition. If you saw me only from the outside, you'd think I enjoyed making him that little bit uncomfortable. You'd be partly right. Not from meanness—more because I was interested in him and wanted to taste all the different colours he could feel as quickly as possible.

"Tell me the story of each of their deaths while we go through the rooms," he suggested. "It scares me. I like to be scared."

For the first time in the conversation, I smiled with pleasure. "Let's play a game then."

"I would love that!" he agreed, before even checking to see what the game would entail. "Your smile lights up your face, Henry. I hope I can make you smile a lot during our acquaintance." He seized up my hands and shook them up and down to better express the intentness of his words. I drew in my breath in shock at the raw sensory graze of being touched. I wasn't sure anyone had touched my hand skin-to-skin like that for a sustained time since Mother's death. I had been shaken by the hand in the way men do, and my father had rubbed me or patted me on the back for a brief moment or two. For some time, I stared at the spot where Arthur had touched me as if I expected the meaning of life to suddenly appear on the palm of my hand like a bruise.

"What kind of game is it?" he asked at last.

Would you like to play with us too?

This story is a kind of fairytale about the less popular roads through the woods. The one where the shady trees and bent figures lurk. Time might not move forward or backwards quite evenly when you're moving around in the crooked wood. By now, you might have begun to wonder if this voice you're listening to is that of someone with something a little wrong with them. I'm not offended. Don't think that. There is *absolutely* something wrong with me.

Maybe you believe in the same haunted life-scape as my Irish forebears, or instead you suspend disbelief when voices from beyond the grave speak to you in the form of text? I believe it's better to let such questions remain open, able to catch the light glaze like abalone shells in the sun, art, and the mythic

OF THE HEART

qualities of life respawning themselves. Fairytales live off a different morality to everyday life. They are sane madness; that's why we're so afraid of them that we gird ourselves against their tangled logic. Usually, we only see them after they've eaten us whole like Little Red Riding Hood's wolf ate grandma and they're wearing us on the inside. What big teeth we have!

Fairytales repeat themselves and go around and around, twisting and contradicting themselves. They're in the past, they're right now, always... Otherwise, if you weren't lulled by the gentle repetition you might notice the sound of history rearranging itself, where a story is told that not only alters the future but the past as well. You might hear the collective gasp that comes just before people stop even seeing the story and step bodily through the text into the slower, richer, sooty music of my world. A former convict woman named Martha taught me that about the witchcraft of storytelling, but we're not at the Martha part of my story just yet.

I was suckled on the witch-milk of Irish wonder tales, so it's easier for me to believe in you as someone of the future, than for you to believe in me, back here in the past. Death works like that. My world straddles the modern world and less well-lit times, haunted by pookahs and beansidhes and shroud wailers. According to Mother, I was myself one of the bestiary of monsters from the murky past. I was not the child that she wanted, nor the one she believed she gave birth to, but a replacement left by Them, from the Other Place where everyone has their feet on backwards, and no one ever cries. Or laughs. Or if they do they do it all in reverse. Her real baby had been taken there, and I was left in his place. Lord only knows what happened to him Over There... Who knew the Good Folk's motive in leaving me there in Hobart with my parents, be it benevolent or malevolent? Or perhaps more dreadful still, ambivalent? My mind, like my world, straddled two realities. I knew of the Origin of the Species; I knew the Catholic church and a lot of prayers; at the same time, I held a fully magical worldview that owed little to church or science. What did I truly believe? Well, whether I believed in faeries never seemed to matter to Them. God seemed to be in a bother about what other gods I am sharing the nighttime side of myself with, though, and I'm just not as into that.

There are certain key stories that drive each era; some live on to become fairytales, belittled; they thrive in the underground among the outcasts. Like mycelium under the mushroom, they link together the deep substrata of our world even when we no longer take them seriously. Mankind can't help rubbing at those themes eternally, as one tongues at an ulcer in the mouth. That's why we'll never fully burn out our forebears' dread of the changeling. The cuckoo in your nest who won't only take from the other hatchlings but will slowly press them to death all around its gigantish form. As my siblings died—and I did not—it was, perhaps, only the master story of Jesus's ayings lodged in my father that saved me from exposure-by-parent, such as was the old cure for a changeling who'd brought a curse down upon the family.

When your father watches people starving to death and raving by the roadside of their hometown—as my father did in Ireland—something in your own body learns of this threat. Even though he didn't speak of it often, my body still knew. It understands the stories about woodcutters who have to leave the children in the forest because there isn't enough food. If one bears the weight of both the changeling story and the starvation story, they are only ever inches away from being left in the woods. Though I had not myself known serious hunger, I understood through the magic of blood why hunger obsesses the mind of our forebears, just as it did the mind of the escaped convicts in the company of the cannibal Alexander Pearce. The land here is hungry. Lands get hungry when there are too many forgotten stories gone into the soil; it turns the gut of the land when it has to swallow them all. Their loud silences create a pulling-inward drop in the soul of a place, right along the fault lines of the memory theft. The gullet of this island rumbles with cavernous forgetfulness.

We don't get to choose the dreams the land has—that will itch at the collective mind of which we are a part. They were all played out while the forest still enveloped Europe. Here the Great Western Wilderness is still hugging us with darkness. The wild forest's presence takes part of our minds back down there to our own stories-on-the-edge of the wild. They bubble under the surface, shards of narrative trying to push their way to getting a breath in a pool full of faces. All the dead are like that, a bunch of stories unspoken, silences held. We didn't get to choose the stories we inherit. They chose us and continue their existence when we pass them down. Sometimes we have to make a human shield of ourselves to *stop* some dangerous stories from being passed down.

I suppose that's how I feel about Mother's story. The story of being a changeling chose me. If I wanted to stop this story, I'd have to make a human shield of myself, because Mother wasn't strong enough to stand in the middle herself.

"It's different to normal children's games. You will need to sit back-to-back with me."

Of the Heart

"Is it a faerie game?" Arthur asked, scurrying to sit back-to-back with me and knocking me slightly with his enthusiasm. Now we are spine-aligned, and as I'm not looking at him, I feel bolder. If you are looking from the outside, you will see that we have slipped our shoes off to sit on the bed and that Victorian Age gentlemen's sons wear socks like everyone else—and also possess feet.

"In Ireland," I began, with a little shimmering feeling of brushing up against the seamy form of a taboo. "We don't call the Good People that."

"What do you call them?"

"Well, that depends what kind you're talking about. There are sidhe, beansidhe, grugoch, merrow…"

"What type are you?"

I smiled to myself. "Guess."

"I don't know enough about them…"

"The sidhe are the noble race of faerie who are the bright ones; the beansidhe is a wailer on the winds who presages the death of people or may be seen to scrub the blood-stained shroud of one who is to die. The grugoch is a wild man of the woods, and the merrow is a sea maiden whose power comes from a little hat of red feathers. If you steal it while she's bathing, she is forced to come home with you."

"Why would someone do that?"

"What do you think humans all crave?"

"Love."

I raised my eyebrow with scepticism. I felt the answer was power, but I thought it was sweet that he thought otherwise. I liked that he believed it, and I wanted him to keep believing it. "You still haven't told me what kind of changeling I am?"

"Master Henry, I don't know you well enough just yet," he replied sincerely. "If it's all the same to you, may I wait until after our game?"

"All right," I said quietly, linking my arms with his so we were held back-to-back. "In a moment, you'll start to notice the feeling that you are sinking a bit and then falling back." As I said this, I very slowly leaned forward and pulled him back over until he was laid out across my back as though on an altar of sacrifice. He went over easily and softly, trustingly. Will you come with us as trustingly? Send your own vision tumbling downward and then readjust your worldview until my down is your up? "You backwards somersault, and I forward tumble through the floor, and the world turns upside down. Now we are sitting in exactly the same room, but this room is different. The first thing you notice is that the clock is still ticking, the same one that is dead on the dresser here. Tick, tick, tick," I suggested the first few and then left the rest to his fertile inner darkness to body forth.

"I hear it," he murmured in a tone of awe.

"Me too." And it was true; it was part of my lone-play that I enchanted myself first if I planned to try to include others. It was the only way I knew how to play with other children. I had learned it from a dead girl I met down near the Female Factory where they once kept the convict women. This girl, Mary, was my only playmate. My parents called her my imaginary friend. Maybe she thought the same about me? "There is a woman sitting in a rocking chair feeding an infant child. Can you hear the sound of the chair on the floorboards?"

He nodded. So unused to prolonged human contact was I that I felt his roused heartrate through his back and was sensitised to his breathing. This contact with him through both body and story was a lot like learning to play a musical instrument. Musicality, of course, is the sole real virtue of the changeling as far as Irish lore is concerned, so my parents had plied me with instruments and lessons from an early age. It was believed that if the changeling was kept happy with enough food and music, it kept them from suckling away the good luck from out of the teat of the family. "It is morning, and the light is coming through the nursery window. What do you see, Arthur?"

I thought he would find it hard to get started, but right from the beginning, Arthur was an amazing playmate. "The woman feeding the baby…she is nodding, almost napping while the child drinks. At the window, an elf child appears and watches them. He doesn't seem happy or sad; he just looks in through the window, like you were looking out of yours when I first saw you."

"Rain is pattering at the glass plane, though the sun is still out, casting a light rainbow in the air. The elf boy is me, Arthur. Walk into the room and look directly at me. That's better; I can see you now."

"There is someone else in the room with us. A girl… She rings a bell, and you come straight through the window as if it were made of pressed-together rice that must be pushed through and separated."

"Turn and look at the girl. She is a child with dark hair. If you gaze at her long enough, her eyes will disappear and turn into the sockets of a skeleton; if you stay with her long enough, white butterflies come out of her eyeholes when she's happy."

Arthur jumped when he saw it; I felt him leap on my back like a salmon bouncing upstream to its mate-and-die fate. I felt him jerk away, as if at the end of a line. He had live fish under his skin. "I saw it!" he cried. "I saw what you said before you said it!"

OF THE HEART

"Yes," I replied calmly. "That is the game. But you must close your eyes again and go back through to being the right way up for this world. Otherwise it's *unseelie* magic; it will hurt you."

When he had done so, we turned to face each other.

"What sort of creature am I, do you think?"

He swallowed down some fast-paced emotion I couldn't place and cleared his throat. "Henry. May I call you that and drop the formality? When she is getting to know someone, my Grandma Mary always likes to pretend she is painting and say someone hasn't sat long enough for her to get a good likeness. Might we be friends? I'd like to return and play your game again."

I didn't really show him much of the other rooms in the house. Because I still wasn't sure who he was in my story, or perhaps even who I was. I wanted him to answer my question about my nature so I myself would know. As the victim of this story, the power was in the hands of others to say what they thought I was. I would never be free until someone released me. Though I certainly wasn't a wooden shape of a boy, left as a faerie stock in exchange for their real child, the story about me had been given to me through violence—believed about me without my permission. So I suppose I was looking to change it in some way, through Arthur's eyes.

The thing with a fairytale is you might be the young girl who has to pass through the wild wood, or you might be the wolf; you just don't know until you've already fully committed. Once you're laid out on the altar of your true story, you are free-falling backwards through the floor. What if, against all seeming likelihood, *he* was the little girl and *I* the wolf? I thought, *You might be the old woman with a key piece of wisdom to hand me; you could be the Prince...* For many years, it seemed to me that I only knew who I *wasn't*. I wasn't the princess, because there weren't any stories with fairy godmothers in them for people like me.

Most of you will wake up maybe twice in a lifetime, reflect on the part that you play, or feel for one precious moment the giddy levity of knowing that you are in the middle of your fairytale ending. Then you'll perceive the heavy fact that nothing ever ends but moves instead, in cycles of joy and sorrow. Those of us who know what character we are and have come awake in our story appear sometimes among you as beggars and tramps, or children, or the mad. Epiphanies of the common place, as ubiquitous as dust in shafts of sunlight. We are always dancing on your peripheries and being passed by as something too insignificant to be noticed, except by the eyes of the pure of heart. We can smell them, those kind of eyes, as soon as they fall upon us. Just as I smelt the dew-on-thistledown purity in Arthur's gaze outside my home, before we even shook hands.

How to show you my world in between Arthur's visits? I don't want you to think you know already because the past is a different beast. When the lights are down, it comes sniffing up close to your feet under the sheets. We think we are dwelling or flashing back, when really what is happening at four in the morning is a delicate overlap, where the past, present, and maybe even the future dance together while human minds quieten. The closest you've physically been to that echo is if, as a child, you ever touched the old, paper-thin skin of a great- or even a great-great-grandparent whose eyes first opened somewhere in my world.

There are certain things about my life that separate my experiences sharply from yours. The woman who washed our laundry came here as a convict. She was Irish like us, and it was over twenty years ago when she got her ticket of leave. Everybody still knew about it, though; some so-called respectable families called it "the taint." Nobody told the person about it. Meaning there was no proof that other people were thinking about it all the time, yet the person likely sensed it. It was talked about behind their back constantly, after all. Unless, of course, the former convict married well and achieved some success; then it may not have even been discussed any longer, though everyone was still thinking about it.

Her hands also told a story. Ronit's hands were red and misshapen from years at the scrub board and the wringer, perhaps also from the cold. She had been with us for over a year when Arthur arrived, which was longer than most of our servants stayed. I had given up trying to talk with her, as she only answered me with "Yes, Master Henry" or "Of course, Master Henry." I would have loved to unlock what lay behind her greenish eyes full of mist and sorrow, but as a child, I was not to be left to my own devices when it came to either seeing all people as people or being innocent of the class gap between them and us.

Death is a great presence in my world. It would have been odd of me to ask Ronit about the fact that she didn't die in the process of getting her ticket of leave, but I think I did it when I was too young to realise it was so. One can assume she was strong, as she endured transportation by sea for months, as well as being locked in with others during times of disease. Sometimes I would consider the many friends our washer-woman must have buried over the years. Although I'm seen as a gentleman, we don't have penicillin, and an infection from a cut could end my life. As far as my heart-ravaged father can tell me, my paternal aunt and her child died of weakness caused by starvation back in Ireland, under circumstances that he has always found too dreadful to put words to. Though I wasn't there, my flesh remembers it; Father and I always have backup food stored somewhere. For these reasons, that death stalks the hindmost; he is rigid about class divides and asserting them, including over the will of the weaker party. If my father was to die, I don't have a backup plan.

To set the scene of my daily activities—on a backdrop of the uncertainty in front of which my story happens—I will give you our day. Early in the morning, we awake and wash from a basin of cold water, except for in winter where we will add a dash of boiling water from the kettle as a luxury. There is a crucifix over the washbowl, and at some point, I will run through motions of crossing myself and repeating prayers. Father seldom speaks of Jesus in daily life, yet the agonised Christ watches me bathe, a silent, sorrowful witness to cleanliness, making sure my nails are clean and my whites are white. If there is a moral to Catholicism that Father particularly agrees with, it is the high importance Jesus would be putting on scrubbed nails, and cleanliness being next to godliness. I'm not sure if it's clear, but my memory oddly associates the cold washbowl and Jesus.

If you were there watching our lives, you would see me put Father's tea water on to boil while he makes breakfast. If we've taken hot water from the kettle to heat our wash water, then I'd have to get up earlier to accommodate the second boil on the wood cooker, in the days before we got two kettles, and later on, gas. In those days, every luxury must be paid for in effort, and tea is the essential kind of luxury—the type that is key to psychological survival in a Hobart winter. I have been a tea drinker for many years; many of my medical remedies contain intoxicating quantities of alcohol and cannabis. I am also entirely in charge of the wood stove, though father splits the big logs for me. We are often able to pay someone to do it for us, though Father likes to save money. He is trained as an accountant, but at this point, he works as a clerk, and apparently despite the economic depression we are inching out of in Hobart, legal practices still want one.

Despite Father's white-collar occupation, his mind still slants backwards like a long, end-of-day shadow, back into the Middle Ages. Though he's not as superstitious as my mother was when she lived, there are a number of prohibitions against me nonetheless. A short list of things that as a changeling I am not allowed: to wind the clock, to milk animals, to touch horses' manes, or pregnant women or their babies, or goats, or laying hens. Though I must say this last one I disobeyed when Father wasn't looking. My person is not to be touched with iron in an active way. Nobody is meant to watch me without calling out my name to alert me they were there, and nobody might strike me more than three times without a calamity befalling them. In general, best not to touch or strike me at all.

After our morning ritual, I see my father off to work where he is in Morton Allport's legal firm; then I feed and release the chickens. Once the woodstove is well and truly roaring, you will see me with a basket walking in my suit, tie, and hat up the road to the bakery and the cheese-maker. I buy some of the ingredients we need to cook dinner, though a lot comes from our kitchen garden. We always have backup food growing and don't rely on our potato crop. On some days, we have Ronit in who does the laundry and scrubs the place from top to bottom. From the age of ten, I was already a bit like a housekeeper, even doing some cooking as well.

See the horses and carriages going up and down the main street of South Hobart? The occasional ladies with their gowns held up, boots just visible, avoiding piles of horse manure, and the spot where a drunk stumbled out of the public house and vomited the night before. There is the smell of fresh bread in the air, making war with the weird acerbic pong of the tannery. Despite the lack of engines, life can be loud, with barking dogs, whinnying horses, people hollering wares, chickens giving out their laying caterwaul, and the clank of carriage wheels. Somewhere near, a blacksmith is hard at work, though this is a less common sound than it was when I was a little boy. Waterwheels still churn in the Cascades River below, which once flowed with more muscle than it does now.

Around me, hundreds of other people are living similar lives, some far more comfortable, some wretched beyond belief. Some children are in charge of other younger children and administering the opium to the toddler to keep it pacified whilst the parents work. I have only myself to pacify. A great many of the suffering are former convicts who have completed their sentence. Gossipy people keep mental records of the families with the taint upon them who are trying to pass off. Hobart is made for the free settler now—now that a stop has been put to the aesthetic blot of human misery regularly expectorated into our port. They believe we can make something far easier on the eye out of this place. A little name change from Van Diemen's Land to Tasmania, and she'll scrub up alright, they say.

If you become me and turn a full circle (no one will really stare much as I'm known for being a bit eccentric), looking out from the bakery in South

Of the Heart

Hobart over the church steeple towards the centre of Hobart, you will see dirty smoke rising from a few industrial stacks that still mar the sky. They are not as active these days, since local manufacturing has begun to give way to global mass production. Where I am right now is not the posh end of town where Arthur lives, but neither is it the bad place (Wapping) to be; it is in the middle. As was said by The Bard, on fortune's cap, we were not the very button, nor the soles of her shoe. We lived about her middle, her privates. If you mention feeling sorry for the destitute, adults teach you to say "but for the grace of God go I," but what they mean is, just be thankful it's not you it's happening to.

Some days I would hurry home to meet with a tutor or a music instructor. I worked hard at cello, violin, and piano, as well as loved literature and history. Though I can't remember if I worked hard at them. For the purpose of our speed-read of my childhood, it matters that you could catch the resonance of the cathedral bells from our home and that sometimes in the night I would wake thinking I could hear my mother's old rocking chair moving on the old floorboards across the hall. This was what gave me the idea, planted in the fecund darkness of my isolated mind, that one of the four walls—or the floor, or ceiling—of the rooms was permeable. Maybe what was on the other side of the wall was the ghost of the earlier house on the spot, the one we lived in originally before the rebuild? On the other side of that wall or floor, they did things differently. Other lives continued along different timelines, or maybe all along the same timeline at certain hours of night. Other fates rocked away in the darkness, rocking cradles, rocking worlds.

As the last one standing of my own generation, I found the fact the Allports had all their children still living remarkable. My father said the famine had weakened our stock, in such ways the iniquities of man tread us down or rise us up for generations, never leaving us alone. "Always having enough to eat will do wonders for the survival of one's offspring," he would say, whilst making a sniffing sound as he indicated the direction to Fernleigh and its teeming healthy Allport children. "Whenever God puts one more Englishman on the earth he subtracts three Irishmen," he muttered.

Morton Allport, Arthur's father, was a hereditary barrister, which in this Hobart-sized world I inhabited was close enough to being a hereditary peer elsewhere. His grandmother was a well-known local artist, and Arthur was going to inherit his father's position as head of the family along with his occupation, just like that. There were no decisions or choices to be made if you were the oldest son of a hereditary barrister; the wig was put on you in the cradle. They lived at the Holbrook Place mansion Fernleigh, but rumour had it they only had half of the place, and some other family was in part of it. To me, whether or not they lived in a whole or partial mansion was somewhat beside the point. We were on the lower end of the middle class ourselves, and Arthur was on the upper end of the middle class. Apparently when you hem humans together in a small and isolated, antipodean community, they start to get really concerned about such things. They bother themselves mightily about who one's parents were and to whom they were related, and what small scandal might attach to such a one. Gossip seemed such tiresome fare to me.

My father in the evening by the coal-fire taking his brandy reminded me: "Morton and I like each other enough because I'll talk about natural history with him, and you boys have hit it off. But they are our social superiors still, Henry. I won't be able to afford to send you away to school at Hortons. The Allport boy's life and the circles he moves in will be very different to yours."

"I don't want to go to boarding school, so that suits me fine, Father. They would only all be Protestants anyway." I said it as much to make him feel better than anything. I was never disappointed in not being able to go to school with Arthur because I had never entertained such lofty hopes. As to religion, well, in truth I didn't care what religion people were. I knew that even whilst trying to allow people to mistake us for Protestants, Father did hold a prejudice against the religion, and it pleased him when I echoed a smattering of anti-Protestant scorn. "But really, it's not as if he's the grand old Duke of York's son, is it?"

Father smiled grudgingly. On rare occasions such as this, he would speak of Ireland. "Back home-home, my old aunt used to say that the folks with airs and graces in Dublin would be made nothing of in London. Such it is down here, Son. We all get free from bondage, and then we make our own new set of lords all over again, because we must fair love the feel of the boot heel on our necks so much." He laughed bitterly to himself, dry and unused in the back of his throat, more of the ache of a long-lost-laugh than a laughter itself.

I didn't turn the lamps on. I only took a candle. This was a little anachronistic as kerosene gave a steadier, brighter night light. It wasn't as though I wanted to unsettle him exactly, but it wasn't as though I didn't want to unsettle him either. In my nightshirt like a ghost myself, I told Arthur of little Aunty Etticoat with the white house coat and her bright hat, who finds that the longer she stands, the shorter she grows.

"The candle," Arthur said immediately.

"Mother taught me that one." I smiled and placed the candle down next to the place where the clock sat.

"Why did your father never just wind the clock back up?" Arthur asked, hands on his hips. In the semi-dark, we gazed at the frozen hands set eternally to seven minutes after nine in the morning, the second hand just on the verge of launching forward from twelve but never allowed to set off on that journey. Truth was, I related to that clock I wasn't allowed to changeling-wind myself. Sometimes in the story, I tell myself about my life (which is all memories are). Mother's clock started to tick again the moment I walked out of my father's home for the last time—and ticked out until I was gone.

"Time stopped for him," I replied, looking over at the shrill quiet of it. "Here in this house, time appears to move on, but to Father we are always trapped in that moment when Mother left him. I know this is true because I still hear the clock going sometimes. You heard it too. It's on the other side of the fourth wall."

We went back-to-back again through unspoken mutual consensus. I felt no fear in Arthur's body this second time, only excitement and readiness. His readiness quickened mine.

"Show me how you came to replace the human baby."

I smiled. The truth was, I had no recollection of any such replacement. Yet, somehow, I was beginning to warm to the story of it—its drama, its imaginative flare.

"I came with the sound of bells out of time, with wild, wild eyes and all the birds stopped singing."

I waited to see if he caught the Keats reference. He didn't seem to, so I made a note later to read aloud to him from *La Belle Dame Sans Merci* while our fathers became inebriated below. It did me good to hear my father laugh. Often, I wished I knew what he and Morton talked about late at night. I think I wished to know the flavour of their humour so that I might learn to make father laugh.

"Are you a boy or a girl?" Arthur asked in all innocence, as if we now belonged to a world different to the one normal people inhabited, one where such choices were entirely mine to decide. In what we were coming to know as *our game*, he extended this liberty, for me to pick whichever I preferred.

"Maybe... But I think for the Good Neighbours, it's more like being both or neither." In this I had, without him knowing it, told him a secret I'd never before shared. He seemed to be content with the idea of my androgyny as if it had made sense to him already. This fact made me feel daring. "I'm a ghost as well as a changeling, you see. When I play my cello up here near the window, I imagine I died along with my mother and sister and have just been haunting here all this time in the belief I'm still alive. Father only still talks to me and sets out plates of food for me because he's long since lost his mind."

Even if I'm not really dead, I become a ghost when I write. All writers are ghost writers. The moment these words are written, the self that wrote them will never be again as it was in that moment. All words become ghost stories from the mouth of the dead—in time, light which has its point of origin somewhere that is now no more, yet the light is still travelling out to you. We are here with you when you read. We are all of those who have become echoes, who exist now only in this parade of signs on a white backdrop, leaping back and forth with miraculous speed between the page and the synapses of your brain. We exist yet in your world; do not doubt it. The act of reading activates us, as does speaking of us. All of the ancestor rituals bleached from us 'till we are Saxon-white have coagulated and bubbled up in squid guts on the skin of a dead tree. So I'm told.

"Do you *look* like you're dead?" I could hear the dread in his voice, and I kept my arms linked through his.

"I don't know, do I?"

"Yes," he whispered. "You have a little of the merrow in you, bluish-pale and dripping water. I believe you could be the voice keening who foretells disaster. Whilst you are certainly of the noble race, I am not altogether unsure that you aren't a feral child from the forest as well."

As he named these qualities in me, perhaps they came to exist only in this moment? It was him that pulled this new me into being. Next, he also pulled out of the game. Afterwards, he said to me, "You're a bit scary, did you know that, Henry?"

"You said you like to be scared."

"I like it a lot." He left the implication this carried hanging in the air. "I think I'm going to tell you about one of my faces."

I frowned. "What do you mean?"

"My names. Remember I told you I have lots?"

"Of course I remember."

"You will see me differently once you know about the ones other than Arthur," he said regretfully.

OF THE HEART

I put my hand on his arm lightly for a moment. It was a brief burn of human contact, which I had to immediately relinquish. The sweet traces of it lingered in the intricate grooves of my fingerprints like a nutriment I could absorb in slow release. "Don't do it then. If you want to be Arthur, just be Arthur."

"I wish I could," he murmured, following me into my dead sister's room.

Arthur fiddled with the back of the rocking chair where my mother used to soothe my infant sister. He couldn't resist giving the chair a rock to make the abandoned nursery come to life, as if the ghost of my mother sat there with her child. "What did she die of?" he asked, changing the subject without telling me his official name. I didn't mind. I placed more value on his dream of himself than I did on what the rest of the world had to say. He went over to the cot. Father was not the sort of man to change things in a hurry, and even though the room had been converted into a guest bedroom, they were still forced to keep company with my dead sister's cot and my mother's rocking chair. Arthur preferred to sleep in my room when he stayed.

"The same thing as Mother. The river fog killed them."

"Influenza or typhoid?" he asked, the matter-of-fact question of any young person of an era where child mortality from disease was commonplace. Despite the ubiquity of death, or perhaps for this reason, it was a topic that obsessed us. To understand us, you had to imagine finding a picture of a dead sibling in a family album and needing to ask what their name was?

"Yes, the influenza-mucous-yellow fog spirit. I saw it lazing around the rivulet less than twenty-four hours before several people in the area fell ill. I dreamed on the night before it happened that my mind was in that mist as it came up through the floorboards looking for them." I beckoned to him to come and look down through the crack in the floorboards where the wind whistled up from below. "Look. Down here, in the basement; that's where they took her. That's where I hear her sometimes."

"You mean her spirit? Is that where we go when we play our game? When you tell me to feel myself sinking down?" I didn't answer because I don't think he fully understood about the fourth wall yet, so it wasn't time. "Was it the Jerry you saw, do you think? I've seen the men riding horses in the mist."

The Bridgewater Jerry is a name given to a particular viscous column of mist that tumbles down the mouth of the River Derwent and into the bay like a galloping column of pale grey water horses. I shook my head, because the apparition had clearly not come from that direction. Though I was glad to know that his mind could see the forms of horses in the mist. Perhaps like me he was a little bit Sighted? Can you be a little bit Sighted? Or is it more like a fatal illness? "No, this was something different again. It seeped up out of the slums downriver with an evil look on its face. It didn't come all the way up from the cove."

Arthur smiled. His slightly turned up nose gave off something a bit pixie-like when he smiled. "Mist has a face?"

"Many faces. Least it does if it can ride horses!" I poked my tongue out at him.

Laughing, he playfully slapped me, but not as hard as other boys did when they would trip or punch me on my way to the candlestick maker or the butcher. I felt for a moment like he believed I was indeed something Other again than either a boy or a girl, that he saw the elf-get, the monstrous-stranger, and that he was alright with it. All at once I, too, was alright with it. The idea that he liked this about me left me with a levity that smelt like fresh linen in the sun when it has caught a sea breeze in its weave. I felt free inside his gaze. Like someone who could attract a great deal of good fortune to his farm.

Later that night, I woke and gained the blurry awareness of being entangled in sleep with Arthur. We were more like a litter of pups than boys; my father and his father spoke quietly over us, one of them holding a lantern. "Ah," my father said, sentiment as well as alcohol blurring his voice. "Makes me remember my boyhood friendships."

"Innocence is precious," Morton sighed. "I remember when I used to be that relaxed. It almost seems a shame to move him…"

"Let him be then, Morton, let him be. Look how comfortable he is! I'll feed him breakfast and send him home on the morrow."

As they were leaving, I think I heard his father say his official name for the first time. It never really seemed like the name of the boy I knew. And until Arthur agreed to be called that other name by me, I would never think of it as his real name—that was his alone to decide. This right to consent we offered each other was like water in the desert. Even in the middle class, children were not asked for their consent in those days. So, having the consent of our fathers, these words spoken over us filled me with a contentment as strong as having fallen asleep before an open fire. I must have gone straight back to sleep, safe in the knowledge that, for now, our friendship had their approval, and the world didn't mean to take him from me just yet.

2

That's what I call it in the privacy of my mind where you join me now. Calling it that acknowledged that I hadn't really been fully alive until I was friends with the boy the world called "Master Allport." I had never gazed into the magic mirror of a true friend. The year after I first dubbed him *Arthur* was a time of strange, new permissions. For the first time, I took him inside my mirror maze and got him to see things inside the things I'd shown him in the first place. Our game intensified. I sensed—though I had no evidence for it—that it was so for him as well. We had each unleashed something in each other's latent capacities. His reading life, for instance, blossomed with radical speed under my fond attention and praise.

In my case, it was with the healthy vigour in his body that he beckoned mine to grow and reach out towards the sun. We were halfway through that First Summer when he first threw his arms around my neck in exuberant happiness and declared in the most heartfelt manner: "I love you so much! You're my dearest friend!" I was so touched by his unguarded expressions of affection that I had to dry my eyes with the corner of my handkerchief. He seemed so vulnerable. If I were a different sort of boy, I could have wounded him savagely, as it appeared as yet he had built little defence against such betrayals. There was never any risk to him from me. For when it came to being told I was loved, if someone had said it to me before, including my parents, then I couldn't remember it. I think I realised early how shared our vulnerability was. After he saw how moved I was by his affection, I was given many more cuddles, as if he sensed in me an orphan puppy that needed more pats than it was receiving.

He took me places where the water was still clean and pure, far upstream of the congealing dog carcasses, blackish-brown slaughterhouse offal, and the odd human foetus that occasionally still appeared in the downstream stews, where the streets at night were hacked apart by influenza coughs. Up higher, beyond the town boundary, the air was thinner, heady; there was less of the psychic mess of humanity sweating in the air around us, and it was out there with him in the freezing cold water that I laughed and laughed 'till I wept for the first time in my life. He insisted on teaching me to swim. In that liquid environment with him, I was entirely out of control of my limbs and existed only in the trust of him, without whom I could not breathe. Whenever I flailed, his hand steadied me; I was never allowed to go under for more than a moment. Just long enough for me to know the intimacy of reliance.

No longer did I heed my father's injunctions not to go into the bush, not to get cold lest my weak lungs couldn't take the shock, not to elevate my pulse rate lest my apparently defective heart clap out. There wasn't a thought of fear all Summer, as if we'd become weightless. He had reason to be bold, for all his siblings and parents yet lived. For me, until then, I didn't know how afraid I'd been since my mother and sister died in such quick succession. Much more unclear were the odd recollections of other siblings who'd died when I was too young to see them clearly in my mind's eye. I was afraid because I had felt alone in a house full of echoes that felt larger and stronger than me. Afraid because I felt all the Irish famine dead clawing up my bloodlines, insecure about subsistence. I had been afraid we would all be eaten, one by one, by those hungry dead, afraid I'd be accused of suckling the life from the household and turned out onto the street, or hillside-exposed, like the changelings of the past. In fact, before I met Arthur, I'd been afraid so often I didn't know it was even called "fear," because it had been there all the time.

It was a feat of sorts, carried out by my young, urgent, growing flesh that wanted the light. It was a feat of courage for me—this hoping-outward, this attempt at fearlessness—in a way it wasn't quite yet for Arthur, who had grown under the sunlight of more privileges. Suddenly, with the fear dissolved from my limbs after being brave and being rescued, my faith in someone else was like an extra muscle. I don't think I'd ever used it before until then. My body was coming to trust Arthur's body. So, my father was no longer the person whom I had to satisfy and placate above all others, the person who would make the decision if I was to be got rid of or not. He was something to be gently humoured and cared for. Someone with whom to share a little of the sunlight and pure livingness of youth that was sluicing off from my pores like spring rain. Consequently, he often favoured me with an indulgent and nostalgic smile during that early time, as if he was again remembering the youth he'd referred to when Morton and he had come into my room that night.

OF THE HEART

Come with me under the limpid moon and long-cast shadows, my breath matching a sobbing heart. We run under cover of nightfall, trying not to look each other in the eye lest we laugh at our own disobedience. The memory knots me up… Feel the way his warm hand—protective and, to be honest, a little bossy at times—guides me about. He knows along with me the elation of finding myself free of my father's house. The Cascade River at night is a patchwork of echoes and shambling drunks finding their way to their night sleep in the bushes. It isn't always easy for me to tell which are which, between the replays of the past and those who are still alive in a physical sense but just as lost. They all look the same kind of see-through.

As it returns to me, this mind assault, the influx of the past collapses me up a little, and I struggle to distinguish the edges of forever. I remember how the rivulet down that end of town smelt like tannery fluids, male urine, and freedom. Bad smells weren't all bad anymore, somehow; they almost seemed a code for escape from the middle-class cloister. Arthur was rapidly pulling me along by my hand, taking me upstream away from it, taking me somewhere purer like he always did. He needed to escape, too, for his own reasons of which I knew little at this point. "I have to show you something," was all he said. Being free meant him drawing me on like this. It was as if he lent me a little of his life force, and with it, I exploded into motion with him. Otherwise, I was more like the piano player in the music box who lies down in the dark most of the time, until someone winds her up and opens the lid.

"Look!"

I smiled because I loved it when Arthur would be excited enough about something that he'd forget he was meant to be an English gentleman. When we reached Shadow of Death Valley, as some people had called the site of the Female Factory in the past, Arthur paused and pointed up past the willow trees to a little shanty of a place not far from the watermill. There were stubs of candles burning on the front balcony—that was what I noted first—dripping wax straight onto the woodwork, stuck on by their own attitude problem. Coming from a world where polishing the brass was a monthly job of mine, it was hard to consider what kind of monster might use wax to stick a candle to their own establishment. These rustic lights seemed to illuminate the path and door as if to invite people to come by at night. "It's a witch's house, they say."

Squinting, I made out the horseshoe above the door, the broom beside it. At the top of the humble overhang and wooden protuberance that passed as a veranda, there was a string of some small bones tied together that made sound in the breeze like a macabre windchime. I knew immediately I was going to have to go inside, because people who decorate their home with bones are my kind of monster.

"Should we...should we try to meet her?" I asked hesitantly.

"We shouldn't just *should*, we must!" Arthur declared.

Every one of the dwelling's wind-whistling nooks was violated by ivy; it looked like a habitation swallowed but only partially masticated. The main differences were the superstitious items and the ghost-echo of the little girl sitting in the tree out the front. I tried not to stare directly at Mary, because I knew if I did, I would have an episode where my second sight would crush me in front of others and cause me to act strange. Then if I tried to ignore it, I'd get a tic. She was stronger here than I'd ever seen her. I wanted to tell Arthur that before we even went in, but I was too nervous to speak.

What sort of person would live within this dwelling, and how would I converse with them? My training had all been in polite society, which was aspirational from my father's point of view. I wasn't as bold as Arthur to just start conversations with former convicts, vagrants, and Black fellows, as much as I had always so much wanted to hear their stories.

"What are you going to say?" I whispered.

"Well, if she's cunning folk, chances are she sells her services. There used to be one such woman back in Staffordshire that my grandmother talks about; she could charm away warts, and you always had to cross her palm with proper silver, apparently. I shall merely tell her I heard that someone operates around here, and that I am in need of such a person."

Terrified by his boldness, I followed with cheeks already pink. I think maybe he liked that it all impressed me so much and played it up. The people who lived in the huts around the abandoned mills were often ex-convicts, rough people who had nothing to do with my family beyond washing our linen. Was it Arthur's higher social rank that made him feel impervious to the discomforts of this situation? *You know they have less than you, don't you? And how do you think they feel about it when you're not there to see?* It wasn't just discomfort I felt around the lower classes, it was outright fear. They had, after all, lived a life surrounded by violence in a way I had not. His confident knock on the front door seemed to further this impression that Arthur felt himself partially in charge in such a

Of the Heart

situation. "Other people are like spiders, Henry," he whispered to me. "They are more afraid of you than you are of them."

I had never been afraid of spiders, so this metaphor fell flat. As soon as the woman answered the front door, I knew we'd come to the right place. Under the marks of character and hardship that lined the woman's face, there were familiar contours, and despite the crop of spun silver in her hair, the last signs of once raven tresses were still in evidence. The hairs stood up on the backs of my arms when I gazed into the knowing eyes of Mary's mother. I knew it as soon as I saw her. There was a rum- and burning heath-scented magic around this woman that I knew nothing of; my very ignorance of all she was and all she manifested took my breath quite out of me. To me, she may as well have been the Gordian Knot.

"Pleased to meet you, Madam," Arthur said, taking off his hat and addressing her as politely as if she were one of the daughters of the gentlefolk of Hobart he'd met at a ball. "I find myself in need of the services of cunning folk. I wondered if you might know one?"

I held my breath at his daring while she regarded him without speaking for a few moments. After a while, she swung the door a little more open and leaned on the edge of it in the manner of a cocky young boy who had more swagger than he did stature to back it up, but who was still happy to fight you. Her whole bearing told a thousand very rough-hewn and crude stories to the observant eye. She crossed her arms and narrowed her eyes, glancing from Arthur to me suspiciously. Slowly, her stance straightened up, as if she were coming to her full height and breadth in the doorway, her body language telling us she didn't care who our fathers were, that she had a knife hidden in her apron, and she'd cut us as soon as look at us. "Who's asking, kid?"

I jumped when I saw the Black man by her hearth fire. At first, I'd interpreted him as Aboriginal; at my second breath, I realised the fellow was in fact a negro. This was a rare but not vanishingly rare sight in Hobart Town—certainly nowhere near as rare as Aboriginal folk had become. Mary Bones took my attention next by appearing indoors. There she was, with shoes on the wrong feet, stronger in this room than I had ever seen her elsewhere. She was standing in the doorway to the one room, twiddling her ringlet hair and singing a stitched-together, mingled nursery rhyme. Her voice came out mixed with the sound of a child's wind-up music box, so that the sound appeared to come from her mouth. I couldn't pay proper attention to anything other than this sound. Mary was trying to show me something under the floor, and she was so insistent about it that the nursery babble and music box's sound became louder and louder and shriller like a rising shriek.

"Henry!"

Eventually, I responded to Arthur's voice as he gave me a gentle shake.

I nodded and closed my eyes for a second, trying to regain my composure. It was embarrassing when this happened in front of other people, especially strange, rather scary people I'd never met before. The music box had the same tune as one of my little sisters, and I wasn't sure how Mary was able to make this sound. What did my sister's music box have to do with this house and this woman?

"Mary, Mary quite contrary…and Pandora," I whispered to myself.

"Is the boy touched?" the woman asked.

"No," Arthur replied. "He's light-shadowed. Gifted."

The woman grunted sceptically. "Yeah, *touched*, like I said. Is this what you came here for, boy? Looking for me to help you turn your poor, weird brother normal?"

Arthur laughed softly for a moment. It was a strange little laugh, and it kindled the beginnings of something in me that I could not as yet name. "Oh, Henry isn't my brother. But yes, I did come here for him. Not to turn him normal, just hoping to find someone else like him, I suppose. People who would better understand his gift."

The effect his words had upon me was enough to drown out what I could see and hear. For a moment or two, the life in me triumphed over death, and whatever grave moss had been seeking all my life to grow upon my skin was vanquished.

"Let Old Moses get a look at you, boy," the man was saying, coming up to me while smoking on a pipe and squinting at me through the smoke. Arthur still had my arm. Mary was singing quietly about cock horses and cockle shells. Moses shakily took out some spectacles and put them on to better examine me. After looking me over, he exchanged significant glances with the woman. Then he looked at both my palms as if reading the lines. He blew a bit of pipe smoke over me, and I started to feel more present, more in my body, less aware of ghost music box voices. I couldn't tell if it was his breath or the tobacco I involuntarily breathed that had this effect.

"Sit down; I'll put the billy on." Though Martha's words were for us, they were also her answer to Moses's wordless question after he looked at me.

"I'm Arthur, by the way."

He didn't need to tell me I wasn't allowed to use his last name in this place; that was obvious. Arthur would now serve as a separate identity for him, someone who allowed him to do the things that Master Allport was not able to.

"Well, I'm Martha; won't that get annoying real quick?"

OF THE HEART

Arthur laughed cheerfully, but it took me a second or two to get the joke. When I did, I smiled.

"You going to sit down or what, faerie boy?" she demanded with her hands on her hips. For a moment, I was startled by her abruptness and just stared at her. It was Arthur who pulled me down by the hand until I was sitting on a tatty mat by the fire. There were no chairs in the room. Moses sat on an upturned box next to the hearth, likely on account of his more advanced age.

"Yes," I muttered redundantly. "Of course...my apologies."

Martha grinned widely with intense mirth brewing around her teeth, which she revealed were blackened with chewing tobacco. As though to illustrate her point, she spat some of the blackened fluid in her mouth into a tin against the wall with amazing accuracy. "Don't you have the cutest little manners ever?" She grinned at me, every sparkle of her eyes a cacophony of insolence. It was clear she was trying to provoke me, as if without me ever knowing it she and I were on different sides of an ongoing war I'd never even heard about. I guess I'd never heard about this war the same way Arthur hadn't seemed to know anyone had a problem with the Irish.

I didn't know how to respond. The glint of animosity in her eye as she looked me over—like a predator trying to determine how quickly they could catch and kill the prey—was something I'd never been hungry enough to understand. Somehow, I knew that; I smelt it, I suppose, with my second sight, which could also sometimes become a second smelling. I could smell the way hunger puts a sharpness in a person, the way privation wakes the animal intelligence in the body in a way my body had never been woken. I knew all that just by being near someone, sitting down for the first time at the fireside of a woman like Martha. Maybe I knew it because my family was hungry before me, and the starving often sing together.

"Henry's quite the natural," Arthur bantered back easily, as if he were born to entertain former convicts and criminals. "My father has put three times the effort and money into trying to turn me into half the gentleman Henry is."

Immediately, I knew what lay behind those words. Arthur had purposely drawn any class-based animosity towards himself rather than me.

"Is that so, Little Lord Toff?" Martha declared. There was a smile on her face, yet her eyes were still narrow. Old Moses just smoked his pipe meditatively and continued to examine me with disconcerting focus. I could feel his eyes on the side of my face like I was a jigsaw puzzle he was intent on finishing and had no intention of hurrying. "And who—or what—may I ask is Daddy Toff?"

I wasn't even sure what she was trying to ask. Arthur seemed to catch on immediately.

"My father?" He grinned self-deprecatingly, adapting easily to the notion that status was something to be ashamed of in these circles. "What are you guessing he is?" Either because his grin was so infectious or because he'd turned it into a magic game, some of the feeling of class warfare began to soften at its edges. Martha sat down herself and began to prepare tea. After a fashion.

"I'm calling you're a doctor or banker's lad," Moses said, looking over his glasses at Arthur in a way that suggested he'd made a prescription upon Arthur's very soul. "One of a big family, so that your Pappy let things go a bit with the younger ones."

I watched Arthur smile; he was suddenly more mysterious and held at his extremity, less about the effusive charm. Always, I was watching. I suppose I hoped to learn from him what to do with people.

"I've got a few in my family, but it's not enormous…I'm also the oldest boy."

"Let me try," Martha leaned in close, peering at him even more closely than Moses had. "Show me your hands." Arthur offered them both to her. She turned them over and looked at the palms first; then she righted them and examined his knuckles. For quite some time, what I felt to be an uncomfortable amount of time, she seemed to feel her way along all the small bones in his fingers. Finally, she spoke. "Your fingertips and palms are very soft; you've done no work in your life. You've held a pen plenty, but you've also been struck many times across the hands…I'm going to call, high up military father."

"My father's in the legal profession," Arthur replied quietly, all the life gone out of his voice of a sudden. I very much would have liked to reach out to touch him, as I was mortified that she had noticed something I hadn't about his hands. "He is indeed strict with me at times. Though he loves me," Arthur added.

"He kicks ten colours of cunting shit out of you, don't he, poor lad?" Something in her eyes had softened with a species of compassion. It was a rough, old compassion, yet it was there nonetheless. I was too in shock from the eruption of obscenity to sit with this truth at the time. Arthur laughed with surprise also, then reined it in and sighed. He made a gesture with his head that was neither a total denial nor a total affirmation. "Maybe about eight or nine, but mostly only when I deserve it. I'm the most difficult of all of his children. He says also the most promising."

"What makes you difficult?" Martha asked, folding her arms as if the question were a test.

"I suppose I've got a few ideas about some things."

"I bet you do, too, eh?" she laughed, glancing at Moses with more subtle communication of the winking kind. "Poor Daddy Barrister's got a little spitfire on his hands, I'd say. And what with having to gentleman you up good and proper, he'll quite put his cane arm out with the effort!" She laughed with enjoyment at the idea of Arthur's father's eventual defeat through beating fatigue. I felt it pleased her, in the world of physical discipline we all lived in, to think that rich boys were also beaten. Her eyes flashed on Arthur again as she poured the dark brew in her billy into some tin cups. "You're planning to break that cane arm for him once you come of age, no?" The sly little look she gave him was full of that mysterious rustic witchery I'd smelled on her when we first walked in. It was made up of one part privation-driven intuition and the rest on cunning.

"I might have thought about it a time or two," Arthur replied, his tone guarded. Concerned that he felt hunted by her correct observation, I came to his rescue as he had come to mine earlier.

"Is she your little girl? Mary?" I asked, quite suddenly. "Mary, Mary quite contrary, how does your garden grow? With cockle shells..." I noticed the cockleshells piled up on the floor near the wall. Martha spilled a little of the tea she was pouring as I said Mary's name. I noticed the flinch that led to the spill, and she noticed me noticing. When she looked up at me briefly, there was a flash in her eyes, which had sharp curiosity mixed with something baleful. It was the hungry look again, the one I knew I'd not suffered enough to understand. I could smell blood, and I had no intention of relenting. This was one law of the jungle my body understood thoroughly: when it comes to having the advantage, you should always follow through. I myself had not been badly hungry, yet I came up from them. "What's under the cockleshells? Did you keep her little baby bones in a box down there?"

For a second, I felt pure pitiless exhilaration. I was entirely elf-get in that moment. The rush was gone when I heard the censure in Arthur's voice. "Henry!" He put his hand on my hand and squeezed it. "Maybe there are other ways of *putting it*," he suggested with exaggerated tactfulness.

Moses laughed and broke the tension, a wheezing old sound. "The boy's good. Too good. Looks like we got ourselves some competition on the block, eh Martha?"

"How did you know Mary Bones was Martha's dead child?" Arthur asked as he walked me home along the river. "Did you see her in the cottage or hear her?"

I nodded. "Saw her and heard her. She kept pointing to something under the floor. I've known her for a long time, and she mainly communicates in nursery rhythms and bits and pieces of old sayings she's picked up. It's because when she…well, you can't call her 'dead' really. When she first came to me, she was a very little, toddling child. She's different to the other dead children because she has been able to grow up. Or at least she has the appearance of doing so. A lot of children died at the nurseries in the Female Factory when they used to use it." I shrugged. "I always assumed that's where she came from. She hadn't spoken much at the age she died, and she has always had those same limited verbal abilities. Mary is stronger than the others. The other ones would all get swept away by time, but not her." I sighed, partly nostalgic, partly pensive. "I never fully understood what made her *so* strong until now."

"Is it Martha's love that keeps her?" Arthur asked.

"Love can do things like that: keep things alive that should be dead."

"Why do you think it is that you can see them?"

Pausing by the turn-off for my walk home, I listened to the icy rush of the water below. "Probably because I'm not long for this world."

"Please don't say that!" He caught up to me all of a sudden and took hold of me, pulled me away from the edge even though there was a railing. "It's an unbearable thought."

"My apologies. I'll not speak of it again." I blushed a little and didn't know what else to say. The feeling wasn't a frivolous one, though, not like being flattered; it was quite serious. I took careful stock of the fact that this was something that hurt Arthur and made note not to repeat it. As we walked back towards my home, I put my arm through his, hoping it would comfort him. "Does he hurt you…a lot…like Martha said?" I asked. "Your father? If you do something wrong?"

"No more than other people's fathers, I reckon," he replied. There was just enough cageyness about it to show that, although physical discipline was indeed the order of the day for children of our era, Arthur had been wounded in his heart as well as his body. "He's good to me most of the time. Sometimes, that's actually the hardest part."

"My father doesn't strike me at all," I murmured, admitting something freakish about my family. "Ever."

"Well, you're a very good boy, Henry. I can't see any reason he'd need to strike you. He's also probably afraid he'll break you."

I looked to see if I was being teased. Arthur used his other hand to extend and examine my fingers that lay across his forearm. Because it was dark but for the moon, it was primarily a tactile examination. There was an affection in the gesture that seemed to rule out teasing. "You're delicate, and he's already lost a wife and his other children."

"I'm not *that* delicate."

"There's nothing wrong with being delicate, Henry," he said resolutely, clearly not willing to back down from his statement. "Perhaps if you did not have such fine fingers, you'd not play as well as you do? God makes us all differently for his own reasons; your purpose is clearly to make music and poetry. Keats was delicate too."

I smiled with slow-kindling warmth that seemed to come up from a mountainside hearth fire inside my chest, where ice melt would soon flow in tear-rivers down my face if I wasn't careful. I could have retorted that Keats, too, hadn't been long for this world. Instead, I got distracted. "You read up on him after I mentioned him?"

Arthur looked at me and smiled; for a moment, his eyebrows jumped up with something almost like a challenge. As if he had every intention of rising to every occasion in excess of my expectations. "Of course. After you read me *La Belle Dame Sans Merci*, I read everything I could find about him. He died with the tuberculosis; it was tragic."

While I struggled to conceal my emotions, we walked on. The poetry I'd memorised by heart was the first place I had found other humans I could relate to, who saw a life of withering intensity around themselves. Having an inner life made me feel safer.

"Did you expect less of me?"

"Yes. A great deal less." I clapped my hand over my mouth, realising this was far too honest. "I mean, no! I mean, not *you*, personally. Just...people. I have learned not to expect extravagant things from...people."

I could feel my father's gaze on me as I cleared away the tea tray. The feeling wasn't as strong as Moses's eyes, so I managed to ignore them for a while. Finally, I looked up and caught the concerned, benevolent expression of my father looking at me from over his spectacles. It was the same mixture of confused pity, sadness, and affection with which he'd looked at me all his life. I guessed from the affection that he had no idea about my night adventures to the homes of ex-convicts and witches.

How I wished I could fling my arms around him and give him a warm embrace of the type that Arthur so often bestowed on me. I knew Father loved me, but there was a brittleness about his physical being since my mother's death, one that made your own body feel awkward and uncomfortable just by being in proximity with it. I didn't need to be told with words that it wouldn't have been proper. After all, I was far too old for it now, if I had, in fact, ever actually been young enough.

"Is everything all right, Son?"

I smiled. The immediate and genuine happiness behind my smile was irrepressible, and I doubt it was lost. For a moment, it seemed as though he would be pulled into an emotion in response, as if the torpor of daily living hadn't quite smothered out his internal vitality just yet. He damped the response quickly upon catching himself.

"Things are better than all right; they are quite wonderful."

He nodded rapidly, a nod that tucked back in whatever feeling came before it and nonverbally told me to do the same with mine. "Good," he replied. And then again, more quietly, "Good." Before I could take the tea tray, he patted my hand briefly, almost absent-mindedly as if I were a cat who had nudged up against his leg desperate for attention. "I want you to be happy, Henry."

I bit down on my lip with a rush of barely contained emotion. "Thank you, sir," I managed to whisper before ducking away with the tray to the kitchen. Thankfully, at that time we had no live-in servant, so there was no one else up but me and Father. It took me a moment or two to compose myself, and I had no witnesses during this process. It is good for a strange child, sometimes, to be told they are a changeling, one whom others mustn't look in on without their knowledge. Somehow it seemed to me that Father had conveyed something much deeper to me than the most basic of positive regard. Or did I make up such fictions for myself? Read layers of wanted meaning into the words of everyone around me? Because I was desperate for some sign they held me in regard? I really wasn't sure. I wanted to be right so much it didn't seem to matter.

I quickly dried my eyes on the corner of my apron and fixed Father his pipe. I knew he liked to have that in the parlour in the evenings by the fire. I'd already taken up baking at that age to give Father something homely to take to work with him each day. Perhaps I was anxious to prove I had worth and purpose, that I could partially replace my mother and thus not be exposed again to the world outside our home. Primarily, I think I just needed some way to show my affection to a man whose whole body seemed edged as if to fend off touch.

OF THE HEART

By the time I took him his already packed pipe on another little tray, he was well and deep into his brandy. "Thank you, Son," he whispered, putting a straw straight to the fire to light his pipe. I waited until the stream of tobacco smoke began to ripple out into the air. The smoky silence seemed too heavy to leave the room immediately. "Allport's son's a good boy," he observed between tokes, grudgingly, almost as if someone had claimed otherwise. I wondered if Mr. Allport himself had claimed otherwise?

"He is," I replied. "He's the kindest person I've ever met."

"That he is... That he is... Good-hearted," Father muttered, sipping from his brandy in between tokes of the pipe. "Pure-hearted." I felt something loosening in him with the drink and the smoke and wondered if I might dare a question. "And that's rare enough in this world." I loved how his accent would start to creep back up from under the carpet where it had been stashed and burr its way back into his tongue with all the old memories; it only ever came back into being when he'd drink. Father was an easy drinker, not aggressive, quiet and melancholic.

"Does his father... Does his father not think so?"

Father laughed softly under his breath in a way that told me Mr. Allport had indeed discussed this topic with him. "He says the boy's headstrong and talks back to him. Often takes the mother's or the sister's side to undermine him... That sort of thing. I think he's too hard on the boy between you, me, and the walls." It thrilled me when Father said that. I loved the expression because it was one of the few times normal people admitted that walls too have ears, and because it meant someone was confiding in me. All I wanted from people were these glimpses into the secret world that lived inside them, but I had no idea of the tools for extracting such confidences. "He has such high standards and expectations for his oldest son. I pity the boy, despite their material comfort. You lads are young yet; it's natural enough for a boy to still cleave to his mother at this age, if he's fortunate enough to have one, and to try on strange notions."

I nodded. I imagined it was so. At some level, I was conscious of missing a mother in my life. When she was alive, so were my siblings, and for most of the time, we were in the smaller house that had once existed behind our own. The ghost of that cheaper original cottage was mingled somehow with the sound of other children playing and my mother on her fiddle. Maybe that's where my fourth wall came from? This sense of the phantom building that stood before the one we lived in later? Somewhere during that changeover, we had gone from being that Irish Catholic family to a middle-class residence of people who once came from Ireland, and if they were Protestant or Catholic no one could remember for sure. At least, that was now what they said where we could hear them.

Early on I'd learned it was the men in my life who had the power to decide upon my protection and preservation. Wearing Mother's apron when I cooked was no accident; I wanted to keep her ghost alive. For Father to remember that I was the last he had left of her. As a sickly, strange child with no mother, I knew full well how tenuous my place in life was. If anything happened to Father, there weren't any backup plans for me beyond the orphan school. No other relatives, nobody to teach me and show me how to use my skills and gifts to make up for my other oddities. If there was one thing I well understood about life, it was that any of us could stop breathing in our rocking chair at any moment. You always had to remember that people could suddenly just not be there anymore, and you must treat them each accordingly. Connection was sacred to me, even when it came to odd little attachments like the one that existed between Father and I.

"I agree, Father," I murmured, both because he could die in the night and because I really did agree. What harm was Arthur doing in siding with someone who must in all situations be the underdog? Although I lived alone with another man, I had enough understanding to infer how life was for women. I thought of Martha and smiled to myself as I exited the room with a polite, "Excuse me." She had found ways not to always be the underdog, and I wanted to learn those ways.

I can date the beginning of the loss of my innocence to Martha's story. There are some stories that allow things access to you, things that can forever muddy the waters of your being. Martha's story was such a tale, something I couldn't help living into even though I wanted to keep it hygienically at arm's length. Some of the pus and sharp-scented women's sweat of that story wouldn't be washing off me in any hurry.

"I don't know if you boys are old enough to hear my story," she chuckled, that deep-throated snigger of hers that hinted at ideas far too adult for most adults. "Maybe you," she said quite suddenly, swinging the violation of her gaze and her finger in Arthur's direction. "I smell it quick! When a boy's not quite a boy anymore."

Arthur blushed under the weight of her knowledge. I wished to rescue him from the discomfort. Perhaps part of me didn't want to, though? As tenderly as I felt for him, even in those days, there was something so intimate about the shared ordeal of exposure. There was such a raw pulse in the air while we shared the act of listening to her story. I learned that if Martha was indeed a witch, then hers was the power to open all the hidden wounds, draw all the thick phlegm of things to the surface.

"Ha! Your blush confirms it! Not all boy any longer. You're spilling your seed already, but you're not even close to becoming the full man you'll be one day... You," she said, turning to me. "You're only just trembling on the sweet edge of it, only just a child... What a lush time! When you don't know the Hell ahead of you, and not much shit piled up behind you. Haven't taken your bitters yet..." Her voice fell away for a few moments, allowing a dramatic silence as she shook her head with some profundity. I realised all at once what a teller of tales she was, what a virtuoso storyteller I was in the hands of! The realisation was humbling. I had not seen the potential for art or artistry in this simple dwelling. When it came to people and to justice among them, I was still learning.

Arthur and Moses sat in profound silence as shadows stretched out longer into the perpendicular summer twilight. Moses toked on his pipe and Madame Diablesse (as he called her) began to spin the dark web of her knowing into a story that would unfold hidden parts until it became an initiation for Arthur and me. "You'd both be old enough to be used by the world if you were girl children, so why shouldn't you get it? My grotty tale?"

Arthur and I were too spellbound to have responded, yet she looked intently from one to the other of us, as though waiting for someone to answer her rhetorical question.

"If you were girl children," she added, beginning to pack her pipe as she spoke, laying the tobacco out along her apron which was stretched like a table by her knees as she sat cross-legged, "and you were the piss-poor class, you'd have had a few men's cocks up you by now already, the pair of you. Oh, don't look so shocked! Did you think it was nice out there? On the street? What did you think the poor girls were selling in the alleyways at night while you sit cosy by your coal fire, or tucked in your bed that your servants have passed a bedwarmer over? Hugs?" She laughed uproariously at this notion. "No. When you come from the lower class, your cunny is good for use before the blood even comes; stops you getting pregnant, that does! I suppose you're thinking it's going to be that kind of story. You're both soft touches," she said, as though assessing us all over again, to make sure we were indeed still soft touches. "You less than him," she said, pointing at me and then Arthur. "Master Barrister's son is the one I'd pull a swifty on to get him to give me money by saying I was in trouble. Ha! So you probably have me pegged for some noble tragedy and wrong-donedness, but you're going to get a different story... My girl in The Factory, Gerty; she came with that kind of story—own mother selling her little girl's snatch to pay the rent when things got tight, that sort of thing."

"Unimaginable," Arthur muttered in disgust.

"Not imaginable for you and your soft heart maybe! But if you only ever believe one thing Martha tells you, believe me on this: if some dirty bastard has thought of it, some filthier cunt has *done* it. Let that seep up amongst you both for a bit."

It did indeed sink up and then in me, this idea, and the implications mirrored out to infinity. I recoiled from them with both horror and sorrow for humankind and all suffering beings.

"But see that's what you aren't going to ever understand, no matter how many stories you listen to; you are never going to know what it's like to find it all too easy to imagine being Gerty, while she bites the pillow in one room and her mother's counting coins in the next, trying to pretend she can't hear you weeping. Because you," she said, pointing a seemingly accusing finger at Arthur in particular, because he was the one that had dared to speak. "You have the fucking luxury to find it unimaginable!" She seemed to regather herself after becoming overtly passionate for a second by slugging down some of the spirits Arthur had stolen for her from his father.

I made very brief and subtle eye contact with him where I was certain we both acknowledged our success in loosening Martha up. Had either of us expected anything could be as loose as this though? That I don't know for sure. I know I hadn't. There was some dark glimmer in Arthur's eyes as he listened to her. Regularly I'd glance for a split second at his eyes while he listened. It was clear her tale had spellbound him. Something in her mess and darkness sung to some half-buried part of him; she spoke to his intense and natural physicality, which Mr. Allport said was like a Black fellow and tried to beat away.

"But when I was a girl, things were far more luxurious for me than they were for Gerty, in that there were no strangers forcing their cocks up my holes each night of the week," she chuckled with dark cynicism. "If you can call that a luxury. We were piss-poor, but we still had a pot to piss in, kept that much of our dignity. A man had to offer up at least a vague promise of marriage if he was going to fuck one of our girls raw before she'd bled. We were posh folk like that," she said with a sarcasm so dry it could have passed muster in banter between educated people. "That was all well and good until Father was killed in a mine cave-in. Ma and I had both feared the Knockers were on him and done everything to turn the Eye back on who'd sent it; everything to get them off him. But it was no good. Sometimes when the spirits of the deep earth decide they want to devour something…sometimes they ain't happy with a thing you offer them in return for their minerals, nothing but human blood. Well, it was like that with Pappy, God rest his soul. They took him from us, and in one swoop plunged Ma and I into begging straits and the workhouse quick-like." She took another break to toke on her pipe.

While she smoked, I watched Moses and admired how stock-still and attentive he was to the tale. He gazed fixedly into the embers of the fire. As he did, I could tell that he was living her words. There was no way to tell if he had heard the story before at all, or whether he'd heard it one hundred times. His patience with his attention seemed like a thing of worthy stone taking upon itself the exfoliation of the wind.

"Thing is, with a cunning woman's trade, you can't wield it so good from the street. People don't want your bad luck rubbing off on them, no one wants to go to a witch who can't even hold a cottage down. That's when your cunning folk becomes a witch—when she can't hold her kit and her squat together! Next thing you knew, you'd be accused, back in the day. So, the trade I'd learned from Ma was no good to me. Some of us have one type of spirit and some another: that's just the way of it. Now…half their fucking problem," she said, indicating the world outside her doorstep with a sweep of her hand, "is that they won't accept that. They want one type of man to be another type of man, and one type of woman to be another type of woman. There are begging types of women, and my Ma was a begging type of woman. And there are *taking* types of women," she said with a significant nod. "You guessed right. I'm a taking type of woman. Some rich bastard has ten times what he needs—you bet your sweet, pure little behind I'm going to take something! Fuck starving while they eat the fill of three! Put that in your pipe and smoke it, barrister boy!" she said, slowly blowing her tobacco smoke over in Arthur's direction.

I don't know if Arthur had noticed the jump between admitting to having a father in the legal profession and a barrister in particular that Martha had successfully made on her own. I suspected she secretly knew he was Moreton Allport's son all along and just let him think he was keeping his secret.

"Before you start casting me as some loveable waif from a bloody Dickens book, think again! Because I didn't just take what I needed to survive—I took whatever I thought I could get away with. I was transported for one out of some two hundred thefts I'd committed. But I never had to sell my cunny!" she declared with some intensity. "And you boys, and you too, Moses! You don't know what that means out there in the world—to a young, hungry girl where the whole world only wants what's between your legs and little else from you. Nothing against the girls that did it."

At least you have something they want... I remember thinking that and immediately feeling ashamed of my own thought, as if her story were already rubbing off on me lecherously.

"Not saying I was all virgin-like when I hit the alien shores of Van Diemen's Land, not even close. But I'd never taken it for money; not that it's the worst thing you could be by far, but it wasn't for me. My poor mother on the other hand; she did everything she needed to do *but* steal, and when I looked into it years after being free, I found out she froze to death in the gutter, still holding out her cup...still begging for their kindness." She spat savagely on the ground, as if kindness could be damned. "Still rather be where it got me. Crowded into some filthy prison, shifted, shaved, poked, stripped, and humiliated. Just like they were trying the old methods in the Witch Hunts, it was. Back then, they was looking for your Mark, the witch teats where you fed your familiar; now they're just looking to make sure you aren't using your cunt to store contraband, so they tell you! But if you'd ever had it done to you, you'd know what it's really about. It's about power, plain and simple. Even with everything else that happened once they marched me down into Shadow of Death Valley." She shook her head with an air of strong resistance in the set of her mouth like a stone gulch. "Still would rather have fought and stole than rolled over and died waiting for their pity. Where's their pity, eh? You ever seen it?" she demanded of Moses.

He smiled with an expression of understated cynicism. "Pity? Think I spotted it once by the banks of the Mississippi, and then some cracker jumps out and drowns it before I could get a proper good look at it."

I didn't know whether to laugh or not. He said it with a dark chuckle, but he had earned the right to treat the topic with humour. I knew instinctually that I had not.

"So I got there, didn't get sick. Spent the first month of the sea voyage terrified all my spirits would have left me as the shore of England disappeared until I saw that damn seal tailing the boat, following us here... Moses saw the same seal, didn't you?"

He nodded. "Boats can't move fast enough to outrun a people's dreams, or their nightmares... Everything follows you to a new land, even the things you wanted to leave behind."

OF THE HEART

"Ain't that just the bitter truth and a half?" Martha muttered. "But in the case of my spirits, I wanted them to follow me. Thought it would be as easy as just setting up again... But once you've been a prisoner, the whole world looks different ever after. You boys don't even know it—don't even feel it—because you've never broken through the invisible wall around your world that protects you from having to touch people like me. To an extent, I lived on the fringes of your world for a time before Papa died. When you been plunged out of it unceremoniously, your guts change forever. The Martha I was beforehand was shaved off along with my long, dark hair, and a new person was born inside the walls." She pointed in the direction of the Female Factory. "I wonder how many times you've tried to imagine what convicts went through?"

"I've tried," Arthur admitted, as if his natural goodness was something to be ashamed of.

"And how did you imagine we felt?" she asked, taking a longer more meditative swallow of the spirits before passing it to Moses.

"Trapped," he said immediately. "Stifled. Suffocated."

Martha grinned. "Na... That's *you* you're feeling, sweetheart," she said, indicating the collar area where her own top button would be if she had one. "How do you even breathe? You can loosen that thing in here, you know? You don't need to be all gentleman'd up to death around me."

I could tell that her assessment of Arthur's emotions of suffocation and entrapment had hit equally as close to his bones. He didn't take up the offer to undo his top button, though. I wondered if he wanted to... Sometimes, it would seem like there was such a pervasive unease lurking below the surface of our society, that one top button coming unfastened could be like opening Pandora's music box. Small acts of conformity took on the power of enormous neurotic attention.

"Perhaps we all do that? When we are trying to feel sympathy? See our own sadness in others?"

It was a profound thought, and it ached in me as soon as Arthur gave it utterance. I loved that there were depths to him that could be drawn out by being around challenging new thoughts.

"Ha! You do it, so it must be everyone! What with you being gentlefolk and so forth." She made a joke out of bowing to both of us. "Let me tell you how it really felt," she said, suddenly serious and causing everyone in the room to hold their breath for a moment as she scanned our eyes, one after the other. "Being a convict is like riding the dragon. You got to stay on top; if you get off, it will eat you. A great, powerful, fire-breathing monster of a thing you have to stay on top of too… On my first night on the inside, I went under, like being held down by a wave at the beach. But Gerty showed me the ropes in the end. She had known The Beast for many more years than I, and she taught me how to see the shape of it. How to keep it between my knees and how to steer. People who don't *see* proper, they would have taken one look at my girl Gerty and just written her off as the human garbage we were all treated as. She was a pretty thing; if you'd cleaned her up and put her in a lady's smock, no one would have known the difference until she spoke. Not like she could help what she was reduced to. Like so many. There was a lice-ridden wisdom about that woman, God rest her soul… Let me tell you. She taught me about the dragon while I taught her about the spirits and the Eye. And before long, I became one of the Flash Mob girls—you heard of them?"

"I think everyone has heard of them," I murmured. The Flash Mob was a notorious female convict gang from earlier in the century; its members had apparently shown their bottoms to Lady Franklin during her visit. "They say some of you were witches."

"Huh!" She spat again and looked back at me with her dark eyes glowering with intensity that was almost as keen as menace. "But don't they say that about every woman they're afraid of?"

Walking back, the silence was so heavy it hurt my chest. Martha's story seemed to sit on us like a hag rides a sleeper during a nightmare. When Arthur spoke at last, his words were firecrackers in the air, a violence done to the night. "Do you get the feeling that Martha *love-loved* Gerty?" Arthur asked it in a way that it seemed a significant question.

"What do you mean?" I asked, frowning.

Arthur glanced sideways at me as if he suspected I was fooling with him or playing innocent. "You know," he said significantly. "Not as in 'romantic friendship' loved, but *loved.*"

I was still frowning. "I think it was quite plain from her story that she loved Gerty."

Arthur smiled at me, then reached over to take my arm and pat my hand as if I was something precious. "I forget sometimes you don't go to school."

His indulgent tone annoyed me. For some reason, I was being patronised, and I neither liked nor understood it. "What do you mean? My private tutors give me an education on all matters of import. I doubt I've missed anything in my lessons that schoolboys are taught."

He was still grinning. "It's not something in the lessons we're taught," he shrugged, as if to offload responsibility for tampering with my innocence. "It's not an academic thing, what boys learn at school."

I summoned the courage I always needed to ask for anything for myself. "Please tell me of it, then. I am humiliated by not knowing it."

"Oh, Henry," he stopped me in my tracks and turned me to face him. "Please don't be! There is no need. I don't refrain to mock you…I'm just so glad you exist. It seems you are someone untouched by the world, and the world is tawdry. I do admire it so, how you sit apart from the common order."

When he said this, he looked upon me with such a sense of affection and wonder in his eyes that I could not bring myself to complain or renew my suit. Because I adored him, I submitted to being the otherwise one, dwelling always upstream in those pristine parts of the river where he liked to take me, when really what I wanted was to follow him into the saltier downstream world, which he already understood so much more than I.

3

My dearest Henry,

Before I left, Martha assured me she was putting the story into a bundle and tying it up with string until I got back, and when she and I met again, she would undo the knots around a new campfire. She really is Nature's poet! I would rather not be at boarding school, I won't lie to you. I have nothing serious to complain of, though, beyond the lack of privacy and missing you. I am counting down the days until the holidays arrive, when I can show you my collection of very singular egg specimens. There are species here from birds whose eggs have not yet been catalogued and drawn. Also, I learnt by heart some poems—at first to impress you, but now also for the joy of it. Oh, how I so miss our talks and how you make me think…

There is nothing like that here. Just the wash and dress routine and lights out in the dormitories. I know I'm lucky to have been born a gentleman's son; I'm not blind to the suffering of the poor. But if gentlemen are what is produced at Hortons, some of these families deserve their money back. There are boys here I would not be friends with were we not together in captivity. What is happening with your cello lessons? Has your father found you a new tutor who can extend you as you wished when we talked last? I hope you continue to take sun and exercise. As much as I would not wish you here with me (it is less than sanitary sometimes, and you would not get enough time to practice; I fear you would go crazy), it worries me sometimes how little your father encourages you to get out and see other people your own age. It sometimes seems you are as much his captive as I am of this boarding school.

Anticipating my return,

CA

P.S.: I have reason to believe they open our mail.

Sometimes, we come awake in an event that happens at all points of time simultaneously; this is why my story is set in the past-present. What I mean to say is, once it happens to you, it happens to you every-when. If it happens, somewhere in the future, you will feel a chill run over you—the one the grandmothers say is the wind passing over the feet of the graves. As your eyes come open in the darkness and your pupils expand, it might be said you know yourself all at once, who you are in the fairytale. You see your purpose like a chain of key events, backwards as well as forwards. Luckily, the asleep people we call the "sane ones" never really remember much about it, if they have an experience of waking up halfway through their story. It takes a lot of effort to stay in your madness, to walk in it daily and refuse to yield it to the pressure of the herd.

My madness—or else my response to the information my senses receive with their cross-hatching and taste-colours—began to truly blossom while Arthur was away that year. Ordinary people would call it the stirrings of coming of age. For me, it wasn't as simple as a tale of body hair and growth spurts. Instead, I awoke startled. Shaken. Still in the darkness, I felt the sweat sticking my nightshirt to my chest as I breathed in and out. A fire—somewhere between tingling and stabbing—was making its way up my spine to my head in hot rushes. I closed my eyes tight with its intensity. Ultimate aliveness alighted upon my brow, causing my eyes to move rapidly under the eyelids, as do those of a dreamer.

That's how the end of childhood announced itself. First, I remember the heat, then the sense of perhaps being outside my body or too large for it. It seems I got up off the bed at some point and walked to the window. Although, I know now that I've entered mythic time, the eternal now—and so *when* I walked there and *how* become less important. There were ghosts against the window glass. Their eyes seemed to grow bigger and bigger the hungrier, paler, and more wraith-like they became with the wearing-away effect of time. Perhaps it happens as they enter the forgetfulness, where people forget to speak of them anymore and their names remain unspoken? The way they negotiated the glass of the window, they must have had hands and feet like little white frogs. So much do they want our attention. Many of them were babies and small children, because over time they had wandered downriver from the teeming death-pit of the nurseries adjoining the Female Factory.

The fingers of the sea were reaching for them; drowned women were calling out their names; they had no choice but to slowly wash away. First, they would cling to any reflection of life, through any window, my mirror, or any luminous crack in the fabric of things that offered a ray of it. In my Irish family, the dead were a natural part of life; not everyone saw them as clearly as I did, though.

Of the Heart

The Sight was a gift-curse, or a curse-gift, depending on how you look at it. Some consider it a frightfully bad omen of your own early death. I could fall into trances, for instance, where I could talk to them. If anyone had asked me, I'd have said that it wasn't death I was seeing at all; it was the residue of life that I was very sensitive to.

In my trances, I would begin to hear the sounds of my brother and sister playing on the other side of the fourth wall that was knocked down to turn our original house into the more middle-class one that came later. When I would hear them—as I could hear them on this night—still playing in Irish, the baby crying, mother crooning…I came to the conclusion that it was because of the missing wall. The dead were not gone; they merely continued their lives on the other side of the invisible fourth wall. The dead existed in the ghost house.

I moved, silent as a moonbeam, across the wooden floor in bare feet and spectral nightshirt. I might have been an echo myself. I was aware of a faint light around me that didn't come from the moon. It seemed dense enough to slow down dust motes, that corpse light around me. I remember questioning how it was I could see the dust motes at all in the low light? That's what was making the dead's eyes so big and greedy: my light shadow. They licked their lips at me through the glass as I came closer. Their sticky-grey frog fingers stuck hard to the glass with desire. My face reflected in the glass didn't seem quite familiar. It was the usual pale complexion, delicate features, and mousy-brown hair I'd been seeing in the mirror all my life. Yet, where my face had always had something faintly pinched about it that was redolent of constant sadness and being stalked by the grave, there was something ethereal replacing it. I felt far more afraid of what I saw in my eyes than anything on the other side of the glass.

Blinking several times to destroy the impression I was seeing, I frowned. The people with a lingering corpse light were crawling away one by one. At first, I wasn't sure if it was merely my ability to see them that was falling away or if they were actually leaving. In the background, my mother's rocking chair ceased its motion and the sound of my sister's laughter whilst at play faded. The sound of dogs unsettled in the distance displaced the floorboard's steady whine. Wind was rising.

Superstitiously, I knew I should look away but could not. Out of the shadows thrown by the trees near the rivulet, a huge black hound with ruddy eyes the size of saucers came into view. For a moment, upon its spectral visage, I perceived the impression of the publican of a nearby inn. As I watched the creature, its nose to the ground, hunting the dead as if these hellhounds were foxes and setting all the neighbourhood dogs up in hew and cry, I knew I was watching someone's secret other life. I held my breath as I beheld it. I was afraid of it—as the black dog is an omen of death—and yet fascinated by the sense of seeing under the façade of daily life.

I think it was in that moment that I realised it wasn't just my house that had a different story going on beyond the fourth wall, where the residue and mould growth of spent lives continues on. There was another life going on below the surface of Hobart, too: a second spectral life that switches on when everyone else switches off. In that other reality, there were witches and conjuremen, hiding behind the faces of ex-convicts and riffraff; there were black hellhounds under the visage of gruff pub owners. There was perhaps something Other—that I knew even less about—living for now below the water-line, yet beginning to rise to the surface of my own face.

We reunited at the corner of Davey and D'Arcy Streets, close to Arthur's parents' home at Fernleigh. He caught me up before I had much chance to see him coming, darting around the corner at almost full tilt. He was taller just in the time we were separated. We were at that age where a boy could go unseen for mere weeks and be visibly different. For a moment, my will was lost to the new strength in his upper body as he lifted me off the ground in playful exuberance.

"Oh!" I cried out in surprise. "You picked me up!"

Arthur took a step back from me and looked me up and down enthusiastically. Even though it was only his eyes he said it with, I felt much as if I was a lost kitten rediscovered by a mother cat, needing to be licked over to be certain it was truly returned in one piece and not injured during absence. "I've been rowing and swimming; it keeps me from thinking too much. You've grown and changed in my absence also."

I smiled mysteriously. It pleased me that he could see the Otherworldly light around me, even if he didn't know what it was he was seeing. "In a good way I hope?"

Arthur smiled, and I liked the way he smiled at me. "Very much so. You look…very well." Always indulgent and kind, I had no doubt whatsoever he'd have said the same if I was on my deathbed with cholera. "As if with a new light beneath your skin."

I didn't say anything because I was too delighted by his ability to exceed my expectations over and over again. As we walked in the direction of Franklin Gardens, I put my arm through his, and he squeezed it warmly to him.

OF THE HEART

"Can we spend the whole day together, and then can I sleep at your house and spend the next day together also?"

I laughed and buried my face against his shoulder for a second. "I was hoping we would." In those days, where we were still—to some extent—boys, this plan for the next twenty-four hours felt, I believe for both of us, like the most complete happiness that could be imagined.

"Can I tell you something that happened to me at Hortons?"

"Of course."

"Can faeries—I mean changelings, in particular—send their soul distances to visit with someone who is sleeping?"

I smiled with relief. Every time I relinquished him to his school, I feared I would lose a part of him, that he would come back not believing in anything anymore, not believing in me. His belief seemed crucial to my existence, as if I would simply turn to dust or sea foam if it stopped. That he could become too old and worldly for our game, or to witness the existence of changelings, was to me a dread. It clearly hadn't happened yet. Arthur had held the slither of magic we'd created between our spines when we'd sat back-to-back, safe. He might have taken it out only when he was alone, polished it, and dreamed with and through it, never allowing the world he described as "tawdry" to come near it.

"I don't know. I think so. I sometimes dream that I fly, especially after my sleep tonic."

"Did you fly and visit me while I was away?" He turned me lightly to stop under the shade of an elm. How would I tell him that I flew to him all the time, even when we were choosing a place to sit under a tree on the lawn, and he was right there already? Such is the extent of the normal barriers between the minds of people and the miracle of it if two people slip through the wall into each other's mental room.

"I do it often. I go to sleep planning to fly in my dream, so I can check you are safe."

Arthur's eyes lit up when he smiled with just as much resplendent warmth and excitement as he ever had. "Because I saw you! I fell asleep in a crawl space to get away from the other boys, and I woke to see you come through the fourth wall that you mention. You looked sexless somehow, just like an angel."

"Look." Pulling back the cloth that covered the baked goods in my basket, I displayed my handiwork. "I cooked for Martha, to sweeten her towards me." I wanted to gently change the subject. There is something about someone asking something too direct about one's elfin origins that requires diversions and flirtations with the truth. What I wanted to say to him, but didn't, was: yes, ask me things, but ask me differently. Ask me slower.

Arthur smiled. "You're clever," he said, clearly accepting my lack of wish to talk about it further with the same sense of positivity that literally nobody else had ever shown towards either my intelligence, or the cunning I'd learned to survive in a world hostile towards thinkers. "I doubt she has access to a gas cooker; she will be very impressed with something not tasting of smoke, I imagine. I just stole liquor from Father again," he added with his rakish grin. "To loosen her tongue."

"Won't you get into trouble?" I frowned. I had become increasingly worried about doing anything to get Arthur in trouble with Mr. Allport since I'd learned of the beatings. It caused me pain to think of it. He was not a huge, strapping lad exactly; he was stronger than me physically, but my protectiveness was towards his softer heart.

"He won't notice," Arthur said confidently. "He only sees what he wants to most of the time anyway; if it doesn't have something to do with photography or salmon farming, there's a good chance he'll miss it. He seems to have obscene amounts of everything. He's too spoilt to notice something missing."

I slid my arm unobtrusively through his as we walked towards the Davey and Macquarie crossroads. We walked in companionable silence, and at every step, I felt the surging sap of the world around me verdant with life. My own body sung in unison with it as my pulse tended from the same fuse as that of the green world. It was only a companionable sort of touch in my era, the linking of arms, yet I fed on the warmth of his skin through his suit coat like a plant does on the sun.

When we knocked on Martha's door, Moses answered. The older but robust-looking man crossed his arms and looked at us over his spectacles as if we hadn't been invited and we were clearly naught but trouble. "Ah, the Marassa are here," he muttered.

"What are *Marassa*?" Arthur asked.

"Twin spirits who bring devilment in their wake…" he muttered to himself, his tone both resigned and grudgingly affectionate. "And all the blessings too." Moses stepped back and hustled us inside with an impatient arm gesture. I don't think he wanted people spotting us. Seeing Arthur grinning at him, he shook his head. "Come inside, Marassa. *La Diablesse* Herself is in here."

"What's he been saying about me?" Martha asked, looking up from where she was seated against the wall with her boots and stockings exposed to the

Of the Heart

knee, committed as she toked on her pipe. "Nothing good, I hope?" She leered at me in that way of hers that suggested she was sizing you up, and possibly having a joke with you, or maybe making one of you... It was hard to tell.

That all changed after I presented her with my basket of faerie food. Outfitted as she was with only a fire and pots and pans for cooking, such things were rare in her world. Her bread was all smoky damper. "Damned if you're not a little wizard in the kitchen, faerie lad," she said, after having immediately devoured a muffin and a lemon tart. She offered the basket around to Moses and Arthur, who both accepted only when she'd taken what she wanted of it.

I sat watching with delight as they consumed my cooking, filled as it was with charms I might have made magic with—concocted out of nursery rhymes and the glimmer of puberty—magic that loosens the tongue and warms the heart. It pleased me that Arthur was eating it even though I'd all but told him what was in it. Of course, Martha was my main target. I wanted her goodwill, and risky as it was to try to charm a witch and a conjure-man, I had a feeling that the black magic of hunger would be working on my side. Already I knew, right down in my stomach, that there was no difference between learning Martha's story and learning her witchcraft.

"You cook better than our cook!" Arthur remarked, taking a seat on the threadbare mat by the fire as if he wasn't at all worried about getting his suit dirty. If I got my clothing dirty, there was a very good chance I would end up having to starch and press it myself. Often, I would try to help save money with tasks such as those, for the high maintenance outfit that society demanded of us required more financial outlay than Father could always manage. We held together the frayed ends of our dignity, striving to grab onto the edges of the middle class. Arthur knew that he could easily acquire more clean clothing, and Martha was told by the world that she didn't need to, as she wasn't marriageable any more. Her gown was dirty in two visible knee-prints where she was always kneeling down to do things, and she didn't have to apologise to anyone for it.

"Thank you," I responded, making a mental note of what Arthur seemed to like the best from the basket so I could cook it again.

"Wallaby stew we've got on for supper's going to look mighty plain now," Martha said after eating her fill with gusto.

"Underneath the second cloth, there are some fresh herbs from my garden if you'd like to use them for your stew?" I offered, very pleased with this smooth opening to getting her to eat the herbs from my special garden where I tended the dead people who had later turned into the green people of the soil.

"What're you buttering me up for, then?" she asked, eyeing me suspiciously. It was like she could smell my pleasure at getting her to eat the herbs, and it put her on her guard. "What do you want from me, eh?"

"The rest of your story," I replied. Generally, I either didn't speak or was immensely to the point. It took me a few more years to get some skills in between these two places.

"So... You're back for more of my filth, then?" Martha's arms were crossed, eyes twinkling, one foot up on the inside of her other leg. Often she would look like this to me, when her shade entered my dreams, dirty stockings and still wearing a gleefully evil smile on her face. She was chewing tobacco flagrantly with her mouth open and grinning at me, reminding me how few cares she had for the world's judgment of her.

"Hell yes, I am," Arthur responded with a charming smile, presenting her with more alcohol. I was a bit shocked to hear him curse like that, and yet, at another level, I liked it. It felt real. As if I was getting to see glimpses of what lay underneath his tightly buttoned surface. I knew instinctually that this was a power Martha had that I did not, this ability to draw the darkness out from people.

She beamed like a young lass given flowers when presented with the booze. "Aren't you the right little gentleman? Lasses aren't going to stand any chance with you, are they? I'd let you court my daughter if she was still around."

Such a strange turn of expression: standing no chance. As if a young gentleman were a big game hunter tracking women across the savannah, before mounting their heads on the wall as trophies after they succumbed to him. For a moment, I wondered if perhaps women made more sense to me than men; maybe I should have been one?

Moses paused to put a bookmark in his book and close it. I made mental note of his literacy and began to think of what volumes I might be able to access from home for him to read. I greeted them with a shallow reflex bow. "Good evening." I'd ceased to care that they sometimes teased me for my good manners. I had adopted them as my eccentricity, of which Martha said all two-headed folk (this was their name for conjurers) had to have a few. It was our way of turning the poison of a bad reputation into a medicine. Having a talking point made you interesting to the public.

After getting her pipe going, it wasn't long before Martha warmed to her tale again. "Thing is with being a convict," she said, interspersed by smoky billows, "it wasn't like any of us alone had a brilliant fancy-pants mind like the quiet one here," she said, elbowing me to let me know the quiet one was me. I couldn't help wondering how she'd come to this high opinion of my mind, as I really was almost silent in the beginning. I was too busy watching and learning. Martha seemed to be able to hear the cogs turning in my brain even when I didn't speak. "But *between us,* we became something. When you're forced up that close with other human beings, something of your essential humanity dies—it's called 'dignity,' I think. I already told you that old Martha died, and the dragon-rider came later. First, she had to know she was part of the dragon before she could ride it. And that's what happened: the hungry gullet of the dragon's mouth gobbled me up. Gerty claimed me on her behalf like I was food. That's what you felt like all the time once you're on the bottom of the heap: food. The one thing you never have enough of is the one thing everyone treats you like.

"Gerty had a sly wisdom. She was my death midwife for that old me, and she taught me how to do things that my old self would have never done. Soon, I discovered that I loved being dead! Everything flowed to me more easily after that. Stopped caring about my privacy. You'd take a shit in front of anyone just like an animal after a few weeks of being dead, because you're fucking dead! The dead do whatever they like. We can have black teeth if we want, and no one can say anything. Takes a bit of time, getting dead, but you get gobbled up by the dragon and start moving as one of her scales. You know you've got fire in your belly then, and your confidence starts coming back. The confidence they knock out of you when they process you. You're stronger than ever because your body extends out past two damn hands and feet. Hell! You've got dozens of fists, dozens of feet! You can't stop a creature like that for long. I started to realise with a thrill that where I'd died something stronger than ever before had slithered out of my carcass. It was more than sisterhood; it was something only the dead understand, those who've been pushed past pride and face and into the wild."

She laughed then and swigged from her rum. "The wild outside! What tosh! The wild was on the inside in those stone walls. May could play the fiddle, and Liza taught us all a whirling dervish dance she'd learned from her mother. I taught them how to stamp the ground and spit whiskey on it for the devils while we danced. And all that, years before I met Moses and ever heard about spitting rum! We made the overseer afraid of us when he'd threaten us with solitary, and we'd take up our dresses and bare our arses to him. Someone I was meant to be working for planted his seed inside me. Didn't get paid for it, so I guess it doesn't count.

"Out of all the laws of man and God I ever broke, the biggest taboo to me was wanting that baby to grow inside me. I loved my innocent babe even though I hated her father. I wouldn't judge a woman who chowed down on Dr.

Patterson's female pills 'till she undid the seed, but that wasn't the way I rode it. Sometimes, you've got to take power slantwise when you can't wrestle it off them face on. So, I took my pleasure in converting his blood into witch blood inside me. I would make that girl, for I brooked no opposition in the world of magic with the high tide of the Flash Mob behind me, powering my work, that girl she would be.

It wasn't long before it got contagious, and Gerty and I had other women outside the ones we danced with coming to us saying they'd been having visions they suckled an imp, or a crow got out of their craw and flew away. The power of it grew bigger than the combination of us. Visions were had so that it's hard to say who had it first. Many of us saw Our Lady of Mercy plant a dove wreathed in roses inside my womb. More than one of us saw the girl rise wreathed in the serpent—rather than treading on him—and pouring out honey upon the soil of this place…

When my little girl was born, caught by Gerty and the others on the floor, people wept and smelled the perfume of holiness. And God knows there were mainly unholy aromas in that place… So you'd notice it alright. Then, of course, they took her from me." The expression went right out of Martha's voice, as if all of her drama, power, and storytelling oomph just slipped right away like a snowflake melting on your fingertips. "And dragon-rider as I was, there was nothing I could do." She paused there for a long moment, forcing us to sit with the utter devastation for longer than was comfortable. "Don't try and look away," she demanded suddenly. "Look it full in the face, boys. Because whether you like it or not, toffy gentleman as you both are, that's going to happen to you one day. Probably not with a baby, but you'll know it before you're dead, the pair of you." I gasped because it felt almost like she'd cursed us with her certainty. "There's no sting that can compare to it. There's no number of beatings you wouldn't take to avoid it. That moment where there's absolutely nothing you can do for the thing you love most in the world… It's so bad you even stop screaming in the end and just stare into the black heart of it…"

Tears were standing in my eyes now. I didn't even dare look at Arthur. We were both frozen with holy dread.

"You won't cry when it happens to you. You won't be able to. Scorched earth doesn't weep. Your hair will start to turn grey that day… They put her in the nursery to be sent away to the orphan home. The one that gives this charming valley its nickname because it kills so many babies. I knew it would kill her, so I didn't stop fighting them. Never had I rebelled like that. I'd always ridden the dirty place with one foot on one side and one on the other. This time

I kicked and bucked and bit; dear God if I didn't use every ounce of strength and power in my body on those sons of bitches... I caused some injuries; I drew their blood for my child. The whole Flash Mob went into outright rebellion for Mary and I. All of us blood-sworn that we'd not reveal anything of the visions we'd seen no matter what punishments they meted out to us. And we held to that, not a one of us giving way under pressure.

"We were ready for them. We knew what was coming. I was like stone when they stripped and shaved me that second time. No satisfaction of a flinch did they see from me. The first time I'd been all cowering and trying to hide my shame with my hands and weeping. Not this time, cunts! I'm ready for your witch hunt! I swung at your damned gallows last time if I'm recalling it all right, but I still got back up and came at you again, didn't I? We had a plan, and I held it tight to me as they marched me away into solitary. I knew what I was in for, in the darkness and the silence, but my baby was out there, and I was made of stone-cold steel for her. You don't understand, of course, any of you! Not until you've looked down at that squalling mess of blood and flesh that tore out of your own body. Or maybe I'm wrong... Maybe not 'till you've really bled for someone or taken a punishment on their account. That's love right enough in a way you can't know 'till you've stood there and said you did something that she did to spare her the pain...

"Well, I went quiet enough into the darkness knowing my girls were out there. We had blokes on the outside who were helping us get weapons in. We were going to kill the superintendent after slitting his Achilles' heel with a scalpel as he walked by on patrol. It all went wrong, of course; you know that, or you'd have heard our story before now. The girls managed to cut him, though... Meanwhile, in the dark of endless solitary, I saw how Death came as a big man to claim my baby girl, and before my very eyes, he touched her with his cock-shaped staff, and she grew up into a beautiful dark-haired maiden with snow-white skin and rose-red lips. Just like in the fucking fairytales." She paused there to viciously attack the beginnings of tears that stung her stubborn eyes. "And I was right enough. Some said they laid off her care to punish me for the uprising. I can't bear to, even now... It was a right mission just trying to get her bones back, but I found them all right. Her strong ghost led me to them, and I scratched at the earth like a wild beast until I was holding my baby again, howling at the moon, more animal than woman, and more mad than sane. Even though I had her bones, I knew that *He*, Death Himself, or something very close..."

"The Baron," Moses added, nodding his understanding of this figure.

"Him!" Martha agreed. "He had claimed Mary for himself. Every spring, he lets her loose to roam above, and she grows up a little bit more each year. I let the girl loose from her bones under the floor and sun them on the grass amid the daisies and forget-me-nots, and I will some of my life-force into her. Only Moses really understands about Mary, so he hangs around more than other people. At night, I take my baby indoors and lay a hare skin over her, waiting for the day she wakes up again."

"So, the girl died in squalor and neglect, the rose cankered in the bud, a proper symbol of this damned-blessed isle, which is one people's apocalypse and our new Jerusalem all at the same time, and something else which is both. If you decide to accept what you both are, you might need to carry forward this flame we've started to kindle. Moses and I aren't getting any fucking younger. And there's no going home for any of us now. There's no England or bloody Ireland or whatever it is I hear underneath your Englishman impression," she said, poking my arm with a sharp finger. I flinched as though she had exposed some essential nerve in me by recognising my Irishness. "Those places are dead to you, and you to them. This is all we have left, even though we're strangers here."

"Take this," she said, pressing an earthenware jar into my hand. "It's a witch's poultice made with flying ointment and soot from the fire of the Devil's Dance given to me by an aborigine woman, plus some fat rendered from a black cat by Moses. If you go to the grave of one who died before puberty anointed with this and lie down, well, pretty soon you'll know if you're meant to be one of our number. You get me?"

I nodded.

"But don't use all of it, you hear? Only use half."

"What the other half for?"

"For your boy," she said, indicating Arthur with her head. "If it happens for you, but only if He comes to you! Then you may guide Arthur there also. But beware: a fearsome connection will be forged between you, so think hard upon it. This is your first test."

I made a point of pretending to tune my cello while Arthur undressed for bed. I'd always make excuses to do something else when he would dress at this age. It was perfectly expected and normal behaviour for boys of this era to undress around each other and sleep in the same bed. There was no logical reason for me to be shy around it as we'd been doing it since we were boys. Glancing up

OF THE HEART

from my cello strings midway through a stroke, my bow-arm pausing in midair, I thought of what Martha had said about privacy, about how it had been taken from her.

What a luxury it was, I realised, this edge of discomfort I felt as my eyes rested briefly on his torso. I challenged myself to push into the discomfort, letting my eyes drop lower to the as-yet-fine trail of hair that grew down from his belly button and disappeared beneath his belt. Conscious of him noticing my attention, I finished the bow stroke, accidentally producing a perfect tone of deep-bellied longing. I brought the note to an abrupt stop in embarrassment at how it exposed me. Could he read sound like I could? When my eyes shot back up to his, I found only a soft, warm curiosity glimmering there, as if I were something he found pleasantly exotic but didn't know what to do with. Breaking the brief discomfort with a smile, he pulled his nightshirt on over his head.

Placing my cello down, I looked at it with mild feelings of betrayal.

"You're not going to play for awhile before bed?" he asked, climbing into my bed and sliding into the same space he'd always occupied since his father first started coming here. I could tell from his voice that he was gently encouraging me to play.

I shook my head before pulling off my own waistcoat and shirt and changing into a nightshirt. It didn't seem a good idea to play cello in front of him that night. When I got into bed and snuggled down into my usual place, he slid his arm around me with the same relaxed affection he always had. My heart ached with gratitude that me staring at him hadn't made him uncomfortable around me. I would rather deny myself utterly than risk losing the ease with which his arm lay across me. There was some sort of wordless promise I made to myself after we'd downed the lamp and he lay close to me: that I would never—could never—risk losing his friendship.

"Henry?" It made me feel strange when he said my name like that. A nameless tug in my stomach marked it out as something far outside the ordinary. The feeling seemed to hint at a memory of something long-buried, something older than I was. It was similar to an ache of nostalgia, when I was in years far too young to truly know that blue-grey taste in the air. Downstairs, the loud carousing of our fathers and another lawyer, Mr. Butler, seemed like it was coming from a different world to the one we inhabited. We inhabited a space outside of time and far beyond the edges of things.

"Yes?"

"Is something bothering you, my friend? You know you can tell me anything... Surely?"

There was a significant pause before I swallowed down hard. "Of course I do," I replied, my voice so thin it was a whisper. His hand searched for mine, found it, and gave it a reassuring squeeze. "Sometimes I think there's something really wrong with me," I confided.

"I think that about myself too."

"What do you imagine is wrong with you?" I asked, my voice edged with tense caution.

"I think I hate everything about human society," he murmured urgently. "I want to live wherever you come from. Will you take me home with you one day? I have a theory that the Devil is everything that the world says you shouldn't love, but you do, in your heart of hearts. All the things they say have no value. I think the Devil…I think he's a Black fella, a convict, or a beggar… or a woman like Martha, or maybe all of those things, every day."

"La Diablesse," I murmured with a faint smile.

"Is this similar for you? What do you feel is wrong with you?"

I closed my eyes. Giving words to my fear felt like the ground dropping away under me; my stomach had fallen ahead of the rest of me, and nothing was stable. Just as I was gripping the bedsheets to brace myself against the anxiety that this topic avalanched through my flesh, the window suddenly burst open, and a rush of furious wind came into the room, hitting the window twice into the wall. Arthur started straight up in shock. I didn't move. The explosion of force I'd felt come from my body left no room for it. For a giddy few seconds, the gust swirled around the room and destabilised pictures on the wall before I skittered across the floor in my wind-taken nightshirt to close up the windows with my arms.

When I turned around, the moonlight cast my shadow before me on the floor, partially enshrouding Arthur as kneeled up in bed in a posture of alertness. He seemed like a sharp hound sniffing the air, well-aware of the magic that had just moved through the room. As I walked towards him, my form swallowing up my shadow with each step, I remembered what Martha had told me about bringing him over. No conscious part of me knew how to do that, yet the dreaming part of me who came from the hungry place, the shadow I inhaled into me as I crawled onto the bed, knew it.

"Want me to show you some more of my magic?" I whispered.

He nodded mutely and swallowed. As I slid my hand around the back of his neck and drew our foreheads together, I consciously allowed the waking at the base of my spine. It started to climb me, and I twitched and convulsed as I brought it up to my head. Every hair was standing on end; I was panting, and a sheen of sweat was beginning to make me cool like spreading sap, which he would later describe in the idiom of our time as ectoplasm.

As my light exploded into his head, I held the shape of his skull in my hands like it was something I was drinking from. I saw myself in my head as slightly insectile, tinkering in music-like ripples with the front of his brain. He moaned softly and pressed his head harder against mine. I started to explicitly see music, then colours and undulating lights that were in fact melody. I began to tap out a beat on his leg, and the light that danced between us supplied the melody. It's hard for me to say how far I took him into that vision with me, but I could tell from the way his bones moved in my hands that he was deeply affected.

"Can you hear my violin playing?" I whispered.

"Yes," he murmured back, not letting go of my head. After a few more moments, he opened his eyes, and I felt it even though mine were shut. "I can hear your cello, too, and your piano."

I smiled, still not opening my eyes. "Nobody ever gets to hear my piano unless they sit in the next room."

"Except me," he said with breathtaking confidence.

I laughed and gently broke contact with him. "You're cocky, aren't you? You may be right. I most likely will let you watch me play one day." Drawing back from him a little more, still smiling, I felt reckless with the heady rush of our contact. "When you really get to know me, I might even let you hear my fiddle."

Arthur gasped audibly. "Oh my God... You can't? You can fiddle? Seriously? That is without doubt the most capital thing I've heard! I want to see and hear right now!"

I laughed. "It's illegal still, isn't it? Just like being Irish..."

"I like the fact that you're Irish. Alexander Pearce was Irish."

"Arthur!" I cried, slapping him. "Alexander Pearce was an actual cannibal, and we prefer it if people don't bring him up. People already say that our kind all ate each other during the starving."

"I'd sooner keep company with Black fellows and Irish cannibals than the respectable Englishmen who collected the rent and taxes while Irish men, women, and children starved by the hundreds of thousands, or the men who shot first at the Native folk."

I favoured him with a sad, loving smile. Slowly, I shook my head and reached out my hand to briefly touch his cheek. "You have an unruly, beautiful heart, my friend. The world won't thank you for it, but I will." I gave him a rapid kiss on the cheek.

He grinned with pleasure. It was hard to tell in the semi-dark, but I think he blushed a little at the gesture. I hoped I hadn't been overly familiar. "Thank you," he murmured. "No one's ever said they liked that about me before."

When I open up my memories, it always feels like coming into a dust-bejewelled room that has been boarded up many years. The floorboards creak under my shoes as I enter, a grown man coming back to examine the detritus and wonder of childhood. In my mind, I blow dust off my cello and run my fingers along the stained ivory of my piano as I walk by. With careful hands that show a line or two—but are still recognisably mine—I crack open an old music box. A toy of my sister's that I'd told father I kept in her memory, that really I kept because I liked it.

A little lady in a scarlet dress sits at piano and plays when the box is opened; the music is halting now with the weight of time that has built up. When I open the box, and the music starts the ruin with its long-peeled away wallpaper, it becomes lighter suddenly, as if someone has pulled back the green parasites that grow over the holes in the roof. The bones of the old place are exposed, and the wind gets inside. Progress continues all around the ruin of our world, which is still etched into every convict pick-marked stone in the foundations. The cobblestone-ghosts of our world, living on under your feet.

When the little woman in the red dress I know as Pandora plays as I open the box, and the wallpaper unpeels, the upholstery unfades, long-dead flowers come alive in long-cracked vases that all reform. Arthur is young again and walking the streets somewhere out there—or in his home just waking for the day. And I...I am walking the streets with my basket in hand, heading to market. It's possible I could see him there, and I am always looking. I'm wearing my Sunday best, even though it's not Sunday. The light I'd seen around me at night seemed to be noticeable even during the daylight now. Nobody except me could see it consciously; still, people were treating me differently all of a sudden. It was as if part of them could see it without their knowledge; some were attracted, some threatened.

Since not long after Mother's death, it had always been me who would walk into town to the market with her basket and bring home needful things. On this morning, fashionably dressed free-settler ladies on the arms of gentlemen passed by me, mingling with the lower sort of middle-class patrons like myself.

OF THE HEART

The poor and ex-convicts, who would always approach the market from its edges, never daring to promenade through the centre as the fine ladies did paraded on the arms of their men. The way they tossed back their hats, you'd think the presence of the man gave them their very right to exist.

Occasionally, I would glance at one of their gowns and find the material and the cut either fine or gaudy, often depending on how much I liked the woman wearing it. The gentlemen I judged far more universally harshly, especially on matters of hygiene and basic neatness. As Father was always saying, you don't need to be rich to be clean. Hobarton was that kind of world, you see, where everyone else knew you, and everyone knew everyone else's business and judged it accordingly. Judgment was in the water. Judgment was the currency. You couldn't get by without becoming part of the leviathan of it, even when you didn't want to be. Or at least, not yet I couldn't, because I wasn't dead yet.

It was early morning that day; this one that arises unbidden from my music box and Pandora's song, one of the vendors had gotten in a great stock of flowers. I have never been one to be impressed by roses from fancy hot-houses. My heart always belonged to the common daffodil. You have to have a piquant eye for beauty to appreciate the daffodil. His song is one of ephemeral beauty. His heart cracks open in the cruel grip of the darkest and deepest frost; from there, his flower is born, slowly, one quarter inch at a time, pushing through ice, in the direction of the light. Long before the first golden eruption, I sense them striving. As if the green life-drive coming out of the bulb seeking light while every bit of heavy earth, harsh stone, and long-encrusted ice seeks to keep it down, echoes part of myself, a bulb planted in a new land, striving desperately for the touch of the sun.

The people around me were mainly part of the ice. Father had told me once that when the middle class arrives in a colony, it becomes conservative, as if desperately trying to cling onto the era during which it last experienced home. Home is always receding when you've come to a colony. Home is always some place in the past as well as across the ocean. That's why he told me the respectable people here were all as frozen as the peak of Mount Wellington, because they belonged to something that didn't exist anymore, a home in the past. They wouldn't welcome anything new that came to disturb them out of their comfortable rut. At least, this is what my father said.

On that day, for a change, I found myself drawn to the hectic-scented roses. They were rich shades of damask pink, deep burgundies and reds so rich I felt like I'd never truly appreciated their intensity of colour until this moment.

"Morning, Master Henry," the vendor acknowledged me with a smile. "Looking for any flowers to brighten up the home?"

In truth, I grew my own flowers to brighten our home, as well as a seasonal garden of vegetables and fruits that assured us regular food. Yet, there was something about the red shades and burgundies of these flowers that put me in mind of Pandora, inside my sister's old music box. I'd never grown those colours in my garden for some reason; they'd always seemed too garish. I would keep yellow because they were a suitable gift for friends and family, white because they were appropriate for the many infant funerals one must attend, and pink roses in case I ever loved someone. A blood-red shade of emotion I hadn't yet known. As I gazed at the Pandora-coloured roses now in the market, they seemed almost lurid. The emotion they evoked in the air had a taste, and it made my mouth water.

"Morning, Mrs. Everett," I replied, remembering my manners and rapidly swallowing the excess saliva. "Do you mind?"

"Of course not, lad! Smell all the roses! They only last for such a short time after all…"

Closing my eyes, I took a long, sensual breath of the scarlet bloom's fragrance. It was heady like love. The spirit of the rose seemed to enter me at the nose and mouth and breathe life into something hidden in my blood. I found myself thinking of my friend Mary, and Martha's prophecy and vision. *Perhaps I can live for both of us somehow.* It seemed like a strange thought to have about the dead girl, logically at least, but the rose's perfume was telling me something about myself that made it seem not so strange. At some level, she had always seemed like myself in female form. I knew that in Martha's story, I was the boy-child with the radiant brow plucked out of a river, but I found it easy enough to relate to the girl who pricks her finger on a spindle and falls asleep for a thousand years. The little girl sleeping in her bones.

Immediately, I knew I had to buy some. Maybe they were for Pandora, or for Mary, or for myself; I wasn't sure. "I would like six of these, please."

"Here you go, dear. Just pay my daughter there."

I took out money and went to pay the younger girl without ever really looking at her. She bent down to force me to make eye contact, and her two blonde front plaits made their way into my field of vision first. Then her face, which was smiling. "Hello down there, Master Henry! And who may I ask is the lucky girl?" Seeing my hesitation, she grinned wider. "Nobody buys red, long-stemmed roses unless there's a girl…"

OF THE HEART

I could feel that this interchange had now caught the attention of other people who were gathered around to look at or purchase flowers. In panic, I made a couple of false starts at answering. "No... I mean... No... I don't like girls." I covered my mouth with my hand a second afterwards. "I don't mean it like that! What I meant to say is..." The girl, who must have been no more than a year or two older than myself, had her hands on her hips in mock outrage. It was totally clear to me that it was in jest, but I still panicked as I hated to be rude. In truth, I had no negative opinions on girls at all. Some of my best friends were women and girls. Dead girls, yet girls nonetheless. "I'm buying them for my piano."

"Your piano?" the girl asked with raised eyebrows and a little mocking smile around her rosebud mouth.

I was committed now, and I thought of what Martha had said about the need for conjuring folk to cultivate an eccentricity. "Yes. That's right. For my piano. She's the only woman for me." I grinned back at her until she cracked up laughing.

"I like you, Master Henry!" she giggled. "I'm Clara; we've spoken before but you were probably too busy thinking about your piano to remember!"

She might have liked me on sight, yet it was clear that my eccentricity wasn't having the same effect on the young gentlemen standing near us, who I knew to be the Butler's and Crowther's boys. They were about Clara's age, and though of a higher class than both of us—being both Hutchins boys as they were—it appeared that perhaps they wished to have the attention she was giving to me.

"Nancy!" You could hear them pretending to clear their throats as if in a futile attempt to cover their contempt for my lack of virility. It amazed me how witty they found this, no matter how many times they repeated it. They were laughing at each other and egging their friends on to come up with others. "Jessy girl! Catamite!" With a snicker, they shoved me in the back, causing me to collide with Clara. Clara cried out in pain and shock as the thorny roses were mashed between our chests.

"Leave him alone, Butler," I heard Fletcher's son say when he saw his friends push me. "You're going to get us in trouble."

As it was, Clara's mother promptly went after the boys with a broom while they ran for it. Fletcher apologised for his friends before running off too. It didn't matter whose father earned more when you were facing down an angry matriarch with a broom handle she's not afraid to use.

"I'm so sorry," I said, steadying Clara.

"It's hardly your fault that they have no manners," she tut-tutted as we both bent to pick up the dropped roses and the coins they'd knocked from her belt. When we both got to our feet, she looked across at me (she was petite despite being older than I) with concern. "Silly boys! They've really discomforted you, haven't they?"

"I'm fine," I said, brushing it off; one did, after all, have to be British. Even if one is, in fact, Irish. I did want to say something more dignified, but it appeared that all my changeling, truth-telling ways were coming to the fore along with the inner light that had settled on me. "It happens a lot lately."

"Well, don't you listen to them, handsome," she said to me with a smile that would have seemed blatantly flirtatious on a girl with less natural sweetness. "I like a man that buys long-stemmed roses for his piano. Here's one to go with your gorgeous blush." She teasingly inserted the head of a pale pink rose into my lapel. If I wasn't blushing beforehand, I certainly was afterward.

"Father? What's a catamite?" I asked the next night over the meal table. Off to one side was my piano, bedecked with half a dozen slightly bruised, deliciously fragrant red roses.

When Father nearly spat a mouthful of my garden peas across the table, I knew it clearly wasn't anything I should have brought up at the meal table. Upon recovering, he explained that it meant a boy who liked girls' things. That hadn't sounded so bad to me.

"Where did you hear that word!" he thundered at me.

I gasped in shock and dropped the cutlery. Father was a gentle, mild-mannered man; it was rare to hear him raise his voice.

"I'm sorry, sir," I muttered. "I had no idea it was such a shameful thing, otherwise I'd not have repeated it!"

"A most vile thing," my father affirmed adamantly. "Who said this to you, my son? Did someone *call you* this?"

I hesitated suddenly. I was beginning to realise how seriously this was being taken, and I hadn't expected that. At some level, I wasn't sure whether it was me or the boys who were out of line.

"The Butler boy, Crowther's son… Fletcher's lad was there, too, but he was telling them to be quiet. But what does it mean, Father?"

Father got to his feet immediately and began pacing the room. "And you did nothing to answer this slander? Was it said publicly?"

OF THE HEART

I frowned at his pacing. This all made me very anxious. I made an effort not to wring my hands as Father pointed out that it came off unmanly. "I had no idea it needed answering, innocent as I still am of its meaning…"

"Of course, of course you are," he muttered over and over again as he paced. "You're an innocent. By God, I'll take my horsewhip to the young hooligans if their fathers do not answer this with like strength!" he declared, slamming his hand down on the table. It felt for a second like we were earlier in the century, and my father was about to call a dual of pistols at dawn for the family honour. In one way, I found the feeling rather nice, because it affirmed my status and importance in my father's eyes. At another level, I knew there was some nameless shame behind what had occurred that I had no way of understanding. The sting of this loss-of-face was what brought the colour to my cheeks and the tears to my eyes.

"I'm sorry, Father."

"You've nothing to be sorry for!" he shouted at me. "You're an innocent, and if their dirty, gutter minds aren't gentleman enough to see that, then all the money in the world won't buy them class! I will see this answered… What were you doing though, Son? At the time? What were you doing when they slandered you?"

For some reason I couldn't explain at the time, my cheeks flushed a deeper mauve. It wasn't only shame that coloured them, but a flash of anger that I could neither word nor would I have been bold enough to do so if I could. *I can now, though.* What had I been doing to deserve it? Was what Father was asking me.

"I was purchasing some flowers," I said quietly.

"Those ones?" he asked, pointing in the direction of the luridly red roses.

I nodded.

"Don't do that again!"

"What? Don't buy flowers?" I asked, confused.

"Don't buy red roses. Actually, no, just don't buy flowers; don't even look at them. Keep away from those boys, and I will deal with this."

"Yes, Father," I whispered.

There was that feeling again, the one I'd felt just before the windows burst open in my room. Nothing happened this time, though.

I wouldn't say it was a matter of doubt, exactly, that kept me waiting with the ointment until after that event. Everything changed inside me after that day at the marketplace. Some resolve inside me hardened; I became more certain of my outsider status. I looked at my father more objectively, considered Arthur's critiques of our society's ethics more deeply. It wasn't the words of some mediocre bullies that wrought that change in me; as I had told Clara, I was bullied often. It was my father's panicked reaction. Without ever needing to be told in words, I learned from his body, from his adrenal glands, that I was somehow in mortal danger from people who thought like those boys did.

Possibly, I garnered, I was even in danger just because people had heard them say it. If Father was practically packing pistols at dawn in response to a mere slight, then I knew something was serious. I could sense his fear for me, and so I felt fear too. There weren't many weapons in my arsenal that I could use to help Father fight my enemies; there was only really one that I knew of. If I was already so sinful when I had done nothing at all, perhaps then I ought to do something to earn their condemnation? Such as selling my soul at the crossroads? I was fairly sure it belonged to the Devil already anyway. Observe! Those who would judge the process through which those condemned as witches in the past must have walked. I find it all too easy to imagine their feeling process. When you are condemned without a trial, there are some of us who would like to accrue some actual sins to go with the ones that were assumed of us by our neighbours. Not knowing the exact nature of my supposed wrongdoing, I figured that consorting with the Devil would have to just about cover it. Perhaps, in this way, I could glean some power to strike back?

I slipped unseen and unheard into St David's Burial Ground around the hour of midnight, holding a stone from Ireland in one hand and the now half-empty jar of witch ointment in the other. Yes, I saw it all clearly even as I walked hunched against the light rain, inside one of my father's great coats that was still somewhat too long for me in the arms. The witch unguent blackened with ash—from the Devil Dance ceremonies where the Native people had danced to try to drive off the white man—was already working its way under my skin. I could feel my death creeping up inside via the pores. The magic of the ash was there to kill my people, they wanted us all to die… They were coming to burn our world down, and nobody would ever hear them or see them when they decided it was our time. It would be like the Black Line all over again, where they only found one boy and one old man. We had taken their land, so who could blame them for wanting revenge?

A paranoia was creeping over me. The shades of the Native dead were everywhere suddenly. The madness of it started in the burning of my skin that felt like I was on fire. What had the wretched convict woman given me? Martha had poisoned me. As I looked around me, there was only the rising night fog that the graves belched up and the sloppy trickle of the open drain that ran amid them; no one living moved but for the rats. Father and all decent folk had taught me that the cemetery was haunted by miscreants at this hour. I was the only wrong-doer walking the graves tonight. I was no doubt going to die here, my soul darkened by the sooty ointment on my skin. I'd be eaten by devils before the night was out. And in my imagination, I saw them sidle up to my corpse on their stumpy black hindlegs. They were devils of the marsupial animal variety, because my addled brain made the linguistic association and factored in Vandemonian wildlife.

By the time I found my sister's grave, I was stumbling between the headstones like a drunkard. I started to laugh to myself in a hysterical pitch when I saw the graves beginning to give up their occupants like a rising sheet of forms shimmering in the fog. I wasn't even squeamish or superstitious about casting myself down on her plot. Tonight, fear was a white-hot thing, not a cold, clammy one. It was the heat that was peeling away down to my bones, like dragon fire trying to expose a glowing, white-hot skeleton. Before I could resist or shield myself from the searing, things began to grow out of me. The bulbs were erupting, and daffodils shot out of my mouth before I could scream. Writhing back and forth and making choking sounds on her grave, I tried to fight as amanita muscaria mushrooms burst out of my stomach cavity and propagated the earth with spores. Roots were coming into or out of me, penetrating me everywhere so it was impossible to tell where I began and the soil ended. My eye sockets were filled with green, growing plants. There was a strong scent of eucalyptus. I could taste honey on the back of my tongue.

Blinded with the green, I felt the sensation of sharp talons like an eagle had landed on my chest. It wasn't disembowelling me; it was just standing. It bent and used its beak to put honey under my tongue, the way a bird feeds its baby. If my mouth wasn't being violated by the spirit of spring—as it gave forth a furious burst of joyous yellow flowers —I'd have laughed. The magic in the Devil Dance ash was only there to kill off the part of me that thought like a white fellow, and I was all right with that. I saw things too clearly to want it any other way. My mind was full of frost and light spangled wattle-down. He who came for me was not the Devil. At least not as the church told you the Devil was. It was merely he whom I'd always seen following me out of the corner of my eye, the man with the hood-covered face who whistled or played on a swan-bone flute at the bottom of my garden.

My muscles released with a flood of relief, because I knew in my heart of hearts that no truly evil being could create music like that with such a simple instrument. For the first time, he spoke to me. "Do not be afraid," he said, as an enormous vista suffused with light and a thousand eyes suddenly sprung open before me. "This is the world, Henry. The part that has been hidden from you, the truth that has been stolen from you. You have been lied to. The apple and the woman who took it were good! Blessed is the fruit on the Tree of Knowledge. It intoxicates, and you were built to know intoxication."

4

The pre-dawn air in our house smelled like Jesus, soap, and dust. I hoped its newly refreshed strangeness would be allowed to silently swallow me so that I could write down what had happened to me—that way, I could relive it, make sure I forgot nothing. The bottom stair gave me away with a groan.

"Henry, where have you been! I was worried sick!" Father came quickly down the stairs, grabbed me between his hands, and looked me over for signs of harm. "I checked your room before I retired, just to make sure your candles were out, and you were gone!"

There was a thing inside me with wings and claws about to go mad against his chest if he didn't let me go. I could feel my colour, hectic and hewn, but there was nothing I could do to tuck away my soul's natural weapons.

"Let me go!" I cried, struggling against his hold. "Don't touch me!" It felt like I'd dropped to my knees to pull away from him. Instead, I was told later I fainted on the floor. Naturally, it seemed to me as though time went down the funnel hole.

When I next remember something, I'm in my own bed, half-propped up with pillows. The door to my room is pulled in but not firmly closed. Father is talking in the hall outside my room with two men.

"Were you able to see whether he hit his head in the fall? He probably has a mild concussion." I recognised the voice of Mr. Allport.

"I think I caught him before he hit his head. He just sort of went down in a slump. At first, I thought he was just doing it to break my grip on him; then I realised he'd gone unconscious."

"Does he remember anything about the night he spent out there alone?" This other man had a slight accent. I did not know this man. His tone sounded inquisitive or even suspicious. It was as if being out alone at night were somehow mildly criminal in and of itself.

"He didn't answer me. He just told me to let him go, to take my hands off him."

"Well, he needs to rest, perhaps, before we can discuss that with him. If he has forgotten what happened to him before he came home, that is very dire indeed…"

The implications of his words were clear. I would need to come up with a story about what I'd been doing that didn't involve graves or flying ointment.

"He was *dirty* when he came in," Father added. "Henry never gets himself dirty! Morton could testify to it. Even when he was a little boy, he presented well. He'd take a shirt off and put it to soak if he dropped something on it, by the age of five."

"Your son is beginning to grow up," the unknown person who I took to be a doctor said. "When I examined him, it was clear Henry's becoming a young man now." A stampede of Martha's talking about being forcibly examined rampaged a full witch hunt through my flesh. Was he looking for a special witch mark on my body that would tell him for certain that I was different? "Often, behaviour patterns change radically for a while after the onset of manhood; it's not uncommon. My German mother used to call it the 'arrival of the stranger.'"

"But it's just that… It's just that I'm worried that…" Father cleared his throat. "Henry's always been…well…different you see. He's functional, you understand? Highly intelligent, in fact, but…"

"I can hear you," I said, clearing my throat afterwards.

"Hello there, Master Henry."

"This is Doctor Crowther, Henry. Morton asked him to drop by to give me some advice." Everything about my father's manner during this exchange was forced and pseudo-involuntary. I could see the grip this Englishman and this German had on him; he felt forced to do whatever they wanted. His faith in his own resolve was so weak he couldn't even make a proper decision for himself about his own child.

I knew Dr. Crowther, mainly from when he charged with mutilating the body of William Lanne, who people said was the last surviving Aboriginal man. Arthur had raged about the whole business when we were boys. At the time, he'd claimed it was against religious lore to defame a corpse in that manner, especially without the person's permission. If I'd ever met Crowther, I had no memory of it before this moment. His eyes narrowed, and I could see him trying on the different dress-up outfits for suspected deviancies, seeing which one he thought suited me best. Why had someone like him chosen to call on my family? What was so interesting about my situation that it had him involved? I felt a hunted sense that he had been told I was a changeling and had wanted to look my body over for signs of my elfhood.

OF THE HEART

"He's normally a good-natured lad, really. Just... He just has a feverish imagination. He's quite a musical talent, perhaps more than our fortunes can truly support as I would, if I were a man of means." It almost sounded as if Father wanted help with me in some way that went beyond getting the opinions of his betters. He hoped that between Morton and Crowther, two of the more influential men he knew of, he would be bequeathed some wisdom on how to father me, or maybe even practical support.

"I am going to have to recommend you get someone in to perform the correct procedures on him. I will give you their card. There's one man in particular. He could save your son before he ends up needing...a hospital situation. I think mainly some hot cuppings and cold water dousing. This will help to wake up his latent humours and warm his system up. On the mainland, doctors are having a lot of luck with that, particularly with the sort of children that get described as...strangers."

"Of course, I will make sure I get him for Henry. Mr. Allport did tell me you would know best."

Crowther nodded, happily accepting my father's fawning, and the passage of sycophancy tied the case up with a neat piece of string. I had been diagnosed with a clear-cut case of Imagination; people started writing off prescriptions for it immediately. Nothing worse for a middle-class boy to be found in the possession of. Nothing a lifetime spent among the bourgeoisie wouldn't cure, though. "I'll get you both started on some strong sleep draught for anxious dispositions. Taken every night before bed, it will help you both unwind your nerves, and help Henry to get ready for his treatment."

Apparently, it was the new flavour of the era. A disturbed person needed to not be stimulated too much, to be allowed rest without seeing any company. The treatments were designed to be uncomfortable but not painful. Like an exotic flower that grows in the shadow of giant opium poppies, my visions bloomed hectically. Under the influence of it, Crowther's body bent thin and hunched, gut-picking; the new doctor was a tatty crow who followed in his shadow.

Then the opiate would kick in. The idea of a fight seemed ridiculous. What was there to fight about? The dreams and visions were before me; they *were* me, my very flesh knitted together by magic. What had I been worried about a moment ago?

Rag & Bone Man

Then the therapies began. I can still feel the cold sheets under my stomach, after I was told to take my shirt off and lie on my stomach. My father left the room the first time. The next time, the doctor asked him to stay. It was hard to understand that part, what the role was in increasing the witnessing of the cupping. The cups were hot enough that they burned my back. Responding with obvious pain was an option I didn't allow myself. Nobody asked me anyway. If there was something I'd learned, it was that one needed to keep one's self on the inside, and the world on the outside. It was harder during the cold water dunking, though. As there is no fully dignified way to come up from having your head shoved down into icy water. You came up gasping, wet, and confused, stripped of your dignity, as if you'd been the victim of some violent baptism.

Thus passed some indeterminate amount of time where my father declared I was now an invalid. I was regularly burned, occasionally purged, and often dunked. It was fashionable for upper middle-class people to have at least one invalid, and Father always did aspire to being upwardly mobile. So, I suppose you could say the move was face-saving, and I'd now become a status symbol and talking point. I would hear him talking to friends quietly about how I was getting help. My era loved a good talking point. Everything was opium-pale, but my mind was heated and brittle as insomnia, my eyes lidless against the dark. So, I tended to hear everything. It was right when I thought I'd start screaming for no reason that his pebble pinged against my windowpane.

If you've ever entertained the idea that such glorious symmetries and poetic moments of perfect timing only happen in stories, content yourself in knowing they happen sometimes in real life also. Maybe only once in a century, but one such moment happened to me. My heart thundered with fear that the sound didn't mean what I hoped it did, until I reached the window and looked down to see him. He was standing not far from where the whistling devil man was wont to stand when He came to play on someone's bones beneath my bedroom window at night. For a second, the thought made me shiver. I wondered if the devil man had led Arthur to me, offering him up like some kind of sacrifice? Perhaps I thought like this because I was again, just like the first time I'd seen Arthur, looking down from an upstairs window at him below?

This time, though, he was approaching from the hidden side of the house. Looking up at me in the semi-dark, Arthur doffed his hat to me as he had on the first night and held up one finger to his mouth in the gesture of silence. I didn't need to be told. Quietly, I closed the bedroom window, my heart already in my mouth and made the torturous, tiptoed journey out of my room and onto the creaky landing. It was the stair that had given me away the night where I fainted, so I avoided that one altogether. All the lights were out, and I hoped that Father was deeply asleep and wouldn't hear me on the stairs.

It would have been worse than whatever period of time I'd been on opium, to know that Arthur had come only for Father to chase him away. Opening and closing the back door behind me was the most terrifying part yet, because at that point, I was so close to him. I was afraid that even from upstairs Father would hear how my heart hammered. Not only would he wake and make Arthur leave, but he would sense what I felt, and how outside the ordinary this all was, and therefore he would forbid it.

It wasn't long after the painful slowness of closing the door behind me that I was grabbed and pulled into his arms. It was like when he returned from boarding school, except where that had been buoyant and playful, this had a drowning intensity to it.

"Arthur," I whispered, my voice weak with gratitude. "You came."

"Of course I did. I've been looking for the right opportunity for nights. Are you all right?" he whispered near my ear. He didn't let me go immediately, and my entire sensorium was awash in the smell of his skin. It seemed I forgot my own edges, just like when we were tangled up together as boys.

When I nodded, he pressed me back so he could examine me in the moonlight. I was barefoot in my nightshirt, and no doubt so pale I resembled the ghost I sometimes felt like. "What happened?" he asked, after he'd finished looking me over. Even in the dim light, I could make out the expression of concern on his face. "Why won't your father let me see you? What is going on in there? I've watched how often the doctor comes..."

For a moment, I feared I would start laughing loudly with anxious hysteria. It seemed impossible to know where to start in terms of explaining what had happened. My lower back was still smarting with blisters from my last extra hot cupping. Their treatment had stunted me somehow. Arthur's maturation to young manhood was racing ahead of mine. Even in the short time we'd been apart, he'd grown and hardened. He had the wiry sort of frame that is often a lot stronger than it appears, and it wasn't going to be long at all before he could break his father's cane arm, should he choose to.

There was only one fact of importance I needed to tell him. It had nothing to do with the burnings and the cold water. "I did it, Arthur," I told him, leaning in to whisper urgently in his ear. "I broke the fourth wall on reality."

"Do you think you can find your way back there?" he asked immediately.

RAG & BONE MAN

"Blindfolded."

"Then take me with you," he whispered back, grabbing my hand hard and urgent.

I didn't let my lack of compliance show as the following days of my treatment regime turned into weeks or the weeks into months. Over time, I had somehow learned to be pushed headfirst into water in a calm manner. The doctor and father both praised how compliant I was. Every day, I became more aware and careful, like a cocoon-transforming creature that prefers to unravel in darkness and privacy and not allow its wings to be seen until the right moment, on its own terms. I went through a full puberty as my father's invalid, the awkwardness of it hidden away from the world. Yet, the whole time, I was planning my future resistance. All I thought about was Arthur's words to me: *Take me with you*. And all I cared about was gaining the power and knowledge to work out how I would make that happen.

When I would wake at night in the sweats of an opium sleep, I would see the whole silvery thread of the story's pattern, the one I was living. My mind was felt to throb and eventually explode and bulge outward monstrously, until I was holding Hobart inside me like a pregnant woman holds her baby. Inside me, I felt the realities of the place in my amniotic. Although I would forget the gossamer complexity of it upon waking, there were certain things I would carry over, like the knowledge that I must bide my time a little longer. With the fullness of manhood would come answers, whether they were the ones I wanted or not.

Father had the tailor come to the house because my old clothes didn't fit me anymore. By the time he and the doctor decided I was well enough to go back out into the world, nothing I'd worn before my illness was any good to me. I had gotten taller. I was thin, though my shoulders were wider. My increasing reach of my lengthening and flexible fingers could cover two extra piano keys now, between thumb and little finger. For some reason, I wasn't outfitted in my new suits until the final cupping had been performed. The doctor felt my opium use was of no concern, as long as everything else seemed to be falling into place.

It was easy in the end, getting Father to agree to let life happen to me again. It all had to do with Miss Clara, the daughter of the florist, and the impact she began to have on our household. She arrived just when my patience was nearing its end. It must have been something about a feminine presence in the house that melted my father, for he would seemingly agree to anything she asked of him with a pretty flutter of her golden eyelashes. "Well, Master Henry, this won't ever do," she said as she swept into my room on the first day of her influence. "I noted your piano was fresh out of flowers. You can't take a woman for granted like that, you realise? Just because she's made of wood!"

She smiled so sweetly as she passed me the red, long-stemmed roses that even father found the gesture entirely appropriate and left us alone without a chaperone. Even the business of giving flowers from a girl to a boy was outside the box, when it came to our world, especially long-stemmed red roses. Her confidence was stunning. As soon as the door was closed, she looked back at me with a conspiratorial glint in her eyes. "The letter from Arthur is hidden in the paper the flowers are wrapped in." She winked at me, making me feel like a participator in a crime of some kind. I blushed, both because of my excitement at receiving a letter from Arthur and out of embarrassment that Miss Clara was sitting on my bed. Women did not generally sit on a gentleman's bed. I admired her pretty blonde ringlets and wondered how it must feel to look like how she did. Her appearance suggested everything sweet, inoffensive, and ornamental, giving little indication of what kind of mind lay behind it. I didn't envy her situation, for all of society's approval. She reminded me of the little porcelain ladies with coiffed hair, which adorned every available surface of our era.

"Thank you," I whispered, regaining my composure after clearing my throat. Unwrapping the flowers, I merely held the letter in my hand and didn't open it. I wanted to read it when she wasn't there. "And for the flowers also," I said, gathering them up after I'd dropped them carelessly all over the white linen covers in my rush to remove Arthur's letter. "Father won't let me buy that kind anymore."

Clara frowned. "Why ever not?"

"I don't really know. It has something to do with those boys who pushed me into you at the market. I think he feels that the flowers somehow provoked them, or perhaps that it's inappropriate for a young man to feel that way about his piano?" There was a subtle dryness to my words; Clara's eyebrows shot up at it. There seemed to be an adult sort of understanding in her gaze, one that perhaps came from the fact she was two years older than me. "Is that why your father won't let you see Arthur?"

I frowned. "No... Why? Father believes I'm very ill because I'm different."

"Not too ill that he refused to receive me..." Her words drained away with an air of significance. I had no explanation for this discrepancy in Father's behaviour, beyond that I sensed he wished to exclude the feeling of magic that startled the air when the two of us met.

"How did he seem, Miss Clara? If I may ask, Arthur, that is…"

She smiled at me with an odd mixture of pity and envy. "I had *hoped* he'd come calling to see me, but it was only to talk about you. He's very worried about you, Henry. Very frustrated and angry with this situation. He talks a lot about what he wants to do when he finishes school."

Although it was with a rush of pleasure that I received the news, it pained me to think of him angry. Arthur's soul was a generous one, and though he had a natural melancholy about him, at times, it took quite some discomfort to rouse him to negativity towards others. "That saddens me," I murmured. Which of course, as far as understatements go, was very British.

Clara patted my hand nonetheless, as if she sensed the discrepancy between the words and the feeling attending them. "If you write him back, I will carry the letter to him with barely any bitterness." She grinned.

"That is kind of you. So, you like him then? If you were hoping he would call on you?"

"Well, of course I like him! What is not to like? Dashing boy, bold, big-hearted, bright, witty, with just a little touch of disrespect for authority."

I smiled at her assessment of him. It pleased me that she noticed the same things I valued about him. "Yes, he is."

"But you don't need to be jealous, Master Henry. He clearly likes you about as much as you do your piano! And notices me like Father notices Mother's new shoe purchases!"

I responded to her effervescent wit with laughter, though moments later it occurred that her statement confused me, and I stopped laughing awkwardly. Should I have been jealous? Were friends often jealous when the inevitable girl came along who would become his wife and take him from his childhood friend? Was that the expected way life moved forward? I really wasn't sure. Part of me had assumed that Arthur and I were forever.

"*Should* I be jealous if Arthur noticed you?" I enquired, to see what she thought, as I wasn't sure who else to ask these kinds of things.

She looked at me oddly, as if I puzzled her. "Perhaps I should leave you alone to read your letter… I'll call again tomorrow to take your reply and live vicariously through you. Master Henry," she said with a curt bob of her head and a shallow curtsey. As she withdrew, I wondered why anyone would want to live through someone confined to his sick room, who was at kindest estimation a bit odd, and at worst a word too unspeakable to be listed in the dictionary?

OF THE HEART

My dear friend,

I deeply regret that I have not been able to manage to get a message to you sooner. My father caught me getting back into my room the other night after I called on you and was rather angry. In a week or so he will forget—such is the quality of his rages, they are blown and spent rapidly. When he does, he will start to loosen his watch over me, he'll get taken up with a project on the grounds and forget. At present, I do what he asks to appear obliging, which is ultimately all that is required to manipulate his good opinion. In the meantime, I will write you and when I can sweeten Father. I'm sure your Father can be easily overcome. If we can just get you strong again, Henry! I don't trust that Doctor your father called to the house one bit, he is the one who dug up the body and hacked off the head of William Lanne, did you realise? He called it research but regardless of the race of a man it was a disgraceful mutilation and assault upon a buried body. I don't trust his family in general and it bothers me that your father does.

When he sees you thriving I know he can be brought to loosen his anxious hold over you. After all, he is not an unkind man, merely fearful. I do believe he wants your happiness. It is understandable when he's lost so much. Still, I fear it does you no good, being cooped up in that house and not getting sunlight or fresh air. I believe him to have (albeit innocently) created this illness in you to assuage his own anxieties. At a deeper level, I believe he senses, but does not know he does, a little of the wild magic that transpired through your person on the night before your fall. I believe he fears it because it is so very alive. Father fears it too without ever having touched its edges. All our world fears it, Henry, that is why I trust it.

Yours faithfully and always,

C.A (Arthur)

I winced as I read his letter. The subtext was as thick as the ghost-treacle around the rivulet. *Rather angry* meant his father had hit him, probably in visible places to the point where he wasn't going out in public until the bruises healed. I shook my head very slowly, a shiver passing across my skin. For a long time, as the electric shock of rage passed, I held Arthur's letter against my chest and tried to inhale its contents through the hunger-ache that stirred and lurched into awareness between my ribs. What saddened me the most was that Arthur really believed Mr. Allport loved him, and what is even sadder is I think he was probably right. Such was the approach to fatherhood in many households.

The father ruled it as the Governor ruled the colony and took out any petty humiliations the day held from those above on those less powerful than himself. Not ever having been beaten, I had no idea how anyone could equate it with love, except in a situation of fear so constant and relentless, it becomes normalised since childhood. With my eyes shut, I followed the threads of the words back to Arthur sending my love and my support, not just the idea of them but the feeling itself. *I'm going to make this all go away. I'm going to make him go away. I've got you...* Silently, I hardened that promise inside of me like forging a weapon, heating it with the cupping heat that still lived a hot little life in my lower back, shaping it, hammering it, and finally cooling it off in the face-dunking basin.

It was a promise that emerged from my very pores after what happened in St David's Burial Ground. That part of me that was infected with the spores of some subaltern intelligence that grifted through the back streets, picking at the rags and bones of the past, collecting the stories of miscreants and rebels, melting them down, turning them into something new... Whatever that vagabond force was, I was of him. I didn't get a choice. It seemed that Arthur did. He indeed seemed innocent to me, somehow, in a way that I perhaps was not. He was choosing to fall where I was already plummeting. For this reason—and of course, because, quite simply, I loved him—I would defend him from the consequences at all costs.

I dug deep into everything that felt slightly crooked in my goblin-marked flesh, the malignant potential of every doctorly mistreatment, the marking of my earthly cells, each with its own little hungry mouth. I took a particularly large dose of opium to mitigate the anxiety that Arthur's letter left swamping up like a bog inside of me. Like the brackish water of wetlands, it rose and invaded the house. I lay on my back, staring at the ceiling, feeling it all coming up under the doors and down from the window frames. It was as tiny as the mouth of a baby, but it was as an eye that looked out darkly from me, the Eye... It was bred and brewed over centuries inside my ancestors, who were full up on bitter dispossession and struggle, and entirely empty of food. The poisons I'd been bred on summoned it into being; I merely cast Their Eye. Flesh memories, traumas stored in blood, muscle and bone, silent stowaways in the night of my being, rose to the surface like bodies three days after a shipwreck.

Mine was the history of the strangeling. It slithered out through one of my ears and went pushing through waters, gelatinous with the rivulet's gore. I saw the traces of the tears of millions that I carried, encoded in hare skins full of

OF THE HEART

broken bones and matted grave fur. It was dirty inside this human heart, like Martha's initiatory story had been dirty. I hadn't come here to be clean.

The second time she came to call, Miss Clara brought a mixed bouquet of flowers for me. Normally, a girl giving a boy flowers was considered off-kilter. She got away with a few inappropriate things over the time I knew her. As the daughter of a florist, she managed to make it seem like flowers were something that just happened to you in her presence, and both our parents allowed us to be alone together without anyone watching us.

"Is it true what people say? That you're magic?"

One of my eyebrows jumped up with mild irony. "Is that what people say about me?" Through my recent sufferings and deprivations, I was learning not to be afraid of their opinions. "Which people?"

"Mainly the servants your father has hired in the past, who all left because you're creepy."

There were a couple of moments where I stared at her in surprise, because she was nearly as honest as me, then I burst into a laugh. "Me? Why am I creepy?"

"Never mind, Master Henry, I like creepy things."

"Well… Well, thank you… I suppose… What did the servants say about me?"

"Mainly that you cause all the clocks in the house to stop at the same hour that your mother died, that you're a faerie changeling, that objects break or move when you're angry, that you can talk to dead people, and anyone who is unkind to you meets with an accident. I think that was it."

"That is untrue about the clocks. That's only happened once that it stopped at that time, and there was no proof it had anything to do with me." The room seemed to fill up with the sound of me not denying the other accusations. I couldn't seem to do anything to remedy that. Miss Clara just started nodding to herself after a little while, as though me breaking off the sentence there told her everything she needed to know.

"I tried to get Arthur to confirm or deny the claim you're a magician at least, if he wasn't going to answer the question about changelings, but he will answer no gossip about you."

"Bless him," I murmured and cleared my throat, trying to conceal the surge in the deep well of my feelings.

"But it may change your response when you learn the reason I want to know, Master Henry. I am particularly interested in the subject because I myself hear the voices of dead people." She looked around as though checking that none of the living, beyond me, were listening, and then continued, speaking more quietly. "And I *taste* them as well, in the air. I feel like the flowers I tend for Mother respond to their presence, wilting more quickly when they are around... Especially the dead that feel unhappy. Like the convicts." Her voice began to fall away in response to me staring at her. "You think I'm a silly, frivolous girl," she said abruptly, getting rapidly to her feet and brushing down her skirts smartly. "Well, I'm not, I'll have you know; I am actually very smart. Despite these," she said, flicking at one of her ringlets as though it mocked her.

"No," I said suddenly, getting to my feet. I was in the chair for this visit and fully dressed, but I'd known immediately it was the first time I'd been standing in her presence since her visits had begun. She was significantly shorter than me now. "I mean...what I mean is... No, I do not think you're silly or frivolous. I have far better observation skills than that. Please sit down; I would like to hear more about how the dead and the flower people speak to you."

She narrowed her eyes slightly, trying to figure out whether to trust my words or whether she was being stealthily mocked. I held my hands out to her, palms up. "Please," I said again, more gently than before. "I mean it; I'm not teasing you."

Hesitantly, she placed her tiny, delicate little fingers into my hands, and for the first time, I realised quite how much I'd grown up of late. Our hands hadn't looked much different in size when I'd spilled red roses on her at the market and she'd reached for her dropped change. I've always had that kind of memory for the key moments of life, the ones that seemed to make the narrative of my unraveling go forward, the type that allows one to write of them in stinging sensory detail.

"Pleased to meet you," I said with a faint smile.

"Why do you say that?" she asked, standing there with her fingers still rested lightly in my hands.

"Because we only just met properly."

My dear Henry,

I have felt you close these last few nights and just now I've managed to get a message to Martha. If she is serious about you and I being what they've been waiting for, I believe she and Moses will proffer us some assistance. On one side, I fear she will consider it but 'Middle Class Travails' and make light of my rich boy tears I have shed before her, but it may appeal to her desire to stick it to men like our fathers... Time will tell and I pray for her help.

OF THE HEART

Moses has been teaching me things that help to shape that desire into something more than a standard prayer.

In the meantime, I continue to feel the aftereffects of the magic that you passed to me with your forehead shortly before the accident. It has activated something in me. Sometimes I dream that I steal into the forms of bandicoots and possums and wearing my rat skin coat, I go about the streets and find the secrets ways into the homes of others. I climb up them in my possum, trying to look through the windows. Always when I dream I'm trying to get to your house, yet though I could easily run the distance right now, from Fernleigh to you, on my human legs, I spend some time feeling lost. It feels like the animal brain becomes more and more dominant the longer I ride with them until I start to lose control of the experience.

Oh Henry... I really do wish we might meet soon so that I can tell you of these developments face to face! Queen Victoria herself set her seal of approval on passionate friendship when she approved Tennyson's In Memoriam poem... What on earth have we done wrong that might be classed as any different? You are dearer to me than my own brother, yet who is harmed in that? My brother never charges me with the lost love or complains of its absence. Even if sometimes, like Cordelia to Lear, I am inclined to love "as is my duty" when it comes to my blood siblings, I've never been lacking in my duties...

You of course have been robbed by Nature of all natural siblings, and mother too, it seems so unjust to deprive you of yet more connections. I'm glad at least that you have Miss Clara and that you are not entirely without company. She is a diverting girl, much too clever for her station in life. She is kind and good also, which of course will also count against her when society does the tally of our sins. No doubt your father admits her to his home because he knows she would make a fitting wife for you.

There I stopped reading for a moment. Probably because I stopped breathing as if nudged hard in the stomach. It reminded me of when the doctor used to dunk my head. Swallowing hard to suppress my reaction, I continued to read.

He would be right, if that's what he's thinking. She seems to have an intuitive understanding of our whole predicament, and being an independent girl would doubtlessly be interested in finding a husband with a mind like yours, regardless of other attendant hurdles the two of you might face. I've read it somewhere (I read often and mentally store up things I wish to converse with you on when we meet again) that one begins to come of age when one considers for the first time that their elders may be utterly wrong about everything, but one only becomes truly adult after you forgive them for it. By this estimate I am a long way from a true adult and spending a lot of time in the former territory. Henry, it is really, truly, difficult not to hate him at the moment. I know he's my father and it's my duty to respect him, but how can I when I know he's so very afraid?

Faithfully always,

CA (Arthur)

That night I dreamed of strange girls with flowers where their sex should have been. I knew from their eyes that they were no more like other girls than I was like other boys. I played music for them on my cello at first, and next on my violin as they became more excited, and they bloomed with a heady eruption of perfume. For the first time, I understood why I called all my instruments by feminine pronouns. I awoke smelling the exotic fragrance of the magnolia and jasmine and something far stranger. It confused me to feel that my nightshirt was sticking to me with dampness.

Immediately, I got up and changed out of the night garment. I knew it had something to do with the feeling of rising and peaking excitement I'd experienced while I played music. I washed in cold water and tried to forget about the whole thing. All the while, whenever I made a splash of water in the basin, I could feel the doctor-hand at the back of my neck, about to push me under. I could hear beyond the dripping water each time the echo of the angel-devil's urgent whisper repeating: *you have been lied to...* To try to drown out the angel-devil's voice, I went into the front room to play the piano. Which was a futile exercise, really, as I'm quite sure I was never so much his plaything as with my fingers on the keys. Again, I would swear I felt someone touch the back of my neck as I played.

After closing the door behind me, I sat down on the stool before her and shut my eyes. Without opening them, I ran my fingertips over the lightly stained ivory. There had to be a way you could scream through your finger-ends into the music. I was made of misty spring mornings with sharply perfect frost patterns inside me, waiting to be catalysed. I was also thunderstorms, glacial shifts, and a hidden supernovas. Only in my music could I show them to anyone. Some part of me had smelt different air and remembered a world where life was lived on a larger scale than the quiet middle-class lifestyle laid out for me. I tried to express the expansiveness of this world without borders or edges, which disappeared into illimitable horizons. Where love alone made a law for lawless men.

OF THE HEART

While I would play, I would be a reed in the current of this feeling, the echo of a world that no longer existed—or perhaps had never truly existed at all for all I knew... It hurt beautifully until tears ran down my face as I played. I would become the whole ache-wound that is the town of Hobart and the sorrows of all of its occupants. Just as the spirit of the opium poppy had shown me. I could feel myself like a seed and incubator also; I was mother and father to this rip down the middle in the fabric of things. Because the devil man who followed me, whistling His tunes, would need someone to hold the door open for Him, I assume. I had told Arthur I knew how to break the fourth wall on reality, and I had partly exaggerated. It may have been more strictly true to say I *knew someone* who was carrying a spoon that could make it as brittle as a sugar glaze.

Abruptly, I stopped playing. Someone was knocking at our front door, and I couldn't play with someone unexpected there. When Father answered, I crept towards the door and listened to see who was calling. All I could catch was that the man had a broad Southern American accent, and his voice was very low and deep like that of some Negro men. My heart jumped up with hope at the thought of Moses. I knew it couldn't be him, though; Moses was beautifully spoken. My sphere of life at the time was such that my only idea of beautiful when it came to accent was a middle-to-upper-class English accent. An Irish one was shameful; a Welsh one, like the way the devil man spoke, seemed yet more provincial, and a Southern American accent immediately invoked for me the spectre of slavery. There was some faerie part of me that saw the presence of iron at the wrist and ankle as an abomination, whether one had stolen a loaf of bread or were simply busy existing in Africa.

"Be off with you!" Father was saying to him, taking the tone he only ever took with his clear and obvious inferiors. I felt a pang of shame in him. "We've no need of you here."

I didn't recognise Moses for a good few moments over his exaggerated deference to my father and his floppy old hat that made him look like he was homeless. "Many pardons, Master, many pardons. But maybe for the Young Master here," he said, gesturing to me with big, loose arm movements that were not at all like his usual body language. He was a closed book of a man to me, the old conjurer; he had not offered up the story of his life the way Martha had. Even Arthur only knew fragments of it from when he'd slip out something about a place he used to live, or the home island of his Polynesian wife. So, it fascinated me to see him in action like this. "Pick a card, any card! It will tell you your fortune."

"I've never heard such nonsense!" said Father, not yet doing anything to get in the way when I stepped forward to take the man up on his offer. Father was the rabbit again, caught in the gaze and mesmerising dance of the rattlesnake. Or was he perhaps a chicken on this occasion? The motions of the snake were sinuous and hypnotic; you could feel him get caught up in them. Now that the devil man had marked me, I truly *saw* Moses for the first time, as our sorcerer's eyes met each other across the threshold. He winked at me from behind his mask; I saw his power fully as if it rippled over his skin like an interruption to the light.

"Pick a card, any card, but beware you Fortuna's eyes are everywhere, young sir! Dame Fortune, she already know what card you're gunna pick before you do. Decisions been made already, see?"

Cautiously, my fingertips—their intelligence awake to tiny differences in vibration—alighted on a single card and drew it out slowly from the pack.

"Don't show it to me! Don't show it to anyone!" Moses declared theatrically. By now, it seemed that Father had just submitted to watching his act, and then begun to rummage around in his pockets for the loose change he believed Moses wanted. "Lady Fortune wants to talk to only your eyes, Young Sir."

I looked down discreetly at the card in my hands. It was the Eight of Hearts, yet the stranger part was that upon it was written the word *Soon* in Arthur's handwriting. I smiled to myself with the romance of the gesture, though I immediately guessed that Moses had performed this trick by having my friend write the word *Soon* on every card in the deck, which were all most likely the Eight of Hearts. Despite being under-awed by the trick itself, the idea of Arthur inscribing every card in the deck with his message moved me.

"Keep what you have seen close to your heart, and don't show it to me." Obediently, I slipped it into my pocket and crossed my arms. I have to own up to some older, knowing part of myself that folded my arms for me with a certain twitch of one eyebrow. My eyebrow and my crossed arms seemed to dare him nonverbally to impress me with his showmanship. Despite the fact my body language was akin to that of something carved in ice, he came and put his hand over my waistcoat pocket where I'd placed the playing card. "Feels like a message of Hearts."

My father glanced at me to see if it was correct, well and truly buying into the performance now.

"Because you have made up the whole deck using Hearts cards," I murmured. It was a new confidence that came of my initiation. I didn't mean to

OF THE HEART

challenge Moses exactly; I just wanted to show him who I really was. My father laughed the complacent laugh of the person who has never deeply valued his son's intelligence , not until it was being used to get one over on someone already beneath his station. It saddens me to admit that I saw this in him, this tendency towards punching down at those beneath.

Moses merely laughed and made some deferential gestures in my direction. "Young Master is very sharp," he said, fanning out the cards to reveal only the tops, which were indeed all hearts. He did so in such a rapid sleight of hand movement that I doubt Father caught it. "But Old Moses, he ain't done yet. You have in your pocket the Eight of Hearts, do you not Young Master?"

"Can we be assured they aren't all Eights?" Father snorted, thoroughly disenchanted now. Moses ignored him. He patted me on the pocket. "Eight of Hearts…the wish of the heart is about to come true…" Suddenly, he turned to Father and took up his arm too quickly for Father to resist. "Let's look at your hand here." He scrutinised Father's palm for a moment or two before making a grave sound. "You've buried many kin. More than you got left livin'… You got a lot of fear. Fear you're going to lose this one too. But you ain't, you know, Master? Not if you're smart. You're going to be called on to make a decision." Suddenly, Moses had Father's arm tightly, and it appeared for a moment that in response to his urgency, he might have tried to pull it away. "Between what people think of ya, and what's gunna keep your baby alive, and if you fail that test, sir… Well, if you make a mistake, you gunna regret that for the rest of your days…"

Father pulled his hand away. "Get off my doorstep," he whispered in a tone so quiet and menacing, I could sense it came from a terror as stark as it was sudden. He'd let some predator species half over the threshold of his chicken coop, and his eyes were moon-wide with the smell of them.

"Oh, don't be like that, Good Sir. Looky here what's that behind your ear?" Moses produced a coin from behind his ear and showed it to him, all the while scooping away one of the hairs from my father's head. "See? Old Moses is harmless…" he muttered, coughing as he staggered away. Father stepped back gingerly from the coughing and closed the door rapidly. Any hint of coughing or sneezing around the house of my father, who had lost so much to disease, was a sure way to finish a conversation with him. I was still mildly stunned by the moment where I'd made eye contact with Moses as he placed my father's hair in his pocket. To me, each of the motions he'd done in taking it were clear. It was in my disposition now to smell out such subtleties and notice what others missed. Moses had noticed me noticing.

RAG & BONE MAN

The door was closed, but I was left hungry—hungry to learn what he knew of how to work people like that. Given what art Arthur already possessed on that front, having Moses as a teacher was going to turn my friend into a force to be reckoned with in the dominant world of men. For Arthur not only possessed likability almost in excess, but an advantageous social position. With Moses' skillset, he could almost literally have anything he wanted. Part of me was excited; part of me feared what having that power would do to my friend's good heart.

"I shall have to speak to someone about these vagrants," Father was raging. "Have them rounded up! Only yesterday there was this insolent dark-haired wench, who I'm pretty sure used to wash my laundry when she was still doing her sentence. That Martha Dunn character your mother used to go and see to read her fortune when you were still a babe in arms. Never did Nellie any good consulting with her, that's for sure. One child dead, one changeling-ed under our nose, and then Nellie herself, God rest her! Haven't seen that Dunn woman for years, but damned if it didn't look like the witch! She just stood on the opposite side of the road and stared at me! To all intents and purposes, she meant to set some gypsy evil eye on me. Like those low tinkers back in Ireland would do. Not moving an inch, just staring you out..." He was clearly Irish-bothered by this at a deeper level, yet was too busy trying to English to admit to it. "And now this cretin! I'll have them all rounded up and flogged!"

"Yes, Father," I murmured distractedly, so little did I take his rage-shows seriously after hearing them for many years and never seeing anything come of them. "Quite unsettling." I excused myself of his pacing and ranting, heading back into the front room. There I took the Eight of Hearts back out of my waistcoat pocket and found with it a small written note with a time and address on it.

My heart elevated dramatically as I considered the implications of the fact Martha had known my mother before I was born. She had obviously known a lot more about me via normal means than she had admitted. If she'd called me faerie-boy, it was less about intuition and more about direct knowledge of what my parents believed about me. In this, I came to understand how confidence trickery played its part in this kind of work. I inferred the meaning of the note I'd been given. With that particular sleight of hand, Moses had entirely gotten one over on me, and I didn't care one little bit.

5

The devil man's voice continued speaking to me in the silences. Perhaps only the young know what it is to anticipate a moment so keenly and with such perfect dedication that every detail of the memory becomes burned in behind your retinas? Luckily, for those of us who are easily possessed by memory, part of us all remains young always. That's only if you've ever been young at all (not all of us have), and you've cared for someone from the bottom of your most innocent heart (as most of us haven't); then you will *know*. I counted the days and fretted away the hours that stood between me and the date and time on the slip of paper.

All morning, while I waited on Father to get off to work, the sounds of making his breakfast and tea all boomed inside my ears, where they were invited in whether I wanted them or not. When I had finally straightened my collar in the mirror for the last time and headed out the door, my newly polished shoes made a rhythmic scrap and clap, scrap and clap. It was so loud to my sharpened sensory arousal that it felt close to unbearable. The way people tend to feel about someone making claws of their nails down a chalkboard. It came between the sounds He would speak, the angel-devil who had come for me, speaking through the sticky fat coating of the ointment that took possession of my hair follicles.

You were made to know intoxication.

I had no way to understand his siren's song beyond those words, only to wonder if Father and the Vulture Doctor were right. Was I indeed ill in some way? Was this sensory intensity a symptom? There was probably a name for it in his big diagnostic manuals. A fever of the brain, a failure in my warmer humours that needed to be encouraged with cold on my active mind and heat on my inactive body. Being called as a cunning man, a crossroad's walker, a two-headed man, a worker of magic... It wasn't just about stepping apart and claiming a different reality for yourself; it was also about coming back in and resisting their counter-spell with everything in yourself. You were fighting for your soul. Though none would witness or cheer for your struggle, the heroism of it would happen in secret; it was still the most crucial battle you could ever fight. It was just as real as feats of arms. At the end of the day, for me, it was as simple and elegant as this: there are two types of people that the Otherworld chooses to rampage into: those who buckle under the weight of their own gift and are proven unworthy to carry the vision, or those who step up.

I never gave myself any option except the latter. It was that white-washedly simple in my world. The love that ripped me open down the middle, coupled with the fire of the light-bringing angel, had been too profound for me to let go of that impact-scorch, not over something as petty as other people's ideas about normality. To know that holy power once was to be forever hungry, forever light-shadowed. Forever walking a long road that would end with me once again looking up into his gaze as it unveiled infinity, or otherwise it would never end. Like some Wandering Jew of the crooked world, I would walk these streets eternally waiting to hear His melancholy-cheerful whistle dogging my step along the alleyways and through the tunnels. Such were my thoughts as I walked through South Hobart towards Miss Clara's home.

There was no logical reason to see a connection between my hooded angel-devil and Arthur, other than Arthur choosing to stand in the same spot at the bottom of my window. Yet, something in me knew that the closest I would ever get in life to the lit-wick of aliveness—that the angel-devil had ignited in me—would be with Arthur. This was *it* for me. I knew it so vividly at that very moment, as I walked up the path to the flower-erupting front garden that announced Clara's family home. I stood there in a sudden rush of fierce tears, dabbing them hurriedly with my handkerchief. The devil man kept saying *you were born to know intoxication* between the quiet sound of drying my face. I knew nothing else was going to be more deeply significant in life for me than this collision. I would give my life for it, if I had to. It was simple, quiet, and pure, like the flaming heart of Our Lady burning away my chest.

"Master Henry, you're here!" Clara flew out through the door and gave me an exuberant embrace. "Come inside, quickly!"

I did as I was told. Or was at least partially dragged into their parlour. Hurriedly, I took off my top hat, which Father had said since childhood was vital to not offending the house of your friend. So keen was he at the notion I might begin courting Miss Clara that he didn't seem to place limits on it. When I'd started taking turns around the garden again, he only had one servant hired to watch me while he was at work. Now there was no one home but me. Despite this, our little ruse would never have worked without the participation of Miss Clara's mother.

OF THE HEART

"Good morning, Master Henry," her mother said. "Look how you've grown! You are looking well; it's good to see. Why don't you come into the sitting room for some tea while I prepare lunch?" She was blonde like Clara, with a more generous form. No sooner were the words said as I was bustled through the door. I hadn't seen Arthur under proper light in some time, and with my first look at him, I dropped my hat. I hesitated whether to pick it up and draw attention to the fact I'd dropped it in the first place. In my world, such seemingly trivial actions could take on huge gravity. The hat was immediately forgotten, because as soon as he saw me, a mixture of immense relief and something like suffering flashed through his expressive eyes, and he rushed towards me. My natural impulse was to do the same, and my body started to. Everything living in my body and soul responded—yet, when I felt his last-minute hesitation and the reining in of his emotions, I adjusted. I was so trained, after all, to squash all the things most alive in myself.

Arthur was frowning, as if he was fighting off crying as he offered me his hand to shake. I took it and shook it. Electric sparks of life sprang from his flesh to mine, and I probably held his hand a little too long. He softened the gesture by rubbing my other shoulder with warm intensity with his other hand. It was so deeply unnatural for him, the stoicism of society. His heart was one that gushed when most trickled.

"It's good to see you," I murmured.

"Oh, don't be silly, give him a cuddle!" Clara insisted, gently guiding him forward with her hand. I blushed furiously and stiffened with mingled fear and want. Gracefully rescuing me from my awkward agony, Arthur rose to her challenge and took me in his arms. It was all I could do to conceal my intake of breath; it was like I was getting access to air for the first time in over a minute. For a few breathless moments, I closed my eyes and revelled in his proximity; as he pressed his chest against mine and squeezed me with a gentle protectiveness, I took a deep breath of the smell of his skin on the side of his neck.

"It's so good to see *you*," he whispered near my ear before releasing me rapidly. Immediately, he seemed to regain his manly composure, which had grown in maturity by an alarming amount in my absence. It frightened me as well as allured me, because I feared that, with this impending end of youth, I might lose him. My eyes coursed over his shaving stubble and the new accentuation of his jaw, the line of hair on the outside edge of his hands, and the fact he was still a bit taller than me. The way his once turned-up nose was a now a little masculinised. When I reached his honey-warm eyes again, I couldn't keep up the act of not showing my entirety to him in my eyes. I had to look away.

Clara's mother had closed the door now.

"Are you all right?" I murmured, tears standing in my eyes.

He nodded in his new toughened, grown-up way. I could see the evidence of the hurt that had caused it, and the determination that was growing underneath it. He waved the whole thing off like it was nothing because he was learning to be British, even though, frankly, we were all Tasmanians. "I'm fine. It's *you* I'm worried about—and that doctor. What's he got you on, Henry? Medication-wise? It's not natural to sleep so much, or to be indoors for so long…"

"Please," Clara said graciously. "Would you gentlemen like to take a seat? How do you take your tea?" she asked as her mother came back in with the tray. She was masterful at this. I don't know how we'd have managed in this situation without her. Swallowing hard in the name of my composure, I managed to pick up my hat and avoid sitting on the tails of my coat. Suddenly, I hated with a vengeance the whole costume and had a vivid fantasy of rending apart the clothes off my own back with my teeth and nails like a rabid animal, ripping off the cravat and gnawing it apart, pulling my waistcoat apart in front of everyone. For a moment, I had a terrifying fear I would really lose control and begin to do it.

I cleared my throat and said: "Milk and no sugar, thank you."

Make no mistake, this is what it's about, being a gentleman. Find everything that is alive and natural in you; do to it as the hounds do the fox.

"Same for me, thank you," Arthur said. His voice was more obviously thick with emotion than mine. He was never as good at destroying himself as I was. I used to say it was romantic of him, his strong sensibility for life… Perhaps it was simply human. There was an essential aliveness in him, a stubborn seam of life that knew somehow at a core level what health and natural goodness felt like, and it wasn't just that—it was also that he stubbornly wouldn't give up on them. The way I wouldn't give up on my vision. It was, perhaps, that he too *couldn't*.

For the first time, I realised, as I politely sipped from a china cup and listened to Miss Clara make desperate but effective small talk, he had as little choice in all this as I did. He was messy. He might have not been quite the kind of freak I was, yet he was another kind. He was one of the age's great obscenities: a man of untidy, unruly feelings, whose spirit would not be broken to the yoke of drawing room trivialities.

"Oh, I can't stand this!" he said with intensity, getting to his feet. His napkin fell on the floor, and I watched it fall. It meant just what my falling hat had meant. It meant order overturned; it meant the coming reign of chaos. I don't know what Arthur would have done to follow through on the feeling of insurrection

OF THE HEART

that came with the falling napkin had Miss Clara not stepped in and deftly manoeuvred us.

"I can understand that," she said, dabbing at her mouth prettily with her own napkin after placing down the lemon tart she was eating. As if this disruption were as natural as anything else. "Because it is such rubbish, isn't it? Let's talk about something *real*."

Her words were like a series of small explosions in the still drawing room air. Every cluttered china dog, every dancing china maiden or praying child, every jostling portrait, each superfluous cheap copy of an oriental clock, every supercilious flower vase, all took an inward breath at her audacity. From the mantlepiece, Queen Victoria herself had a sour expression.

He shrugged and instinctually sat back down, the air around him seemed to hold the life-weight of a storm surge. "I'm game."

In some ways, the dream of the night after is louder even than the memory of the day. It clangs as a flesh-wound, one that was carefully buttoned down and starched over while we'd waited for each other. Neither Arthur nor I spoke of what we'd endured during that separation. Yet, in the sitting room at Clara's house, it seemed to mingle between us, simply with this new shared breath. A nonverbal story-sharing that each of us breathed in and used to account for the changes in the other. We both tacitly understood the new inhibitions the other had developed. I think he knew my confinement had been hurtful, and I wondered what he had passed through during that time.

That night, I took a lot more opium than usual, as I didn't imagine I would sleep without it. My dreams came rushing up through the pipes Father had recently had installed in our kitchen sink. There I am, in that timeless place, standing on the Southerly side of the rivulet with my back to Ridgeway, half-silhouetted against a sanguine sky. Arthur is facing me. Neither of us moving or speaking at first but standing still like a faerie stock, arms at our side, made of wood and stuffed with straw. "Look what I've made, Arthur," my voice is elf-flat without expression and only a faint touch of pride. I have no idea what I mean until a second later.

With my hand, I gesture to the side and behind me. Like one of the Four Beasts of the Revelations saying: *come and see!* I smile. With my own eyes, I never see the flames rising over the ridgeway, nor the houses all ablaze. I see it reflected back in Arthur's darker eyes. I see the expression on his face change to one of dismay as the reddish glow of rising Hell and peaking desolation lights up his complexion. Behind me, I can feel the heat and the conflagration of the mountain as if it was my own heart catching on fire and bursting through my chest, much as the most unrepentant of witches of old must have died on the pyre.

The rush of the feeling is indescribable. I am on fire, and yet I feel elation flecking through my pain; it is a rushing into being, and all of my seedpods crack open amid the intensity and spill life into the black devastation of this beloved devil country. It isn't me that spills. It is something that has gone inside me. At the moment of uncontainable ecstasy rushing up my spine, Arthur throws back his head—the flames of insurrection bathing him satanic-red—and howls at the blackening sky. I think I hear a volley of echoing cries bouncing around the valley, where others lie waiting for this moment also.

With a jolt, I'm back inside Time.

It's remarkable how dreams can do that. Just stop everything all over again when you enter their hieroglyphic language. Startling awake in my bed, I found myself sticky again. That feral cry of Arthur's was still lurching in me as I got up to perform the ritual of washing. The sounds the water made were as thick with the devil man's voice as they had been the day before. An extra cold basin of water put pay to the tingling heat the dream had left in my flesh. I dressed myself uncompromisingly, as if buttoning myself down were my absolution. As I did, my mind turned to the day before and I heard again Arthur's words: *I'm done.* He hadn't explained himself beyond those words, spoken as we parted. He hadn't needed to.

Was there something wrong with me that I had felt such exultation to feel our world burn? I didn't know, yet I could not quite bring myself to feel sorry. Sorry was a feeling I was rather tired of feeling. These were the people that were trying to take away my vision. And without it, I'd be as dead as most of the Black fellows who set fire to the homes of the whites to protect their connection with the land. I sympathised with what one might be prepared to do if their life, home, and loved ones were threatened. Only after I'd set fire to the white fellow in me with the soot from the Devil Dance could I have understood the movement in Arthur's face—from anguish, to understanding, to exultation, as his eyes reflected the blaze of our world burning.

I put those thoughts away inside Pandora's music box, along with all the other strong things that would have to learn to hold their breath for that little bit longer, before the hand of power would release them. When I came down the stairs, I spent quite some time composing myself and preparing myself. It was raining lightly outside, and you could hear the wind on the shutters announcing the arrival of something ragged and unsettled. The step of my shoe upon the stair paused midair just the moment before the knocking began. My hand gripped and squeezed tight to the banister. Already my heart was galloping away with all the king's horses. I didn't move from that place halfway up the stairs.

It was as though the suckling ghost of my mother held it firm from purgatory below our stairs. I could hear Father's angry step as he went for the door. No doubt he expected to be greeted by more of the recalcitrant riffraff of Hobart, someone he could express his own littleness at, coupled with his desire to have flogged. The last thing he expected when he flung open the door would have been to find a gentleman's son there banging it so raucously. "What the devil is going on?" Father declared.

"Henry!" I heard Arthur call out around him like Father wasn't there. I was moving fast, down the stairs and into the hall. As soon as I set eyes on him, I could read the whole story from the torn open buttons on his shirt, the beginnings of his black eye, and his frantic breath. I knew every precise detail of what it meant. I could see that the day had come, just as Martha had long ago predicted, when Mr. Allport raised a hand to Arthur and lived to regret that he had done so.

"Now you know very well your father doesn't want…"

"Damn my father to hell!" Arthur thundered with his new grown-man's voice.

"Now… Arthur, if you could just…" Father's voice fell away as I brushed passed him. How impregnable the strictures of society can seem until a moment such as this one… When you challenge them and find they have nothing with which to back themselves up but your fear. Or perhaps I just shut all the sound out, and so it only seemed like Father had stopped speaking as I stepped out into the rain?

There wasn't any hesitation in this embrace; it was done in the teeth of everyone and everything, and it felt better than anything I'd ever known. All I could hear was my heartbeat suddenly jolted by his chest colliding with mine and jumbling them up together, before dancing madly with his beat, more rapid still than mine. He was sweating, and I loved how his skin smelt in a way I'd never enjoyed any animal thing. I wrapped the flat of my forearms around the back of his neck because it was the only two places where skin was showing on both of us, and there I could get his sweat on me. If the wild feeling that went through my body when I played piano had a smell, it would have been like that of his skin, like ozone and the thirsty earth and moss after rain, with a pinch of salt.

"I'm never going to let you go again," he told me near my ear with a passionate intensity that sounded almost like a threat. The way he dug his fingers into me when he said it was so hard it hurt a little. I didn't hear Father's voice again until he made a move to grab my arm and pull me away from Arthur. My eyes had been screwed shut tightly, feeling the rain all over our skins. I didn't fully understand what happened at first. One minute, Arthur was holding me in the street and Father tried to touch me to exert his authority over my person, and the next moment I was pushed behind Arthur, and he was standing pointedly between my father and I. Nothing was said; there was only the sound of Arthur's ragged, wild breathing in the stunned silence. The significance of the gesture seemed to crash through space for a few moments, and the frayed ends of fate threads rearranged themselves in response. The gesture of physical defiance was raw and obscenely savage, out of place in our class and era, shrill like the highest, harshest notes of the violin. The air tasted of vivid purple.

Father held his hands up in a gesture both placating and partly submissive. "Don't do this," he murmured. When he spoke, his voice and the sad expression on his face belied another emotion, one of reluctant sympathy. "You've got such a fine future ahead of you, lad. You could help to build this place!"

"No!" Arthur snapped adamantly, shaking his head and holding me behind him with his trembling hands as if he feared I'd be manhandled from his grasp. Nothing about his voice or demeanour suggested he was capable of full self-control at this moment. I was terrified and in awe of this bold species of resistance. "No!" he cried again, as if answering more than just my father. "Not without Henry…" he muttered it like he was only just realising the truth of it. Afterwards, he started to nod his head with a new certainty. "Not without your son, sir… He has every bit as much right to that fine future you speak of as I do. More, in fact, as he is far more talented, and I won't—I *will not*—go and have it without him!" By the end of his speech, his voice was thick with emotion that was fast becoming hysterical tears. My father looked distastefully at this unsightly excess of feeling happening in the street. Something in my stomach crumpled me like a fist in my guts. Taking off my coat, I wrapped it protectively around him.

Father sighed, defeated by a stronger will than his own. "Well, I suppose you better come in then, where no one can see this unhinged behaviour," he said grudgingly. "Just prepare me for what to expect when your father comes looking for you?"

While he spoke, I brought Arthur inside, shut and locked the door behind us.

"I don't think he's going to come here trying to bully me anymore," Arthur replied. I took out my handkerchief and passed it to him.

"What happened?" I whispered.

Sighing, Father backed away. "I'll set some sweet tea on to boil," he said, disappearing into the hall. It seemed he wanted to get away from the crash zone of us.

"I have the wolf from the fairytales growing in my belly." Arthur smiled bitterly and shrugged as if he had simply arrived at that part of his monster-tale, and he could not fully answer for his gut-creature. "I guess? He just hit me one too many times, Henry."

As soon as we'd gulped down the unpleasantly sweet tea Father made us for shock, I hustled Arthur away upstairs to my room. Whilst he didn't prevent us this privacy, Father did call out to us. "You're too old to share a room, and during the day, you keep one foot on the floor at all times!"

"Yes, sir!" Arthur called out to my father; we were already most of the way upstairs, and he looked at me with an incredulous expression like my father had gone insane.

"I don't understand what he means by that?" I queried Arthur as I closed the door to my room after him.

Arthur rolled his eyes. "He acts as though you are his daughter."

I pursed my lips bitterly. "No, he doesn't. If I *were* his daughter, he would be keenly trying to marry me off to you, along with a great number of chickens and a few very special abalone shell paperweights to secure the deal."

I thought Arthur might laugh, but he only smiled sadly. "If you'd but been born a girl, Henry, he wouldn't have needed those things," he said quietly, a bittersweet poignancy lingered around these softly spoken words. His words left me with a spasm of delight, followed by an ache twice as wide as the girth of the initial pleasure. I cleared my throat and returned my mind to the matter at hand. "How much damage did you do to him?"

Arthur sighed and looked quickly away from me. Stuffing his hands into his pockets in the posture adopted by common lads, he went over to the window to look out. Rain poured down the pane, seemingly in time with each shard of fresh pain that I felt at not being numbered among the cloven gender who would not have needed a single paperweight. "I started taking pugilism lessons after I got into a fight with some boys my own age." I frowned at this revelation of Arthur's, although, at the time, I didn't fully grasp the subtext. What I did know was that this was part of the pain-narrative that had put the new inhibitions in his body. "The result being that I no longer get into any fights with boys my own age. Father knew about it. He was paying for the lessons, because he hoped it would toughen me up, and he felt that if I was going to continue to behave in such a singular manner, I would need to learn to stick 'em up... Guess he just didn't expect me to do it to him."

"So, you've bruised him on the face?"

"Yes. I may have hurt one of his arms a bit, too, when I restrained him. He's too proud to be seen outdoors looking like he got the worst end of a physical altercation."

Mentally, I was tallying how long it was possible he would leave it before coming to look for Arthur. Or would he send someone else from their family to do it for him?

"This is why I don't expect him here any time soon." At this, Arthur walked over to my bed, slipped off his shoes and pointedly sat down on it with his legs crossed under him and both feet up on the covers. "My grandfather is too weak these days to come around and try to force me out of here. No one in my family will talk about it; they'll pretend it didn't happen like they do with everything uncomfortable or unsightly."

"Rebel," I accused with a smile and a twitch of my eyebrows, pointing to his recalcitrant feet, which were off the floor.

He laughed. "Indeed! I warrant I have half-impregnated you."

I laughed, too, at the absurdity of the idea of myself pregnant. Yet, his comment returned my mind uncomfortably to the strangeness of my opium vision where I had dreamed I held the minds of Hobart in my wet-inside belly. Was it Father acting out some strange fantasy of my sister living on through me? *Actually* pretending I was a girl? I did bake for him and wear Mother's apron. Puzzled, I came very close to trying to phrase the unwordable question I'd liked to have put to Arthur. What was it Father worried we might do if Arthur lifted his feet off the floor? But it's very hard to ask about something you have no words for. I didn't let it trouble me for long; I was far too exuberantly happy to have him there with me in my room at all. My heart had come to expect so precious little when it came to joy and closeness that it didn't take much levity to fill me to overflow.

I dampened a clean washcloth at the basin and laid it tenderly on his swollen face. If only we had some ice in the house! The tenderness I squashed up into a ball and pushed on into that act was tremulous. I took off my shoes and knelt on the bed to get closer to him while I worked. He looked up at my face the whole time as I cooled his wound and smoothed comfrey ointment onto it.

OF THE HEART

Near the end of the task, I glanced into his eyes at last. There was some strange new expression in them, something full of animal knowledge coded in a language I didn't speak. His pupils were dilated. "It doesn't really hurt that much," he said, when I was all but finished. "I cherish being taken care of by you, though."

I smiled, flushing faintly. "And I like taking care of you." I got up and put away my ointment and washed my hands to cover their tremor. There was silence for a while as I rinsed out the cloth and hung it up to dry. When I turned back, he was watching me. There was something so intent about it, something so patient-predator that I didn't know what to do with the sticky urgency of it. Sometimes, I fancied my own veins contained greenish-white plant sap and not livid human blood at all, as if I hadn't been encoded with the right mammal instincts to understand human signals.

"I have a plan, Henry. I'm going to make everything all right."

I trusted him utterly. Such was Arthur's unique magic with people. He had a way of saying things with such certainty that there was no question of not believing. No wonder Mr. Allport saw him as having a fine future in law.

"I believe you. I have a plan, too, Arthur."

"What does yours involve?" he asked me.

"Killing your father with my mind. It appears to me that when he hurt you, he forfeited all of his rights to a merciful death."

Arthur laughed. "That's sweet of you." He said this like he really believed it. In truth, it was anything but sweet. It was primitive, in all the best and worst of ways. "What does your plan involve?"

"Father will not tell me what to do anymore because he now knows he can't back it up physically. He hates to lose and won't want to lose again, so I imagine things will change. I'm going to start stepping out with more different girls and give in to his desire to start grooming me for partnership in the Practice. All of these concessions will grease the wheels for him to accept the fact that in my spare time, you, Miss Clara, and I, are going to bring Spiritism to the respectable folk of Hobart. We won't be cutting Martha or Moses' grass because our clients will be drawn from the middle and upper-middle classes, which theirs almost never are. You will have a trade, my dear friend. And when you can both make our own money, *nobody* will get to tell you what to do anymore."

His plan was giddy like a precipice before me. Arthur was good at seeing his way to how things like this could work. He had his family's fiscal luck-force in his pocket and a great eye to the main chance. Towards the end of his speech, I reached across and took his hand in mine, lacing my fingers through his. We sat like that for a little while without speaking.

"I will do this thing with you," I said at last. "But first…" I turned to look at him. "You have an appointment with the black-faced man at the crossroads. I must take you to where it happened to me, where the fourth wall split and spilled itself all over me. There I will present you to him, as Martha told me to do. First, you must be lathed in the witch unguent, with the ash of the Devil Dance ceremonies. All this must occur before my training can go any further, and I will not feel ready to become…the person you speak of…without some more of Martha's instruction."

"Tonight then?" He smiled with a slow, warmly kindling enthusiasm sparkling in his eyes. "Because I'm ready."

6

Until I was there, walking with him arm and arm along the exact way I'd walked at my initiation, I didn't know how personal it would feel. During my own initiatory vision, I'd witnessed Martha and Moses making the ointment that had been, at that very moment, soaking into my pores. I saw them pour in the ash from the Devil Dance. I saw them put in the plants witches ride with certain charms I felt sure I'd remember the words to but didn't, plus the fat of a dead man hanged at the gallows. Then, as it cooled, I saw them split the batch to make two separate doses for Arthur and I. This was like giving him half of my fire, I instinctually understood. *Fire of my own fire, breath of my breath, blood of my blood, bone of my bone—stronger than all bonds, this bond that binds us.*

As we headed towards my sister's grave, I saw the enormity of this gesture Martha had asked of me. It frightened me a little; I will own that. It frightened me to feel the threads of my destiny becoming tighter around me, binding me into future outcomes that would all be the result of this action. Yet, I couldn't back out because I'd seen him make an irrevocable decision of his own to stand by me, one that he couldn't take back. He still bore the bruises of that decision on his cheek and no doubt on his heart. I knew I was giving away something of myself that no elf-boy would ever give away. It was tantamount to a selkie's loss of her sealskin. But there was no question. I'd have given him everything.

"This makes us closer than kin, you understand," I whispered to him. "It's something more binding than marriage, more profound."

"I understand." That was all he said. It was perfect and enough, as always. Sometimes, I feared the way he always knew what to say. I feared that it was more a great *willingness* in him than a true understanding of me. I'd been said *no* to by the world so many times I began during those days to fear with Arthur that I was experiencing a form of trickery. Regardless of how deep his understanding went, he passionately wanted to understand me, and that was more than had ever been offered to me anywhere. So, I would accept it. It was a risk I would just have to take; thus I imagine begin all true loves. If such things indeed exist.

"Do you feel the effects of the ointment yet?" I asked him, as we passed between the graves and the open running sewer of a place it was in parts. Arthur didn't seem perturbed by the environment one bit.

"It's coming up on me by the moment," he said, leaning a little more on my arm as I guided him to where he would have to lie down. "When I look at you from the corner of my eye, I see nothing but light."

Almost as soon as he'd spoken, his legs seemed to go out from under him, and I had to settle him down on my sister's grave, like tucking in a child. When he was on his back looking up at the sky, perched above my sibling's skeleton, I knew he was now where I had been when I'd seen the angel, who held my hand while I took my first steps into the Otherwise. Arthur was looking up at me with wonder as though I was that angel for him.

I was afraid. But I did not leave.

Thus developed the embryonic bud of the two of us... I held his hand until his eyes closed, and I could sense his vision turn inwards towards the source of his own truth. I couldn't have worded it at the time, but I knew that although I had used my vision to cut a door for him, what he saw once inside would be unique to him; it would be his own vision. In wonder, I reckoned—during those long, fretful seconds, minutes, hours—where I had to await the completion of his incubation, on how Martha must have known in her crude wisdom the process of maturation I would have to walk through to bring her instructions to fruition?

It was probably not until then that I saw how her teaching me had begun a long time ago. I had been reckoning only in time spent in her company and not thought of the time spent experiencing what she had laid out for me. Knowing that something planned for me by my elders gave my vision part of its power was both humbling and inspiring. I was all right with being just a link in a chain, a knot in a long, ruddy-coloured thread; I didn't need the gold chain of the ancient occultists; this was enough. There was comfort in it. It kept me strong while I waited to know if Arthur would also be strong enough to walk through the door I'd cut for him. It lay open upon its hinges, though it wasn't a door made for any mortal man to traverse.

When I saw him, at last, attempt to sit up, I bent over him. He gasped and blinked a couple of times, gazing at me with an awed expression of total beatific trust. I watched the air he'd taken in turn to mist with his out breath and slowly leaned down over him. As I did, I held my breath and let the virtue of my vision fill my lungs. When my lips reached his, I exhaled my breath into his mouth, and he breathed it in deep. A holy communion of a gasp.

Of the Heart

Then something existed that only moments before had not existed; it was a new story made up of what was me, touching what was him, and creating a third thing. I was about to withdraw and tell him to hold the breath in for as long as he could, when he slid his hand around the back of my neck and prevented my retreat. Pressing my lips deeper into his own, he kissed me. I wasn't sure if he even saw me, so in a state of spiritual transport was he. Whether I was me at all to him, or just the figment of some fading vision of his guardian spirit who was doubtlessly a woman, I don't know—but *he kissed me...* What else is there to say? Leigh Hunt addressed Time thus: "You thief, who loves to get sweets into your list, put that in! Say I'm weary, say I'm sad, say that health and wealth have missed me, say I'm growing old, but add that Jenny kissed me..."

Arthur was my Jenny.

Whilst his mouth was on mine, and his tongue sought mine eagerly, I couldn't consider whether he really knew what he was doing. My body's cobbled-together defences came unraveled. I couldn't breathe with the shrill, insistent rush it sent through my touch-deprived flesh. He tasted to me like food must have tasted to my starving Irish family. He drew back for breath. I pulled away from him, still panting, and looking for my penknife so I could put the mark on him, like I was meant to. I didn't dare look him in the eye. I felt like it did in dreams on the mornings when I'd woken up sticky.

"I need to mark you," I muttered, fumbling with my penknife. Though the words I wanted to say were something closer to: *I love you.* He didn't say anything but offered me his left arm, wrist up, as if I intended to let his life's blood, and he meant to eagerly allow me. Turning it over, I found the outside of his little finger and made a gentle nick there. I wanted to show him with my hands that this was how it was going to be, that whilst I saw that he was someone to offer a main artery, I would never wilfully harm him. His givingness was safe with me; I made that promise directly to his skin, veins, and muscles.

I squeezed it 'till a droplet of his blood ran down his finger and onto the soil, and then marked his forehead with the mingled blood and grave dirt. Lastly, I put his finger in my mouth to suck the blood off. How I wanted to taste his blood...Where everything he was was made liquid. As I sucked the blood off his finger, I felt Arthur make a sharp intake of breath. Without understanding of what the act simulated that had made it provocative, I gave myself to that enthusiastic suckle in full measure. From his response, I learned something unspeakable. I was starting to hear my own body's quiet voice whispering out from the soot I'd rubbed into my skin with its delicate slither of bone knowing. Not knowing how else to lean into that edge, I cut my own finger. When I placed my little cut against his lips, he clamped his mouth over my wound and sucked my blood eagerly.

"Now, get up and swear what is between your hands to our angel-devil and the mistress of the moon."

I watched as he knelt beneath the thin column of moonlight, took off and opened his penknife, and laid it at the feet of the moonbeam. The wind got up and rustled the graveyard trees, moving around the sluggish night fog. When he got to his feet, we stood there together for a little while without talking, his eyes full of the new depth of a man who has broken through the fourth wall on reality.

"I can see them everywhere…" Arthur murmured, taking my arm and pulling me with him while he turned in a slow, full circle at the crossroads of Murray and Collins Streets. All around us were the echoes of the dead who seemed to wander up from the hospital and down from the gallows, following the ghost roads, evading the hellhounds, eventually finding the rivulet to try to quench their unquenchable thirsts. Moses told me once that they weren't meant to mass around like that.

Mother had always told me that the dead thirst like the living, only they have to make a long, lonely walk to their eternal rest. Those who gave victuals to others in life would be offered water; those who had not would walk without it. Buried without shoes as many were, they would only be provided with a pair if they had shown such kindness in life and given a pair of their shoes away to a stranger. For this reason, I always gave things to them, in the hope that someone would hold out their hand for me when it was my turn. The little whooping cough children, and the women dead from childbirth, the young men hanged, I didn't discriminate; I poured whiskey at the crossroads for all.

"Is this what it's always been like for you?"

It was one of those questions that you don't realise you're waiting for.

"Yes." Our breaths were turning to mist in the cool night air, and I could see how the warmth in it attracted them. Perhaps I should have been frightened. I wasn't. Perhaps I wasn't truly me anymore as we continued to turn in slow circles, with our backs to each other. Something older in me had consumed the younger me whole, like a snake whose gullet is engorged with the writhing carcass of a younger animal. Slowly, I was digesting earlier-me in my stomach juices and taking on his nutrients and his habits, so I could learn to pass myself off as the uninitiated Henry.

Arthur linked his arms through mine, pulling my back in tight against his. "Look, we've become the two-faced man at the crossroads," he said, finally ceasing to rotate and leaving us so we were each looking along one of the deserted night roads. "This is how it's going to be from now. I've got your back."

My lips pressed together tightly with emotion I swallowed down hard. Because I couldn't answer through the lump in my throat, I leaned my head back against his so it was touching. I knew he was still intoxicated by the after-effects of the ointment, yet it didn't matter. Silent tears were spilling from my face so that I could feel them running into the collar of my shirt, and he had my arms so I had no way to wipe those tears away. I left them there to run down and drop as an offering to the hungry-thirsty dead. The youngest ones first, the ones who are still hungry for their never-tasted mother's milk. Next the ones who are thirsty for their never-tasted first love's kiss. *Yes, you can have a little of the edges of my feeling. There is enough of it to go around, by Jesus, Mary, and Joseph... Little Mary and all the other tiny ones like her who never got your first kiss of love, have some of my happiness.*

Arthur kept making rapt sounds of wonder as he leaned his head back against me to look at the stars, which he saw for the first time with the eyes of a fully made cunning man, laughing with rapture at the beauty of what he saw. I should have told him to be quiet, lest we wake the neighbourhood, and they witness our immense eccentricity, but I didn't because his joy was slick all over with beauty.

"You have my back in this world," I whispered, leaning my head right back on his shoulder as he was doing on mine. "And I have yours in the Other."

"Deal."

"You make me feel so safe."

"As you do me."

It was only later I was to become consciously aware that we weren't the first to stand thus or swear such words to each other. That other story is part of one of the forgotten faerie-tales, the exiled ones that hail from the more crooked and twisted byways of the Enchanted Forest. There are some stories that mankind just isn't ready for and so is always trying to forget as quickly as possible afterwards. The wind will not allow for that though. He rushes through at such moments, when two people stand at a crossroads and swear an oath to become a two-faced man. He swallows us into the miasma of memory, just like being caught up in the riding mist-men of the Bridgewater Jerry, or going under in a room-temperature river of molasses.

The trees and the old stones keep on whispering the forbidden faerie tales; they just don't say them loud enough for the average person to catch their phantom drift. But when you step out at night and fall silent on silent streets, one's younger human identity looms so small in the lamplight. You begin to fall in step with your shadow. To such folk, the wind is always talking, and the forgotten-dead become white noise on the backdrop of life. They took my story away, you see, and many like mine. Your world is built upon the bones of silenced tales. They still haunt the edges of the unspoken, packing a punch of charge from keeping quiet for so long. They would like to talk now. I think I'm going to let them.

Some nights, the Rag and Bone Man starts tapping out a tune on his hollow bones—he is a hollow bone himself. The renegade wind makes memory-music on his ribcage. He's a gallows haunter. He's the Pied Piper of Truth. Because when the Rag and Bone Man plays your bones, all the buried stories get up and start speaking in tongues. These words exist at all, like all stories, because sometimes the dead come back. And sometimes, they come back not as comforters, but as accusers. They come to point their finger and moan, naming the ones who did them secret harm, naming and shaming those who erased them.

"I want something," Arthur said, rolling over onto his stomach and fixing me to a corkboard with the warmth in his eye. My stomach dropped two flights. I didn't know what it was he wanted. The answer was yes. Though I had known him since we were boys, there was something deeper below him now, as if the ointment were still seeping in ever further into his system by the day, colonising his bones in the end. I knew him better than anyone did, and yet, in another respect, there were a great many unknowns and a lot of unexplored territory, a lot of adventures he had about which he didn't tell me everything. There was a little spark of mystery he carried; it glimmered in his eyes.

"And what is that?" I asked, turning my head towards him and seeing between us the daisies in the lawn of the Botanical Gardens, the fresh green shoots of the lawn made bright by the sun. My eyes might have mentioned to him that whatever he wanted was his. They might have told him I'd give him anything he wanted, but I had to try very hard not to unclench my teeth across this fact.

"I want an honest answer."

"That I can promise you."

"Do you like yourself, Henry?"

He caught me off guard. "What do you mean?"

"Just that. Do you like yourself?"

"I hadn't thought of it."

"Think of it now, for me." He had a way with statements like that, where he managed to deliver a command so deftly it never even seemed bossy.

"I...I suppose I'm not a bad person in any particular way. Yet, how can I like myself? I'm too inside myself; I don't experience myself as something to be liked or disliked. I just *am* this. I'm aware that other people don't find me particularly charming."

He laughed gently and reached for my hand in the grass. I let him take it. "There are a lot of bullies in this world who cannot stand for anything different or fine to exist in front of their noses. You are something better than charming; you are *real*. I would take one real friend over a crowd of unreal ones. Charming people are usually just master manipulators."

"You yourself are a suspiciously charming person, Master Allport..."

Arthur rolled over onto his side. "That's because I'm a master manipulator."

I flinched slightly. At this age, though, he didn't draw back from it. He was interested, too, in touching my intimate spots, even the ones so sensitive they flinched. "In your case, though, you never need fear it, for what I wish to manipulate you towards are terrible things like being in good health, getting to fully use your talents, and liking yourself."

"I'll do those things for you," I murmured. He was right to be cocky, as he had all the power in the world. I felt no resistance to the gentle and firm touch of his tuning fingers on my strings. Yet, I didn't do the things he asked, I realise, not the liking myself part. Arthur probably knew me well enough to realise it. It wasn't clear to me that I'd been dishonest. There was no way for me to know I held my own life and worth as light as air, as I had never occasion to experience anything different to which to compare it. Things had been that way as long as I could remember. How early did I first hear repeated, I wonder, the tale of my monsterhood?

The story where my parents' real beloved baby went missing down by Cascade River, only to be replaced by me? Me—this cold, loveless thing that seldom smiled or laughed—lacking in whatever charms make people feel maternal or paternal. How soon did I first hear my mother rue the day they took her real baby? Who can unpick the whole unkind tapestry of my self-neutrality? Suffice to say that whilst I didn't actively dislike myself, I was convinced I held little value in the world. Convinced of it though I was, I didn't fully understand the reasons why—or even know I thought like this. Only Arthur had ever been convinced of my value or seen in me things he found delightful. So, in his presence, I opened, warmed, and allowed my sense of humour to express itself freely, my imagination rolling out in waves.

"Besides, you *are* charming as well as all those other things," he added. "It just takes the right person to put you at your ease."

As we lay there, holding hands on the grass, Arthur had begun to fight to hold onto the most vital connection of his young life. I couldn't see that, though, for without meaning to ,I had already begun to count my future in years rather than decades. It was already clear to me there would be a time ahead when I would no longer be needed. Arthur's life would be moved forward for him in a direction that would not involve me. At that time, I would simply turn back into seafoam, with none of the mess and fuss of death. I would revert to thistledown and blow away on the wind. Children would make wishes, blowing into the air the substance of my thistleguts.

Being presented as a Gentleman of Magic in the homes of the wealthy was a little like I imagined it would be. Awkward at first, but once I relaxed my reserves, I was shocked to discover it was very natural to me, almost as much as playing music was my *langue maternelle*. It was easy, mainly because Arthur had constructed a persona for me, one that basically instructed all to be both in awe and slightly afraid of me. This part of it—conjuring me forth as a mystery being before I was revealed in the flesh—I can only assumed happened on advance visits. Once he had set the scene for me, people accepted my idiosyncrasies as a sign I was legitimate. Sometimes, I had to stop and wonder at how correct Martha had been on that point. All cunning folk were strange in some way, yet if you knew how to ride your peculiarity, you could convince people to be impressed by it, rather than revolted. That was an art form that was natural to Arthur.

"What can you tell me of the fate of my Aunt Teresa? She died when she was only a young, unmarried woman, and sometimes…" The woman paused; you could see her cheeks start to flush as if she were about to unravel a tightly wound knot that had crept up into her guts and tangled tight. "Sometimes, since her death, I feel her slip into bed beside me. I hold my breath until I feel it subside. I've always believed she's not quite…settled in death."

Arthur began to prepare me, using his pocket watch as a trick piece to indicate I had to be hypnotised to revel the wishes of the dead. Whilst I pretended to be put into a trance, I was already in enough of one to sense Mary Bones coming towards me. There was a luxury to this, being allowed to spread out a little into what I was. Arthur moved his position to behind me with his usual sense of gravity, as if we both were very professional and preparing for a circumstance of some occasion. It was both of us that made it happen. I couldn't have let go like that without him behind me. When I cast backwards into his arms, there was no act in it. It was like that first day in Martha's cabin, where I'd nearly passed into a faint from hearing Mary Bones. For the first time in my life, someone was getting me, letting me…unfurl my monster from the hole inside my back.

When my head came back to look at those around me, I was a little girl who died in poverty and malnutrition locked away from my mother. I was that very little girl who Martha had not been able to nurture. I was all the hunger and all the dry bones of her, and every convict child who died in Hobart. "Teresa, Teresa, Teresa," she muttered through me. My voice came out high like a girl child's. Clara's pen could be heard to record what I was saying. "She's with you still all right. Making that damp come up in your hallway… Drinks up a serve of you every time she climbs into your bed. Drinks up all your kisses with your husband. She doesn't disappear like you think she does, though…" Mary's voice had a sing-song tone about it, as it often did when she got excited by attention. There was no way I could control this. I was, she was, we were, a happening. "It is you who disappear into a long rest when she comes. Drained by her wanting of life."

On another occasion, a big, rich, generous sort of woman with an ample breast and wonderfully bright outfit called Mrs. King, reached out to me like I was her own son. It was in the aftermath of me bringing through her son who had died long before her. The woman's eyes had tears in them, as if she could still see something of her lost boy in me. A shadow or an echo of his life. "You are not as some say at all; you are a true angel." Before I knew what to do about it, I wasn't just embraced; I was pressed to her bosom.

Sometimes, I would give them advice about how to gently move their beloved on, or to perform one last task that needed doing, or feed them in some healthy way. Sometimes, the dead had simply hid some money for their child and died before they got to say where. Sometimes, they simply weren't content with the life they'd been allowed to live before death, and the living needed to perform a task to expiate the burden of survival. Some part of me had inherited notions of the guilt that came with surviving. It was an Irish thing.

I was surprised to discover compassion that flowed from me like milk. Oddly, in those moments, I sometimes felt my nipples leak a little fluid. It was not enough to be noticeable on my shirt, under my waistcoat. Yet, it was there. Like some feminine stowaway, a rogue mothering instinct, a partly residual form of possession. Sometimes, halfway through that feeling, I would catch Arthur looking at me with the most intense expression. I would start to hear my mother's rocking chair on the floorboards of our home then and think of how, when I'd tried to touch my mother after she died, her saliva had dribbled out onto my hand.

These salons are stamped into me as a series of perpetual fallings backward into Arthur's arms, a long collection curated out of my surrender. On a walk home after such a séance, where I had gone limp against him, we saw the Rag and Bone Man coming towards us in the distance. The night was faintly misty. I'm not sure if that was because of a true mist or a fireplace fog, yet it concealed the man's identity and threw an extra, larger shadow of his against the damp orange glow of the road. "You are like him," Arthur remarked. "You're the spirit-world version of the Rag and Bone Man. You make your living by taking away the rags and bones of people's feelings for the dead. What do you do with them to transform them when you get home, I wonder? Do you have to turn them into something else just like his shop does?"

7

Our Shelley summer is imprinted with reading aloud to one another, his voice, my voice, weaving, layering. We explored the temperate rainforests around us, and the Romantic Age, at the same time. They seemed equally real to me, the land and the time of our parents' youth, as if we traversed through both on foot. Arthur would row us somewhere mysterious; we'd put on a billy for some tea, and then immerse ourselves in the laver craters of other people's minds. Most of them were dead, but through the doorway of the book, they suddenly got up and started shouting, ranting out their passionate dreams at us.

Like Byron and Shelley, we rowed a great deal. In the manner of the Lake District poets, we were walkers and swimmers. We went camping and climbed the mountain and there were always books in our knapsacks, crooked little windows into somewhere else that we flung open when we rested from the track. Through them, our lives and imaginations spilled out across the world, suckling on strangeness, foreign emotions, rage, horror; we lived and read aloud to one another of weird, extreme passions. I found inside my breast the monster tit of Coleridge's Christabel and that sight to dream of, not to tell.

Being able to call myself a man was seared in the day Father showed me how to shave with a cutthroat razor. It didn't matter that I'd been shaving for a time without mentioning it to him; it was the personal nature of the whole thing that made adulthood official. I didn't cut myself, and so he never needed to show me again. The brief moment of physical intimacy passed as rapidly as all such things did with Father. Thus, I assumed, had concluded my childhood. Lacking in ceremony though it was, my young manhood came with attendant changes. I worked some days—or half days when needed—on the accounts or at the reception desk. Contrary to the suspicion of some of the wives, no clocks stopped working in my presence, and no milk was soured during my on days. The goblin-milk my secret teats made was kept for the evening hour.

RAG & BONE MAN

The fact that I managed this semblance of functionality carried with it privileges that I held at high enough value that I'd have done anything to appear normal. Even though it took a great deal of self-control, I laughed woodenly at the jokes of the other clerks, secretaries and accountants, who were no more witty than they were interesting. There were no women in the office, so most of these jokes were about genitals or women's breasts. I spent most of the day with the works of P.B Shelley, hidden under my desk and reading secretly when I finished my work before it was due, which was often.

The most important thing was that my movements were no longer fully controlled by my father. I had no need of his doctor or his prescriptions now. The only truly necessary opiate was for Mr. Allport senior to not prevent his son Mr. Allport Jr from walking me home up Davey Street in the afternoons. If Arthur was waiting outside after finishing his work at his father's Practice, and I at mine, wearing his suit with his hands stuffed into his pockets as if he were a tradesman's son, then everything was all right. When we met, like the humming-bird my touch was light. His was firmer. For the brief moment of contact with him, I fancied the wolf in his belly growled and stirred. You could feel it, this bundle of animal energy tied up by his waistcoat like it was caught in a knot around his middle. It made me leave my hand on his shoulder and give him a little squeeze of sympathetic understanding. *I know what it's like to be confined*, my hand said mutely to his shoulder. "Are you all right? You feel...tense."

He patted my hand softly through his glove. As always, he seemed to notice and appreciate my concern and tenderness for his body, a part of him to which not many people would have any longer shown these emotions. In truth, my physical instincts told me to run my hands over his shoulders and press out his tension with my thumbs, but I couldn't do that on the street through his suit coat. "Oh, it's only work. I haven't had enough time to shake him off before I got to you."

"Is that what he's like?" I asked, sliding my arm through his as we began to walk through seemingly mutual agreement. Davey Street had a bit of traffic on it at that hour, so the clop-clop and rattle of the horses and the carriages they pulled formed a background drone on our talk. When conversation was at its electric height between Arthur and I, my mind would become so excited the sounds and other faces around me would seem to fade into a hushed white noise, as if a funeral were passing through town. "Uptight? Tense and alert, a young wolf ready to fall upon the opposition like a sheep that's wandered from the fold?"

OF THE HEART

Arthur didn't answer for a time as we walked. I felt I might have cut too close to the bone. "I'm good at it—being him. I don't want to talk about him, though. I'm good at him," he said again. "But I don't *like myself* when I'm him, and I don't see how we can truly fight to live if we don't like ourselves. It's vital."

He was hungry, this stripling wolf inside my friend; I would see the glint edge of him in Arthur's eyes sometimes when he'd smile or scowl. There was part of me that believed it knew how to handle power like that in a man, being one myself.

"Why don't you get rid of him then, if you dislike him so? Become Arthur full-time?"

"How can you even ask me that?" He pulled me to a stop, just across from St David's Burial Ground. "*We* need me to possess social power, Henry. However else can I help you otherwise?"

I wanted, for a moment, to pull back my arm and tell him I didn't need helping, thank you very much! I had no wish to be anyone's charity case. But, quite simply, he meant too much to me. More than my pride meant to me. When I say this, I don't just mean that maintaining his positive regard was important to me, which is what many falsely name love. I mean that I would not wound his feelings if I could avoid it, even to the detriment of my own. So, I took a deep breath and then exhaled my momentary chagrin, giving it away to the wind like another of my silent and unnoticed love offerings.

The thing was, I suppose, half the people I knew as a child were dead already, and it didn't make sense in such a world to speak harsh words that might be regretted later. Tenderness with each fragile, mortal, frightened one of us (who even remotely deserved it) seemed the only worthy response to our shared predicament. I squeezed his hand and smiled for him, drawing him back to walking beside me with a gentle tug. "Forgive me, my friend," I murmured. "I don't ever doubt your intentions or your loyalty to me."

"No, please forgive *me*. I was abrupt. It just pains me to imagine you believing that I ever wanted to be him! Or that I don't want to just become Arthur right now, and the world be damned. I do. I want that with everything that's alive in me. It's so important to me that you believe that… Just because I have many faces and names, I still only have one heart, and it's yours."

I swallowed down the lump in my throat and squeezed his arm. My emotion was as much for his growing eloquence in his sincerity. This was one good thing about *him*, the young solicitor that I never got to really meet, that was creeping through into my Arthur, this new verbal dexterity.

"I believe you. I suppose it's just…I want to know both of you."

"He's but a means to an end for me. I don't mind being nothing much special in particular when it comes to history. I'm happy to be thought of as a collector of rare things, oddities even, but someone who can spot that which is truly fine. If I'm remembered only for discovering your genius, and the rest they say about me is foul, that will always be enough for me."

"Don't flatter me, Arthur. I'm not someone you need to charm—"

"I'm not flattering," he declared so adamantly there could be no argument. "I'm just telling the truth. I believe that's why they left you on Hobart's doorstep, the Fair Folk. You're here to help stitch together a culture for this displacement, this fracture in the natural order of things we call a town," he said, indicating the young city around us.

I laughed, though not unkindly. As we passed the army barracks on the left, I quietly slipped my arm out of Arthur's while we walked. It wasn't that it was particularly unusual for young men of The Age to walk arm-in-arm. My concern was that I had a tell, and my tell was how much I liked it. I felt myself to be under more scrutiny than most people, especially around the kind of masculinity that thrives among the regimental men. Since our strangely passionate behaviour in the street had been seen, taunts and harassment had become commonplace events for me whenever I went out on my own. It was so common, in fact, I don't think I bothered to remark on it to Arthur. "I don't know that a lot of the city agrees I'm such a precious gift to humankind, Arthur," was all I allowed myself by way of complaint. "Though it's certainly touching that you think so."

"That is their blindness to overcome," he asserted with conviction. "They aren't meant to understand you; it's part of who you are. You are designed to be always far ahead of your time—like Chatterton. Just as how, when we were boys, you told me you were from the place beyond, to the West, past the horizon and always further, further on."

I reached for his arm again and squeezed it softly, drawing it in close to my body. "You're very sweet," I said quietly. In truth, my stomach spasmed with sharp flecks that left me queasy. "If I have ever mistrusted you a day in my life, it is only because you are so very good to me, so very…better than I knew to wish for…and it has been quite…unique to me to be treated with such kindness."

"It is the same for me. Nobody has ever behaved with such a tender regard for me as you do. People have wanted something from me fiercely—wanted fiercely for me to be something they want… But my feelings existed nowhere in it. You've taught me what it means to use the word *love* rather than *like*, what the difference is. I know because of you that what my parents call 'loving' is a misuse of the word. Also, that friendship is indeed the highest, noblest form of passion. I am not so very good, though, Hen. Not as much as you think. I just know how to be sweet with the sweet, and bitter with the bitter."

The conversation had taken such a heartfelt turn that I thought of making some reference to the warmth of his behaviour towards me on the night of his initiation. Yet, I did not. This fact looms large across my fate like many other unspoken knots of sensations. Despite the frustration of retrospect, I still fully recall and understand why I couldn't ask. Part of me was far too afraid he would say he didn't remember, and if something definite was said to kill the delicate stowaway Hope… I wasn't sure I'd survive it. It was better to enjoy the memory of it when such a thing may never happen to me again, I told myself. We embraced affectionately as we parted, and I kept the slither of hope bound up right next to the shard of fear, silently cutting each other in my chest.

It was to my crooked-teacher Martha, dragon-rider, I went to unravel the knots I felt left in. Who better than her to teach me how to find my balance atop the terrible beast of reputation as it took off under me? People weren't just talking about Arthur and I now; they were linking us with the séances, with old, cunning ways, and people like Moses. I remember how, on my first lone night walk with Martha, she took me to the Police Station, down at the wharf-end of Davey Street, and taught me a form of divination that involved interpreting the shape made when one spat a mouthful of black chewing tobacco up the wall. This act, she told me with immense glee, served a dual purpose, the first being prophetic.

"And the second?" I asked somewhat dryly, as I attempted to clean my face with my handkerchief and only succeeded in spreading the obsidian goo further afield. Later that night, at my basin before bed, I found some still lodged in my ear. "Let me guess; is it…defacing public property by any chance?"

"Ha!" she elbowed me vigorously as if I'd made a great joke. Our connection had reached the point by this stage where she actively enjoyed my sarcasm, and I had reached a space of neutrality with her relentless obscenity. "'Sticking it to the pigs' is what we call it, faerie-boy. Because if it's my public fecking property seeing as I'm public, why can't I deface it whenever I want? Eh?"

I didn't have a rational answer to her, so I conceded the point. It was often like that with Martha—just when you were primed to write her off as a thoughtlessly overcooked pie, you'd spot some crusty black wisdom in her filling and pause before tossing away her offerings. If the Police were indeed public servants, why did they treat some of that public with more respect and others with complete contempt? I had heard many stories by this time—from both Martha and Moses—about what went on beyond the soft, damask wall around the middle class, built about me since birth with decorative chintz cushions and doilies. Whomever the Police worked for, it clearly wasn't Martha, because she was regularly harassed on suspicion of soliciting with no other probable cause than being an ex-convict female standing in one place for too long.

"Seeing as your balls seem to have finally dropped, we should have a shindig one night after Moses is finished with Arthur. We've got some bad rum, an outdoor fire, and Moses's mouth organ; 'bout all you need for a party. I'll teach you how to hold your liquor and cheat at cards and dice—essential skills for any cunning man."

"You have a singular method of instruction, Martha. I must say."

"Well, someone's got to loosen up that tight spectral fanny of yours!"

I slapped her on the arm. This was a regular form of nonverbal communication by this point. Love was expressed by this tar-spitting, whiplash of a woman in various degrees judged on how hard she elbowed or punched you in the arm. The harder she did it, the more you were wheedling your way into her heart.

"Can Mary come?" I asked. "She is still one of my best friends. I work with her each time I address the dead at a séance."

Even though I didn't look sideways as we walked, I could sense her pleasure. I knew what it was to have the dead hold a major role in your life that few people ever understood. It pleased me to be able to reach out to someone else like me and say to her, I see her too. Did the fact I could see her mean she was real? Or was time all just mixed around in my gullet? One day would I cough up a handful of fish innards and part of Mary's clavicle? What mattered was that Martha shared my slant-wise gaze.

"You're a good egg, faerie-lad," she muttered. "A good egg." I didn't say anything else for a while. There was a sense in me that the good opinion of a woman like Martha meant something more solid and real than that of a dozen women of high society. She was a judge of character that few I've known could equal, and damned if she wasn't a hard marker as well! If she thought well of you, it was likely you'd worked hard for it and were vigilant in maintaining it, for it was hard to win her regard, and easy to lose it.

I don't recall seeing that as a flaw in her. I was just pleased that she set some kind of standard for me beyond simply repressing myself, which was the only achievement my father had seemingly ever wanted for me. "I'd have invited

OF THE HEART

Miss Clara too," I added. "But I don't think she's ready for the rum spitting and party hats on children's skulls."

Martha snorted. "Flower girl? Well, if she doesn't like herself a set of kid's bones and some rum spray, what's she want with our old, crooked ways then?"

"I think people like her imagine Spiritism could be made respectable," I ventured tactfully. Under the surface, Clara was so much more than respectable. What I didn't fully take in at the time was how fragile her position in society was. As the daughter of a Cascades brewery worker and flower seller, for her, absolutely everything rested on her appearance of virtue.

"Fuck respectability!" Martha spat in the gutter with some enthusiasm. I made a mental note to ease Clara in for a bit longer before arranging their acquaintance. With a certain degree of strategy, I changed the topic.

"Martha? Would it be appropriate at this point for me to ask you about where your Craft came from? You said your mother was a cunning woman… Was she taught by her mother?"

Changelings by nature are always emotional orphans. I desired a sense of lineage of some kind to replace the lack of connection I felt with the sensibilities of my surviving parent. "Yeah, grand-mum learned it from a tinker man whose caravan would stop on the common across from where I grew up."

"Where was that?"

"Northumberland was where I was picked up from, but I'd been around a bit. But those tinkers…they are from nowhere and everywhere. They keep the old magic circulating—them and the Gypsies. Like the vital bloodstream of the land." She glanced sideways at me, that leer she'd give sometimes when she was looking to see if she'd uncovered a vein of snobbery in me. "You too posh for tinkers then? Bet you're thinking: why the hell didn't I go off and become some gentleman magician; this low wench has tinkers in her get up! Eh?"

I shook my head and shrugged. "I'm Irish Catholic. Who am I to judge?"

"Well, Jesus, he loves the wretched of the earth more than the respectables anyway."

"You believe in Jesus as well as the Devil?"

Martha laughed. "Well, a girl's got to hedge her bets. Nah… It's more like what Grand-mum's tinker man used to say: Jesus has got the Devil hidden under his hat. He's a two-faced man, that one, he's where we get the term! How could the Son of God be anything else but a likeness to God Himself? Have you seen this world we live in? It ain't one thing nor the other; it's equal parts joy and sorrow… Life ain't black and white, so why would God be?"

"Equal parts? Do you really think so?"

She must have caught the mournful tone in my voice because she didn't mistake me for protesting in favour of optimism. "It's just people don't speak of their joys like they do of their hardships, Henry. Some because they're afraid to tempt fate through boasting of it; most because they say pleasure's a sin. Yet, suffering is noble as long as you don't fall to the very bottom of the heap."

I laughed cynically to cover the fact I was thinking of the joys I never spoke of in life, which were many and intense beyond words. "This is very true what you say. Yet, I also wonder if I'd deem life even close to fifty-fifty had I been born amongst the Native people? Or would I instead decry the world as an evil thing, my current view being unfairly bolstered by my social privileges? It intrigues me after your experiences that you still rate life so highly."

She snorted. "Well. I've fought for it, I guess. Means more to you, the more you have to fight for something."

My dear Arthur,

I wanted to return your extravagant compliment at the time of giving, but was keenly aware you would shrug it off, laugh at me, and say I was too kind. Here on paper I feel braver and say how stimulating I find your company. You will ask for particulars and so I will name them in no particular order. You have a far better mathematical sense than I do. You might call your gift for numbers dry, but it's this aspect of your thinking that makes you relentlessly logical in debate. And a man who may overcome his enemies with words and wit is far superior to one who must rely on violence alone.

Furthermore, you know where every country and capital city in the world is, and what it's called, and what manner of people live there. You can comment knowledgeably on the customs of tribes no one else I've met even knows of, least of all cares about. Martha tells me that I must make peace between myself and the ghosts of the Native dead, and you are the only person I can think of who can guide me deeper into the land here. You know, my friend, as if by some rogue instinct, the longitude and latitude of sensuous space. What I know is the cartography of dreams. Nothing I am skilled in yields to touch or receives fingerprints, it melts upon the daylight air. I write maps of unknown worlds, and fill them with the names of faerie cities measureless to man. I can play several instruments (none of them a dulcimer) passing well, but you can play people, and you are a virtuoso of surpassing skill. Bringing forth fine

OF THE HEART

harmonies I'd not have known dwelt therein, even upon some broken down instruments with hardly any strings left. You are an artist of this world we live in here in our bodies, whereas I am the artist of future worlds as yet undreamed of and perhaps forever a little out of reach. It is the job of my world to call to yours like a siren, one that means you well.

This is why your friendship is as necessary to me as air is to fire. Before I met you I had already read through Father's literature collection from end to end, every poet, anything about art or music. But I left all the natural sciences and geography untouched, I took no interest in the history of furniture or human costumes. Nor did contemporary clothing much interest me until I intuited how you use clothing to express yourself the way I do with music. The day I realised your entire presentation from cufflink to trouser crease was a performance—a performance of the myth of yourself, a stubborn refusal of the mundane, an assertion of form over function, of art over ordinary life—was the day I came to share your love of men's clothing.

The only time I spent on the other volumes in Father's library was in fascination that my quiet parent had once collected them. I wondered if he acquired them merely for show, to prove we were intellectually bourgeois, or whether his interest areas were really once this broad? What had shrunk them down to their current size? It had been years since I'd seen him read anything but local newspapers and ones he gets sent from home. The remaining books are artefacts in my family's largely unknown story that starts somewhere in the North of Dublin (I'm guessing this only from accent rather than abundant information) and terminates here, at the bottom of the world.

These things were never interesting to me in and of themselves before you arrived. Physical items of this world were just a thick coagulation that lay between my perception and the dreaming quality of things, like an obstacle. Until you introduced me to their inherent mystery. I came here with violent intentions towards reality. Knowing you has taught me finesse in my response to the tactile world. And your passionate love of my music has given me discipline in honing what nature gave, because each piece I teach myself I imagine playing it for you.

Though of course I know it's too early to assess the long-term effects of our friendship at an intellectual level (unformed as our life's work and contribution to the world of art and culture still is), I know in my bones our connection is formative for me. I hope for you also.

Your devoted friend

H

My letters are well represented by this one. It found its way into the Library of Luminosities. The place where all the forgotten letters and burned books go to live-die.

Crack, crack, crack, went Moses' walking stick on the gate of St David's Burial Ground. *Let me in,* he said without words, to the dead. Arthur and I removed our hats. Arthur had been slipping about at night in a flat cap with his shirtsleeves rolled up and walking with a swagger. Through sheer demeanour-shifting, he was managing to not be recognised. Martha dipped them a little curtsey, with a kind of respect I'd never seen her pay to the living. With a creek of the gate, we all entered the memory-soup.

"Used to be different, in the old days," Martha lamented. "Back when there was more of us. You could go see Billy Allison at the British, but old Nokes was the best for healing. Now most of them old folks just good for getting grave dirt from, and a few old recipes in the memory banks. We're a dying lot, us cunning folk. A dying breed."

I watched Moses almost hop between the graves, as if the dead gave him a borrowed agility. As he went, he poured rum into the cracked open and sunken earth graves where coffins were partly exposed. St David's was in a state of disrepair and overgrowth, which made it an increasingly easy place to perform nefarious acts of any kind. "Rise like lions after slumber," Moses muttered to the dead and began moving strangely as if dragging one foot as he walked the circumference of the area we were gathered in. "In unvanquishable number. Shake your chains to earth like dew, that in sleep have fallen on you!" Quite suddenly, Moses' voice rose and was run through with command; I was shaken and chastened by his considerable oratory power, which reminded me of a trained actor. "Yes, shake your chains to earth like dew, that in sleep have fallen on you. Ye are many, they are few…"

While he spoke, Martha was laying out Mary's bones on her rabbit skin and blowing into life a small fire for the dead to warm themselves beside. It was simple as far as rites went; they poured roads of water like a crossroads up to fire they'd made, and then the living people sat in the dry patches and broke cakes, silently eating and drinking with the dead. Martha spat some rum onto the fire, and the spirits thrilled to it.

"Moses?" I asked when the work was done. "Why do you use that quote from Shelley's *Masque of Anarchy* for the dead?"

OF THE HEART

Martha grunted in a way that suggested my book learning was a source of irritation to her, but Moses had a glimmer of a smile around his mouth. The older man kept his feelings and thoughts close, though I suspected he secretly liked books. Yet, it did not necessarily come through in his explicit communications. "Did you not listen to the words, boy?"

"Of course," I frowned, as I knew the words off by heart.

"Then you can see how it's appropriate for them."

"I can see how they are many and could rise in unvanquishable numbers; I'm just uncertain who the few are. The living? Why would we want the dead to rise up against the living?"

Moses poked at the small, smoky fire with his stick and got his pipe out to pack while he was considering his answer. "Not just *any* of the living. See…" He paused to light his pipe, and when he'd drawn smoke from it, he leaned across to blow it onto Mary's bones. Such offerings of rum, breath, and smoke seemed to make her whispering louder. These days, I was better at managing the layered realities. "When someone has passed through the transformation of death, they sometimes have better vision than they had as breathers. Death gives them a perspective on what really matters in life most of the living haven't got. You can see outside of time when you die, see it all at once if you want to. They know we're all going to rot down on the same soil, great and mean, man and woman, Black and white… Death, he don't discriminate; he digs the same size grave for all."

Moses chuckled to himself at the thought of it. "Yet, be that as it may, some of them have something they have to do, some unspent energy, some stored-up message, and they can't get done dying until they've passed it. Sometimes, there's no chance for them to really get back at who they needed to, so then you need to harvest their rage or their pain and direct it to someone who has done something like what was done to them. Sometimes, it's vengeance the dead want—it is, right enough, and we sorcerers let them have it. Sometimes, they point fingers and name names. William Laney would point his fingers at old Crowther if someone hadn't stole them and catalogued them."

I shuddered. Crowther's advice had led my father to hire the doctor who had held my imagination's head under water until it gasped for vital breath; this made the whole atrocity that happened to the body of William Laney seem far too close to the surface of my skin. It was part of my skin, in fact, this thing that had been done to Billy. And to all those considered the least in our city, it was done to me; it was done to Christ himself, and it made Our Lady of Mercy weep tears of blood.

"Their whole family needs an appointment with retribution," Arthur muttered. "I'd also be happy to see most of the Fletcher's family trip and fall under the same carriage." He had a whole complex set of grudges against people and families of the city by this time. My Arthur, who had been born one of the best-natured people I've met, had gradually become—through his love for justice and hatred for hypocrisy and bullying—someone who had a sizeable hit list of folk he wished to get even with. In part it, made me sad; yet I had to own it was a reasonable response to the doings of boys and men. As much as I missed aspects of his lost innocence, I loved him for the purity of his hot black heart.

"Those among the crossroads dead, those who still see clear…they could help you undo these corrupt men of influence," Moses murmured, toking on his pipe and throwing the statement out there almost noncommittally, as if it were not so much a suggestion but a mere teaching. "But as you boys have seen, they need some things from the living. They need one who died before they died to organise them. They need someone to become St Peter with the keys, opening and closing the way for them—otherwise, they all get themselves in a tangled mess of intentions."

"I think I need to learn how to wear the faces of the dead, the same way I can with animals," Arthur said. "How do you think I should start, Moses? If I could take over the appearance of a dead man, of a living one at their rest, the way I can with a bandicoot…"

"Need yourself a spirit-bridle," Martha said. "It's called 'hag-riding,' and it's hard work. You won't be able to bridle the same man again for a while afterwards because of the struggle they put up. But if you find one who *likes* to wear the bit…" She winked at Arthur conspiratorially, as if she expected that he understood well enough what she meant.

"Well, the living are harder than the dead," Moses added. "I'd start with someone who is willing, preferably among those who are best known to you."

Arthur immediately looked at me and grinned.

"You're going to ask for permission to take over my body, aren't you?"

He nodded and laughed. "May I have the honour of this skin-walk, Master Henry?" He offered me his hand as one might extend their glove to a lady in a ballroom.

"Of course," I replied softly, taking his hand.

"Aww, God bless his soul," Martha was saying to Moses in the background. "So trusting… Ahh…to remember what it's like to have trust in a man without borders like that…"

OF THE HEART

"I get into someone's head best via the ear," Arthur explained, almost sheepishly. Sitting before him with my legs crossed, I leaned my head forward until my ear gently touched his.

Martha immediately got to her feet. "Not like that. Jesus' hairy, pink nut sack, you gentlefolk are inhibited!" As she spoke, she pulled Arthur's knees apart with her hands and shoved me down so my bottom touched the ground, and I was forced to sit closer and lift my legs over his. I was naturally flexible of limb, so the posture wasn't physically uncomfortable. "Now, move closer to him, Henry, and relax your bloody legs! Look, like this, just let them go limp." Despite the involuntary protest from the anxiety my body carried that sent flares of tension through my muscles, she managed to get me sitting with my legs loosely cradling his hips.

"Well, we are drilled and punished and taught to be inhibited," Arthur murmured, a defence put forward on behalf of the uptightness in every gentleman everywhere. "It's another of our middle-class virtues, apparently."

"You need to serve some time, my friends. That would loosen you up about other people's bodies."

"I don't think that would be my style. I think I'm the sort of man who, if going to commit a crime, chooses a capital offence."

"Is that so?" Martha bantered with him. "What will you go down for, barrister-boy? Love or murder?"

Arthur shrugged with a certain species of recklessness possessing the air that moved around to accommodate the simple gesture. "How about love *and* murder? Better hanged for a pound than a penny, as they say?"

"Always been my attitude too. Now, Henry, just..." She looked my body over critically. "Just try and relax, would you?"

Arthur put his arms around me. "You can lean on me." He drew me in close. "Just try, and let me support your weight."

It was harder with the others watching. Arthur didn't seem to mind a smattering of gazes upon us. Sometimes, I wondered if his soul intelligence had turned being observed during transgressions into some kind of thrill. As soon as I'd done what he asked, my senses came alive. A tugging ache of rippling light travelled through me. As I let him press his ear shut tight against mine, images of the sea tumbled into my skull. I almost pulled away. Sounds like the rushing of the ocean inside a shell raged into me. There was a sticky entanglement entering my ear and invading my synapses. It was gelatinous, squid-like, full of suckering, seductive tentacles that eventually enveloped sections of my brain.

There was nothing but the rushing of the microscopic sea that lived inside the spiral of a cosmic shell.

When he began to retract, like a wave pulling back, leaving your feet abandoned in the trails of sand and disorientation, I felt him leave a bioluminescent blue light behind as he withdrew. He left me with a spangle of electric sparks that were caught up in the tingling, alive fabric of his being—and seemed to become part of mine also. An involuntary isolation that had seemed to divide me from others all my life had been breached. I buried my face in his collar to hide my exposure. He held me for some time. Moses—and even Martha—had a rare burst of good manners and delicacy, busying themselves with packing things up. They pretended not to be paying attention when Arthur took his coat off and wrapped it around my hunched shoulders. I shivered at how deliciously warm the fabric of his coat felt inside. "Are you all right?"

I nodded but wasn't sure whether it was true or not.

"I hope it wasn't grotesque?"

I cleared my voice. "Not at all," I whispered, shaking my head.

"Good. Wearing your skin is like drinking music."

My dearest Henry,

Your letter moved me inexpressibly. To weeping, in fact. And though I wanted to reply immediately and tell you so, I couldn't quite find myself in words for a few days. Sometimes, Henry, it seems like words are moving towards me slowly, from below, passing through that ghost treacle you used to say rises up from the river at night.

My sensibility isn't moved so strongly by your compliments because I am unused to praise. I am praised inordinately by my mother, to the extent it holds no satisfaction, for it is too easy obtained. And almost never by my father, even at the times when I may flatter myself thinking I'm deserving of it. "I am myself indifferent honest, but yet I could accuse me of such things that it were better my mother had not borne me," as Hamlet would say. Like every man, if all accounts were laid bare. I am no more the miscreant my father believes, than I am the paragon my mother sees. I've put their faces on long enough to know they act out these parts merely within the stage of their own minds. They do not actually see me. Only reflections of themselves, distorted, sometimes reversed or inflated.

OF THE HEART

No one had ever really, truly, looked at me before my very first conversation with you. At age ten, you looked at me truly from the first breath. It's only now I see how you doing so was a sweet blessing and a curse all at once. Forever after, I will know what it feels like to be looked upon by the eyes of someone opening themselves to knowing and loving all of you. It's a feeling I don't know how to conjure words for. The words evade my hands in the dark waters as I trout-tickle for them. I'm a patient ghost-fisherman, but all I've managed is these words about how I don't have words for the way you've spoilt me. Being seen as so very good by you, so worthy, and not for worthless things in this case but for the very things I myself most value, makes it become true. Your eyes have made me a better man.

Ever yours,

AA

The trees that grow here in Van Diemen's Land are largely full of highly flammable oil. Eucalyptus is a fire-lover, a courter of the lightning bolt. I understand these trees. The similarity between them and myself is too uncomfortable sometimes. Being in the bush isn't always calming to me, unless I find myself higher up in Sassafras forests. The cooling difference of the deciduous European trees that grew at Fernleigh were also a relief to me, as I leaned my forehead against an elm whilst I waited for Arthur. It wasn't that I was stalking around his parents' property or spying on him. He and I had arranged to meet halfway, and he was a little late, so I had kept on walking. Though I didn't dare to go up to the door and knock, I did creep up through their grounds along the route I knew Arthur favoured. Finding a vantage point where I could see but not risk detection, I leaned against a tree and waited. When I saw him at last, he wasn't wearing a top hat or gloves. He was jogging across the grass between us with his tie on loose, and even the top button of his shirt was undone.

"Quick!" he said, nearly running into me with his enthusiasm. "There's no one in the house for once. Come and see my home. I shall like it better once you've been inside it."

I let him take me by the hand and run me up to the back door of Fernleigh. There was a brief tussle on the step where I insisted on wiping my feet, while he wanted to drag me straight over the threshold. Of course, I imagined some poor servant cleaning up after me, and the idea of leaving a mess in their home mortified me on behalf of this unknown person, rather than because it belonged to rich people. After all, we were taking the back entrance, the path used by tradesmen and servants.

"I want to show you something in particular."

We moved over expensive Persian carpets, passed some landscape paintings in gilt frames. When I glanced through a door, I saw a golden upholstered chaise lounge. As they were an everyday thing for him, Arthur didn't give me long to appreciate my surroundings before dragging me into a room and closing the door behind us. He pulled open a drawer in a Huon Pine cabinet and inside revealed a collection of tiny and medium-sized shells. I smiled to myself with a rush of the warmest affection. Of all the expensive art and artefacts his family owned, it was something of no material value that Arthur wished to show me.

He held up one of the larger cowries to my ear so I could hear the ocean come roaring into me, as it had from his own ear in the burial ground. "Grandma Mary likes to say that seashells are little houses for dreams. We have some from beaches all over the world in here. You can hear the ocean and its dreams from nearly all the corners of the globe," he told me, still holding it there. "Though, of course, the ocean doesn't have any corners. When I was a boy, my nanny read me *The Sea Maid,* and I started to imagine the shells in my mother's collection were things she'd taken away from people, like the sea witch takes the mermaid's voice away from her payment in the story."

As he replaced the cowrie shell into the cabinet, I cocked my head on one side with curiosity. With my fingers, I explored the shells from far off beaches, and with my eyes I explored the side of his face. Being a musician had taught me to be skilled at paying attention to more than one thing at a time. "I thought you got on well with your mother?"

He smiled wryly without looking at me. It didn't give too much away, but I felt I spotted something faintly ironic in his expression. "Mother loves me a great deal. It does perhaps sound ungrateful to say anything else. She has, after all, been so often the one to stay my father's hand from striking me."

This was the first time Arthur had made unprompted reference to his father's physical abuse or to complicated relations with his mother. Before I could stop myself, I had taken his hand in mine comfortingly. "You're allowed to feel whatever you feel."

He looked down at my hand in his, seeming to regard it thoughtfully. After a few moments, he stroked my fingers lightly with his. As though on automatic reflex, my flexible and sensitive musicians fingers opened wider to accommodate his between them.

Arthur sighed. "If only that were true…"

Sensing that the conversation was taking a melancholy turn and wishing to be of comfort, I retained his hand in mine and with the other took out a different shell to listen to. "In this one, I can hear the voice of a maid servant your mother took it from because she was pretty and used to sing, and your mother was afraid your father's eye would rove towards her. This one, on the other hand…" I began, selecting another and moving closer to him to allow the delight and wonder of the story to spill from the shell, through my body into his. "It holds the dreams of an old whaler who chased the vision of the Fata Morgana mirage off the coast of Brittany. Can you hear it?"

Instead of answering, he brought my hand up to his mouth and kissed it in a chastely tender sort of way. "I hope that you remain always this innocent. When we are thirty-something and older, I dream that you will still tell me stories and make ordinary things become extraordinary—that we will still be playing Our Game. These days, holding onto it seems to me less and less a game and more like a battle. Tell me it will be so, that we can remain here?"

I wanted to say something to reassure him, but I was left unable to speak. It was as if the sea-witch had stolen my voice. When I didn't reply, he continued. "My grandfather always says that a man shows his highest regard for his love in how long he is willing to court before obtaining her in marriage. In my experience with girls—"

"Which I don't wish to hear about," I said, a little more abruptly than I meant to, trying to take my hand away. This response of mine took me by surprise; there hadn't been time to find an avenue for its repression before it was spoken.

He resisted my reaction gently. "Please," he murmured, looking down at my hand with such sincerity that I couldn't bring myself to pull away again. "Let me finish. I have found what Grandfather says to be true, in that I've not felt sufficient levels of romantic regard to wait for very long. I experience best the high ideals he spoke of in our friendship. He told me when I met the woman I should marry, I should only do so if I wanted to change absolutely nothing about her. If instead of hoping that things improve with the passage of time, you hope it touches her not at all. I feel—" He broke off abruptly at a sudden noise. I was immediately on my feet.

"I think someone's coming!"

RAG & BONE MAN

He was on his feet also, carefully replacing the shells in order and closing the drawers. "Quick. They're coming up the servant's entry; let's slip out the front."

It was after that I began to write poetry. Perhaps it was the magic of an unfinished conversation; something that tumbled out of the shell into my ear; that sense of something as yet undone that sparked my word-flood? Something in the messy tidal grit and mucous-full bleeding red interiors Arthur had poured in when he entered my ear, both from in the graveyard and via the dreams that ratcheted me raw... He had opened me to a new nocturnal, mammalian, lunar aspect of my being. Opened my chest wider, so that the words could pass through me like I was an echo chamber—or a hole in a megalithic rock. Sometimes, I felt like nothing at all but a hollow, whistling bone. Other days, I knew such a stinging longing that only a mild self-harm that drowned it out could satiate the black maw between my ribs.

My poems were full of forces of nature entering and transforming each other; my writing never spoke of human acts, hands, faces, arms, legs... They spoke of shattered light and the bleak thrill of the tree whose sap is harrowed to resin by the sharp lash of the lightning strike. My poems were written inside a zone in which I seemed isolate—and yet I was not isolated. I longed for him to again pierce the shell that had grown around me, to blur and wear all our edges away again. The poetry was to set the tone of our Shelley Summer, as we were wont to refer to it.

It was over this time that we took out a safe-deposit box where we could leave each other messages and gifts. It was rare for either of us to check it without finding that the other had left poetry, baked goods, sweets, notes, books, or pressed locks of each other's hair. Such things followed the sentimental fashions around friendships of our era; what was unusual was our mutual dedication to the practice of surprising and delighting each other. We both overflowed now that we'd found someone who appreciated us. With Arthur's bigger budget behind him, this meant a lot of new books he'd heard me mention I wanted, clothing that always fit me perfectly because he liked to recheck my tailoring measurements regularly in case I'd grown. He liked to know the exact measurements of things, he said.

Among cunning folk, Martha taught me that the practice of taking the measure gave you a magical link to that person. Knowing this, I let Arthur measure me often; he also had my hair, which, from a magical level, was like owning me. As Martha had noted, my trust in him was without borders, as was his in me. To preserve that trust, as it was the most sacred thing in my life, I committed his beautiful letters to the flames when I'd read them, even though it broke my heart to do so, not wishing to chance any threat to his social standing.

8

When I use ghost hands to open my old music box, Pandora starts to play, and all of the furniture in my room comes back to life and reassembles again. It was as if the Victorian Age were merely a pressed flower that survived between the pages of things because of Time's accumulating weight, packing in its virtue so things never decayed. Each time, I let my legs or my mind's eye carry me back there to my old house; no matter how many layers of dust with the smell of an antique store have piled up upon our memory, there are always spectral daffodils in a vase on my piano. There are some kinds of flowers, after all—those associated with miracles—that never fade.

It was probably just before I started burning father's shirts with the iron on purpose, that it happened. The timeframe doesn't quite stack up with total accuracy, so you might need to indulge a historian of feelings for dating things via the genesis of particular emotions. As Oscar Wilde put it (his fame and infamy were yet some years away at this time), "One can live for years sometimes without living at all, and then all of life comes crowding into a single hour." How true this was of my story, and perhaps for all our stories, whose dreams far outlast the colour of our faded days. How many of your days are a simple, relatively tight routine? Where nothing actually deviates terribly? The kind of days where you woke up, ate some porridge and a piece of toast with tea, pressed your shirt, went to work, performed the same routine as the day before? Came home, ate dinner, dressed in your nightclothes after a nip of Scotch, smoked a pipe, and went to bed?

I was sitting at my piano playing, which was what I usually did after practicing. Playing was the part of the session where I leant towards the songs I knew well and could play with wholeness and emotional fullness. It occurred one frosty early spring morning, as I went through the motions that I usually did at that hour. The three parse curtains were open to let the light in, but the lace ones were closed, just as my eyes were. Decently dressed in a waistcoat and tie—just in case anyone called on us while I played—with the buttons at my neck undone, I had my tie loosened because of the physical exertion of this work.

My shirtsleeves were turned up to the elbow, and I'd broken a light sweat. I'd never have left the house in this state. My hair was loose about my face. When I put my head forward while playing, my mousey-brown hair was long enough to hang to my jawline.

It was a rebellious gesture, to be sure, my hair—a little nod to the Romantic Age. When I was outdoors, it was normally hidden under my hat or tightly controlled with a hair product. But when I played, I loved not having any constrictions about my person. Heat would start coursing through me, so soon I'd have a sheen of perspiration. The reverie that held me during playing was sensuous. The hypnotically repetitive piano refrain came from the deep wells of me. It lapped at the shores of my awareness, and then it moved out of focus like a wall of aural space receding from me. When the tide of that sound pulled away, I would feel grit, like all the sand and tiny shells of me were being sucked towards the infinity horizon. Waiting for the tide to come back in, I'd play a refrain until the new notes started to come—it was only then I realised I was beginning to create a flourish—and then the rush would overtake me. If I pulled that rising thrill up the back of my spine and in through the back of my head, I could keep that power circulating through my body.

There, for a moment, the wall of sound would make its watery retreat with light dancing over the ripples. He carried me still through these parts, my hooded light-bringer, but I couldn't feel him again until the music would well back to a gush point. The sensuality of it—that I now identify as an erotic haunting of music—possessed me. So used to being left alone in my oddness was I, like a kind of sacrificial victim, that I didn't hear Arthur let himself in. By the time I noticed him watching me, I startled with the uncomfortable feeling that he'd been there for some time. The recognition of this fact caused panic, one that had a little something to do with the part of me my parents named "changeling," whom they say in Ireland should never be watched without their knowledge, and a little something also to do with human shyness.

"I'm sorry!" he said immediately, discomforted and flustered when he saw he'd been rude. "I didn't mean to…" He held out to me an abrupt gash of yellow, as though in compensation for his lapse in manners. "I brought you flowers."

I got to my feet and took the flowers from him uncertainly. It was clear to me, after a few seconds to get my breath, that these were daffodils, not simply a shriek of succulent, wild joy wrapped in brown paper. Normally, tears did not flow so readily for me, but my breast was already heaving from emotion and effort at the keys, and there he was all of a sudden, bringing me my favourite flowers. I couldn't remember whether I'd ever told him how I felt about the daffodil? In the language of flowers, a gift of daffodils means hope, because hope is stronger than the harshest winter and can crack on through frost. Had I told him, or had he somehow guessed? I still don't remember, and after all these years and tears we've been through, I really don't know if it matters.

"Thank you!" I covered my mouth with my other hand and stood there with them.

Father walked in. I turned my head quickly away so he wouldn't see the tears in my eyes. "I'll just put these in a vase," I muttered. As I exited the room and closed the door to the sitting room behind me, my hands trembled. I hoped neither of them would notice there was a perfectly serviceable vase on the piano already.

I heard Father say something to Arthur, and I paused to overhear them. Arthur said something quietly in response, which I didn't catch.

"If that is indeed so, why would you encourage him?" I heard Father snap at Arthur.

"Because it made him smile! Don't you think it's important he smiles sometimes?"

I frowned and pressed my ear against the wall to hear Father's response. "Of course I want him to be happy, but I also want him to be *safe*. If you love him, as I believe you do, then you mustn't endanger him in this manner again."

"I do love him indeed, sir! And I would never do anything to put him in danger! It's *innocent*."

"It better be!"

"It's innocent," Arthur repeated again firmly. "*Henry's* innocent. You must know that…"

"It won't stop the gossips. Every woman on this street will know very well what daffodils signify, and don't think because I'm a widower that I don't know they're a hope signal. You know I think you're a good lad. I've always liked you. But please, if you truly hold my son in high regard, do not bring flowers to this place again!"

I scuttled quickly away from the wall when I heard Father about to exit and raced into the kitchen to find a vase. Why was everyone so afraid of flowers? What was so bad about hope? The thought stayed with me for the rest of the day. It stayed with me after I walked Arthur home in the evening. After I said goodbye to him with a poignant smile and press of the hand and stood alone in the dark for a little while.

That night, I took my opium for the first time since I'd been seeing Arthur regularly again. I dreamed the house was overtaken by brash-coloured blooms of red and yellow. There were other colours, too, mixed colours, clashing colours, blooms and perfumes that had no respect for notions of good taste and symmetry. A riot of blooms, which in their growing slowly picked the masonry apart and exposed the roof of my room to the raucous stars.

I was hanging out a billowing white sheet on the clothesline when I heard his approach. Usually, I only washed our smalls at home, as laundry could be cheaply outsourced. We did our own intimate wear mainly because my family had always been too superstitious to entrust objects with our sweat or other body fluids on them to the women of the convict class. Sometimes, my bed linen fell into this category now, too, so it was a bit embarrassing to me that it was Arthur coming down the path, whom I'd been dreaming about when I despoiled the sheets.

They were hung near the old elder tree in our garden—the one that had the faces in it—and while I worked, I would talk to my mother. When I was a child, I believed my mother's soul had gone in there, which was why you couldn't cut the elder or burn her wood. The Elder Mother was much like the graveyard mother of the Fair Folk's kingdom. Her root system, like the whalebone structure underneath the berry-stained gown of the faerie queen, was holding the dead to her blossomy bosom. No, you couldn't cut the elder without cutting through the flesh and blood of the dead who'd gone up inside her, and if you burned her wood, the souls within would shriek in torment.

"You are going to have to stop sneaking up on me like this," I remarked, without turning around.

It would have been hard to say how I knew who had come down the garden path behind me. Perhaps it was nothing supernatural at all; just that no one else ever did it but him? Real magic is like that, liminal and strange, hazy around the edges so that you just don't know where it ends and other faculties begin. Until it isn't. At other times, there is a magic that sears right through you, so that your daily life seems more of the illusion ever after than the things you saw and felt. The question of whether it's divergence or madness becomes moot.

"And why is that?" Arthur asked. There was a playful challenge in his voice sometimes of late. Where I would feel his power expanding outwards from his chest, so that his presence would begin to fill the space we were both standing in, meeting mine, and pressing in on it.

Of the Heart

"Faeries don't like it," I answered, turning to face him, the white sheet trying to embrace me in the wind like it was a wayward shroud. Just below where we stood, you could hear the rivulet in full gush. For a moment, the sheet felt wetter against my flesh than it really was, soaked and pulling me. "It is our place to creep up and watch, not to *be* watched."

"Is that so?" He cocked his eyebrows faintly and crossed his arms. There was a crooked smile at the corner of his mouth for a moment. It seemed like the ghost of someone else's smile. "Well, consider this your invitation to creep up on me sometime. I dusted myself with fern seed and everything, but the invisibility magic clearly hasn't taken. Anyway… Let me make it up to you by helping with the laundry."

I smiled ruefully at him. Sometimes, he was so thoroughly good that I suspected him of insincere people-pleasing. It felt like he was saying just what I wanted him to. The world had taught me already to be suspicious of excess kindness, and no one I ever met was as kind to me as Arthur. "I'm embarrassed enough that you found me doing it, let alone letting you help me with it," I protested.

"Nonsense," he said, bending over and taking out a wet pillowcase. "There is no shame in being able to do for yourself. I am the one who should be embarrassed, that I barely have to do so."

When I reached out to prevent him taking up one of my sheets, my loose shirtsleeve was pulled back, and he caught sight of the bandage I was hiding underneath. With guilty speed, I retracted my arm. Before I could get far, he'd caught my wrist in his hand.

"What happened?" he demanded. The moment I hesitated, he tightened his grip. "Henry? Answer me!" I don't think I'd ever felt him be so fierce with me. For a moment, I could barely breathe. When I still didn't answer, he took my arm and began to undo the bandage to see what was underneath.

"It's nothing," I muttered. "It was an accident."

"Rubbish!" I jumped at him raising his voice to me. He had my arm, and there was no point trying to wriggle free. I felt like a hare stuck in a trap, as the teeth of exposure closed around me. "These are self-inflicted!"

Although I started to shake my head furiously, I never quite managed to verbally deny it. It hadn't been as if I'd tried to kill myself. It is little easier now to put words to why I'd started cutting myself than it had been at the time. Arthur seemed so frustrated by my inarticulate response to his questions—which was mainly to start shaking my head—that he didn't seem able to be properly verbal either. "No!" he said finally, shaking his head very adamantly, tears burning rather than melting in his eyes. "No!" He shook my arm up and down. "No, Henry! Do you understand?" he demanded with great intensity, as if he had in fact said something far more profound than a simple negation. It began to rain softly on us. I couldn't even feel its chill. My skin had no sensation whatsoever. It hadn't had a lot when I'd cut it either. I was slightly outside my own body, screaming in.

"I'm sorry!" I gasped, crying freely now. There was no containing it. These were violent, messy tears. The sort one cries during the onset of heartbreaks and tragedies.

"No!" Arthur repeated, grabbing me hard around the shoulders and giving me a shake. Even in his extremity of emotion, the way he handled me was harder than a gentleman would handle a lady, yet never as hard as he might do to another man. Always, Arthur treated me as something else. As if I were something outside the common order of things. When he looked at me, it no longer mattered whether the changeling story about me was truth or fable, because I became a magical creature in the path of his gaze.

"Don't *ever* apologise…" It seemed that shaking me had to be interspersed with hugging me very hard before shaking me again. Suddenly, in his almost mute frustration, he seized on a way to communicate to me what he felt. Reaching into his pocket, he came out with his penknife.

Immediately, I found my voice. "What are you doing?" With all my strength, being somewhat greater than the average woman but still apparently less than Arthur's, I tried to pull his hand away. He successfully resisted me. "Arthur, stop it!"

"This is how it's going to be from now on!" he declared, as he forced the blade down onto his own wrist in the place where I'd done it to myself. I cried out in pain as he cut himself. "No!" I wept, utterly disconsolate. "Please! Stop!"

Despite my protests, he cut himself three times the same way I had, and blood welled out. "Anything you do to you, I will do to me! Do you understand?"

I nodded through hysterical sobs. Something shifted in Arthur so that he took in for the first time—the state I had worked myself into—and he moved to comfort me. He pulled me into a hard embrace, during which he bled on the back of my shirt. It was raining harder now, as if the sensation of wetness and clinging material I'd felt earlier were manifesting in the air, as if my emotions were sweating out the rain. All I could think about was taking the bandage that had been wrapped around me and using it to staunch his wound, yet he held me too tight to say or do anything. It felt for a moment like his chest would swallow me into a great oceanic glut of salty feeling and shifting emotional atmospheres.

OF THE HEART

Perhaps in an even more profoundly human way, he was light, and I was a still sun-catcher crystal. When the light hits the prism of the crystal, it shatters. In its destruction, the light becomes numerous colours, different faces of the same light. To the world, this phenomenon is known as refraction and colour, and it's perceived as beautiful; yet to the light, it is destruction. "Don't leave," he whispered urgently, like it was a secret he couldn't keep inside. "I *can't breathe* without you." So, I took a deep breath and calmed myself for him with steely resolve. I reminded myself it was me who had come when he'd opened his eyes in St David's the same, just the way my hooded angel-devil came for me. There was a responsibility in that fact. I had a responsibility to hold together for him.

"Nor I you," I whispered.

"You won't have to!" he declared savagely, forcing me back from him so he could see my face. His eyes were burning with passion, and blood was seeping through his shirtsleeve. "I'm not content for you to just survive and endure like this! I'm going to make a better world for you. I'm going to make you a world where this"—he took my hand and lifted my injury up higher—"doesn't need to happen anymore. I'm going to change people's minds, change the law even if I have to…"

I wanted to believe he could change the world just because he willed it. Still, the hardness of my faceted edges was on an inexorable collision course with his light. There was some part of me that had known with a growing horror, from the beginning, that my love was going to leave permanent scars on him.

"I've thought it through with some depth," Clara announced while we strolled in her mother's flower garden. I would help her with the upkeep while we talked, and I never minded that she went into long periods of silence. "And I believe we need to start courting, Henry. Before you object to the idea, please consider the ramifications for all of us. Once we have been formally stepping out together for a while, you will only need to ask Father for my hand, and he will accept you immediately. Then when we are married, I shall be able to travel anywhere I want—to anyone's home in your presence, and Arthur's, without a chaperone."

I frowned. "This is perhaps not the most romantic of propositions I've heard, but certainly flawless in its logic."

"Surely you jest, Master Henry?" I could always tell when she wished me to know she was displeased in some way by reverting to name and title in the manner of those who are unfamiliar. "I know far better than that whom your heart belongs to, and it's with full understanding of this fact that I make the suggestion. All I ask from you in the arrangement is my freedom, and the standing of a married woman. Of course, we would have to make our way in the world somehow. We would be able to do that together if we were married. For while Arthur's dreams about taking over Hobart one séance at a time are all very well, how may a girl engage his plans without a husband? It is one thing for him to risk his respectability as he so often does! The world will judge me more harshly."

Arthur often said the world could go to hell, yet he was the first one to say how important it was for him to hold onto some social power. So, I considered her words. I thought about what it would be like to be her, as closely as my limited knowledge of women and their bodies would allow. I came to the conclusion that, if a loveless marriage felt to a woman like not being touched felt to me—if it would be anything at all like the sharp longing I lived with daily that had caused me to cut into my flesh—then I would not do it to her. I *could not* do it to her. If manhood had any meaning for me at all, it was in this willingness to bite down on what is hardest to hold back for the best interests of others.

Her arm was through mine, and I used it to bring her to a halt in her step and turned her around to face me. "Clary," I whispered, slipping my fingers through hers in the way that Arthur would sometimes do to me. I shut my eyes hard for a moment or two. "You have shown me nothing but kindness, and I cannot... I *will not* repay it by stealing your life from you like that..."

"Henry—"

"No, you must hear me!" To my surprise, I'd taken her between my hands on either side of her shoulders, not roughly at all but a little firmly. "You deserve more."

"That's all very well, but do you think I'll get it down here at the bottom of the world in this smug little nest of corruption?" she asked, gesturing in the direction of the town.

"You deserve your own proper love story!" My throat thickened as I admonished her about what she deserved. The part of me that wanted the same thing couldn't bear to see her lose the chance to do what I couldn't do. "You deserve to fall in love and find the man you want to spend the rest of your life with and marry him... You deserve..."

"You're not listening!" It was the first time I'd ever heard a well-brought up girl raise her voice in this manner, so I fell immediately silent. "I'm telling you

OF THE HEART

that what I will *get* in reality isn't what you are fantasising about, Henry! There's pretty much only one man in Hobart capable of giving anyone what you're fantasising about, and his heart is already spoken for!" I had never seen her express so much passion before, and it made it feel easier to breathe around her, knowing she too had a pulse as strong as mine. "Some lucky people just meet that one person who sets their world on fire, and it's mutual and all-consuming, and it's incredibly rare. Most others of us have a lot of different crushes, but nothing like that—and one day our father suggests someone, and we allow ourselves to be passed as property from father to husband... Who's to say the freedom and comradeship you and I could offer each other is so much less than that?" she demanded. "Who's to say it, Henry? If we are both happier, why must it be fairytale romance? I'll happily take our wonderful friendship over those empty-headed boys out there!"

I took her in my arms and embraced her. "If you think it will help, I will start stepping out with you, yes. But marriage... Why not Arthur? He at least feels all the instincts."

"Arthur loves you!"

"But he likes—"

"I'm not a child, Henry. I know what he *likes*. But he *loves* you."

"Be that as it may, what good does that do either of us?"

"I don't know that it's all so hopeless... Once we are married, it would cast nothing improper upon either of us for your bachelor friend to lodge with us."

"Arthur must stay a bachelor his whole life on my account? How many other lives shall I ruin in the process, Clary? Perhaps if we think it through, we can contrive some way to widow your mother, and strangle all the puppies of Hobart for my cause as well?"

She burst out laughing and wiped at the tears of her previous high emotion. "Oh, Henry... I do adore you... But no one is murdering any puppies. Arthur is already a strange one. He was never going to fit the mould with or without you. I myself am a medium, and the daughter of a very independent-minded female Spiritualist and florist; I was always going to go off-road a little too."

Ah, but she had no idea how far off-road Arthur and I had already gone. How would she react when she met Martha and Moses, and I started telling her of crossroads pacts with devils?

"So, it's settled then? We're getting married."

"Courting! Yes." I confirmed.

"You'll need to ask Father, of course, but really, it's a formality; he has been hoping for it since we became friends."

"Really? But I'm...strange..."

Clara shrugged. "A strange gentleman is better than a normalish working man, I suppose."

"Perhaps we should attempt a kiss under the circumstances?"

She grinned. "Now who's Mr. Romantic?"

"I thought that a solid enough lead-in," I murmured, as she pulled me closer. She smelt like talcum powder and babies and a hint of girl-sweat, which was tangier than boy-sweat and not unpleasant. Her lips felt soft and strange, as did the way her neck bent backwards and went almost limp in my hands. Once I adjusted to this fact, it was easy enough. I kissed her the way I wanted to be kissed by a man. I tried not to think about how it had felt when Arthur kissed me, disassociating myself from my body and my own needs as if it were my mere puppet and I its master.

As I walked home afterwards, I remember feeling empty behind my breastbone. Without warning, I started to run; it began with a jolt of sensation in my legs that made me think I might outrun my own shadow. Quickly, I realised he'd somehow gotten ahead of me as I ran, for the Rag and Bone Man was coming up the path towards me. The vision of him hit me at the same time as the waft of the smell from the tanneries, associating him in my mind with corruption. He grinned at me, a devilish thing close to a leer. It was only the knowing glimmer of deeply adult things in the eyes that prevented me from immediately seeing my own older self. When I'd been younger, his resemblance to myself had been less apparent, but now, stopping on the corner of Gore and Upper Macquarie Streets and staring, I saw myself, yet much altered.

The Rag and Bone Man lifted one eyebrow with a certain disdain for my slowness. "You finally caught on to who I am then? I thought you were smart?"

"I am. You know because you are me." I nodded to myself. It all made sense.

"I'm a you that still *could be*." The tattooed miscreant winked at me, tucked his hands into his pockets, and leaned back against the wall in a posture that reminded me of how the prostitutes down at the dock stood. The blatant, cocky nonmasculinity of it startled and confronted me.

It was only when the pebble pinged off the outside of my arm that I became aware I'd been openly talking to myself on the street corner.

"How about you go and check yourself into the madhouse, Crazy?" a voice yelled out.

Before I knew what happened, that lurking figure from the shadows with the shady grin pounced and jumped onto me. That is the only way I can explain having turned towards my tormentor and screamed at them "How about you go fuck yourself, you mediocrity?" at the top of my lungs. I'll always remember—in a disassociated sort of way, as if I'm not quite me—how I laughed when I saw the shock and loathing in their expressions. It was as if I grew stronger from their disgust and fear and drank their poisons for fun. For a moment, while the Rag and Bone Man was walking in step with me, I *was* the Other Me. And I laughed at the thought of enemies.

Arthur and I were sprawled on my bedroom mat in the sun. Father had set rules against me getting into bed with Arthur—or him sitting on my bed—except for with one foot on the ground. So, we'd just taken to lying beside each other and cuddling on the floor instead.

"So, did you like it?" he asked, stroking my hair behind my ear while we spoke.

"I'm not sure."

It was the most honest possible answer to how I felt about kissing Clara, but Arthur thought I was being coy. "You can be honest with me, Hen," he admonished me gently. "You know you can tell me if you hated it." After a moment, he added, "Or if you didn't…"

I shook my head. "No, I *am* being honest with you. I really don't know. I wasn't thinking about what I like or don't."

Arthur frowned in the way he did when I puzzled him in worrying ways. "What do you mean?"

"I suppose I was just trying too hard to know? I just focused on her and what I thought she might like. I don't recall feeling anything beyond wanting to please. It wasn't clear to me, though, whether I was doing it right or not."

Some emotion moved through Arthur's brown eyes, as a shaft of sunlight and dappled shadows move on water. "We should practice on each other, to get better at it."

Trying not to choke audibly in response to his words, I stopped breathing for a little while. I tried to laugh. If he'd said this so casually, he must have meant for me to find it humorous. "And you're going to simulate the experience of kissing a woman for me?" I asked sceptically, hoping my tone would cover the quaver in my voice. "*You?* You're not exactly feminine-feeling…" Shyly, I touched his stubble, which was the beginning of his first beard. But he refused to find it funny.

He made very intense eye contact with me, holding it just over the discomfort point and into the place where my eyes started to water. "Surely, you've been watching me closely enough over all these years? I'm more than a little adaptable."

"You *wear* people," I accused.

"I like to call it 'harmonising.'"

"Call it what you will, but you're still…" My joke disappeared when he lifted my hand to the side of his face. He pressed it gently, his head leaning yieldingly into my hand. His body perfectly copied the way Clara's head and neck had moved in my grasp the day before, even though he'd not seen it. Without deciding on it, I pressed my lips down over his. How do I describe the homecoming? The yellow rush of the first daffodils against the end of a grey winter? The sound of a mountain river in full gush when you are warm and can smell wood smoke? Words break apart and fray around the visceral cut of this memory. He met me timidly and receptively before eventually succumbing to a full, enthusiastic surrender.

When our lips finally parted, I whispered thickly to him: "This time *you* be the man." It wasn't a gentle request. It was a demand rising up from a thick knot of want in my stomach. Even though we were grown up now, we were still playing Our Game. This time, we weren't just trying on different faeries and monsters (or perhaps in truth we were?)—now we were trying on different genders.

"What manner of man would you like me to be for you, Henry?" The question carried so much heft, it felt like it was a hessian sack full of stones he'd offloaded into my hands, and I was almost winded by the impact.

"*You*," I said as I pulled him closer. "Secret you, holy you, behind all your names and faces—you."

Arthur appeared to find this request daunting, as if he had to think about it, the same way I'd been unable to answer his question about kissing Clara. What exactly was secret Arthur like? Very seriously, he pushed me down onto my back—as if I was not to move until he said so—and slowly came down over me. He didn't let his body fully press against mine; only his chest and stomach were used to drop the weight of his will onto me. "You're the only one who has ever seen him," he whispered. He looked deeply into my eyes while he reached under my neck and took control of my head. The kiss was fierce and hard, with unnervingly sharp attention.

When he pulled back, his breath was coming in and out as hard as mine. It was awkwardly out of proportion to our stated intention of kissing practice. Quickly, I reminded myself that this was an example of his power as a face-

OF THE HEART

changer. He was being the man with me; that's why he'd pushed his tongue into my mouth with such desire. He noticed my sudden recoil at the thought he was pretending and became awkward and embarrassed too.

"Wow…" he muttered awkwardly, sitting up and brushing himself down. "Just…wow."

I nodded. There was nothing more that could be said. Neither of us wanted to look the other in the eye, because it felt like if we did, we'd be forced to discuss how we'd just felt a perfect thing. A little, fragile slither of paradise that had come off in our hands for a minute like a melting icicle. Beautiful yet ephemeral, it would melt, but before it did, it would cut us both to the quick. For a brief moment, I utterly believed this was shared knowledge that had passed between our bodies without words. I would doubt it again once he was gone.

"What did you mean?" I asked quietly. "When you told Father our love was innocent?"

Innocent of what? was more precisely what I'd meant to ask.

"I meant I feel nothing towards you of which I am ashamed. Little does your father know it's lawyer-like of me, because I also believe there is no such thing as a love for which one should feel ashamed."

I took in the full implications of this bold statement. "But what of…say… incest?" I suggested.

Arthur shrugged defiantly. "What of it? If they each love the other, who am I to say evil of anyone? Or claim that their private morals somehow objectively affect me and mine? No, this is half of what's wrong with the world, Henry. Busybodies with opinions everywhere, convinced that too many things warrant their judgment. I have no respect for all the stones thrown in this glass city of a town. When I move out from Father's home, you will see; I will give them all something to gossip about."

9

Clara's father huffed out an enormous cloud of smoke like some large, complacent lizard, which seemed to envelope the entire room in a miasma. The worker's cottage near the Cascades was a snug affair, so the men having a room to ourselves left all the women and children hustled off into the kitchen or bedrooms. The way I had been brought up, this seemed lacking in chivalry. As it was, I—who was the guest—felt my good manners forbade me to make comment.

With a hand gesture, he encouraged me to drink up the cheap brandy he'd poured me. "I mean, correct me if I'm wrong, as you two fellows are gentlemen of learning, but to my humble consideration, it's all feminine fripperies." His voice was an unpleasant shade of orange to my ear-eye. Like his person, his voice lacked in the simple grace of pink, yet didn't have the courage to be red.

"What is that?" Arthur enquired, frowning a little as he leaned over to pick up and drink from his brandy. I watched him while he wasn't looking at me. I watched the way his hands moved and how he touched objects. The manner that he had of crossing his legs in a seemingly relaxed way without disturbing the creases in his trousers.

"The 'Spiritualism' or 'Spiritism' or whatever they call all that tapping on tables and seeing ectoplasm? Don't tell my wife I said that, or I'll not live a happy man, but I consider that it's a purge of their naturally emotional temperament, as you would well know as men of learning," he declared confidently, in the tone of a man who might have read a book once and consequently thinks a good deal of himself. "All this seeing of spirits and hearing of voices stops them suffering hysteria, so it's good for them, really. And it's mighty good of you gentlemen to indulge their natural weaknesses; God knows I'm a martyr to it myself in this house full of them."

"On the contrary, my friend. I believe in it myself," Arthur replied coolly, with flecks of clear defiance in his less-than-friendly tone. He was always faster with this sort of thing than I was, you see. My resistance—when it slowly rises to the surface—is quiet, considered, and total. It took me a few moments to process where I intended to stand in a situation, but once that place was chosen, you would have to kill me to budge me from it.

"In fact," I added. "I see spirits and hear voices myself. So perhaps I suffer hysteria too." Though I didn't mention my imp-teat leaking witch-milk, I felt the nipple graze on my shirt. It reminded me I had some kind of stowaway connection with the feminine. Also, Arthur was right. It does feel amazing when you start to say no to bullies. The satisfaction of knowing I didn't care what this man thought gave me a new strength. This pleasure was greatly added to when Arthur made eye contact with me. What I saw in his eyes was approval that bordered on admiration, yes, but it was flecked with some other warmer emotion, something with an edge of life in it far keener and stronger.

"My apologies!" Clara's father was saying. "If I'd known you were believers yourselves, I'd never have been the type to make fun of it."

Yet, he was happy enough to make fun of Clara for it—in front of the man courting her, at that. It left a bad taste in my mouth, like that of chewing on wormwood leaves. It was something I had no idea I felt passionately about until that moment. Why shouldn't her dignity be upheld the way I would have upheld my own or Arthur's? I could understand no reason to the contrary. Rationality itself seemed to be on my side. I spoke again before I could stop myself, and the Rag and Bone Man was up inside me, with his knowing smile and his tattoo-marked skin, shamelessly declaring himself Otherwise to the herd. "Do you even see how smart she is?" I barely more than muttered under my breath, the quiet sound thick with insurrection.

"Beg pardon, who?" he asked.

"Clara. Your daughter." This time, my reply was clearer. It seemed to ring out in the smoke-filled air. "She's a great deal smarter than you."

Arthur made a sound as if he was choking on his brandy as he tried to repress laughing with shock at my audacity. It wasn't really that audacious when one understood how people like this man ticked, which I had begun to.

"Of course, as you say, sir! I mean, you sirs are the educated ones in the room after all, and if you see that in our Clara, well, clearly it's there." While he made vacillating hand gestures, I merely gazed at him and offered nothing to either affirm or oppose him. In the face of my ambiguity, his confidence in his perspective came apart like tissue paper in water.

"It is," I insisted. "She's quite remarkable, especially given her humble beginnings, with hardly any of her own books."

Arthur and I made eye contact again as he watched my future father-in-law apologise to me again. The man said sorry to me even whilst I insulted him, and by the end of the brandy, he loved me twice as much as he had at the conversation's inception.

They were night-drunk, the goblin sorcerers of the trees, wearing their possum skins. During conflict, they made a sound like millwheels turning in a flooding rivulet. The whicker-hiss was sharp against the night bush, with its self-flaying eucalypts. For some time, I stood with my eyes closed, my nose filled with the riot of damp, clear scents of the land after rain. I had been making my way to the wooden shed when the unquiet thing came through the trees towards me. There was a clammy rise of the hairs on my arms. My feet were bare. The wild seemed to tingle through my skin. What had it felt like to be among the first people to arrive here from Europe? To hear this unfamiliar sound and try to place it to a beast? This was why I had to be still, close my eyes, and try to place myself there. Sometimes, this was how ghosts would begin to talk with me.

Spooked by the feeling, I considered walking swiftly for the house. By this point, I'd learned enough about being haunted to know that fearful behaviour would more likely make them follow me back to my room. Sometime around three in the morning, I'd wake to the feeling of their gaze on me. I turned instead in the direction of my discomfort; post-flying ointment initiation, I had found myself able to do this. There was more than one possum watching me. It seemed I was slipping back further, through the veil of ectoplasm that walled out the past from the eyes of the white-fellow seer. *What if they aren't possums at all? What if they are the changed form of the Black fellows, coming to sniff me because Martha put the ashes from their Devil Dance in her ointment?* Few things about the ghosts of white-fellows made me nervous, even the children. Beyond that seal of apocalypse that fell over the way of life of the humans who were here before us, there was a mind-land where in the past we'd have plastered the words: here be dragons.

The lunar flash of their eyes in the dark quivered with an unhinged energy, something yet to touch the ground. I held out my hand to it, to that feral unfinished-business fuse I felt linking the body of the animal to me. I held out my hand to the life I felt quavering behind that seal. The possum came down cautiously towards me and inquisitively sniffed my fingers. When my fingertips twitched with the buzzing piquancy of strong sensory connection, the creature jerked back and looked at me with moon eyes. I fell into them, journeying into a work of fluctuation, tides. I was all but washed away.

Martha always used to say that Old Master Puck (who was old before the world began yet young as the spring morning and only one face of St Peter at the crossroads) appears to his people seven times a day in different ways. He usually goes unnoticed by those who don't spot the extraordinary playing out in the world of the ordinary. My mother used to tell me of how, in Ireland, we have the Pookah too. In Ireland, he has a strange sense of humour. Rather than the demonic black goat form of the Welsh Poucca, our Pookah is a six-foot-tall white rabbit. My theory is that Puck reflects the pushed-down parts of people, and in Ireland, things just became that bad that our Puck dances between the terrifying and the hilarious.

Maybe this possum was Tasmania's Puck. Able to get into nearly everything, adapt to the city we'd built, to be one of the seven perfectly ordinary things that is actually perfectly extraordinary? Maybe Arthur's bunyip he saw at the Great Lake was a Puck as well? Who knew what the extraordinary was capable of? As I thought this, the small fur-sorcerer stood back on his hindlegs and regarded me. His eyes showed a foreign type of intelligence. I smiled. Or, more correctly, I laughed—the secret, quiet, ripple-of-joy laugh that comes up only from one who is all alone and witnesses a wonder.

"Arthur?" I whispered tentatively. Only because his beingness and his behaviour was marvellous to me, and marvellous things had all become clear to me through Arthur. It seemed he had struck a dart through me via which things of flesh and red blood became miracles to me. Afterwards, I looked around in a hunted way, checking that Father had not witnessed me, nor had anyone wandered down to use their outhouse and witnessed my eccentricity. If there is some true witch-mark that makes some of us hear the voices of the dead and of animals, then that mark comes loaded with ancestral fear. Those of us who came before ourselves, those who were stripped, pricked, examined... For those were us as well. All of those dead ones live on still in people like me; perhaps that's the first thing you see with your Second Sight. We are always looking over our shoulders the moment after we perceive a miracle, to check if we got caught picking the extraordinary into our pockets.

The possum continued to stand on its back legs like a small man. Slowly, I extended my hand again to the creature. Almost immediately, it extended its little prehensile hand in my direction, sharply rimmed in claws. I shuddered at the alive touch of his hand that felt like the sensorium of a thousand possums reaching out to understand the hand of *homo sapiens*. For him, it is the shape of the hand that has murdered many of his kind. He was brave enough to reach for it. Yet, also as of late, there was an old lady a few doors down who would secretly leave apple cores and other things out for him. Sometimes when I would watch her, and she didn't know I was watching, I would see her tempt the possum closer,

OF THE HEART

until he was eating out of her hand. Our hands were confusing for him. As big and without natural defences as to us his hands were small razors.

My dearest Hen,

Your latest letter about the possum brought the naked sublime rushing into my study like the wind from a storm stirring up Vitalism. I indeed try regularly to practice jumping from the mind of one animal to another, with the aim being riding it to you. It's something Moses tells me to do. There are two reasons: one is that you neither lie nor exaggerate and he trusts you to say yay or nay. The other is because…well…the work requires a warmth in the blood for its power. I feel I dreamed in Possum! As one might dream in a blue palette. Could swear to it that you touched me, or I touched you… I miss you a very great deal and the feeling was too big for rat, and maybe too graceful for brush tail possum?

What I wanted was to come to your door wearing thylacine and reveal myself to you through opening the yawning snake-like jaw of my head. In my imagination, you would look down its throat and see the whole world there, just as one might were it one the gods of the Hindus. You'd smile then because when you saw all the different faces in his gullet, you'd know it was me, and that you'd finally seen my real face.

Believe me yours evermore,
Arthur +++

Every now and again, Arthur, Clara, and myself would arrange to do a séance with just the three of us. I'm not sure whether Martha had told us to do it, or whether maybe Moses had suggested it to Arthur? We started to develop our own repetitive practices that made sense to us all, and we achieved that situation from practice.

"Before we begin, it has become traditional that we should all share one of our secrets," Clara said. The candle on the spirit table flickered slightly, which was of interest to us all because no draft had been felt.

There was an uptake in Arthur around secret-sharing time. The flash of his eyes and the jump in his Adam's apple evoked for me a flash of an image of newly shed blood, dashed across damp autumn leaves. I could smell the blood and the leaf-rot in the air.

"Ladies first." Arthur gestured with his hand as if he meant for her to walk through a door in front of him. He seemed to conjure for me a brief flash of the image of a door. It was my front door, the one he'd walked through first the night I'd met him. Part of this happening was my Sight opening up for the evening. The other part was the habit the two of us had made of him as conjurer, and me as seer.

Clara poked out her tongue at him, and he grinned with something Puckish in it. These evenings would bring his good-devil close to his pelt surface and into his glittering eyes.

"Sometimes," she began, her tone of rebellious daring, "I grind up disgusting things and put them in my father's food, and then I watch him eat them."

Arthur almost choked with surprise and then burst out laughing with amusement tinged with pleasure. "How have you waited this long to confide that in us, Clary? *This* secret is made of sheer gold and pearls."

I on the other hand wanted the particulars of the crime. "What sort of disgusting things?" I needed to know.

She shrugged. "Dead flies, beetles, little bits of dead rats, that kind of thing."

I smiled. It was that slow sort of smile you do when truly delighted, in a low-key way, to find something familiar in a person when you weren't expecting it. "All right," I agreed. "I will pay that."

"What's your secret, Henry?" Arthur turned to look at me abruptly.

"What's yours?" I surprised myself by countering him almost as abruptly. For a moment, the dimly lit, close environs of Clara's sitting room felt claustrophobic, as if something were about to get knocked over or spilt. All of the little ornamental china dogs had become full of jittery ghosts that had accumulated there over many such evenings. I wondered if they had meant it to work out like that? The ornamental china dogs? Perhaps, I wondered—to disassociate from the way reality seemed to waiver at the idea of being asked for my secrets—we all have our own agendas. For this reason, I knew this unease was good, because this feeling was the door to the unknown beginning to creak on its hinges for me.

Arthur didn't hesitate nor break eye contact with me. "I have a great number of secrets," he said quietly and firmly refusing to blink. "I'm nearly all made up of secrets. The one that comes to mind at the moment is my attraction to strange things like freaks, people with something odd about them. My father points out all these pretty girls, and I like them well enough, but what I'm more interested in are people with lazy eyes. I like the weird smell of age that clings around people's ancient keepsakes, especially anything that has beadwork done on it that captures the smell of the eighteenth century. I like…I like things that are different. Like dwarfs and ladies with only one leg."

Clara laughed as if Arthur was hilarious.

"What?" Arthur said. "How is liking too many things worse than putting bits of rats in your father's breakfast?"

"I didn't say it was worse… Just… *Interesting,* that's the word for it. You're a character. Mother says a woman of substance should seek out the companionship of men of character, presumably whether they are dwarf-fanciers or not."

I laughed and Arthur laughed, too, pointing at me accusingly. "Don't you laugh; you haven't told us yours yet!"

For a second, I experienced a constriction of the throat. There I was again. I was back in whoever among the swaths of blackened dead that went into building up my red blood; the ones who had been hunted. What was their fear? That I would do the elf-get thing, and I would behave as True Henry, the one who could not lie… "Sometimes I see myself," I whispered, as though this secret came up unbidden and almost unrecognised by me, the way possums must have been unrecognisable to the first newcomers. "From the outside, I mean…" Even speaking of him aloud seemed to give the Rag and Bone Man more power. Just sitting there in the room, about to perform our séance in the low lighting, I could see him again coming towards me out of the rain or fog. The wall seemed to disappear into this vision. The hollow bones he'd collected were clanking in his sack dully with his steps. "But it's not me exactly. The Rag and Bone Man… He's like another version of me; one that's seen harder times. He talks to himself, I used to think. He talks to me now sometimes, too, the Rag and Bone Man… His words are strange; he's not like other men."

"A doppelganger," Clara gasped with alarm. "Such things are deemed ill-fated."

"Don't say that!" Arthur snapped and touched the wood of the spirit table to diffuse any ill-luck she might have conjured forth.

"It's an omen of death in Ireland," I agreed. "Seeing yourself."

"What do you think he wants?" she asked, seemingly more interested in my potential ill-fate than she was in Arthur's discomfort.

"I don't know yet, but I think I'm going to find out soon. He's had some wearing in, but he only looks to be in his twenties. So…"

"Well, why do you put dead flies in your father's food?" Arthur demanded of Clara, crossing his arms. "How did he upset you so much?"

"Don't. Please," I said, holding my hand up. "Please don't harm each other with words."

"I don't mind," she said, almost abruptly. "I can talk about this just *fine*. The thing is, I don't know why, *Arthur*. It's so strange, because he's lovely to me most of the time. You couldn't wish for a kinder father, yet sometimes when his back is turned, I am filled with such ill thoughts of him that I cannot account for their intensity. Sometimes, I worry that he speaks ill of me behind my back. Other times, I worry that doing something like that to someone without knowing why makes me a bad person."

"And sometimes you don't?" Arthur asked with a raised eyebrow.

"And sometimes I don't," she agreed softly.

Naturally, I thought—and I imagined Arthur did, too, given how her father had spoken of her when she was not present—and began nodding to myself. In this secret, above all others, I could feel the edges of Clara's gift and how it—like Arthur's and my own—had a monstrosity hiding in it. Perhaps each of us had already begun to feel this out about each other? It felt that way. I sensed it in that little bit of meanness Arthur showed Clara for tossing around the idea that something might happen to me. I sensed it in the almost brash way Clara had dealt with the darkness that arose in him and in her, as well as in myself. Maybe no one else except me saw the full significance of that moment... It is one of the greater tragedies of life that we so rarely do.

My music, the type I turned over and over until it became its own thing, was the lovechild of my ragged doppelgänger, and Arthur's eighteenth-century beaded purses. It began to well up out of a feeling of persistent sadness, leeching up as a startling eruption of feeling. I fidgeted some music into being the way some children play with spinning tops. I'm not sure if it was even my music, of course. How to say what comes from any one person? Or was some music just formed from the feelings of the dead all around me? It was rapid, this jump I seemed to take, to what Arthur said was composing. Music was erupting from my pores in sudden cool sweats, on the day when my belly emotions became parts for cello. Music happened in the background while I was having internal fights with myself about whether it would be possible during the crescendo for me to switch to playing my violin like a fiddle? Could I carry it off with the vigour of resistance to the class-divide over music? Or would I stumble with my confidence, and it become a musical joke?

Colour started to transform in response to my feelings turning into music. Sometimes, it seemed like all my senses were bumping into one another, mak-

OF THE HEART

ing raids upon the other's jurisdiction. Scents evoke colours for me, sometimes to visible appearance. Colours, but only the very special ones, sometimes also had a certain scent. Suddenly, the world of music took on a new dimension for me. Now feelings could be identified best by which instruments were active, and I began to feel them all. There was a violin in my heart and throat, a cello in my guts and hips, a piano in my arms and legs. Sometimes, I would feel my violin start to get raucous and double-play my strings, shuffle-bowing me into a hidden disorderliness. It was one that didn't even require opiates. I might say to Arthur—were I a particular type of sad—when he would ask me how I was feeling, very cello. What I wouldn't tell him was about how there was sometimes a fiddle inside me. The fiddle had become my next secret…a secret that involved the common Irish genius for wild sound.

What was happening required the presence of an audience to ground its charge. At the very least, I needed a pianist, a cellist, and a violinist so that I might bring it into being. Otherwise, would it not sound strange overlapping each other? Was I just imagining I could do this? It takes an ensemble to say certain things to certain people, or even an orchestra; otherwise, why do we even bring together these musical ravishments? To bring into the world of sound an entire musical experience that, as far as anyone can prove, has never existed before? One couldn't hold onto the ocean of such a power alone. Once some musical feeling that wants to express itself wants out through you, it will Caesarian its way out of you. When it can't spill out into aural space, it begins to build up, a kind of backlog of potential energy.

When forced below the waterline, it must emerge elsewhere to seek breath. A forgotten refrain is never forgotten quite but seeps up through the fault lines in broken hearts, often in some other part of the world entirely. You have to break first to let music through. To truly hold what the Irish called the "imbas forosnai," illuminated inspiration, you had to sink into darkness with the stone of grief upon your chest, held down like a daffodil bulb in the freeze. We all know what has to happen to the bulb when the shoots—white at first but later green—begin to seek the sky. Father didn't want to know what happened to the bulb; he didn't want to see it in my face, nor my posture, so he wouldn't let me perform my music in public whilst I lived at home.

It almost seemed like I had called in the strange attack made upon me one afternoon while I was walking up Davey Street. Perhaps it was that they were the same boys I'd told to go fuck themselves? I don't claim to understand how average folk think. Though the boys responsible were of a higher class than me, they were nothing if not mediocrities. They stepped onto the path as I was heading up towards Arthur's house to meet him.

"You should go home to your own part of town. You don't belong here, papist."

"Didn't you hear him, Irish scum?"

They were other folk like as Arthur's people, the sons of barristers, doctors, and politicians, English in origin. In my stomach, I could feel a core of grit like a witch-ball rolled out of broken shell-shale and flint chips. Gentleman's son or not, I was Irish, and like all of my people, I was the progeny of those who survived. *Millions* perished from starvation and disease; people lived on grass and gnawed on exhumed human corpses before dying in ditches at the roadside, but not my forebears. I was the product of the toughest of the tough that Ireland had to offer, who faced off against a millennium of invasion, famine, and plague. The stubborn tilt of my chin bore silent evidence to my lack of intention to drop my eyes or duck my head.

Perhaps because of my predecessors, who had scratched their way along my inside arteries, I would not hear him speak of them so. There was no way I was going to risk damaging my hands by punching him anywhere hard. I'd never been in a real fight or been taught how to defend myself, so I can only put it down to something ancestral that I naturally could throw a proper punch. I gazed down at his throat rather than his eyes for less than a second before I hit him. The precision of my aim dropped him to his knees, spluttering. "I heard you."

For a moment or two the others seemed to be in silent awe at how I'd laid out their leader. I expected to be punched back. There must have been something about me that made them hesitate. They started taking turns at shoving me. The one I'd punched shoved me in the chest. I braced against it, but I still took a half-step backwards. Immediately, I stepped back into the place, I'd been standing without any change in facial expression, but my eyes met his with fierce, unflinching resistance. It seemed my eyes dared him to do worse.

"What?" he yelled at me, shoving me again hard. "What are you staring at like that?" The boy who was standing behind me shoved me back in the opposite direction, so I didn't even need to do any work to stay level and non-reactive. It was clear already how unnerved the main bully was by my response, or absence of any. The tension of our extended eye contact was becoming unbearable to him, and I could feel him break behind his eyes. "Stop staring at me, freak!" he yelled at me, working up his rage to have the courage to really hit me. I saw the fear flash in his eyes like an open wound as he slapped me open-palmed across the face. It stung, and I blinked once and pressed my lips together firmly. I didn't move an inch. My pride was at least five times bigger than my slender frame.

"I think we should leave him alone," one of them was saying.

"There's something wrong with him, chaps. I think this is…wrong." The nail-chewing one backed down when the leader spoke.

"Well, of course there's something wrong with him! The crazy nance-boy thinks he's better than us!" I knew he was going to hit me again by the way the air smelt acrid with male fear. Although I didn't move, I let myself shut my eyes for a second. He backhanded me across the face a second time. The blow was dizzying and knocked my head to one side. I tasted blood. I'd not had as much experience in being beaten as some boys my age, and I was shocked by the intensity of his knuckles colliding with my mouth.

Slowly and with a calm from down deep inside my backbone, I turned my head back to the centre and looked him in the eye. The other boys were beginning to back off. There was something in their postures of both fear and respect, as if by not reacting to their abuse, I had shown myself unable to be cowed. Yet, they wouldn't oppose the leader, so there was discontent in their ranks. While I looked at the boy I'd traded hits with, I very slowly licked the blood off my top lip where my nose was bleeding. I smiled at him in a wooden sort of way and revealed to him my bloodied teeth. The feeling in the air was changing, and it was coming from me.

"Say something!" he screamed at me, as if my very silence and ambiguity was a horror one could fall into and flounder, going under.

"When you hear the big winds in the treetops, crashing through as the bush as the Wrageowrapper comes down from the mountain, you smell his animal scent on the breeze; that's what the aunty says. When she stalks down the rivulet with her maireener necklace in her hands, the cannibal trolls slide down the hairs on his back and scatter all over town…"

"What in God's name is he talking about?" It was clear that though my storytelling was catching them up with its sadness-mist, most of them, while confused, wanted to hear what I was saying.

"…See the thing is with the red-hatted cannibal troll, they can only live while their caps are red and wet with human blood and tears. They wait until someone is hurt, especially someone who never harmed them. They drink suffering and fear and the outrage, it makes them grow to troll size, it excites them so much." While I was talking, my eyes were far away behind their heads, looking at something they couldn't see. He shoved me again. I returned to my position.

"What are you going on about?"

"I see you," I muttered, looking back at him at last and meeting his gaze again. When I spoke, my voice was low and filled with a quiet intensity. "You *will not* get to taste my fear." I spat blood in his direction.

"Cut him!" one of them yelled. "Cut him above the breath! My grandmother says that breaks their power."

I had shamed him in some way he didn't fully understand, so he had to hurt me; he broke off a thorn from the hedge and slashed me across the forehead with it. I felt the blood run down over my nose and into my mouth. There was a cry of satisfaction from the others. He felt empowered to really hit me then. It was a closed fist this time, and I did not weather it very well. Punch-drunk, I slipped down onto my bottom. Perhaps I would have started to fight at that point, once they cut me above my breath? I don't recall if I knew before then that this was part of how witches were stripped of their ability to cast a curse? I probably would have started fighting all at once with sudden fury like when someone tries to manhandle a cat, if he hadn't arrived.

He came up fast behind the other boys, grabbing a handful of their hair in each hand and hitting their heads together. Already, the lead bully was stepping back with his hands up. "I didn't mean anything." Arthur glanced at me, caught sight of the blood all over my face—and the fact my eyes were running with tears from a glancing blow that partially caught my nose—and immediately hit the other man in the jaw. By the way his chin jerked up and his head back, I knew Arthur had knocked him out while he was still falling. Two of the young men tried to scatter. Arthur grabbed one of them before they could escape and threw him face-first into the hedge. It was only now that everything was moving so fast and the air was full of the iron of Mars that I began to shake. Only then did I feel safe enough to let the fear seep to the surface of my skin.

With the other man's arm locked up behind his back, Arthur pressed the man's face into the thorn of the haw, so it was cutting him the way he'd cut me, until he made sounds of submission. Arthur whispered to him, "You tell your friends, when they finish running away like the contemptible, revolting, miserable, cowardly pieces of human excrement that they are, if I ever see any of you so much as *look* at Henry again, I will find you, and I will hurt you in every way I can think of. I will destroy you legally, socially, and financially, and leave you broken men. I will literally take everything that is yours from you, piece by piece, so that I will live to urinate on your pauper's grave. Do we understand each other?"

"Yes!" He ran away as soon as he was released without bothering to check on his unconscious friend. Arthur was pale, and his hands were shaking. Although he said nothing to this effect, I sensed he did not particularly enjoy violence. There are men for whom petty violence holds some interest; it seemed he wasn't one of them. He reached for me to check me over. I waved away his concern, even though it was probably justified as I was having trouble getting to my feet.

"I'm fine. Is he…is he…all right?" I gestured to the unconscious man.

Arthur turned him over onto his side with his foot, which revealed that the man was breathing at least. He was starting to come conscious.

"He forfeited any right to my concern when he drew blood from you." He took out his handkerchief and wiped my face. Seeing me bloody pained him, I could see that in his eyes, and for the first time in the encounter, I felt something from inside my own body. With a tangled unraveling, I let him take me in his arms and fully released the breath I'd been half-holding in a shudder.

10

My dearest Henry,

As you are always encouraging me to write and flattering me that I'm somewhat good at it, I thought I would record for you on paper last night's events. There was a bit of blood on my hand I didn't find until later in the evening after I'd come down to dinner with buttoned up shirtsleeves! Mother pointed it out with distaste but never enquired whose blood it was. I still don't know myself whether it was yours or his. It was hard to stop thinking about what happened and I didn't even spot it. I think my parents have just given me up as a rake and nay-do-well and will offer me no further resistance.

That night I awoke with a start at 3:00 am because I thought I heard music. For a moment, I was struggling with my sheets and blankets in panic because it meant danger somehow, that sound… It was getting fainter like you were walking away from me, and I felt so very cold, like I was Lord Franklin numbly giving way to a polar death in the arctic waste. Immediately I thought of you and your fiddle that I've never yet heard you play, even though you tell me that in secret you do. But upon fully awake alertness, I found only silence in the room and the distinct feeling of being watched. I started and looked around.

Leaning against the opposite wall I spied the figure of a man with a hood partially covering his face. Very softly, he began to whistle a melodious yet somehow eerie tune to himself, as if filling in time while he waited to be noticed. My body went to spring to its feet to confront the intruder, but it was as if he placed a casual hand on my chest without seeming to close the distance between us. It was strange. He must have at some point…moved, that is. Perhaps it just happened too quickly for me to be fully aware of it? Time and space were out of joint. The geometry of common objects didn't quite add up.

Although he appeared to exert not much muscular force, I couldn't move. I tell you, I got a good enough look at him at this point. He did a number of out of the way things, yet I know he was a man, as you and I are men, and that he was not made of ectoplasm but flesh and blood as we are. He was taller than me, and his arm that he extended to touch me (which was mostly bare, with tattoos visible that one could only associate with some far-off historical barbarism) showed great muscular definition. I knew, my whole body knew, that I was not in the presence of a dweller within the walls of civilisation. It thrilled me. Something about his presence put me in mind of the wild Black men you see in paintings, but his bone structure would be most readily equated with the Nordic facial type. He raised his other finger to his lips to make the hush gesture at me. It seemed likely he was a bushranger, and we were being robbed; yet I intended to let him take whatever he wanted.

The wolf inside my belly did nothing but whine and whimper with excitement and submitted to whatever glamour was upon it. If he was a bushranger, he was also a magic-man, and I was ready to get up out of bed and follow him. If he'd asked me, I think I'd just have put my boots on and got my coat. After that, wherever we were going, all I know is I would have taken you with me. I want to say that I was ensorcelled by his gaze, but try as I might, I cannot remember it, not even the colour of his eyes. Beyond that they were striking, and this vague racial grouping, I cannot altogether gather back up from my memory the image of his face. Very slowly, he came close enough to me to whisper. I may not be able to conjure his face enough to sketch him, but I can remember how his skin smelt. That's the other way I knew he wasn't just a spirit, or if he is, then spirits are not as we have been told! He smelt of healthy male sweat, the ozone left after lightning and rain in thirsty earth, with a hint of burnt honey at the edge of the scent. My mouth watered, and I experienced the most confusing desire to bite into his arm. I feel embarrassed admitting it, as I know how violent it sounds, yet it was anything but. Or if it was then the Eucharist is violent also.

"Are you ready?" he whispered, his accent was strange, yet he didn't speak enough words for me to identify it.
"Yes!" I whispered back, though I'm not sure it's true, as I never enquired what I was agreeing to.

For a moment, he pressed his forehead down across mine, and I felt like I was branded, burned, and shocked by a bright flash of light in the eyes, all at once. When I opened my eyes, he was gone, but I knew it meant I belonged to him, or with him, in some way. I checked through the room for him and at the bottom of the window below. So full of unknown potentials had he seemed I checked under my bed and above on the bricks outside and the roof as if I imagined him to be some kind of bushranging ninja!

What is he, Henry? Is this the angel-devil you speak of?
Do you know? I feel that you do.
Does this sort of thing happen to you?

Of the Heart

For what purpose do you feel he has come to me?
What have I said I'm ready for?

Believe me yours,
Arthur +++

When I read Arthur's letter, the hairs began to slowly rise on the backs of my arms. I watched them prickle and stand up. It fascinated me how gradual it was, this response of waves of hairs coming to attention. This experience of Arthur's, it confirmed a connection with my hooded devil man who could produce talons from his hands. I wondered what had prompted this miraculous manifestation for Arthur? Was embodying ghosts part of his genius, as music was mine? I couldn't help wondering if it had something to do with Arthur having stood his ground for me against the sons of families on friendly terms with his father? Had my Puck, our Robin Goodfellow, sensed the rebellion of decency? My forehead and nose had run with blood for half an hour after the attack, but despite being blooded above the breath, I didn't feel diminished by it.

Father saw my bruises. He wanted to know the names of the young men who had hit me. When he heard their names, he looked ashamed. It was the look he had when he realised the target of his wrath was above his sphere. I nodded to myself, after he left the room. This was as I'd expected. The kind of retribution that Father would have gone looking for wasn't what I wanted or needed now anyway. For a few nights, I played over the scene in my mind again and wondered if I'd not hit first would it have all played out the same? I felt proud of myself and wished Arthur had seen it all before my moment of shame. I wished he hadn't arrived just in time to see them knock me onto the ground with blood all over me. As much as I cherished his rescue, I also wanted him to know I could viciously punch another man in the throat and take hit after hit if I had to.

Meeting after dark is unlike meeting by day. The things that shadow us daily but do not fully wear us—the hidden parts, like night blooms, unfamiliar smells—come on stronger at night. I caught the scent of something feral in the air. As if we'd made some mutual but unspoken decision to only communicate by way of profundities and to utterly do away with common niceties, Arthur didn't greet me when we met. Instead, he came up and stood across from me in the dark alleyway, leaned up against the fence and, as though taking his time, lit up a cigarette. We were wearing long black coats and black hats. By day, these were gentleman's costumes; by night, we were skulkers. Lifting my head a touch, I paused to watch him. He gazed back at me as he exhaled slow plumes of smoke into the air.

"You saw him," I confirmed. "That was him."

"I thought so." After this, there was a long silence. He didn't begin to talk again until he'd finished his cigarette. "You know…" he began quietly. "When we were boys, and you used to read books to me…"

Cocking my head on one side with enquiry, I looked askance at this nostalgic topic direction, poised as we were to deliver an innocent girl up to the witch's campfire and all things ungodly. "Yes…?"

"When you first read *Wuthering Heights* to me, it didn't speak to me deeply, even though I wanted it to because you loved it so. I enjoyed listening to you anyway."

I smiled, still with a little confusion around the edges of my expression. Arthur was starting to become quite unpredictable. There was no discernible pattern to his behaviour anymore. This new erratic quality unnerved me. I liked the touch of fear it aroused in me. It felt like anything could happen around him. "I know. You found it hard to relate to Cathy and Heathcliff, you told me: if they love each other so, why aren't they kinder? It was so adorable that I forgave you for not favouring one of my most beloved books."

"It didn't capture my imagination *at the time,* is what I mean to say. But afterwards, when you read me *Jane Eyre,* I understood Jane immediately, and through her, I think I understood Mr. Rochester, and from Mr. Rochester, I was able to access Heathcliff. Through Heathcliff, I found Byron, and through the little streak of meanness in Byron, I was able to find Cathy… These days, I find that most days *Wuthering Heights* is closer to my mental atmosphere than anything else. I think I understand what it is to feel something so fiercely it's almost aggressive."

For a moment, he paused and took in the way I was looking at him. "What?" Why are you looking at me like that?" He ducked his head in a way that, when we were boys, would have suggested self-consciousness, but it was hard for me to imagine that type of shyness on Arthur as a man. Was it possible that he might still flourish beneath the light of my approval and wither at my disapproval, as I did at the touch of his?

"I was just enjoying your words," I said, looking down. "Very deeply. Please go on."

OF THE HEART

"Well, I got to thinking that if that's how you opened my mind and heart to different human characters, through literature, maybe it works like that with other people too? Perhaps there is a Martha in a book that Clara loves?"

"This idea intrigues me." Now that he'd finished smoking, I wanted to cross the distance between us and greet him, but as some time had now elapsed since we met, it would seem like an awkward excuse to touch him. Sometimes, I think that as I got older, my fear of touching him too much made me touch him incidentally a lot less than I touched others.

"Well, if you and I were simply to be thought of as characters like Jane and Mr. Rochester…"

"Which would I be?" I demanded to know, crossing my arms and repressing a grin.

Arthur laughed. "Well, I already told you how I relate to Jane, so… You'll have to try for the grumpy Byronic hero in this analogy. Surely through us, she can access Martha and Moses? The way I did with Cathy and Heathcliff?"

"I hope so," I muttered. "I think you're right. Whoever we like in books, it is because something in them calls to something inside us that has not had the chance to bloom, or maybe to scream. If I like these people, it is because inside me there is also a convict, and a commoner, a rebel that never yet got the chance to rebel, a woman ill-judged by society, and a thief who never yet had to steal, and a Black man…" I pulled up my excited outpouring short because I could see him looking at me intently.

"I love you!" he declared passionately; he was always one who had no choice but to blurt it out. It was the sort of thing he used to do when we were young. An un-self-conscious way of being that he'd had less access to of late. I was so taken aback that I just stared at him until both of us broke the gaze off uncomfortably because we could hear Clara coming down the alleyway.

Immediately, my heart was beating harder. Knowing the direct consequences if Clara was found out of her room with us by night gave a piquant edge to the rusty taste of alertness under my tongue. I went to meet her, and Arthur followed. As habitual night-walkers, the streets of Hobarton held no unfamiliar terrors for us. I knew it would not be so for Clara. After bullying and fighting, I understood the privilege of the freedom in our walks more so than Arthur did.

"Are you ready?" I asked her, as we came to a stop before each other. A dark-coloured riding cloak with hood inconspicuously covered her bonneted hair. She did not make eye contact with me; she took hold of Arthur's arm as if he were her safety and anchor in the situation. Normally, I'd have offered her my arm. Instinctually, I knew it wasn't my place to make her feel entirely secure tonight. I had echoed my tattooed angel's words unconsciously, yet I saw the reverberation of this phrase go through Arthur's flesh like a shock of electricity, even in the semi-dark.

If anyone tries to tell you the difference between the classes lies purely in levels of refinement or intellectual polish, they are missing the point. There is an immediacy about life—an urgent keenness—to being in the presence of the poor who live on the knife's edge that is entirely missing from the middle classes. If you think I imagined myself their superior, you haven't been paying attention. Moses possessed a natural refinement about him that arose from personal idiosyncrasies rather than background. In a similar sense, Martha was rougher than the childhood she'd arisen in. It is part of being cunning folk that your personality is too big for the world's containers, so Martha told me. They would always try to break you to fit you in anyway, one picked-off leg or arm at a time, even if it had to be into tiny pieces; most people lived as these kind of bits and pieces. We had come there on this night at the appointed hour of midnight, to learn how to break the boxes we'd been put in—break them with hidden knives and jackhammers—rather than have ourselves picked apart.

Martha never said this was what we were here for, mind you. I knew it at a flesh-deep level; this was a sword dance, this work, and you had to learn to get faster and faster at it if you were to succeed. I trusted the still partly unspoken rebel in Clara to allow her to hear Moses' gentle and wise voice rather than feeling the fear of Black faces her parents would have trained into her. I trusted her intelligence to realise she'd been lied to. Most of all, I trusted her kindness. It was much like how I imagine one feels towards a sister. Already, I had learned by this tender age that nothing mattered so much as kindness does. Perhaps it was the jumbled and nightmarish memory of having witnessed the last public execution by hanging when I was a child that cried out against brutality… Or was it perhaps the lack of overt kindness coupled with the ubiquity of death in our lives that gifted me this early perspective?

Years before, I had believed that truth was beauty, and beauty was truth, as Keats had said. By this point, if I had a religion, it hinged on kindness and bravery, because I had not always been strong, and death was always very near, cozying up to you with cloying hands. Because, as a child, I had seen a frightened human soil their clothing as they were executed. Because my mother's

OF THE HEART

corpse had drooled on me. Because whenever I stepped out of my house without Arthur, I was often mocked, threatened, or hit simply for existing. For these reasons, I now had begun to understand that Keats was right, though beauty meant something different than I'd thought at fifteen. By the time I was a man, I picked my friends in reference to kindness above all other things, with intelligence or wit coming in a close second. Tonight, we would see how well my judgment had developed. My concern was more for Martha and Moses than it was for Clara. It mortified me, the idea of bringing a snooty, rude girl onto their turf who would treat them as curiosities or demean them. It didn't matter how many people had no doubt done these things to them all their lives; I did not want to be part of it.

As we walked along the river in the dark, I could taste Clara's fear in the air. The scent of her fear rippled through my stomach in a feeling that had both tenderness and fierceness in it. I felt some wordless communication pass between my body and Arthur's; I didn't understand it with my mind. Yet, I received the message in all my nerves and webbing of flesh. If I'd had to explain it, I'd I've had said it was something to do with readiness in case something went wrong on the way, and we needed to physically protect Clara. It was something I hadn't felt in myself before. The feeling jolted me with its primal iron-ore; it bypassed personality, daily impulses, and quirks, going straight to something fundamental about being a man that I hadn't understood until then. Although I had no words for it, I knew then that, although not all men were equally masculine when a girl like Clara was in danger, one would naturally use their presence and strength to step up in her defence.

"Why does it...magic...have to be scary?" Clara asked in whisper.

"Because life is scary." I shrugged. In that moment, it seemed an answer that contained infinite depth if she wished to explore black waters. The terror that is life's other face is an ever-receding depth that beleaguers the mind with infinite doubts, with new crushing limits and the breathless possibility of the smashing through of those limits also. Perhaps I could have shown her with my music? The ever-swelling ingress of the crescendo that kept trying to get written through me, one that never gives itself to our satisfaction and yet, finally, through a number of gentle retreats and teasing returns, it ripens into soft, swelling fullness. Then, of course, there is sadness: the soaring violins giving way to the maturity of cello, which brings us the aching sad of the heart's wear and tear, the mark of the grown-up. As a boy, you love like violins, but as a man, the cello grazes you out from the inside.

For me, magic was terrible for the same reason that music, words, and art are terrible; they each whisper into the ear of the soul. They flicker lights on inside the hidden caverns in us. In these caves, there are no Abyssinian maids with dulcimers or even women wailing for their demon lovers; there is only the stark, primordial echo of yesterday. There is the building pressure of the accumulating past promising us those dams are going to break one day, and all the dead voices will start escaping through the words, the music, and the images; because these are the cracks through which the Otherness looks back at you. Life is meant to be scary. It is not meant to feel comfortable.

Noting that Clara didn't seem altogether satisfied with my response, Arthur came to our rescue. "Once, when I first began to learn magic just from being around him, Henry told me that when people are afraid, their skin exudes a substance that is delicious to spirits."

"Is Henry like your teacher, Arthur?" she asked in a respectful sort of tone. "You speak about him as though he is…"

"Absolutely," Arthur responded immediately, then appeared to think about the rest of his response in a more measured manner. "Moses is my *mentor* in certain arts. Yet, when I consider the word *teacher* to myself and all of what that means, one spirit on his journey through eternity to another, if you understand me?" Clara nodded that she did. "Then I can only think of Henry, and the way he opened me. He opened my mind to this other dimension of reality which before had seemed a dream. I felt like I'd seen behind the backdrop on a stage—as if everything I'd thought was certain and important in this world was merely window dressing on a larger, far more epic story."

As we walked, Arthur took my hand in his in the darkness. He walked with Clara on his arm on one side and held my hand on the other. I felt it was his way of personalising his words about me whilst I happened to be present. I slid my fingers through his, to hold his hand in the way I instinctively felt was more intimate. I squeezed his hand, because I wanted to tell him that he set my mind on fire like my vision made the ridgeway on fire. That the man he was becoming thrilled me utterly. Even though I'd seen him coming into being for some time now, this man he'd grown into right before my eyes…

Slowly, and at last, I was starting to learn what kind of fairytale I was in. It was a story full of towers that must be scaled on the edge of terrible voids, thorns too numerous to count, and it left the sanguine taste of the utter refusal to give up on the back of my tongue. It was a twisted narrative; our tale contained metaphors of sleep curses and the power of a true love's kiss, hearts caked in Palaeolithic ice sheets, and a long, slow melt. Caught between this collision of ice and heat, the poor little daffodil bulb would have to give way like a cracking human skull, to let the flowers come. Yet, all I had to express the beauty and fearfulness of our monstertale, or the pain felt by the daffodil bulb as the first hairline fissions opened up in him, was this hand squeeze. Therefore, when he squeezed me back, it meant everything.

―――

For a long time, I had wanted Moses' story. He only let go of it in little clutches. Sometimes, he'd make mention of a coup, and Arthur would ask where and when? Haiti, Moses would say, then make some other close-ended response. Sometimes, he'd speak of being a sealer and that time he almost caught a seal woman by accident. After a time, you knew he wasn't going to tell you what you wanted to know most. It was Marie Laveau's albino python Zombi who got him talking in the end. He slithered up through the conversation where Clara tempted and pulled until she got what she was looking for. I watched her in fascination, although I knew I could never draw on natural sweetness like she could, at least perhaps only with Arthur; I wanted to learn from her artfulness. It was the sovereign art of how to extract a tale from an older man who has been etched all across with suffering.

"It was like that in New Orleans in those days. You could dance all night to Dr. John Bayou's drums and fall asleep in some strange room. That's how conjure first got up inside me… Laying out there in a stifling humid room on some cushions on the floor. Can't remember, to be telling you the truth, whether it was just the exhaustion or being ridden by the Baron like I was the cheapest old pony at a children's birthday outing." He stopped here to laugh at himself in recognition. Arthur and I glanced at each other briefly. Neither of us wanted to move a muscle in case it broke Moses out of his sharing reverie. "At the time, I didn't realise it had happened. I just danced and danced until I felt like I collapsed. Someone was watching me, though, taking notes on how strong I was ridden and how many times. It was no accident that I ended up right where I did that night." He took a few tokes on his pipe.

"I'm not sure if I was given something, if some kind of powder or *gris-gris* was put up on me, or in my drink. Because I thought I was awake when Zombi started slithering down from his perch on a chair."

"Who was Zombi?" Clara asked. It was so bold of her to do so; Arthur and I were strenuously avoiding being too interested-seeming on purpose.

"He belonged to Marie Laveau, the Voodoo Queen of New Orleans Herself. Zombi was like the Holy Spirit or a grand loa in the form of a familiar animal. It was Marie's cushions I found myself passed out on." He said the woman's title like each word was a separate statement of her power. "Zombi came up really slow. I couldn't turn my head to look at him as he came up on me. There is a sound a good, thick python makes when it moves… There is also a way it feels with its cold gaze on you. This is why I think they put tricks on me, because I wasn't able to move to prevent it coming up onto me."

Clara shuddered theatrically. "I think I would skip that part of the process if that's optional."

"If you can't handle a massive snake up in your lap, why be sniffing around people like us?" Martha asked, a bit confrontational, a bit of eyebrow, a bit suggestive. Often, it was hard to stop her talking. She nipped the edges of Clara's heel, yet even Martha did not seem to want to cut in on Moses.

It didn't work on Clara, though. "What did the snake do when it climbed onto you?" she asked with such intent interest that it didn't seem like she'd ignored Martha at all.

Moses paused. I knew Arthur and I were united in hoping he would start to talk again, as we had discussed in private our strong desire to hear how he learned what he knew. He cleared his throat, and we all waited. "Strange thing is, Zombi didn't *do* anything. He came up my thigh and onto my stomach and chest all cold and heavy, and he just…lay there. For a long time. What seemed like too long a time. When I say he was heavy, I mean he was six or seven inches across ways. He pressed you down like a nightmare. The odd thing was that *his skin spoke* to me." Moses' words were almost a whisper. I felt his breath-memory in the air, as if he'd conjured the feeling the snake had given him. He laughed to himself, under his breath, as if at some joke only he understood. "His skin itself told my skin I was conjure-man. He showed me how he was once part of Damballah, the world snake, whose scales were tossed across the night sky to make the stars." Moses gave a little gesture with his hand that seemed to evoke throwing the scales casually across the heavens.

"I couldn't move the whole time. He brought his head up over my face and just rested on my hot skin. He never tried to wrap me up or swallow me; he just wanted me for my body heat."

"What did you do when you could move again?" Clara asked.

OF THE HEART

Moses threw his head back and laughed. I don't think I'd ever seen him quite so animated. "I ran like hell! Never went back there again. But Zombi...he came with me. Or at least a ghost of him did. Whenever I would wake in the middle of the night, I would feel him slithering up onto me again. Every time, I would try to struggle, but like a hag-riding, I was pinned down to the bed. One night after I'd had way too much liquor and hashish, he swallowed and digested me."

"What happened then?"

He shrugged. "I don't remember. Mainly, I tried to get away from the conjure-man's fate. I went places that smelt like winds of oceans that put the sweet rot smell of New Orleans behind me. At first, it seemed like he couldn't follow me over water, Zombi's ghost. I was a free man, so there was nothing stopping me. There were a lot of seaports and other men's wives during that period."

"Oh, Moses, you're a devil!" Clara upbraided him, her tone partly facetious. "Hush your wicked tongue now. I'm a good girl; I'll not hear such things."

Martha was laughing in her low, wheezing manner. "This one's got a bigger pole up her clacker than Henry!"

"I do not! Henry's is far bigger!"

Martha cackled with amusement. "You're probably right, but what you be wanting with us, I ask again, if Moses' philandering bothers your pretty head?"

"I suppose one says what we're taught to say until we're comfortable enough to say what we really think..."

"I don't. Fuck what people taught you. What kind of girl do *you* want to be? Better yet, what kind of woman do you want to turn into?"

Moses got to his feet. "I need to follow a call of nature, my friends." He dipped his black hat and shuffled away into the darkness.

II

It was years since the opium poppy had crashed through my veins and cracked up my bones like I was made of eggshells. Every now and again, she and I would have a moment of reuniting when things got hard—though I had never invited the gold-topped mushroom over my threshold. After a few visits to Martha with Clara, it was decided we would do it. There would be a sabbat: a conjure-feast of wild, exiled magics. These mushrooms we were going to eat, unlike the opiate or the hashish, came from the soil here. It was part of something alien, just like us.

"We've put them in hashish butter," Martha told us before we sat down to eat them together. No one was allowed to talk while we ate. This wasn't hard for me, as I competed with Moses for being the quietest, but soon I understood why we weren't to speak. This was a Dumb Supper, eaten for the dead—maybe for the dead inside ourselves, as well as those outside, bringing Zombi, Mary, and Gerty back to life… The bitterness of the mushroom tasted like death. They were going to take me to—and maybe would only go one more time to—a place I hadn't been before. They started networking inside me, mapping me, making me part of their new territory. For a moment, there was a great rushing-up from my feet, and I was afraid of its strength.

When I look down, all of a sudden everything is *now*. My hands are covered in a coloured pattern, like reptile skin in the various hues of a stained-glass window. Light shines through the scales. For a moment or two, I'm worried I will burn away like I'm made of rice paper that got too close to the candle. When I don't, a state, ruthlessly fearless, begins to quicken in me. In it, every present tense sentence runs into every other one until they pile up into a catastrophe of time-scale. For a few moments, I know the whole thing, how my story began, how it never began, how people say it began, and how it ends, and why it never ends, and how people will say it ends. There's an aftertaste of warmth beyond the bitterness, a pulsing connection with these Other-others who stand in the circle. The people, and the tree people, the frog spirits, the ghostly boobook and his haunting cry, and the possum-goblins.

I see the small people watching me from the trees. At first, I think they are the ghosts of dead children. From their facial expressions, I know I am wrong. *Every time we change, we look smaller and smaller to you, because we're further away.* The feeling of their gaze jolted me out of my presence-tense interruption of time. Or was it when Moses started on his drum? I could sense the ancestry of that beat, moving through the skin of the drum. As if old John Bayou were there when Moses evoked that introductory beat. It seemed to stir and wake everything, or perhaps bring everything and everywhen to the party? Each of us began to move in our own individual yet infinitely connected ways. Nobody seemed to need to announce that this was what the drumbeat was for. Moses' movements were governed by the drum, and yet he was amazingly able to dance and play at the same time. With Martha, you seemed to watch her just drop down all of a sudden, like watching a crow land on a carcass and right itself into the entrails.

One of Them, the little folk, beckoned to me. I knew better than to go with Them. I sniffed at the air. What sort of animal was I turning into? In dreams, I had flown but never with any sense of my shape. Tonight, I was something of the mammal genus, for the first time, something with a keen nose. The scent of the small people was like the stripped-away bark of the sassafras trees, dew, sadness, and dried flowers.

This is where we changed you. Right here, right now, tonight. They spoke straight into your mind like a persistent, dripping tap you couldn't quite block out. I started to twitch, my head going down to one side, over and over again.

"Changed me into what?" I whispered aloud into the air. The idea that anyone else human could hear me didn't enter my mind.

Stop pretending to be human.

"I'm not pretending..." Yet, as soon as I said it, I tasted the metallic taste of a lie against my tongue. Again, I looked down at my hands. Now they had become fully see-through, and golden light ebbed out of me into the air. I was quite abruptly full, again, of the sense this had all been planned a long time ago. All of it. Me coming here to Martha and Moses, and each part of their heritages that stacked up into them turning up here in Van Diemen's Land. Arthur and I bringing them Clara... Each was a piece in a puzzle I was given to understand— and able to. For a moment, at least. I had the feeling all over my body that usually accompanies the hairs standing up on the backs of one's arms and neck, and yet it didn't feel like I had hair.

Frantic and hungry with wonder, I glanced around me. I saw Zombi climbing up Moses' body, until they had merged into one man-snake figure. It was a slow, heavy-serpentine motion that happened in the background of the drums, with the conjure-man balancing both. My eyes settled on Martha, who was wearing nothing but a slip now, with even her dress being something in the way between her and the savage divine. She had raven wings scratching and itching their way out of her back, while she strove to pull her feathers free of the skin, as if it were a mere imposition, this human casing. Long peels of her skin came off in her hands. She dropped down onto her haunches and hopped around and twitched with crow-life. I sensed with awe that it was she herself who had consumed the eyeballs of fallen warriors upon the battlefields of yore.

I watched the magical build hit Arthur like a wave. He seemed to catch the magic, and it washed right through him. Was he the shroud in the hands of the washer at the ford? Something with the resistance of water moved through him. He stumbled, and in waves, he came forward as different animals. First, he tried to keep some control of it. As he went along, the cutting loose became central, as he realised that no one was staring at anyone else. The others were in their own experience, except me; I was somehow in my experience and his, and Martha's and Moses', at the same time. After the release for Arthur, there came the strut, the need, and the right, to show off his power. Each face, each dance was different every time, until he had showed, without words, the way he'd swallowed the whole bush and every feral life in it.

Clara danced still, committed but not quite caught up by the outer edges of the skirts of the dancing woman of the sabbat. Her inner weirdness not quite ready to show her face. The illusion that she was always being watched was still there with her, blocking her. *This is what you do.* I was told. *You are a conductor through whom music is made.* Moments later, as though in response to the voice of the elf-people, my own body contorted forwards. My arms arched backwards, strained against the grain of natural movement into some uncivilised power move, like the wings of an animal that moves fast in the air. Whatever it was, my inner animal had decided to open my skeleton and climb out my back and rip my arms up.

The bush Themselves was a teeming person-presence. It was as if it were a superimposed backdrop covering an incandescent reality behind it—one that I must tear through to get at it, to hold the real in my hands. Behind the human idea of trees, was *Trees;* they had minds, shared and connected minds, and their own idea of themselves. The desire to rip it back—like Martha with her feathers, peeling her skin like after a severe sunburn—was primal. Was I dancing away from the golden mushroom spirits, or away from myself, or was this instead a seduction of myself, and circling back to my always-present-tense centre? Reality seemed to spring backwards away from me like a hare. It stood panting, waiting, its eyes wilder than the moon. I heard Arthur's voice calling my name as I watched the hare panting, taking on the sound of a man desperately running through the trees, searching for someone. For some reason, I thought of dogs and a search party scanning the bush for a body. There was a humming of alarm in the air and in the hare's hunted eyes.

Clara was half-laughing as if she were trying to restrain giggles. When my body returned to the upright position, she turned to me, and I saw that she was holding her dress up in her hands the way a baby child might expose themselves. Her dress was floral and whimsical, far more elaborate than the one she had arrived at the circle in. Then I saw it was not a print fabric at all she was wearing; they were real, living flowers somehow woven together to make a dress. She lifted both skirts and petticoats right over her head. When my eyes dropped lower, there was only the bare, white hipbones and pelvis of a skeleton to be seen where her lady-parts should have sat. I watched as she peeled off not only the dress, but her entire skin.

Finally, the glowing pale skeleton stood in the path before me, making a gesture of silence at me with one bony finger, before bounding off through the trees, as light as a rabbit. My eyes went from her retreat to the discarded woman skin that lay on the grass. Deflated, the blonde hair upon the scalp looked liked the wig of some ghastly doll. The breasts and other areas of fat or muscle alone remained filled out. I reached out for the skin. Before I could try to put it on, I heard Arthur's voice whisper my name, as if he was standing right behind me. Picking up Clara's discarded skin, I felt the texture in my hands like it was a new outfit, one I wanted to try out for how it would feel against my skin. Did the Good Folk own human skins like this one they could wear when they fancied a change? It felt soft, heavy, languid.

I jumped abruptly, as I felt I was being watched. To my eyes after a startle, Arthur now looked exactly like he normally did during life, except that his eyes had gone from warm-brown to almost yellow. Were they the eyes of the thylacine? The animal he'd said he wanted to change into, but had not yet done so tonight? For a moment, about when I blinked, I thought I saw his whole jaw come open like a snake's or a Tasmanian Tiger's.

"What *are* you?" he whispered. "What were you before you came here? Merrow or sidhe?"

It seemed that throughout knowing him, he'd been working on this, the question I passed to him the first time we played Our Game. He'd broken down this original question over time, to only two types of faerie that I might be. The wise but cold sidhe, or the merrow, who may well take you deep into the water so you cannot get back out. As if my sinuous slipping into the skin-membrane were an answer in itself, I held his eye contact while I put Clara on. *This is not who, but what, I am.*

It was far more explicit, somehow, than a disrobing. Putting on her woman-skin spoke a whole other cryptic language beyond words than merely appearing naked before someone. Arthur watched me, and his eyes narrowed, the yellow shade of his eyes turned to something brighter and sharper, a predator gleam. Whatever this creature was, he had a jagged eye. Beckoning to him with Clara's tiny forefinger, I lured him. Tonight, the bush became a place of deep mystery among those singing trees. I pulled him to me and kissed him with her mouth. I pulled him to me with years of not pulling him. The animals of him shimmered and rippled over the surface of him, one by one. What he'd learned from each of them was clear in touch. I felt them, with Clara's fingers in his fur, his feathers.

Strangely, he was taller than me by some degree, which didn't feel as right as I'd hoped it would. Surely, the right way for me to love him was like this? As a woman? In this totally real imaginary space? His body thrilled to it. Or did it thrill to Clara? Or me? Again, we touched the perfect thing that had quavered over us when it brushed past as we'd practiced kissing. When he gently shook me to consciousness, I was laying in the leaves. I looked up at his face confused. He had been above me where I'd been, too, so now waking to look up at him was like seeing him in layers.

"Henry! Are you all right?"

"Of course," I replied breathlessly, still in a zinging state of full-bodied arousal. "Why wouldn't I be?"

"You were unresponsive for a very long time there."

Slowly, like the rising magic of the sabbat that pulled us back in, we let first our eyes and then our hearts be drawn to what was still happening. Moses was playing on his drum, a different beat now, a more insistent and complex one. He was beside the fire, and around him went the freed bodies of the two fever-ridden, dervish things that were Martha and Clara. They were dancing the crazed dance of the mushroom people with their skirts as high as their hips. Clara made a high-pitched whoop of exultation and lifted her skirts higher, revealing her underwear just as she had shown me her bones. For a moment, as she passed our side of the fire, I swore she looked right at me, and her wild eye rolled upon me in its frenzy. There was something roguish and knowing there that made me feel as if she'd looked right through me, that she knew what I'd done with her skin only moments ago, and I was the one that was naked down to *my* own bones before her.

RAG & BONE MAN

While the others spoke and laughed through the coming down, Arthur and I didn't join in. They each told the story of their visions, and they were braided together into something whole. Nobody seemed to lead after a time; all their stories sat together. Earlier Arthur had sat down behind me and lifted my head into his lap. When he did it, I remember how I smiled without opening my eyes. It had been years since I'd lain my head on his thigh like that while we would sprawl on the grass and read books or talk. His touch had been different of late, though it was hard to say since when. If I did end up in such a position as this one, I could sense he didn't quite know what to do with me. His self-consciousness leaped from his body into mine. Tonight, it was all suddenly different. Though, of course, it wasn't spoken of, he touched me after the sabbat as though he too knew what had happened in my vision—as if he'd been there too. As if we were lovers.

His fingers fiddled with my hair, my ears; they found out my half-undone tie and my loose wrist buttons.

"I know," I murmured. "I'm a mess."

"I like it."

I opened my eyes, looking up at him. What I saw made me feel the edge near us. "You would!" I laughed, turning it into a joke. I looked over his attire pointedly, as he was just as ruined as I was. "You never have to press your own laundry!"

Playfully, he gave my arm a slap.

He was all you've ever wanted... I think it was Them who spoke in my head. Those six forlorn words would echo and echo again. I would whisper those words to myself and wonder at their meaning; they were so powerful. Yet, life is not singular. Life is an erupting multiplicity, just like the story that was woven together by our coven's visions. It was a life I came here to know. A terrible, a frightening jigsaw of pieces put in random-seeming places, yet all fitting together nonetheless... It jarred my aesthetic sense, delicate as it still was in some ways, after the release of the sabbat. Yet, I felt it clearly; part of me wanted to get dirty. Part of me knew that I'd come here to learn to love the world, and the world wasn't something petty like *clean*. Now I was being cut open by that love, and other powers were pouring on stigmatically through the wounds.

"What did you see, Henry?" someone asked me. I didn't have to answer because Clara realised the time and how late she was out, and the risk she was taking.

OF THE HEART

"Arthur? Would you mind ever so much walking me home?" Clara asked, as the conversation between her and Martha terminated naturally.

"Of course!" Arthur said immediately, as if suddenly remembering with a great shock that he was meant to be a gentleman, as well as all the behavioural expectations involved. Gently, he lifted my head again so he could get to his feet. I moved to allow him to be faster, watching him offer Clara his arm before she stood. These were all ingrained instincts that I had been raised with myself, yet it was not without a pain of regret that I let him go. I loved to be near him when he'd been active or running and his skin was warmed, and he smelled like him. His natural smell had something of ash, salt, and a tang not unlike sandalwood in it.

"I should be doing that for her," I murmured.

"You stay there, Henry," Clara said, waving the matter away. "You're having a bit of a rest there, and Arthur has his shoes on."

It wasn't until then I remembered my shoes weren't on... At what point I had abandoned them, I couldn't remember. It felt very strange to be in a black suit with bare feet—creepy somehow, as if I were a corpse laid out on the grass. For some reason, that thought linked easily to the next. I sat up and went closer to where Martha was sitting, as I watched them walk away into the shadows. "Martha, may I ask you a question?"

"All right. But have a bit of this rum first; it will set you to rights with the other stuff you've taken."

I did as she requested and swallowed some of the offensive-tasting liquor without showing a flicker of distaste. She was right; I needed it to summon the courage to drag this question up out of the deep harbour of myself like an immense anchor. "If two men love each other... What I mean to say is, beyond kissing and cuddling...in bed, what do they—"

I stopped because Martha's face had contorted into a twisted smirk. She struck me on the arm like I was being a fool. "You're playing with me!" A moment or two of waiting for me to smile passed by, and slowly, her grin faded. "But you two are already... Surely? After that night in St David's? That was the before-play..." Her voice fell away into uncertainty, and finally, she started to shake her head. "You're not... You honestly don't know? Do you?" She was looking at me with something between pity and wonder, as if I were a mystical beast with a broken unicorn horn, or a fairy she'd found in the dirt with a torn wing. "How can that even *be?*"

I didn't know what to say. The feeling was one of both helplessness and humiliation. "All I know is that the man mounts the woman front-wise, unlike with other animals, and this I have gleaned from passing the ladies of the night with their customers."

"Your father hasn't told you a thing beyond this?"

"Of course not. Nobody speaks about things like that. Well… I mean—"

"Toffs don't speak about things like that, is what you mean. Well, they pay friends of mine to do things to them there are barely words for, and in their hypocrisy, they keep their children ignorant! It's abuse, is what that is. Clear and simple! May not be like a beating, but it's abuse —neglect, of the mind." She shook her head angrily. "It goes up your bum, Henry, for the love of Our Lady! Not to mention all the other same things a man and a woman can do with the hands and mouth." She made a vivid hand and mouth pantomime of this behaviour for me, in case I'd missed some of the implications.

"In…in your bottom? You mean with the man's member?"

She nodded. Her expression had become one where dismay seemed to dominate over wonder. "This never could have gone on so long if my daughter had lived…" she muttered.

"But…but isn't that dirty?" I could feel tears thickening in my throat, and I tried not to let my voice shake. Already some thick, icy miasma of knowing was creeping over me. Things were starting to make a deathly sense.

Martha shrugged, as if the matter didn't seem so important. Of course she didn't understand the fear of dirt a middle-class boy with family dead of disease would feel. It was the fear of catching something—and of death, death of whole families, which was so often close and linked to times of poor sanitation. It would have done the poor no good if they had made the connection, but we who had the ability to respond to our own mortality in some empowered fashion had concluded that cleanliness was indeed the exact same thing as godliness. "Not unless you want it to be! Just got to bathe first; nothing a bit of soap and water up there can't fix."

I barely heard her. *This is why they hate us.* "So that's what a catamite is?" I asked dully, as if some of my spirit had been broken along with the knowing of my supposed crime. "Is it a word for both of the people who perform the act or just the receiving man?"

Martha shrugged. "Don't know that one. It's also called 'sodomy'; they call it that too. Didn't you know just from your urges? I assumed you and Arthur had been at it for years until I saw you fumble around with holding each other in the burial ground. I figured it would happen afterwards if it had not already. Our Lady of Mercy!" she said suddenly, as though realising something. "If you don't know what it is, then you don't know it's a capital crime…"

Of the Heart

I stared at her for a while, the confusion in my face slowly giving way to a kind of cold understanding as I remembered Arthur's joke about committing a capital crime. I started to nod. "Of course it is," I murmured. My father's fear and pistols at dawn behaviour also made sense. The "innocence" comments about me made sense. Everything made a horrible, dull-edged hurt in my chest that was the very essence of sense.

"They'll kill you both for it if they catch you," she added. "Fine gentlemen or not."

"Yes," I replied, almost in a whisper now. "I know what a capital crime is. Would you excuse me, Martha? I need some time alone."

She tried to stop me as I got to my feet, grabbing my arm. "Don't run off in that spirit! You might be a nancy, but you're our nancy! And there's a damn lot of things I do in a day that the law doesn't know about; it doesn't mean you can't both—"

"Please," I said, with as much grace as I could muster, as I was on the very edge of losing my dignity and didn't want it to happen in front of anyone. "I really need to be alone. Thank you. I'll call again soon." I brushed my clothing down convulsively, half-bowed to her and Moses before walking quickly away with no shoes on. The knobs and screws of nature hurt the soles of my feet. It worried me not, as I had become quite disconnected from them.

When I had reached a suitable distance, I stopped, leaned against a tree, and allowed myself the sobs I felt would destroy my ribcage if I didn't let them out. I was afraid I'd scream and tear my own flesh open with my fingernails. It was lucky they were so well-manicured, because they would have at least sliced into my palms in the effort to hold control in with a clenched fist. My face was burning with the humiliation of my protracted ignorance, the one they had called "innocence"; my chest felt like it had a frozen lump of lead lodged in it. There was a confused response quickening through me even as I wept, as if my heart would break. Was that what Arthur had been thinking about us doing when he gave me that long, hard stare?

Anger was upon me next. One so black and terrible that I feared my eyes were filling to the brim with liquid tar, a black flood running through the streets of Hobart until it found my father and wrapped around his legs, dragging him bodily into the Underworld. I felt my fingers grow sharp like falcon claws of elf-dart, and I hit the tree behind me a few times in my frustration. How could they? How could he have kept me ignorant of my own nature in this manner? Worse still, how could people be so unkind as to see a crime in it? All I wanted was Arthur's happiness. I'd have sacrificed my own for it ten times over. Yet, my Hobart, a being I'd once imagined had me, would now no longer hold me in its arms. An intense sound of frustration tore from my broken voice box and cracked where the higher sounds of childhood were forever lost to me.

I didn't even heed Martha coming towards me through the trees. It didn't matter now anyway. It didn't matter if tears, blotches, and mucous stained my face, and another saw it. In the eyes of society, I was already one of its most abhorred and unclean creatures. What was the point of hanging onto the illusion of my dignity? I may as well just let go of that ball of wool and let a cat make a cradle of it.

"Henry, now you look here, young man. Don't you be crying and laying down before your enemy like this! I didn't teach you so you could be a quitter."

"You don't understand!" I yelled at her. Raising my voice was so uncommon for me that I could tell it shocked her. She closed her mouth and just looked at me and then opened it again. "I'd do *anything* for him…" I murmured more softly, as if I expected that the poignancy and horror of this fact—and its juxtaposition with our legal system—should be plain to her. "If that isn't pure, I know of nothing in this world that is."

She forced me to be held by her, hushing me like a disconsolate infant. For a second, I felt—pressed to her bosom—as if I'd become her deceased daughter, Mary Bones, with such aggressive tenderness did she coddle me. It became clear while she did so what I had to do. I swallowed down hard on the cold reality of it and nodded slowly to myself with a quick, sinking resignation. Sometimes, love means refraining from expression to protect the beloved. I thought then of how the man I saw die when I was a boy had wet himself in his last moments, under the influence of the rope at his neck, and his brain getting switched off. This was something I don't think I'd remembered so clearly until that very moment. "Thank you for telling me, Martha." I straightened my clothing again, even though I had no shoes, gathered my composure with an icy discipline, and forced my legs to walk me home.

My gentleman died somewhere on that walk home. Struck his fatal blow by Martha's words, he bled out along the walk between South Hobart and my home. By the time I got there, his coat had become frayed at the elbows; some of the stitches in his costume were giving way, showing the first hint of the rags they would one day become. If you looked carefully through the loosening threads, you could see a hint of bone. In my vision, it had been Clara who turned into a skeleton, but really that had been me. What made it home and in through our front door didn't belong to my father's world; what slunk through the back alleys and up to our door, his hour come at last...he didn't answer to the laws of man. He was something the elf-get left behind when they took the real child off into the woods.

When Father found me, I was sitting alone in the dark with my bare feet up on the low table by the fire, smoking some of his tobacco thoughtfully. I was still wearing the same filthy clothes I'd gone to the sabbat in; my tie was loosened, and I think some buttons on my shirt were missing. As far as the Rag and Bone Man was concerned, I was still overdressed for this place. One dresses for company after all, in accordance with one's regard for the person.

Father jumped when he entered. "Henry, what are you doing sitting alone in the dark? When did you start smoking?" You could hear the fear in his voice. I sniffed the air, as suddenly I was convinced I could *smell the sound* of his discomfort. When he shone some light in my direction, you could hear a new doubt creeping in. "*Henry?*" I looked over at him and continued to smoke, blowing a plume of it in his direction and never removing my dirty feet from his furniture. In answer, I just slowly shook my head. I let him sit with my refusal to be his Henry, with his fear of the changeling behind my eyes, the cuckoo that grew and grew until it squashed out his other children. My eyes narrowed as I watched his fear quicken further. "He's not here anymore."

His heart was beating like a rabbit's. I could hear it. Unconsciously, he took a step back from me as if he meant to go for the door, as if he suddenly feared I meant to hunt him. "What's the matter with you?" His skin looked as sickly pale as cottage cheese.

Slowly and very deliberately, I put my cigarette out on the side of the hearth. "About Henry..." I muttered. "There were some things I think he needed to know. When were you planning to tell him what he is?" I asked. "Did you think you could keep him a safe little child forever?"

The fact I was discussing myself in third person chilled the inner superstitious Irishman inside my father, the one he was too ashamed of to own up to in public. It made him feel like my changeling had taken over and arrived to seek vengeance. To me, it only seemed appropriate under the circumstances that we discuss things as if Henry were already dead, as there was no hope for him in this world. I watched my meaning push through the necrosis of fear till the gradual realisation of what we were talking about came upon him. You could see a mixture of sadness and queasiness in his face along with his fear now. The fact that what I was physically—viscerally—disgusted him was not lost on me.

RAG & BONE MAN

With a sigh, Father sat down across from me, casting a disapproving look at my feet as he passed. I found myself wondering when the last time he'd actually seen my feet would have been? How strange it was to some part of me that was a citizen of the natural world before the human, that we two men shared a dwelling, where I cooked for him, sometimes I even pressed or washed his clothes, and yet I had no idea what his feet looked like... What was wrong with this world I'd been born into? That I couldn't remember the last time where I'd walked barefoot through mud or over grass, feeling the good earth beneath me, and tracking green-stained footprints across the mats on our beeswaxed floors? When was the last time I'd left behind a rebel carpet of moss and flowers with my print in his hallway?

"I was trying to protect you from...your problem."

One of my eyebrows jumped up sceptically. "My problem?" Shrill violins were going mad inside my brain. I was afraid glass would shatter from the intensity of their shriek. Or perhaps my father's heart would just burst like a ripe grape? "What if I don't find it to be a problem? Isn't it then revealed as, in fact, not my problem, but *your* problem?" My tone was both dry and cold. What else can you expect when you're made of bones, and the wind blows through the holes in your coat? Father would never have been able to hold his own in verbal debate with me at the best of times, and my sense of good manners and fair play had previously prevented me from making this fact clear to him. That was all gone now.

"I did everything I could, Son. Why do you think I got all that cupping and medicine for you when you were coming into manhood? I was trying to make you normal!"

Being reminded of the doctor burning me with hot glasses and dousing me in cold water to improve my humours, his keeping of me sedated...that did nothing to improve my temper. I was only now asking the kind of questions that, when unspoken, had been flinging open the windows, stopping the clocks, and snuffing out the candles for most of my life.

"I ask you: what if it's not a problem for me? Then your only answer is to tell me you tried burning, drugging, holding my head under in cold water, and isolating me, yet it didn't quite break me?"

He sighed heavily and wouldn't look me in the eye while we spoke. It was clear I had something he was afraid of catching. It came from the same root as the middle-class fear of disease. When he spoke, his words came out tight. "I've always known you loved other boys. Ever since the Fletcher's boy used to hang around before you met Arthur. A man swung for unnatural vice down at the

OF THE HEART

gaol when you were still a wee thing, and even if you can avoid that, there's no avoiding the hellfire you'd have to pay for the sin. So, I wanted you to see what could happen to a man who does that!"

"I remember!" I cried. "You made me stare at it and told me to look well upon the wages of sin. As the man was strangled, he lost control of his bladder. People laughed. It's hard to say if he was still conscious to hear their mockery as he left this world. You feel like that was done in the name of a god who is love?"

"I was just trying to keep you safe from this latent perversity in your nature, Henry! It was clear to me even then you weren't quite right. Don't look at me fit to blast me with the Eye! It's God's law, not mine, that says it's an abomination in the eyes of the Lord! If it were up to me, I'd have God take mercy on the sinner, as it seems to have been with you since the beginning, so I doubt you chose to be this way, but what is my view on it worth in balance with those of the Kingdom of Heaven, before the laws of man and God?"

"'God's law'?" It occurred to me during that exchange that my father placed the views of the world over his own views—and would place them over his child's views and his child's soul. "Well, you know what? Damn God!" I shouted at him loud enough that the china ornaments rattled on their silly doilies on their repressed little tables with half their hidden, lascivious legs. "Damn any god who makes me this way and then judges his own creation! If he knows every hair on my head, then he knows every affection of my heart or urge of my loins!" He jumped and cringed at my raised voice like a woman or child who suffers continued abuse from a husband or father—in short, as if I were a monster. "What has God to do with us faerie people?" I asked under my breath, more to myself than him.

I raised my eyebrows at him in the way that betokens an expectation of an answer. None was forthcoming. So I got to my feet and picked up the backpack I'd left leaning against the chair. For the first time, Father noticed the bag, and immediately he was on his feet. Before, there had been distaste in his eyes; now it was replaced by panic at being abandoned.

"What are you doing?" he cried, trying to block my way and making ineffectual little attempts to placate me with his hands. "You can't leave. Where will you go?" I ignored him and picked up my fiddle in its case. "But…but…" You could see Father's eyes darting frantically around the room, as if he hoped to alight on something that would give him an idea of how to influence me. For a second or two, he looked helplessly at my mother's portrait on the mantelpiece and then over at my piano. "What about your piano? And your cello? You'll go mad if you can't play…"

"They live inside me."

"Henry, stop!" There were tears standing in his bulging eyes. For a moment, the nature of my perversion, my problem, and even the abomination he'd declared I was, along with all his trained-in disgust, dissolved. Before him, he only saw his child—his last living child—walking away from him, just like the Black conjure-man had said I would. The spectre of dying alone was longer than the fear of the church and even the much more primal fear of gossip. Dying alone had pointy, dry fingers that scratched at his neck and needled him more keenly even than my sin. I swallowed a soft, old ache into my gut. My gentleman was dead, so what else could I do but bury him? When I opened my coat, you could see right through my chest and out the other side now. Drafts played around inside my ribcage.

"Besides, no one has need of a classically trained cellist where I'm going, Father." These were my last words to him.

With my pack on my back, still dressed in my disheveled black sabbat suit, with my violin in hand and some boots on, I walked out of my father's house—never to return. What would come back later was little more than dust in rags. As I walked away, the wind came after, eager to blow through me and turn me into another instrument with which we could replace my others. Somewhere in the deserted alleyways, I could hear my devil-man whistling a tune so sad it sounded as if he alone understood and carried all the sorrows of the world in his knapsack, as he kept pace with me in the seamy dark of Hobart's streets for two blocks. He was always the sort of man who favoured the homeless.

12

When I left, I walked down Liverpool Street in the direction of Wapping, the poor end of town where a cluster of pubs and looser establishments stood. Maybe it was because lodging would be cheaper there, though I think part of me also remembered Martha's tales of Liverpool Street taverns being owned by cunning men in the past. I took a leaf out of Arthur's book and popped a flat cap on my head to adopt a more working-class appearance. I wanted to blend in and find a room with ease.

The Brunswick felt as though a den of red-eyed hellhounds were hidden away inside the walls. At night, you would hear the uneasy horses shuffle and whinny at the breeze in the stable when it came galloping in during the witching hour. People didn't seem to look you in the eye for very long at that place. Arriving as I was with a bag on my back and a fiddle in my hand, I looked like any other travelling musician, hoping to play for some coins. My intention was to move on to somewhere cheaper in Wapping before anyone came looking for me.

In the sweat-stained, yeasty interior of a room above the public house, the back of my head opened up like a cowrie shell. If you could pick me up and hold me to your ear, you would have heard the ocean reverberate through me like the sound of a bull-roarer. It was necessary, I told myself—while the waters overwhelmed me and filled up my senses—because the *imbas forosnai* (these words in savage Gaelic alone enflamed the fire that was in my head) requires the churning of the grief-fecund sea. My work, had it survived, should have appeared a precursor to such voices as Fiona Macleod and W.B. Yeats. Little did I know that, along the Celtic fringe, there were others coming whose work would seem to link the literary legacy of Romanticism and Modernism.

With one foot in the Romantic past and one in an obscure, perpetual Modernity where the West had not yet become like a forest in dark where all the dogs of Europe barked, there were to be other Celtic orphan poets like me. Had I lived longer, I would have known how a faerie woman named Fiona Macleod wrote the works of William Sharp through him. It was during those days that the bulk of the poetry leaked from me like a manna that would only bloom out of someone's necrotic blood. I was postmortem already. I was Him now, even if it was only when I wrote. Boney fingers scratched the page with all of my futurity echoing back at me while I ghost-wrote myself out of existence, and my clothing began to become shreds of half-unwoven cloth.

The feeling so overwhelmed me that I had to check my reflection to see if I tangibly looked like I was beginning to decompose. Sitting in front of a poor-quality looking-glass in the guesthouse, I wondered what had I been so afraid of. I had almost strategically avoided sitting like this and looking into my own eyes for years. My features were not unattractive, in a pale, austere sort of way. There was little softness in them, and yet the hard edges of my bone structure were elegant. My nose was straight and fine, my cheekbones visible, my eyes a bit deep-set and of greyish hue. Though Arthur told me that on a fine, sunny day, they appeared almost blue. *I haven't been looking because, until now, I couldn't recognise myself.* I smiled at my reflection. Everything changed when I smiled; there was a kindling sweetness that embarrassed me. I got up and moved away from the glass and that boy in the mirror with the flirtatious smile. *Have I been smiling at Arthur like that all these years?* The thought made me uncomfortable, aroused.

I took a perverse pleasure in the sullied feeling as I flopped myself down onto the unhygienic bed. With one hand, I reached out and rifled through my backpack looking for my laudanum. My writing began to come on like something between a Venus flytrap and a flesh-eating bug as soon as I'd taken it, thieving my attention from the hungry want between my legs. It was only when I came conscious after the composition glut did it occur to me that, all these years, I'd been taking opium to ignore that very same feeling. God... When I started thinking about it, the pitch rose to unbearable. It seemed now my understanding was at full bloom; I didn't just *want*, but I needed him. As if I was Pygmalion's statue, I needed Arthur to bring me to life with the press of his body on me, in me—to touch and be touched everywhere by him in a frenzy of adoring hands and breathless kisses. There just weren't enough hand squeezes, chaste embraces, or stolen kisses to wring this feeling out of me like deep, stomach-shuddering tears. My body demanded to be reddened with hot, jagged life.

It followed hard upon the desperate sticky mess of this new, explicit wanting that the nightmares began. At first, I thought they were the product of shame for admitting what I was, or sometimes shame for fighting what I was. Next,

OF THE HEART

I considered they were brought on by the trauma of the execution by hanging I'd witnessed as a child. By the third pondering, I was forced to live through being torn from Arthur's arms by an angry mob and hanged, my last memories before a broken neck being the sounds of his anguish as he struggled against them to get to me. I knew then that it must be something more that stalked me in the halls when the boards would go creaking.

The horror I felt in witnessing the torment in his eyes before they shoved a bag over my head left me certain I was gazing upon some terrible possible future for us. Was I being punished for my impure thoughts? Or was this a possible thread of futurity? A way my path might go if I continued to flirt with my own destruction? For some reason, in the midst of this confusion and anguish, I wrote like I'd never written before. Perhaps my *imbas forosnai* thrived on this denial of the senses? Or perhaps one needs to be exposed to the uncertainties of life to really come alive? Amid filth and a cocktail of mixed intoxicants, I wrote. On the second night, I slept under the stars and was in the grip of such a strong chemical symphony I barely registered cold or discomfort. By the third night, I began to write wild poetry about tracking the Devil through the streets and byways of Hobart, and the conversations I envisaged having with him at different locations. I followed a trail he was leaving me in the form of poems. That is why they call it "inspiration," meaning to in-breathe, because when I'd walk past a place he'd occupied only recently, I'd breathe in the poetry that the hob-man exhaled. It was how we were communicating! A back-and-forth exchange in the language of faerie, not in the common tongue of man, but a communion of art between two mutual admirers of each other's work.

One moment he would be a bird, the next a beggar man; I would see him seven times every day. You had to be cunning to find his phantom words in a place. His poems didn't look like other people's poems. I was coming to learn that they smelt like the docks late at night, where the salty seamen drop anchor in our deep-water port. If you were going to sniff out the traces of them, you had to be there while the fog was coughing up the dregs of the night. You had to have a hungry thylacine in your belly and the entire horizon behind your eyes. There had to be wild horses in your hips and birds in your hair. I'm not sure exactly what I was eating at this time other than mushrooms and the odd apple.

I would pick up curiosities from the places where I found his poems. I was the Rag and Bone Man now, picking through people's leavings, looking for the tear-rich traces of their lives, hungry to understand, hungry to earn my human soul, hungry for my chance to win it from the Devil at the crossroads with my fiddle. Picking around for stories and meaning was more important to me than eating regularly. I think I played the Devil at the crossroads on a few of those nights. Who won, I'm not altogether sure.

When I found other people's letters or postcards, I would invent stories—secret stories of their lives, the parts that don't get left in the correspondence. I imagined all their secret lives to be as colourful as my own. For was the essence of my age not the buttoning-down of the social self so you were all alone whilst forced constantly to be with others? What monsters and wonders lurked below the surface of that realm was another question. This standard flower seller, that standard lawyer, or this beggar… Who were they when nobody was looking? Some small things I collected; others I sold to the bone grinders and fat-melters who made fertiliser and soap from the gristle of other people's lives.

All there was on my person when I left my father's home was my fiddle, an empty notebook, ink, pen, a copy of Tennyson's *In Memoriam* that Arthur had bought me, a bottle of whiskey, a change of clothing, cannabis and cocaine extracts (to manage different parts of my creative flight), leftover faerie mushrooms from the sabbat, a deck of playing cards, any money I had managed to save, and enough laudanum to kill a particularly drug-resistant oxen.

I had time to be alone with my body in the guesthouses I stayed in. I discovered that my skin was alive all over. I felt more sorrow than shame for my aching, tender, untouched flesh. I stripped off all their words of abuse from it. Peeled off their disgust like a false skin, as Clara had removed hers. I didn't need it. Instead, I sought understanding of the mystery that lived in my hips. Memories of Arthur's touches and kisses—mingled with the thought of the act they would kill us for—were more than enough to lift me into sensory transport. After I'd discovered myself, I replaced the bridge in my violin with a flatter more appropriate for fiddling than classical. If I was to play rowdy music at taverns and whorehouses for money, it was no work for a virgin, you understand? Folk music like that is salty and carnal at its root. I had always felt like a middle-class boy pretending to be Folk when I played the fiddle, until that moment when I changed my bridge and crossed it, thin as a hair…

I started wandering around the docks at night looking at the sailors, as if I was picking goods at a market. Using the tricks Martha had taught me to work out if one of them was like me, I tried to find myself a man who didn't matter to me. I thought about Charles Fletcher, the boy my father had mentioned who'd formed a crush on me as a child without my understanding. Immediately I banished the thought, because even though we were no longer close, he still

Of the Heart

mattered to me too much to put him in danger. He was a decent young man with likeable quirks. The man I picked would have to be somehow less than that.

For money, I played music in the taverns at night, or in strange picturesque places like atop a wall near the rivulet. People would put money in my cap, which allowed me to eat enough for survival. When I'd found myself some romantic perch with my fiddle, I'd play sad, old Gaelic tunes that had all the salt tears of the Atlantic in them, calling on the green-grey-glas ghosts of my homeland to pervade the air. In the taverns at night, I'd play reels, or I'd use my fiddle as a violin to sarcastically play something classical before ripping it up into wild Irish music. I seldom spoke to anyone except my instrument. It was part of my eccentricity. I doubt many people knew my name. My life would disappear softly, like thistledown.

There is something liberating about falling from grace. The upper middle-class boys who had tormented me in the past wouldn't dare approach one who had fallen through the invisible social net. They would pretend to not see people like me. So I moved without interruption or hindrance among the dregs of society. There was something about my vagabond fearlessness and the over-heated drug glaze in my eyes that made me immune to real menace. Whilst I was regularly shoved, and people shouted slurs at me sometimes, most of it barely touched the surface of me.

I only got into one serious fight, and the shock of my sudden and unexpectedly fierce aggression ended the encounter in a few seconds. When you make people uneasy, they tend to leave you alone, and the word gets around that you're crazy. I once heard someone describe me as "the mad fiddler." It seems that predators can smell the dangerous unpredictability of a man who has no concern whether he lives or dies, and they steer clear of you.

I watched for some time from below until I saw Arthur move past his new bedroom window. It was harder creeping up at Lebrena than it had been at Fernleigh, now that his family had moved to a different mansion on the other side of Davey Street. It interested me that Mr. Allport Senior would have called the house the Aboriginal word *Lebrena;* it made me wonder if his son was beginning to prevail on him in some areas? Moreton had always taken an interest in the Natives at an anthropological level, including collecting some of their bones. He had not normally tendered them the kind of instinctual respect Arthur did.

RAG & BONE MAN

If anything, the new place was more imposing than the last, constantly moving with family and servants. Through patience and stillness, I had come there unobserved. Turning my collar up against the cold and damp, I stood resolutely without shivering. It was in my nature to be nothing if not stoic when it came to this love. *When it comes to him, I am carved out of diamonds.* Waiting was part of the magic; the pressure that carbon is subject to in the process of becoming adamantine. I didn't mind if I stood there outside his house for hours. I didn't care if it rained on me or the hostile skies bruised me with ice. It would all show up, all that sacrifice, in the tensions my fingers held and released into the music.

When I saw him through the window, I stopped breathing. He had invited me to creep up on him, after all...but it was different watching him now that I was no longer fully an innocent. As I watched him move around in his room through the sheer curtain, my stomach cramped with the thought of the secret touches I wanted to give him. After allowing myself a brief throat-constricting rush of craving, I said a firm *no* to my trembling innards. True love does not seek to endanger the beloved one. The feeling I had was of such pure, blazing service to this feeling that it brought fierce tears to my eyes, such as must come upon the martyr who goes willingly to their terminal glory, robed in light. As well as I could, with held breath, I waited until the best moment before alerting him to my presence.

When the tiny stone pinged on his window, Arthur's response was instant and frantic. To see his reaction ached down into my bones and resounded there like a deep, old sonic boom. How seldom is urgency met with its like? *It would be so much easier to say no to the most vital thing inside of me, had my feelings not been so completely reciprocated.* Within moments, he'd thrown his bedroom window open, and relief was sluicing from each of his pores. He was so emotionally naked in that moment that I experienced the desire to throw my coat around him again, to shield him from the world. I could see he was about to run downstairs to get to me, so I held up my hand to indicate he must stay put. I could see his Adam's apple jump up and down as he tried to swallow his feelings and confusedly sought with his eyes the reason for my request. There was no denying it; I knew as I saw his face through the window that he loved me to the core. I wanted to feel the typical rush of joy at this rare and wonderful reciprocation, but that joy had not been allowed me by the world.

Pointedly, I lifted my violin to my chin and raised my gaze to meet his and undid the two top buttons on my shirt. (Things were about to get warm.) If I couldn't touch him with my hands and mouth in the ways I wanted, I would do him with my music, full of raucous and relentless waves of feeling. With the first protracted note, I'm not sure he realised I wasn't going to play classical violin with my newly altered instrument, but on the second motion of my bow arm, he knew—I could tell in the way he drew his breath in hard. Finally, he realised, at last I'd let him come into the parlour of my secret music.

How open I was before him while I fiddled that wild Irish reel! How utterly naked, despite the physical distance between us… I held eye contact with him. I played it faster with more flourishes than I think I'd ever played anything, and it was all because of that driving intensity in my bones; it was all because of standing in the cold rain and wind, waiting. Over the distance between the window and the ground, I wanted him to feel me. I played until perspiration gathered in the hollow of my exposed throat, and within me there were feelings that smelt like burning horsehair, and strings broke inside me under the pressure of all this life—as well as on the fiddle.

Of course, it was too raw, green, and alive for it to be tolerated for long in this neighbourhood. Morton appeared and shouted at me to go away and be quiet before he summonsed the law. I laughed at him and began to walk a little way off. There was an eerie sense of being at the crossroads. In some folk stories, they talk about fiddling duals with the Devil where he tries to win your soul. Yet, I had a feeling that changelings like me needed to play with human passion before we would be dispensed a human soul in the first place. Perhaps that was what I secretly came there that night to do? Only a human beloved could ever be the judge of your offering.

"Henry!" Arthur nearly knocked me off my feet with his urgency as he met me and dragged me into a hard embrace. "Thank God you're all right… I've been looking for you all day and yesterday! I thought I'd suffocate." It was clear this was no exaggeration, because he was close to overcome as he got the words out. For a moment, I couldn't speak because my throat had thickened, too, with hot, sharp-tasting tears. How good it felt to be in his arms! I thought I might cry out in pain when he eventually let go.

"I thought it best not to be seen around you in public in the daylight now that I'm not respectable anymore."

He held me back from him and examined my face with almost brutal intensity. I found myself thinking of how he said he'd found his Heathcliff of late, probably since he'd cut himself in front of me to demonstrate how Heathcliff loves. This, of course, had all been part of our game where we played in different personas with each other.

"Fuck respectability!" he all but growled through his teeth. "It's just another word for a slow death. Come," he said, taking me by the arm as if I was to have no choice in the matter now that I'd been found but to go with him. "It is beyond farcical that you have not yet been inside our new home. My apologies," he murmured, remembering his gentleman and brushing down my arm where he'd grabbed me. "May I?" he asked, extending his arm to me as though I were a well-born lady he meant to escort into a ballroom.

I raised my eyebrows. "Now? Of all times? I'm covered in…nature." I laughed at the euphemism, and so did Arthur. But I couldn't deny him my arm any more than I could have chewed my arm off at the shoulder. He squeezed my hand as we walked, and I could feel that his palm was sweating.

"I don't care what you're covered in; you are what my senses drink and live off. That music you just made, Henry! You'd defeat the Devil himself on his own instrument! And I am so very proud that you're my friend." I was moved beyond words, but still I hesitated near their rather grand threshold. Arthur came up closer to me then. "I won't let them be rude to you. Nor will I allow you to sleep places where you aren't safe…"

I was already shaking my head and backing away nervously. "I'm fine. I don't need…" *Charity.*

"Please!" he grabbed me, then retracted his hand and pressed his lips together with suffering. "I'm sorry. I don't mean to force you. I just…I can't bear for you to go. I know you will think me weak, or needy, or…"

"I don't think any of that."

"Then *please!* If you won't come inside, I will have to follow you to wherever you are sleeping and linger outside until you let me in, or someone arrests me. I haven't the slightest pride in the matter."

I sighed with capitulation. There was no question of letting him see where I was staying; he'd have had a fit. "Fine," I agreed, letting him lead me out of the world of consumptive, late-night coughing and hacking through the walls and rising damp, and into the splendidly well-lit servant and bustling environs of the Allport family home. Even though I wiped my feet, I felt sure that mossy footprints full of insidious spore-life were greening their way into their parlour and along their hall with my every step.

Arthur gave instructions to one of the servants to have some food brought up from the kitchens for his guest and set about drawing me a hot bath. At first, I made futile gestures of resistance. Was I hungry? I can't even remember. When I sensed the fierce pleasure in service he felt when caring for me, I stopped protesting. He did things for me as if he himself was hungry—hungry to do them. Because I well-understood that feeling of gleaming service instinct, I wouldn't resist. Instead, I stood there with my arms folded over my dirty and disheveled clothing, playing with one shoe with the tip of the other in my awkwardness, watching him run me a bath.

When he was done, he came over to me and slipped off my coat, hanging it up on his coatrack as if my rags were, in fact, still worth worrying about. I flinched when he began to matter-of-factly undo the buttons that hadn't yet been broken from my shirt. He felt the stiffening in my limbs as he went to pull the shirt off and paused. His gaze jumped up quickly to meet mine and search my eyes. Although my heart was nearly in my mouth, I didn't look away. When he slipped the shirt off, his eyes went straight down to my chest and stomach. He must have been able to see how fast I was breathing. Arthur didn't seem uncomfortable, though; he paused to remark on my physique. I felt as though he wanted me to be comfortable and relaxed with this intimacy and was challenging me to meet him there.

"You're so exquisitely androgynous," he murmured, his eyes passing lovingly over my pale flesh. "You appear, like the Witch of Atlas' hermaphrodite, to have the graces of both sexes and to possess the defects of neither."

I didn't know what to say to such an extravagant compliment sent in the direction of my hidden skin, these parts of me that few had ever seen and were in my view a bit emaciated. It was true that I did not possess a great deal of body hair, and my form contained a mixture of hardness and softness, but it had never occurred to me that anyone thought these features desirable. "You're very kind," I whispered.

"Excuse me, Master Allport, I have the food for Master Henry." The servant's voice from outside the door made Arthur start back from me as if he'd been caught in a crime.

"Thank you, Frances. Just leave it on the table." Arthur pulled across a colourful painted screen to give me privacy. I closed my eyes and all but felt Arthur's hands on my waist, coming up behind me to peel up the singlet I wore under my shirt and pull it off over my head, undressing me and grazing the skin under my shirt with his touch, as no one had done since I was a child. In truth, though I wore no singlet anymore and he didn't touch me, I felt it. *Make me human*, I would whisper to him as he did it. Yet, in reality, I slid into the warm water gratefully, despite this fact. I had modest and disciplined expectations when it came to the scraps of happiness I'd be allowed access to in this life. My skin where his fingertips touched my collarbone was still singing; such things were small jewels, pearl-like mercies and moments of stunning clarity that I hid away in the secret bone cages inside my heart chambers.

"I made sure your father didn't notice me slip in and out of the larder," Frances added more quietly, in a conspiratorial tone.

"God bless you; you're a woman of depth and substance, Frances. I've always seen that in you. I'm forever in your debt!"

You could almost hear her blush from behind the screen. I had an inkling based on her accent and station that Frances had never received such extravagant compliments from a gentleman before. "Oh, Master Allport, what a silver tongue you have… You say the sweetest things!" I rolled my eyes. "I brought up this clean towel for Master Henry. Get the poor boy dry and fed!" The servant swept back out, leaving us alone.

Arthur left the door to his room door ajar and busied himself with picking out clean clothes for me. I now saw the subtext in this behaviour that I would have missed only a month earlier. Behaviours that had once seemed incidental—such as the screens and the doors left partly open—I now knew were to protect us from being accused of wrongdoing.

"Laying it on a bit thick out there, weren't you?" I asked dryly, as he entered the space to present me with the clean towel.

He laughed; it was his soft, husky laugh that started in the back of his throat and told tales of adult knowledge. "Only a little… She's genuinely sweet."

I looked at him with raised eyebrows until he got up and began to busy himself again as if my silence had refuted him, never coming close enough to plainly see my naked flesh. Not like he did when he taught me to swim when we were boys. "Well, I do and say what I must, Henry, to protect that which matters most."

"Mother, this is my dearest friend, Henry Callaghan."

For a brief moment, Mrs. Allport condescended to glance in my direction before looking back at her son with blatant adoration and indulgence. Eventually, she came back to me. "So, you're the famous Henry my son has been talking about nonstop since he was ten?" She was a small woman. Dark, and much like Arthur's, her facial features were fine and attractive. Still, there managed to be something where time had pinched her face around the mouth that changed the overall effect.

Of the Heart

"Mother—" Arthur blushed a little.

She waved away her son's embarrassment as if he were a child rather than a man grown. Her eye colour was a little fairer than Arthur's and possessed none of his natural warmth. I felt I was being appraised, summed up, as potential food might be measured for the pot. It wasn't hard to tell—she was a wasp or a praying mantis in the way my father was a rabbit and Moses a serpent. "My son is a deeply warm-hearted person," she began to explain to me, as though, somehow, I might have missed this during our substantial decade as best friends. "His judgment isn't always the best, but just look at him, would you?" She gave his shoulder an affectionate pat that might be more properly described as a feel. It was odd and over-familiar to my way of thinking, but then, what did I know of mothers? "He gets away with a lot because of his charm."

"I'm standing right here," he reminded her, giving me a look that seemed to mutely say: *this is what she's like all the time, do you see what I suffer?* I looked for some sign that part of him enjoyed her adoration but couldn't find it. My newly attuned instincts around human intimacy told me he genuinely found it uncomfortable.

Mrs. Allport ignored his protest, as she seemed to ignore a lot of things to do with his comfort. I glanced briefly around the room but tried not to take too much interest in my surroundings. I didn't want to appear to be gawping in a graceless manner at their home, but some of the art on the walls was exquisite. I was also very impressed by his grandmother's harp. My gentleman might have bled to death, yet I'd been well-brought up, once upon a time, and my interest in all matters artistic made the Allport household a place of great interest. That person I used to be had the benefit of a classical education, after all—and such a great interest in Master Allport—that some degree of scanning my environment was inevitable.

"What do you *do*, Henry?" she demanded. Seemingly, she had run out of steam with embarrassing Arthur and decided to switch to me.

Arthur didn't give me time to answer. "Henry's a genius," he said. "That's what he *does*. I'm planning to discover him. That shall be my arts patronage contribution to the cultural life of Hobart. Don't you think that's a sign that we've *arrived* as a family, Mother? When we can afford to not only practice but patronise the arts? I want to be part of really laying down a unique arts culture here, and Henry is going to help me."

She sighed. "You know very well that's what I think, because you got all your Romantic notions from me!" she declared with a complacent, self-satisfied smile. "Have you ever heard the story about what I wanted to call him as a babe if Morton hadn't prevailed on the matter?"

"Yes, ma'am." It peeved me that she kept asking me questions and telling me things that suggested I didn't know practically every hair on her son's head. I bit down my hostility.

"So, what manner of genius are you?" she demanded, scrutinising my face as though it should have been obvious to her in some way. "I'm not sure whether I think you *look* like a genius." Her eyes took in my whole appearance critically.

"And what does a genius look like?"

I think Arthur picked up on the thin vein of sarcasm in my voice and immediately rescued me. "Henry's an accomplished poet and musician."

"When you say 'musician,' I hope you don't mean that crazed, wild music someone was playing outside earlier?"

I blinked once and smiled to cover my surge of nationalistic pride and anger. *English bitch.* "I play classical cello and piano, as well as in the traditional style of my Irish family. As someone who can play the violin both in the classical style and as a fiddle, I can tell you that the skill level required is in fact comparable."

"Is that so?" She looked at me with clear distaste for having rubbed her nose in my Irishness, but I didn't care. What did I have to lose now? "Well, you really are very talented, aren't you? And you play all three instruments well?"

"Quite tolerably I'm led to believe, Madame."

"Henry is far too modest," Arthur objected. "He is one of the best musicians in Hobart."

"Hardly an onerous title to maintain," I murmured.

Arthur ignored me. "Especially with his cello... As you know, Mother, I'm no musician, but I have a good ear, and I know talent when I hear it."

"Let me have a look at you." She took my face in her hand as if I were a child she meant to examine. There was certainly no by-your-leave in her words. I was there to be touched, prodded, questioned, and examined in any way that pleased her. I could feel she wanted me to know it, as this was a demonstration of her power. "Far too pretty for a boy," she declared after examining my face. "Somewhat Romantic sort of face, though, suggestive of sensibility and perhaps a poetic gift... Reminiscent of the features of Keats and Shelley." She let my face go with a sigh and turned in Arthur's direction, flattering him with a smile. "I'll have someone make up a guestroom tonight for your genius, and we won't tell your father he was ever here. Understood?"

Of the Heart

As her bustle turned adamantly in our direction, it swooshed her gowns along the shiny floor, as if her whole costume were a broom sweeping away one's shadow—and with it your luck force.

"Never mind, Mother. I can settle Henry myself."

She paused and turned to glance back at her son pointedly. *"I insist."*

I was hustled out the next morning, before Mr. Morton Allport could see me. Also before "Master Allport" and myself could be alone together long enough for me to tease him out from under his buttoned-down waistcoat prison. There was only a little flash of Arthur allowed to ripple through his home-face. It came in the form of paper he pressed into my palm while he shook hands with me upon leaving. Even though the stoic gesture had been done beneath his mother's watchful eye, neither of us had any problems passing a note during a handshake without her awareness, even though I hadn't known to expect one. Such was the natural physical harmony between our bodies. I believe there are some married couples that could not anticipate the other as I could Arthur, and he I.

As I walked away down Davey Street with my backpack on, I unfurled his note. Life was too precarious now for the deferral of pleasures, great or small. I would gorge immediately any intimacy I received from him, in case I was dead ten minutes later and didn't get to read his letter first. The dreams of my own execution hadn't ceased. It was hard to live any other way but in the moment when you gazed upon what appeared the peak of possible mental suffering. What I had seen in Arthur's eyes while he watched them kill me would haunt me and follow me down every blind alley I took in life. The only thing that really mattered to me at that point was finding a way to avoid making it a reality.

I was living moment to moment, so I didn't have to think of the necessity of a future that involved never touching him. Once I would have set out tea and made myself wait for the perfect environment in which to read his note. This one I read whilst walking with a hammering heart.

"Strange friend, past, present, and to be.
Loved deeplier, darklier understood;
Behold I dream a dream of good
And mingle all the world with thee…"

—Lord Alfred Tennyson, *In Memoriam*

RAG & BONE MAN

I refolded the letter and pressed it to my chest. From it, I hoped to drink the fire of his mind that had dried itself into the ink, through my chest wound of unsatisfied hungers. To me, it seemed he said things through the Tennyson quote that could not rightly otherwise be spoken.

"This is enough," I told myself aloud as I walked. "This will have to be enough." Again, the anguish in his eyes during my nightmare lashed my awareness to blood-slick rawness. I shook my head in adamant denial. *I swear to you, my love. I shall not allow it. No matter what I have to do. You will have my heart; some other less precious man, my body.*

The sailor held my arm from behind as he took me up the stairs of The Hope and Anchor. It felt more like I was being led up to the gallows in an arm-lock than into a romantic liaison. Perhaps it was the taint of death that got on us like black mould from the history of the executions only blocks away from our location, which made it hard for us to look each other in the eye? I fancied part of each of us was silently apologising to the other in the case that we turned out to bring about each other's death.

If I'd been taking care of myself, I would have told him not to touch me 'till we were behind closed doors, but I wasn't. I wanted to fall. People saw him marching me up the stairs like a captive of war, claimed as booty and being taken up to the captain's room to be shamed. I wanted them to see what this man was going to do to me, and I wanted it to feel dirty. Part of me hated him, after all. It wasn't his fault he wasn't Arthur, I knew. I'd picked him primarily for this fact. No doubt I wasn't me to this random sailor either. I wondered, as he pushed me through the door and into the room, if I was not also some other boy he'd longed to get beneath him, back when life and love were new, and he was too? When he still knew how to blush, as I did now, when he turned me around to face the wall, rather than risk seeing my eyes.

He came up behind me and pressed me with his body against the peeling wallpaper. It smelt musky with hops and old ghosts trapped inside the walls. Knowledge jumped about between our bodies and told a story of sharp mutual denial. Now there was just the fight with the clothing in the way and the revelation of my awkwardness with intimacy.

"You ain't never done this before, have you?" he asked me in broad cockney. There was an irritated tenderness about his tone, as though it was against his better judgment that he asked at all. I tried to focus on the cockney accent Arthur could put on.

I shook my head.

He sighed heavily at the hassle of it, but at the same time, he reached around my body and caressed me in a way that seemed to belie the message of irritation. "Just relax," he half-reassured, half-commanded me. "I'm not going to hurt you."

And he was right; he didn't hurt me. No more than I wanted him to, at any rate. Yet, at the last minute, some rogue impulse shot from my heart and put up a brief involuntary struggle, right before he pierced me and all thought drained from me. My body gave so easily and sweetly, it was almost as if it wasn't a sin at all. The hungry goblins in my flesh didn't seem to care who he was or what the law said.

"That's the way… Nice!" He was encouraging me and laughing good-naturedly at my yielding responsiveness. "You weren't half in need of good cock, were you, eh?" I closed my eyes tightly and imagined he was Arthur. Once I built up the visualisation of it, I felt fire shooting up my spine, and my legs jerked involuntarily like the hanged man's heel kicks out at the air in the dance macabre. In a hot, wet series of spasms, I was birthed as a human, part of the red-bleeding, baptised in sweat, semen-stained, multiple-armed, many-headed, seething mass of humanity.

Like an infant, I was shivering and cold and never more alone when cut free from my neck-wrapped umbilicus. The other man, whose name I never knew, gave me a firm pat on the back, like they do to get the infant crying, redolent of rough-tenderness. "I hope that was all right for you?" Perhaps it was the way I was hugging my knees to my chest with my arms and hadn't pulled my trousers up, as I continued to sit on the floor, that made him hesitate. "You get what you needed?"

I nodded without looking at him. I wondered what the protocol was? Did I say thank you? Yes indeed, you have served your purpose adequately, and my tension is alleviated? Or was I meant to feign some sort of polite affection?

He crouched down in front of me and turned my chin to face him with his hand. "Hey, you all right? Didn't break you or anything, did I?"

I shook my head again.

"You're a pretty lad. All right. Well… See you around the place then, I suppose?"

I nodded. My newborn humanity felt too raw and preverbal for words. If I'd had words, I might have grabbed his arm before he left and asked him to tell me who I'd been for him, when my body was underneath his? Whose face had mine transformed into for a few seconds when our eyes first met down at the docks, and I'd seen his pupils dilate? Whose name had he tried not to say as he pounded me anonymously? Maybe I could have told him who he'd been for me; we might have drunk our sorrows out and even cried a little, at how broken and ugly life really was. But I didn't do any of that, because I'd gone out looking for the man who didn't matter.

I had hardened myself to the thought of other humans watching me die without pity or remorse, having lived through it in almost nightly dreams. To have them instead jeer and throw things at me. I expected it to be a bit like dying and being bullied at the same time. Bullying was relatively familiar, though I wasn't sure what to do to prepare myself for death. I had hardened myself as best I could for it, but sometimes in my nightmares, I was forced to watch the other man I'd lain with die first. It hurt a lot less if we didn't have drinks together first.

13

Poets are always changelings. Like the cuckoo in the nest of their century's discourse, their voice comes at you slantwise and knocks you off your guard. Their numinousness, their ambience—or to use a more modern term, their *vibration*—has the timbre of another time, an alien quality. As if the past or future both were looking back in on you somehow. The changeling myth belongs to all of us outsiders who see with Other eyes, not only to those whose birthplace hugs the pounding Atlantic in her thighs. My Other eyes, ears, nose, fingertips…all of my mixed and cross-purposed senses that were always running over the top of each other with a kind of guileless haste, all of them *knew*. To the eyes of normal folk, I was a deviant, sleeping in his own artwork and drug-use remnants, occasionally breaking out in an unexplained sweat. It was probably the diseases of the common folk starting up in him already. They would have crossed the street to get away from me to avoid the miasma of the consumption I was sure to carry.

The goblin man had crept up into my hideout, dragging me up the stairs of the cheap guesthouse and through the complicity of my human flesh, already partly of the goblin nature, injecting me with his venom. Now, as I sweated and twitched, my dreams were absinthe-fumed, murky green, and venal. My spirit did combat inside every cell in my body, fighting for my life against the smallpox spirit and the yellow cholera mist. I fought for the right to the inviolate light I carried in my heart, sparked from a pure source in the land far across the Westward seas. In my body, I had to convert this poison—the diseases of my age—and make them work for me, or I would be consumed by the great spreading nothingness of modernity.

Sometimes, while I fought for dominion over myself, I would wake soaked in dank sweat and scrawl words that came up from the dreg places. The words crawled out of laudanum bottles and the wet tunnels of the city that dripped with chthonian echoes. I was down near the stews, you see. Near the tail-end of the rivulet in Wapping, just above where the abattoirs voided the blood and shit-tubes of animals straight into the life-vein of the town. The words were my rudder among the echoing cobblestones, dog carcasses and fetid dreams of poverty. When I was conscious, I stared at the words as if they could nail down reality. As if the shifting threads—the code behind the universe's apparent outward form—were being nailed into place by my words at a node point.

Love. It was a single word that kept circling around me like a hyena who senses the pre-carrion phase. Words were not always comforters. Some test you to your edges. Some are thylacines with their ribcages showing through their skin and their jaws disjointed, wide, ready for when the fight's gone out of you. *What does it mean to say you are in love?* Do we, by this implicitness, admit that Love has eaten us? Like Little Red Riding Hood's wolf devours her in the form of her grandmother? That she's a being which we enter and move around inside of once we've pierced her mystery? What if everyone else really knows this already deep down? This hint of archaic worship of Love as a goddess? A goddess who demands her sacrifices. And what worth has she today in the eyes of the mercantile men masturbating over their capital gains, the sanitised and respectable women flushing lysol up their cracks to be closer to godliness?

Much less than fear, it would seem. We lived in an age where you could be rewarded—if born in the right place at the right time—for coming up with psychologically crueller ways to punish another human being for petty theft, but you could be put to death for an act of love. Love would triumph in the end, I told myself. Just like she would triumph in my flesh and bloodstream, putting to flight the rising sickness, bringing the demons of my age to heel with a well-cut phrase, and always reaching for life and yet more life. Such thoughts and wild dreams were wracking me with wonder and dread when something papery hit me in the back of the head.

"Wake up, Henry," a familiar female voice said. "I've been reading the poetry you've written." It turns out it was my own work I was being hit over the head with. "You are indeed a genius. A dirty, undisciplined, unkempt, substance-addled genius." Her words of loving abuse were punctuated by another hit on the head with the papers. And I hate you."

"Thank you," I muttered, without lifting my head from the table I used as a desk where I'd fallen asleep upon yet more of my own writing.

"Don't thank me!" she exclaimed, throwing the poems down on the table beside my head. "I just had a pimp try to recruit me to his team of lady companions for only the very best class of gentlemen on the way up the stairs, just so you're fully cognisant of what type of establishment you're unconscious in! I shudder to consider how you're living and what you're subsisting on." I

OF THE HEART

could hear her voice thicken with emotion here, and I sat up, rubbing my face with my hands to try to clear my head of goblin seed.

"You shouldn't be here," I managed to get out, a frown of concern forming on my face. I began to shake my head as the full realisation of what she was saying was kicking in. I got to my feet suddenly. "What are you doing, Clara? You can't be here in a place like this, with someone like me…without a chaperone."

When my blurred vision began to clear with some blinking, I was able to see she was standing in front of me with tears in her eyes and her feet planted defiantly. "Why not? You are!" she wept. "You've ruined both of us! You're my fiancé, and now…"

I held my hands up. "We are not engaged, Clara! We are…we were… stepping out."

"But we agreed to marry! And I am not going to let you go this easily!"

It felt like my heart was caving in on itself, and through the wound torn in me by my new humanity, sorrow flooded in. I moved towards her and took her in my arms, tucking her weeping little face in against my neck. In my arms, I rocked and soothed her. "I'm so sorry," I whispered into her hair, tears stinging my eyes. "But I just *can't help it*…" She didn't ask what it was I couldn't help, and I didn't elaborate. It was better that way; when it wasn't questioned, it stood for all the things that had led to this moment that were not my fault, but the whole world wanted me pilloried for.

"It didn't need to be this way, Henry!" She hit me on the chest with some intensity with her little fist. I wanted to take her little fist in my hands and kiss it, even though it had lashed out at me. I wanted to kiss it for the life-instinct it showed, the fight she had in her, to fight with everything she was for the path she'd hopefully carved.

The tears that were standing in my eyes slowly coursed down my cheeks. But they were not tears of sadness. They were tears of fierce pride and defiance and fiercer love. *How hard I could fight for this—for those I love—if it was anything else I had to fight against other than myself.* "We could have made a life together! Father will never let me marry you now… You've ruined everything!" She wept furiously.

I nodded, accepting the punishment of her words. It seemed everyone agreed I deserved it; who was I to disagree? "I'm sorry, Clary," I whispered. I don't know what I was sorry for.

Sniffling, she took up residence on the chair I'd recently vacated, moved aside some empty laudanum bottles and cleaned her face with her handkerchief.

"Remember when you were still an invalid, and I brought one of my sister's old dresses around and dressed you up? You thought I was just being silly to cheer you and get you out of bed, but really, I wanted to see you like that."

I frowned faintly, but I didn't interrupt her. The change of topic was confusing to me, and I wasn't sure I understood why she'd gone from yelling at me to remembering this snippet of sentiment.

"When I'd managed to convince you and done your makeup, I remember looking at you in the glass over your shoulder and thinking you were the most beautiful, strange, sexless being I'd ever seen. When I looked at you, my own features seemed too small and dainty somehow, my body too squat, as if you weren't trapped in a single sex like me. I always knew, Henry... And it wasn't *him* I wanted... Not really. I love Arthur; he has a beautiful soul, and his love for you is admirable, pure, and noble... But it was always you."

What I wanted to say I had no words for. If it had felt wordable, I'd have told her that I never felt so free with her as when she treated me as if I were almost another girl. I wanted to say that she didn't need to choose between the two of us anyway; part of me *wanted* her to want Arthur the way I did. Because perhaps then someone would understand—perhaps then someone could look after him in those ways?

Something old and strange inside told me that I would find new ways to love and understand him by being part of his love for this girl who had in turn become part of our love. I imagined him able to do the things for her that I might not be able to do, and it made me smile. All the while, I thought about what it might be like to touch her in the gentle ways that a girl might touch another girl, as I doubted I could do to her the female equivalent to what the goblin sailor had done to me.

"Which is a pity for me," she concluded. "Because you told me the truth the first time you ran into me at the market; you don't like girls."

I frowned. These words stung more than the ones that had been yelled at me earlier, and they were brutally ironic under the circumstances. How could I tell her I was having improper thoughts about sharing her with Arthur? You couldn't explicitly tell a well-brought up girl something like that.

"I do like girls," was all I said instead.

"It's too late for those kind lies, Henry. This is me. I know you. Arthur is in quite a state, by the way. He's beside himself ever since you last left his place and didn't tell him where you were staying. He's combing his way door to door looking for you. But it seems I anticipated you better than he did on this one. I guessed that you'd be actively trying to ruin your reputation."

OF THE HEART

I closed my eyes. The pain that coursed through my chest felt like ice water had escaped into my interior, snow-melt water from up high on the mountain, pushing in at my ears, my nose, my mouth. "God…" It truly was a prayer rather than just an exclamation. *Devil, Angel, One who is more complete than me, I pray you, have mercy on him.* "Please let him know I'm all right. I just—" *It just hurts so much to look at him now.*

"You just *what?*" she demanded, getting to her feet and putting her hands on her hips. "You're just going to break his heart?"

Maybe if the poison hadn't been in me, fighting me for each breath, if I hadn't have been coming down off a few substances, I might not have fallen apart the way I did. Bursting into tears was the least of it. I couldn't stand; I could barely breathe. Clara was on the floor with me, stroking my back and nursing me through the fit of panic and grief that threatened to crush my ribcage. "Oh, sweet boy," she whispered, as if she had only suddenly realised how deeply I felt all this. No doubt there had been no warning in my facial expressions. My whole life, I had been taught everything was better in than out, and now it seemed, when I'd obeyed, it was assumed I didn't feel. "Breathe… It's going to be all right."

But it wasn't. All I could pray was that, whatever price there was to pay for loving as we did, it would fall on me and not Arthur. "I can't stand it," I sobbed over and over again as I rocked. "I can't stand hurting him, and I don't know how to stop it!"

Clara sighed, as if she were older than her years. "Darling… Arthur is an intense personality—like you are. He feels everything so very deeply, and he *wants* to. He doesn't feel alive unless he's in a tumult of ecstasy or heartbreak. You will never keep a man like that away from his pain. Sometimes, I think he likes it as much as you do your opiates. Yet, he is not passive in his suffering, Henry. Even now, he is organising to move from his parents' home. He has things in boxes—or his servants do at any rate!" She laughed. It was brittle. She was trying to crack a joke, but I was a long way from a smile. I felt a chill going into my bones that reminded me of the saying the old Irish folk have about the wind blowing over the feet of the graves.

"When he's settled, he wants you to go to him at the place he's taken at Sandy Bay; he's going to send a carriage for you. There's an important conversation he needs to have with you."

Rag & Bone Man

Darkened inside to make our rendezvous more inconspicuous, the carriage Arthur sent to me felt like the death coach. Emily Dickinson would write of that same vehicle, and her stanzas well describe the mood of journey to Sandy Bay that night:

> *"Because I could not stop for Death,*
> *He kindly stopped for me;*
> *The carriage held but just ourselves*
> *And Immortality.*
>
> *We slowly drove, he knew no haste,*
> *And I had put away*
> *My labour, and my leisure too,*
> *For his civility."*

The sound of the horse's hooves scraping and clopping the road seemed louder than normal in my ears, muffled as my senses were by the thick velvet night. My heart seemed to keep a syncopated rhythm with the horses' feet. Every hair in the grave-pit of its pore stood to attention. My hair—that mammalian leftover, that inborn presence of ancestral wisdom—knew my fate was to be decided that night. Some instinct in me, which always chose hope and reached for the light even when doom was certain, allowed me hope. Hope is the finest, most excruciating of porcelain scalpels. Unlike despair, which cuts deep and takes our breath away like a punch, hope keeps all his cuts near the surface, where the rich nerve endings are, precisely flaying one layer of dermis from another. Yet, I chose it. For the last bit of the journey, I allowed Venus to awaken the angel's lust in me, of the type that spawns the mandrake.

I envisaged—though I knew it was covered in *no, cannot,* and *mustn't*—that he was bringing me to his home to say we would run away together. In my mind, he told me he couldn't wait anymore, and as soon as we began kissing, helpless hands were tearing away ties and tight buttons. Finally, my bare skin and mouth were on his. So totally did I give myself to the fantasy of it that I no longer cared where the carriage was taking me. As Emily concluded of the death coach experience:

> *"Since then 'tis centuries; but each*
> *Feels shorter than a day*

OF THE HEART

*I first surmised the horses' heads
Were towards eternity."*

The driver's face and arms were made of bone. In my mind, Arthur kissed me. *Say I'm weary, say I'm sad, say that health and wealth have missed me, but always add that he kissed me.* Ah… But my words are running together with those of others now. That's what happens when you start to die; all the hard edges of your individuality wear away like holes through a hag stone. With it, what was unique about your voice is sucked up into a vortex of rushing sound that clammers with the static force of the spoken and unspoken words of millions.

It is not without meaning that I haven't attempted to render any of my own poetry here. Though I could, if I wished, show you that I really am all they say I am in that department. I could write strong poems and insert them here, but they would not be *the* poems. The ones that I wrote are lost, along with the unique edges of my voice, the hands that wrote them, and the voice that spoke them aloud into the silent, screaming air. And that is as it should be: the tension of it, the unspeakable unfairness and pain of it that cries out to heaven (so it seems) for retribution and justice… That very tension carries the rich fruitfulness of blackened sacrifice. It is the black manna that will fertilise the next chapter, and so I offer it up freely: the hushing of my voice. For the greatest and most courageous sacrifice for love is never merely giving your life; it is to, when necessary, remain silent. My poetry, which can only be imagined, booms in the unspoken, sacrificed to the abyss, reverberations seething on down there, and…well…they change things.

We walked inside in near-darkness, the polished wood floorboards loud under the hard heels of our shoes until we reached one of the long hallway carpets. I stood quietly looking at him while he closed and locked the front door. The place seemed empty of servants; the only sound when he stopped moving was the ponderous tone of a grandfather clock puncturing the stillness. We moved towards each other in a harmony of fierce agreement. He held me for a long time. It wasn't frantic like before, but long, hard, and deeply fathomed. It seemed that with his chest alone he conveyed to me wordless secrets. In his arms, smelling his skin again and feeling the warmth of him through his waistcoat, my want of him crested over my head like a wave at the beach. My resolve faltered so that I doubted, had he initiated greater intimacy, if my will would have been equal to resisting it. In my mind, I recalled when I'd been struck by such a wave at the seaside in childhood and forced down—down for the count against the sandy floor, sand and salt stinging in my eyes, ears, nose, and mouth. I was there again. The same wait for the crush of it to be over, the same bursting lungs, and the sense of my own comparative weakness in the grip of a titanic force of nature. *I can't breathe! I can't breathe!*

"I can still fix this," he murmured as he released me. It wasn't an accusation like Clara's words had sounded to me (not that anyone could blame her, for she was as helpless in it all as I). There was nothing but tenderness, protectiveness, and the grimness of a man who knows he goes up against a strong enemy when it comes to a fixing.

"How?" I whispered.

"I'm so sorry; please take a seat through here. I haven't even shown you inside properly." He cleared his throat and began to light some candles on a side table. Unlike mine who was naught but bones, Arthur's inner gentleman was still kicking for air. "I've forgotten my manners."

"Forget them then." My voice seemed to cut the air. With its abruptness, our eyes met. The air palpitated with fizzing life. For a few moments, the thylacine was in Arthur's eyes, and they were reflecting back to me the burning ridgeway. A wild power was making a play for him at desperately high stakes. His gentleman was under threat.

"I can't. I have to…" He cleared his throat; the inner battle seemed to be fought somewhere around his Adam's apple. "I have to hold on…to things like that, so that I have some power to protect you, if… If the worst were to happen. You know how important my legal connections could be… Isn't that what you need from me, Henry?" His voice was almost a whisper. The mellow-pulsed ticking of the grandfather clock in his front room was the only sound in between our words. "Above all else, you need me indomitable, do you not? Is that not what I'm meant to be in your fairytale? The hero? The faerie knight who saves Una from the dragon?"

I smiled wanly. "'Oh what can ail thee, knight at arms? Alone and palely loitering? The sedge has withered from the lake and no birds sing…'"

"'I met a creature in the meads, full beautiful, a faerie's child…'"

When he used the gender-fractured Keats quote to answer me back, the floor seemed to drop away from me. I knew I was looking into Arthur's eyes, but I was also looking into the eyes of my devil at the same time. The threads spun out all around me with dizzying fractal complexity. I bit my bottom lip at what I saw. Neither of us moved a muscle, for we sensed the frayed rag-and-thread-skirt of Hard Fate brushing up against us. This was not the green gown of Dame Fortuna, who scatters coins, hearts, and free kittens in her wake. No, this was the haggard visage—she who hides under her hair and pushes to the front from time to time.

"There's death waiting for us down all of the paths," I whispered. It seemed my breath turned to vapour in the fast-chilling air. Perhaps it was because Arthur had forgotten to put a log on the fire for a while. Yet, the chill pattern of it rising between us seemed far more sinister. "It's all around us, on every side... Some are worse than others..."

"I know," he murmured back, and I could hear his voice crack even though he swallowed hard. "I feel it. I'm going to fight anyway."

Slowly, tenuously, with every *no, mustn't,* and *shalt not* repeatedly beating me across my open palm with a cane, I extended my hand to him across the space between us. Every one of these blows that had been landed upon Arthur's hands by his father—and upon other people like me all around the world (that continue still)—made my fingers tremble like leaves seeking sun. Once I had extended my hand towards him, wrist upturned in self-offering, it was clear what I meant in doing so, and there was no taking it back. It was the same wrist I'd cut into in the past and let blood to try to release this feeling. It was different to how I'd ever reached for him before in our lives, and he felt it. He must have.

Arthur stared at my hand, blinking several times, his breathing quick like when he'd run to my house. An battle was being fought in his bosom of which I could only see the outward manifestation, but it seemed to strain and stretch and fight with fists inside his tight buttons. Tears formed in my eyes as my fingers extended out into the chill air, blindly seeking to know if there would be mercy, utterly exposed if there was not. Faintly, with a deep meaning expressed in his eyes, he nodded to me in response to my unasked question, but he did not take my hand. "First, I must tell you—"

My hand shot back down like a sparrow knocked out of the sky by the stoop of a falcon, so total was the shut-down. Silence fell. The ticking had stopped in the background. Even though I tried to compose myself and hold onto his nod, I had to turn my head away. "Tell me what?" My voice was so small in the air, it was barely audible. Still, the dermis-scouring hope injected her thorns and hooks into me. I had not known such pain was possible, as to hope for him to say he wanted to be with me and fear he would not.

"I've asked Clara to marry me." I'd like to say it was like a blow, but really, it felt totally numb at first as all large injuries do, while our brain processes the shock. After a few seconds, I placed my hands unconsciously on my stomach, as one who is winded. He was holding his hands up and moving to cross the space between us. But there had been only one true opportunity to cross that space, and it involved grabbing my hand. I could feel the ebb tide taking the moment away from us, secreting it for some other time and place, in a sea cave somewhere, off beyond the horizon. "I hate to have done so without your consent on the matter, but fast action needed to be taken to safeguard reputations and see off rumours."

"The clock's stopped ticking," I muttered, turning the word *clock* over in my mouth because I'd forgotten what it was for a moment. I was afraid my legs would go out from under me as they had at the guesthouse. "No, it has. Listen!"

"Henry," he whispered, drawing closer still. "*Sweetheart...*" It pulled and tugged me from heart to loins to hear him use that lover's endearment for me, but I was too afraid to let hope scrape me open. "Please...please don't pull away. I..." He stopped speaking then, because I did pull away. Not because I wanted to, but because my anxiety levels were rising so high and shrill that I felt I might have to run from the room and check what time the clock had stopped on. "If there's any mercy... God, please, I beg you don't walk out on me and wander off where I can't find you!" I paused at the sound of thick suffering in his voice.

"Why?" I shrugged and laughed hysterically, crossing my arms over myself. "I'm not needed in this equation."

"Rubbish!" Arthur grabbed my arm hard. "Dear God, Henry... Look at me! *Please?* Look into my eyes. You can't really look at me and not see how I need you? There are a lot of things I want in my life, but I *need* you."

I closed my eyes and refused. "You should just marry Clara," I whispered. My words felt like cold silk because all the blood had left my lips. I had gone limp, allowing him to move me around in his grasp.

"This is what I'm trying to say! I'll marry her and then quietly move you in here—"

"What will you tell people I am?" I asked with a sudden strange calm coming down upon me.

"Sorry?"

"What will you tell people? You two will be a married couple, and I will be...what?"

"I don't—"

"A servant maybe? Upstairs, of course; I'm wonderful with linen."

"Henry!" Arthur physically shook me. "I don't give a damn what people call you! To me, *you are all.*"

OF THE HEART

I nodded. On the surface, I appeared very calm. I even reached out for him and soothed him. Oh, how I loved him… I let myself wallow in the stolen joy of it, as if I myself were already a ghost, getting to taste the edges of another person's love story. Touching his face and hair, even calming him with a soft, lingering kiss on the forehead, it was all possible because it didn't matter anymore if he knew—if he felt in my kiss the love the law would kill me for.

In my hands, I felt his stress beginning to release. His eyes closed, and his lips slightly parted with the pleasure of my touch; his voice came out softened, and his grip loosened. "If you but say the word, I will call the whole thing off, if you don't want me to do it," he murmured. "Just tell me what to do." I took his hand in mine, the one I'd extended to him, and because spiritually, he was my responsibility, not the other way around, I tenderly kissed it. Inside, I was gathering my courage together for him. Somehow, for him, I would bear it. I would stand there in the church and smile on his wedding day.

"I trust you," I whispered with my eyes closed. "Do whatever you think best."

That was when she found me. My body was coming up Murray Street and rounding the corner onto Davey; the previous night at Arthur's house was where my heart and mind were. After all, he had not grabbed my hand, but he *had* nodded when I reached for him… It was unreasonable to expect another to understand that my simple gesture had meant I was free-falling through space, nor the leaden plummet in my guts when he didn't catch me. He was a unique being travelling his road, too, I thought to myself as I walked. With his own inner drama and symbolic understandings of life, fully separate from my own. That was the thrill of it, after all, the shadow-play of sameness and difference. I resolved that I would not expect him to somehow jettison himself in favour of entering my story. No, real love called for something more yielding. It called for me to learn him slow and thorough with growing discipline—and for him to learn me fast and crazy, hold-your-nose-before-they-shove-your-head-underwater-style. Our inner narratives would dance together, and we would take turns in whose was leading.

In his mind, perhaps it was I who had failed to understand the significance of something he'd done or said last night? Did his nod mean as many volumes as my held-out hand, yet it fell on my deaf ears? He had called me *sweetheart*…? With a spirit of diligence, I resolved to learn—and surrender my internal and specific vision of perfection in favour of—whatever shape his idea of perfection made when it crashed up against mine, and we made a mess of each other. Both would have to break, and the pieces would find a new rhythm together. I lay my idea of perfection at his feet in offering. *Show me what perfect looks like to you. Tell me the meanings of your internal symbols, and I will learn to move inside those stories of yours, and I will love them as if they were my own.*

As I approached the corner, my steps sped up. Whenever I passed the places where they would hang people, I would try to get by them as quickly as possible. I had this sensation of rising panic around executions that, if I lingered too long, the fictions of my age (the one an era tells you to justify structural violence) might wear thin and snap. If that happened, I'd have to no choice but to act as if other humans were, in fact, being murdered right on the other side of the wall. What other choice would be open to anyone with normal levels of moral sense, if they saw a murder in progress, than to run towards it, attempting rescue? Crying, *Stop! for you murder your brother! Look! Ten fingers, ten toes, two arms that desire to hold and be held, two legs kicking at the air, one neck like yours to feel the burning choke, two eyes to see fear in… Look! For you are killing your very own self. You are but branches upon the Tree of Life hacking at your own roots, damaging your own life spring. In the name of all holiness, hear me!*

"What a fortuitous coincidence."

Because I'd been hurrying to escape the cripplingly wet scent of fear and the tarter aroma of hypocrisy (thou shalt not kill but do unto others as you would have them do unto you; judge not lest you be judged so that you love your neighbour as yourself, because it's easier for a camel to pass through the eye of a needle than it is for a rich man to enter heaven, and let he who is without sin cast the first stone), I didn't see her until I'd heard her voice. When I did, I came to an abrupt halt.

"Mrs. Allport!" In an early, trained impulse, I removed my hat.

"Good afternoon, Master Henry. May I take a little of your time?"

"Of course." I frowned, perplexed by her asking my permission for something I assumed she'd believed her right. When she met my eyes, I saw there concern and even an anguish that I'd not been expecting. She was only a tiny woman in stature, and it was impossible for me, at least it was that day, not to experience a protective sensation.

"I'm worried about my son, Henry. I don't know who else to talk to but you." She blinked a few times, and some tears appeared in her eyes. Immediately, I softened a bit towards her. She might have been a pretentious, social-climbing snob with far less prepossessing intellectual endowments than she believed of herself, but I couldn't doubt her love for her son—and in that, our interests were united.

"Of course... Anything I can do to help him, I would always do... What is... What is bothering you in particular?" It took some courage to get the question out. The boldness of me asking this of someone like her wasn't lost on me. But what else could I do? If there was a chance something was happening for him that I didn't know about, where he needed my assistance...

"Good." She nodded to herself and almost seemed a little relieved. "I'm sure you have heard about his idea for this very non-advantageous match with the flower seller's daughter?"

I doubt she missed my flinch that answered her words. Immediately, I looked away. It was highly unlikely a hanging was actually in progress within the walls beside us, but I fancied and feared there was. How I wished we could have had the conversation elsewhere, but she was blocking my path of escape.

"Of course," I replied. I was working on being able to think about the betrothal without crying. I understood Arthur's reasons and believed in his intentions. I still wasn't quite there yet when she caught me on that corner, and I was immediately blinking very quickly. "He does tell me things, yes."

I could feel her eyes excavating my response to her words with the precision of a stinger. "Well, you must see that this idea is no good for him?"

I shrugged helplessly. "I don't feel it's my place to say."

Tears were forming in her eyes now. "His life will be ruined, and she will be the end of any chance he has in normal society. On top of it all, he tells me he intends to patronise your artistic efforts by having you move into their home once he's married!"

Even though her suffering was certainly a distress of the privileged that few in our society could relate to, it felt sincere enough. This woman loved Arthur and wanted what she saw as the best for him; I couldn't blame her for that. After all, all I wanted in the world was what was best for him too.

For this reason, I crossed the class divide and reached out for a moment to gently touch her arm. It was the lightest of touches, but it was redolent of compassion, and she didn't seem to take it ill. "I understand. He is very wilful. And I think, perhaps, he will never be fully respectable, ma'am, if I may be bold enough to say so?" I'm sure my obvious love for him shone through in my face. "But I don't think he will ever be entirely *disrespected* either. Your son is such a fine man—such a decent, kind man in a world full of indecency... That can take one far in the world. I can't help thinking that the people who matter will see his character, the gossips will grow tired of old rumours, and he will still make good in the world. Honestly, Mrs. Allport, I do believe he could charm the birds out of the sky, and he is very clever, too; doors will open for him because of his talents, not because of the occupation of his wife's father."

She gazed upon my naivety with a stoney calm. After blinking once at my credulity, I thought a faint smile formed around the edges of her thin lips; it felt a little predatory. "Indecency?" she murmured. "It is fascinating to hear you use that word in particular... Almost as if *you* are something decent... As we stand beside the yard where your particular perversion could land my son."

I don't think I moved or emoted very much, but I recall the involuntary way I sucked in my stomach. My shoulders rose a little higher. It was a faintly vulnerable posture that seemed to quietly request her mercy. The blow was so precisely aimed there was no coming back from it, no witticism to cut down my detractor, not a single attempt at self-defence. "Don't think people aren't talking, Henry. People have seen you picking up men down at the wharf, and now they'll talk about my son in connection with you." She stepped closer into my space, and her eyes narrowed. "How do you feel about ruining him? You've known him since he was but a little boy... Do you really love him?"

I looked away from her, and tears stung my eyes, pressing them shut hard for a moment as I nodded. "With all my heart."

She nodded in a businesslike way, as if to say this was as she had supposed. "I love him, too, you see. More than anything in this world. He is the sole joy that's been allowed to me, with a distant, preoccupied husband and little of any affection. Ever since he was born, he has brought light and warmth into our home. I will be damned if I'll let you take him down with you on your plunge into infamy and death. Do you understand me? If I have to, I'll destroy you. I'll destroy your vulnerable, old father, and this flower girl, and anybody else you care about. Remember how Tennyson said that nature is red in tooth and claw?"

I nodded.

"Do you know what happens in nature to something meaning harm who tries to get between a mother animal and her young?"

"But I'm not trying to get between you, Mrs. Allport!" I cried. "I would do anything to protect him."

She sighed as though she meant to be more reasonable now. "I'm sorry to say it. This is harsh in its own way, I know." She patted my arm. "Perhaps you don't have a choice in how you are. But really, when you get down to it, if you can't help it, and if you really do love my son as you say, then you'd go and kill yourself before you risked him ending up in there. Wouldn't you?" To illustrate her point, she pointed towards the hangman's yard. "I know that sounds cruel,

OF THE HEART

because you're too young and naive to know the truth is like that sometimes. You're just not needed here, Henry."

I blinked several times trying to process this casual brutality. I muttered something distractedly to her along the lines of: "I'll give that idea some consideration; good day, ma'am," before putting my hat back on and walking away in a daze.

14

My mother's maternal grandmother was my only non-Irish forebear; she came from the island of Anglesey. Through my mother, I encountered her Welsh stories about the death coach and the Margen, the personification of death. I remember as a child, when she would repeat the Irish stories, she would always end with this Welsh lore fragment. As if it were a strange shell fragment or other oddity from a far-off shore that washed up upon the beaches of Éire, she would embark on her mother's tale with some superstitious awe in her tone. For, just as with she and I, the grandmother had died when she was young, and the stories were part of a small, precious memory bank.

"If Margen wears the horse's skull…"

"The *Mari Lwyd*," my mother corrected me. "The grey death mare of winter."

"If Margen wears the Mari Lwyd face with antlers atop and a black cloak, then that's all a mask, isn't it, Mumma? What does the death mare look like underneath?"

Mother had smiled mysteriously, as if she—so close to death as she was without knowing—had a special understanding of Death's secret face. "Oh, I think he looks like a very handsome man with smouldering dark eyes! But the Welsh say, because they're strange on the other side of the pond, underneath the black rags and bone face, Margen looks like whatever desire looks like for you."

Even at that tender age, my skin prickled at her answer. I understood somehow, in my bones that would not make old ones, exactly what desire looks like. You would need to know this about me for it to make sense when I tell you the anticipation of fulfilment that went with me as I headed to my father's house. Never before had I felt so close to realising the unwordable longing, to quenching the unnamable thirst, to breaking the fourth wall on reality. Once and for all… Everything around me looked so crystalline and edged with light.

I had rested so much of the unknown wanting on Arthur, it had killed me. Knowing didn't help. Too deeply had the dream that was dreaming me sunk its story into him; too deeply had he accepted it in; too deeply had the sense of him imprinted on me as to what love looks like. To sever him from my longing would be the cutting of a main artery. He was not only the chosen path to the divine that had been laid out for me to find in life; he had also been the mirror in which I had been able to catch a glimpse of my own divinity. So, it wasn't as simple as saying: what I was truly looking for lay beyond the horizon and always beyond. No, there are some human truths that are simple and humble. And the simple and humbling truth is that Mrs. Allport had caught me a lucky blow in a fatal spot. With this one perfectly aimed dart at my secret fear of being unnecessary... Who killed cock robin? *It was I*, said the sparrow, with her little bow and arrow.

As I rounded the corner onto Macquarie Street, my heart was quickening with excitement. Fulfilment of the unspeakable felt at hand. At some level, I knew I would have to take action to make my exit from the world as gentle on Arthur as possible, but no part of me was fully able in that mind-state to make a realistic appraisal of his suffering. Whenever I tried, all I could see were flickers of the horrific execution of the man I'd witnessed as a child. Part of it seemed to have been blocked from my memory until Mrs. Allport's reference to the yard beside us began to pull smell and sound shards to the surface. They mixed themselves in grotesque shadow puppetry. Vividly, I recalled the scent of the man's fear as they strapped weights to his feet to make him die faster. My father's voice told me again: "Take note, Henry. For such are the outcomes of unnatural vice." Or at least, that's what I *remembered* him saying now that I knew what it meant. Violently, I pulled away from the memory. In the action of doing so, I pulled away from my moral responsibility to the man I loved, who also loved me.

I pulled away from the weightiness of truth and in the direction of desire. It was time to see under the mask of Margen, and in doing so, I would make silent testament to a love I was forbidden to express with life, leaving only death as an alternative. It seemed to me that if, in returning to Faerie, I was choosing to break his heart, it was only in preference to his heart, followed by his neck. Every now and again, I kept hearing Mrs. Allport's voice: *You're just not needed here, Henry*. They were words that struck into me as witch pins. Something intrinsic in me came here to *serve*, and if it wasn't *needed*, then it may as well return to where it came from.

Having checked that Father wasn't home, I let myself in with my old key. Just as the locks had not been changed, neither had my room. Shrine-like, as if his child had died instead of become a pervert, the room had been left as I'd last touched it. I wondered if he'd told his friends that I had died? But, as I have said, my mind-state did not allow for considerations of realistic outcomes. There was no room inside me for being touched by my father's grief and dedication,

Of the Heart

or to see it as desire for my return. All I could think of was faking the diary entries I would need to convince Arthur that the faeries had taken me back to my always home. Arthur and I had always lived in and out of stories, after all. This would just be another chapter of Our Game. Stories from folklore all the way to the heights of English literature, with our own stories weaved in and out of both. It wouldn't be too hard to build this story-refuge for him. He would be safe there—safer there than with the cruel truths awaiting him along the fate lines where we might otherwise trip the wire.

Even in my half-dead state, I spent some time over it. It was going to have to be convincing, because my beloved was no idiot. This was a fact about him I took pride in. As much as he would want to play along with my last fairytale for him, he would not allow himself if I did anything to give the game away. I smiled nostalgically as I penned it into place; this was a soft love act I performed for him. My words were to be gentle, lingering strokes that trembled forth from beyond the grave to bring him some last comfort. It would be the final chapter in Our Game, started so long ago that it's never really over. I wept a little then, with the idea of this as my final love act. It felt so cold by comparison to the real thing. I was careful not to smudge the ink; if he smelt grief on the pages he would know. It had to be convincing to Arthur that, for some weeks, I had been having encounters with faerie beings that I feared might abduct me. It wasn't really a lie. I had such encounters all the time. Where I should have written—if I was fully truthful—*nightmare*, I instead wrote *vision*.

At the time, I didn't comprehend how futile my efforts to protect him were. You cannot remove from another person their most profound connection in life without pain, no matter how powerful the story you replace it with. Yet, in those days, I didn't know there was any limit to the power of stories. I didn't yet comprehend how beloved I was, or the extent of the joy Arthur took in me; that is much of the tragedy that happens when the world sells you a story that you're worthless. Most of my life's work and my diary were left on the desk in my father's house, along with iron keys, my fob watch, coins, and anything else metallic I had about my person, whether iron or silver. This was part of the story also, these keepsakes. For stories aren't told only in words, but in the placement of ordinary-seeming objects, and in silent hand squeezes given under cover of darkness. The leaving behind of iron would tell both Father and Arthur a story that the nonsuperstitious wouldn't be able to hear.

Wildly, I found myself gazing at the table of items and thinking of how he would find it beautiful in the end, once the shock wore off. It was pure art, after all, and I picked Arthur because he had fine taste in all matters artistic. His connoisseurship could never be in any doubt. He would swallow my narrative as if it were an act of passion. We would be together forever in this story, which he would step willingly into—in an act of self-offering as total as my own. This time, I would hold my hand out again, and at the last moment, he'd seize it firmly in his. Our stories would both burn up then, as soon as our hands met, in a eucalyptus inferno that would leave our love able to grow a new third story that belonged to both of us, out of our grief-blackened, fertile hearts. It would be beautiful and terrible, a destruction that would presage new growth.

Such thoughts were as far from human as my intention to shed my livingness like it was the final strips of material on a weather-worn cadaver. I wanted the good earth, and old stones, and the sweet-singing river to unravel all human things from about my person, for I had found this realm wanting in many ways, and yet, at the same time not wanting me. I left my father's house without even looking back and headed along Upper Macquarie Street with these kind of thoughts spinning me around. The weather coming down from the mountain looked dark and threatening by the time I passed The Cascades. The brewery looked forbidding, like a harsh stone face against the slate sky.

A rough, shambling Wrageowrapper-wind was coming, tumbling through the feet of the mountains after shrieking in the Organ Pipes above. It made me shiver when it touched me, and I leaned in. There was no surprise at all when the rain began—and began hard. My key magical workings had always been in times of rain or thick, damp mists. It had obviously been raining up higher for a while, as the rivulet was quite a river on the day I left behind my human. I followed Strickland Avenue only as long as I needed to before descending to follow the river upstream, where it would be less likely that I could bump into anyone I cared for. It was unthinkable to put anyone through the trauma of finding a body.

All I had on me was roughly enough laudanum to finish off a sturdy racehorse, as I had already consumed the bulk of the oxen-killing dose I'd been carrying around earlier. Luckily, considering my tolerance for the opiate, it was fortunate that I had a few other substances I planned to throw into the mix to help me get where I needed to go. When the rain began to come hard and stick my clothing to my back, it seemed appropriate, and I didn't fight the cold with shivering. I let it begin the work of blanching out the redness of life in me.

Underneath the Margen's bone mask and the ragged black cloak of the shroud-sodden death mare, my desire was waiting. I'd get there best on the black dragon wings of opium sleep. After all, I'd spent so long chasing the dragon, and until now, I'd never really caught up with him. Today, or tonight, or however long the dance and, finally, the twitches of mortality would last, I would see his face. I would unmask the terror that was my innermost being, and no more would I sheathe my light in flesh. It was with eager feet that I left the byways of Man and took to the paths of the forest, the green ones who alone seemed to welcome me. They did not ask me who my father was, or what country he came from, or what church oversaw my baptism; they didn't ask me the sex of the human I most loved, or the nature of the love act I desired with him. Their faceless faces were, like Dickinson's horses, turned towards eternity and not, as Arthur had put it, eaten up with trivialities. The trees were deep in the long dream, their perspective on history wider, deeper, networked. They had seen all of it, and like me, they were both world-weary and eternally fresh.

The rushing of the river drowned all other sound, and I was far from the haunts of man, so I jumped onto a rock and cast my hands up towards the dizzy sky.

"Beloved! I'm coming!" I cried out to the path ahead, grasping onto a branch to steady myself. Having said the words aloud to the bush, stated my intention, there was a further quickening of excitement, which thrilled through to my finger-ends. I clambered down off the rock and picked up my pace along the path, almost running at times. "It's all right; I'm coming back!" I shouted breathlessly. "Hold the door for me; I'm coming back!"

As the rain tenderised my flesh, and the river began to destroy itself against the rocks in a mist tumult, spectres rose. Flash floodwaters were rising that night, as if in answer to my call. I wanted them to take me apart the same way my love for Arthur had wracked and ruined me. Perhaps they were the Minsters of my Madness, these ghosts; if I went inside the humpy, would it be the cannibal tent from which I would emerge a shaman? My mother was walking beside me on the path for a while, dragging her wet dress in the dirt. There was no horror that could appear that didn't have its perfect counterpart inside my heart. There was nothing of the darkness that was foreign to me, and nothing of Death's face any longer held disgust or fear.

"You came to me from a dirty little fly in my drink," the dead woman whispered to me. I only nodded; this was known to me at some level. "Drank that faerie spore down before I realised. Son, you really should have been a daughter; then none of this would have happened."

"I'm on my way home now, Mother," I muttered. Pausing, I took down a little more laudanum and another handful of pills. There were mushrooms from both the shining and the goblin courts inside me. My body had become the poisoner's alembic; I would burn right through it because I knew who I was now. He was a fly—the one that had brought me here—a messenger from the realm of corruption, maggot-rich. His insect tongue had been tickling the petals of the grevillea, and his feet carried the scent of the hawthorn blossom, that to some smells of sex and, to others, like death. Mother had swallowed me down, and I'd grown inside her. When I was out, I witnessed in a way I'd not remembered 'till now, that the faeries had taken my real mother away while she was still lactating and replaced her with faerie stock. The creature who walked at my side was no more my real mother than I was my father's real son.

"Martha the witch saw the corpse light around you right from the start. She tried to warn me."

Memories blossomed inside me in response to Mother's words; I ceased to hunch or shiver against the cold, or even to dislike the water filling up my boots. I walked purposely, shoulders back, like a man on a clear mission. As I walked, my fingers flew open from their clenched fists at my sides. Elf-shot arrows seemed to shoot out the ends like sharp, chilly glass. It was the spite I'd held in for so long. While I walked, the rain itself formed a tunnel of sorts across which my mind could roam all around the streets of Hobart. Even whilst I still negotiated the edges of the rivulet, I was seeing a busy part of Macquarie Street. There, my inner eye focused on the face of one of my past bullies. I saw it all as if I had stepped out into his sight from across the road. Like an apparition, I appeared to him, somehow, when nobody else could see me. Distracted as he was, holding eye contact with me, he didn't even see the horse and carriage.

It seemed like his eyes were still watching me a long time after his body flicked out from the horse's chest like a toy, and his head whiplashed against the cracking pavement. Still holding his far-off vista gaze, as the panic surged around him, I smiled. With a soft, sticky sound like spiderwebs rubbing together, I drank whatever cream there was to be found skimmable in his used-up soul. From the blood of my enemies, I would make my story stronger. As I walked along the Strickland track, the elf-darts from my fingers all found their targets, a consummate symphony of hatred thundering down on the ones who had wronged me. They would hear my music one way or another. Mr. and Mrs. Allport, and all the people who had shoved me, hit me, spat on me, and taunted me as soon as I wasn't respectable. All of them would have their wooden eyeballs turned backwards, and their lips stuck together with gossamer glue.

The black surge of malignancy ebbed at last as Mother and I approached The Falls. She had walked with me all that way, like Our Lady Mary following her son Jesus as he's forced to carry his cross to the place of execution. It seemed she encouraged me to go into the temple and turn over all their money-lending tables; it seemed to me that the faerie woman, who had supplanted my mother since my birth, seemed to understand the nature of my sacrifice. For it was she who led me to the pool before The Falls where The Margen crouched with her horse skull face, where it seemed she gathered water to wash something there in the water—something white and sinister.

The way it moved, at first, seemed impossible and contorted, until I realised the horse-skull was on backward, and I was in fact looking not at the face but at the back of a human being. Slowly, the bent-backed monstrosity turned with her threadbare cloak falling back in the watery puddles—and then all at once in a flourish. I heard male laughter, of the exuberant, impolite sort. It was a wild sound of exultation that echoed in the valley. The puckish entity threw off the cloak; he looked at me as if we were engaged in an ancient game rather than a life-and-death moment. Perhaps this game was a little older than the one I shared with Arthur?

When I stood still and stared at him, he shrugged, as if to say: *Well, if you aren't going to greet me, then...* He took his ease against the faint shelter of the rock ledge and adjusted his hat. For him, it was a fine time for nonverbal camaraderie about the fierce Tasmanian weather, which involved rolling his eyes and looking up philosophically at the rain as if to say, *But what can you do?* He gave the impression he was quite used to being wet and cold. While he took out and lit up a miraculously dry cigarette, I looked over his person rapidly. From the pistols in his belt and the way his oilskin coat had been partially mended with obvious wallaby leather, I suspected he was a bushranger. Perhaps I should have been afraid of him, but the tattoos I noticed on his hands when he lit his cigarette tugged on a memory of something Arthur had told me about a visitation.

There was an easy, supple species of masculinity about his body that was quite out of the ordinary for my era. With his arms folded, he was leaning his shoulders on the wall with his hips allowed to jut forward slightly, as if he were blatantly directing attention to his manhood. Realising I was staring, I looked hurriedly back up at his face. He was examining me quite intensely with his head on one side, as if I were a puzzle of some kind. I drew my breath in when I met his eyes. They were green, and their expression was somewhere between cocky insolence and warmth, but most of all, they were familiar.

"Want to see me shoot a hole through a sixpence while it's up in the air?" he asked with boyish hopefulness.

One of my eyebrows arched involuntarily. I shrugged. "Is that meant to be impressive?"

RAG & BONE MAN

He grinned good-naturedly and closed up the holster on his pistol. Despite a few scars, a mild tooth chip, and a good dose of weather, he really was an uncommonly attractive man, but that on its own has never really impressed me much. "All right, all right. I've got something better," he said, holding up a finger as if to request I wait while he rooted around in his pocket, perhaps looking for loose change. After some rummaging, he came out with a slender whistle, which appeared to be made of bone rather than tin; he lifted it to his mouth. As I followed his hands with my gaze, half-hypnotised, all the hairs on my body stood on end as I fully recognised my devil-angel.

I wanted to rush straight to him, but I know that isn't how Our Game works. It involves a sleep of a hundred years and tangled vines and a waking so slow it's more of a glacial thaw. There's a hero who has to cut his way through the overgrowth of time that's formed around him during his own journey. He feels like he's late for their rendezvous, and he's always both late and right on time. The sound of a clock ticking, and then suddenly coming to an abrupt halt, heralds his approach. Back at my father's place, I fancy that my pocket watch—along with all my iron and metal objects—stopped ticking at this moment, the way the clock stopped for Mother. Breathing in deeply, I held his gaze as he began to play. As deeply as his eyes affected me, I still paid attention to his fingering of the delicate instrument.

I smiled when I recognised he was playing the same reel I'd played on my fiddle under Arthur's window. There were numerous flourishes, which took us away from the signature tune and down an avenue full of melancholy refrains about sorrow that wears holes through stone with its persistence. His working of the humble instrument for so much feeling, together with his technical brilliance, brought tears to my eyes. It was all I could do not to tear the instrument out of his mouth and shove him up against the stone behind him, before all but forcing him to take my tongue in his mouth. I imagined how he'd laugh in that crazy way of his, as if me trying to push him around was nothing short of adorable. He'd bring out all my fierceness and open a tender artery in me, which would never stop gushing.

In his eyes, I saw that same feeling reflected back at me, 'till I couldn't tell whether it was my desire or his I was seeing. The patience in the gut of his wolf glimmered as a lust dance held a big glut in check for greater satisfaction at some later time. He was a thrill-seeker who'd lived for hundreds of years, and in so doing learned how to best time his thrills for the ultimate rush of the century. When he finished playing, he lowered the instrument and raised his eyebrows. "Impressed yet?"

OF THE HEART

"You're Welsh," I observed, to avoid saying the truth, which was that I was deeply impressed. "Like my mother's grandmother." Though I've always struggled to lie, I am very good at truth evasion.

"*Yr wyf Cymraeg,*" he agreed with a nod. "But I move around a bit; you might say I'm a traveller, an everywhere-man. Part of a hidden company of poets and weirdoes. They call us faerie men, hobs… I'm Robin Goodfellow, but I've had so many names, you see: devil, outlaw, saviour, hey-you, hob-man, bush-ranger, puck, and get-the-hell-off-my-lawn." He doffed his hat to me. "At your service," he added with a wink.

I frowned. "Well, you're very charming, but I still don't remember how I came to know…someone like you?"

"Can't help good luck, I guess?"

I raised my eyebrows sceptically. "Quite. Now, can you remind me what my proper name is?"

He laughed and then took a final, long drag of his cigarette before discarding it. "Gods, you harden my manhood when you're posh." I stared at him in partial incomprehension until he laughed harder at my naivety and incredulity. "It's a shame you didn't wear the apron today, that one you bake in at home? I would have liked to have abducted you in *that*."

"What's happening?" I whispered. His knowledge of what I wore in my own kitchen was unsettling. For a moment, it felt like I was hearing him through water in my ears. There was an ill feeling washing through me, a cold ripple of nausea in my stomach. It was the first time I'd been aware of having a stomach or being wet for quite some time now. Perhaps it wasn't only me but the glamour he'd cast upon me that was taking on water? When I looked back at my devil, there was a sudden sorrow in his face. He was achingly beautiful when his eyes deepened with sadness. There was a depth there as profound as the Atlantic. He pressed his lips together with empathy. "I'm just trying to make the best of a bad circumstance and keep you calm until it's over. I can't bear for it to be ungentle…"

Immediately, I knew he'd been keeping me busy with his music and his offers to shoot holes in coins because he didn't want me to look behind me. His glamour wasn't quite strong enough to hold my mind inside its confines. When I swung around, I saw my body lying face-down in the pool of water, floating. With a cold jolt on the chin, I knew all the way through my bones; I felt the fall into the water and the cold rushing into me that was becoming my cause of death.

I swung back around to look at him. "Am I dead?"

He shrugged, still leaning casually against the stone wall. "I don't know," he said, making a gesture with his hands as if to explain a fateful circumstance that could go either way. "How dead do you want to be?"

I spent so long looking at my abandoned body floating on the surface and not moving, all logic said I was dead.

"What difference does it make?" I murmured without once looking away. There was something magnetic about the scene. "I've been down there for too long now anyway… Even if I wanted to… My brain could be damaged."

Without warning, the everywhere-man tapped on the surface of the fourth wall with his finger. The air made a sound as if he'd touched a lucid screen, and everything froze around us. Slowly, I looked about me at the raindrops held in the air where they no longer moved to fall. Everything except the angel-devil and I had paused. "That will give you some time to think about it," he said, still leaning on the rock and seeming immensely casual about this bending of reality. "Come here," he said, moving towards me. Although nothing around us moved, the frozen state of things did not seem to apply to me, as I was able to step closer to him. When I did, he reached out to me and drew my forehead against his. His fingers felt calloused and rougher in texture than Arthur's. He did it just the way I had once done with Arthur. For the first time, I fully understood the chain of influence I was a part of. *We are part of an unbroken circle of hands reaching out to each other and hands catching each other, sparks of fire jumping from body to body, from forehead to forehead.* "Let me show you," he murmured. Immediately, a great wall of fear like a tidal wave of light coming down on me crashed into my brow.

"I can't stand the strength of it."

"Then I'll give you some of mine," he told me firmly, refusing to relinquish his hold on me. "I can unbind you from restrictions of time and place."

For a moment, I was passing through a nebula of such power and brightness I was blinded. Then, just as abruptly, I was in a room with Arthur and Clara. It was apparent that they couldn't see me, and that I was somehow a silent witness to their conversation. Although unseen, my being was mingled and mixed with Arthur's sensory awareness somehow, so that I almost felt as he felt, tasted the tea he was drinking, felt my tie was choking me to death. My fingers fiddled with it in a way that was generally far more like me with my clothes than Arthur with his.

"Why didn't you while you two were alone together here?" Clara was saying; it was clear they were talking about something that felt awkward to them both. "I mean…I know you actively *see* girls… With Henry, were you afraid you *couldn't*? In the heat of the moment?"

OF THE HEART

Arthur shook his head immediately. He placed the cup down on the saucer. I could feel his hands were slightly shaky on the teacup. Something had rattled him already, and he didn't know what. His palms were sweating. When was this event happening in time? In the past, or the present, or the near future? Did he sense that something was wrong with me? "Hardly. We are not lovers in the usual sense, yet the strongest erotic feelings of my life have all been with him." I felt how little Arthur expected to be understood, how little he expected mercy for the feelings he was admitting. "If you don't mind me being so frank?"

"If we aren't to be frank, then what is the point?" Clara managed to look casual about it to a degree; yet I sense now, as I hadn't before, the slight catch of her breath. I could sense her sensuous interest in hearing more. I knew it because Arthur could read these cues, where I could not. He could tell she liked the romantic—or maybe even the *sexual*—idea of he and I. "Have you ever had that type of feeling for other boys? Boys other than Henry?"

Arthur shook his head. How my heart ached with love for him that he didn't shake his head adamantly or say goodness no! Or any such indicator that he was proud of being attracted to girls. He denied a more general attraction to our sex simply, as if it meant nothing to him one way or the other. "No, not like this. I remember appreciating the physiques of other boys at school but not the way I look at Henry. I've never been in love with a boy other than Henry, so who knows? I'm attracted to girls. I'm just not in love with a girl. I'm in love with Henry."

Clara put her hand on his arm kindly when she noticed he appeared agitated by the conversation. "It's all right, I don't judge you, Arthur. Love is love; no one with a heart could say otherwise. I will say, as your friend, it is one thing to feel this way, but if you…well…if you do indeed decide to act… It would behoove you to be sure you aren't being more poetic than practical, if you catch my meaning? You're not envisaging Henry's a sexless faerie creature under his clothes, are you? Because I imagine it would be very hurtful to him if you have idealised—"

Arthur held up his hand and gently brought her speech to an end. "Oh, don't worry, I already know it will work," he repeated again, reaching for his cigarette case. "When you don't act on something but feel it so deeply, you find other ways to read a person's body. Everything from how Henry cooks to how well he handles fire and creates warmth, and of course, how he writes and plays music tells me everything." I could feel his churning nerves as if they writhed in my own skin. "See," he said, his voice calmed by the tobacco, as he meditatively exhaled the first breath. "I may not have made love to him…" He smoked again, as though building up the courage via the head-rush to say to Clara what he truly felt and make eye contact at the same time.

"But you can be someone's lover without having done so. I have *known* Henry as I doubt anyone else will again. I've paid so much attention to all the little tells... I know his body, its generosity and capacity for fierce surrender, its hunger, and its bravery, from doing everything with him since we were children. I know exactly how he would make love from being near him while we ran, climbed, swam, cooked, built warmth, played music, wrestled, and read poetry together. And I can tell you without the shadow of a doubt: our bodies would work together...we *will* work together..."

Clara shook her head in slight bewilderment. "It sometimes seems you worship him more than love him. No human being is perfect, my friend."

Arthur shrugged. "I cannot answer for it. Beyond to say that, to me, he is like getting a suit delivered from the tailor that fits in every spot and requires no adjustments. So, when I fantasise about him, he's not a sexless faerie, or whatever, under his clothes. No. Besides, I've seen him naked plenty of times."

"What will you do then?" Clara asked grimly, as though his words confirmed for her that there was no other way out of the situation. "Run away with him?"

"If it comes to that, yes."

"Where?"

"Anywhere I have to; whatever it takes to keep him safe."

"Then for the sake of all of us, do it soon, Arthur!" she urged.

"I've packed a bag... I suppose I just imagined it a different way, that we could all be together without needing to run away like we were guilty of something. I know...I know what you're saying, Clara. I should have done something about it long ago. I want his pupils dilated from passion, not from opiates where he's half off his head! I want him to know he's safe, that I've got everything under control, that he can let go of all the anxiety about people coming to kill us, for God's own sake... Is that so much to ask really? I feel he's on high alert when I touch him, and who can blame him? I am too. I'm here to protect him, yet as things stand, if I express myself too freely with him, I could become the cause of his death. I want better for him than some furtive, guilty, criminal act where we are trying to evade detection. I don't want him to have lived his life on the run. Yet, it needs to be somewhere far from man and his false laws, somewhere where only the stars can see and—"

"What if the perfect moment never comes?" Clara asked abruptly. "I'm sorry to be blunt, but sometimes I fear you're a dreamer."

OF THE HEART

I swallowed down hard and tapped the fourth wall with my finger. I'd seen all I needed. Everything went still and quiet. Arthur and Clara were frozen in time, as they always would be for me now, as for everyone who dies young. The echo of voices and laughter canned forever in a time capsule of memory. Every now and again, the fragrance of my beloveds, like pressed flowers in old books, will still drift to me in antique stores, and I start to wonder where the time goes…

It took a little while for the full significance of what I'd just witnessed to take up residence like icy river water in my chest cavity. Even after it did, it took me longer still to put into words this knowledge my devil had shown me. *He was just about to tell you.* The cruel irony of this fate that has been mine and Arthur's has often led me to wonder if since Romeo and Juliet there has been another such sublimely unkind example of bad timing than the death I chose for myself? Worst of all was thinking of what it would feel like for Arthur, to have come so close to acting. To have already begun to tentatively pack a suitcase for leaving and to have been too late… By a couple of days…

There was a big part of me that wanted to stamp my foot and demand to know why my angel-devil had thrust this painful knowledge upon me? But that self-pity came only for a moment, because my mind came next like a thing hungry for life—for a way out. It frantically started scanning through threads and strings of code that represent probabilities and inevitabilities, trying to find a way out of the box I was in, trying to determine by opening that box, if I was indeed alive or dead.

"No!" I muttered to myself as I paced up and down the frozen drawing room, hitting my hands hard against the invisible fourth wall of reality like it was a cage. "No! No. I am not going to let it end like this! I'm just not." What was the point in being smart if I couldn't solve a simple, unsolvable fate equation and make Lazarus rise and walk? What was there to do but summon my devil-faerie-man? Somewhere in the deep wells of memory, I knew how all this worked. I only had to say his name three times. "Robin Goodfellow. Robin Goodfellow. Robin Goodfellow!"

"Yes?" he replied, suddenly appearing sprawled with his hands behind his head and his legs up on the chaise.

"There has to be another way," I whispered, my tone snatching between awe and horror. Drying my eyes with what I imagine must have been a wholly imaginary handkerchief, I came up to Arthur in his pressed flower state. I touched his hair and pressed my forehead to his. To accomplish this, I had to climb onto his lap, straddling him in a way more intimate even than I'd done that night in St David's with Martha's prompting. It was weird to feel myself on the other side of this experience. After all, it was me who was usually frozen still and waiting to be roused. This time, I was the awakener who would have to stir him with my virtuoso performance, as my devil had once brought me to life like a Pygmalion's statue.

Arthur was the one caught underwater now—or beneath layers of ice—his lungs bursting for air. Finally, I was the hero of my own story. It was me who plunged into the depths, swimming deeper into the darkness than I'd ever gone down before... *So dark my faerie eyes can't see in here... I'm swimming blind, but I'll keep going 'till I feel you, even past the point of no return. If you keep on sinking, I will dive so deep into that abyss to get you so we might both be lost.*

"I know you don't think you can hear me," I whispered to him, without disturbing a mote in the dust patterns that were caught and fixed in the air around him. "Most of you can't. But somewhere, deep in there, I know there's a part of you that knows my voice, and I'm talking to past-you and future-you, at the same time. The water's coming in, beloved... It's all coming down. It's time to fight like it's what you were built for. Don't worry. You don't need to have this all under control—*nothing* is."

The *yes* exploded from me with frantic power. My eyes flew open underwater, and my limbs thrashed out against heavy, sodden clothing. My body jerked backwards in a spasm before striking out with failing limbs for the water's surface. Life was fighting in me—life I wanted, air I wanted, and fight? I had it, buckets of it, and passion, I *was* it, eons of it, clawing, fighting, amniotic sack bursting, birthing, dying, black hole devouring, super novaing, yes, yes, yes! *Yes* to life; I said it, fought for life, swam for it. Life, I did it. I did it for him, all the way down to the bone, and again, again...

The light above was still so far away, and my vision was fading. The Well of Oblivion was reaching for me and stripping off my memories. Was this death or birth? My lungs were full of liquid, and the top of my head went *pop* goes the weasel. White light eruption and memory going bye-bye down the plughole of dreams. Eyes pushed inward, compressed to petrified wood. Ears full of cotton wool, gossamering up my nostrils. I never saw the thousand scattered bubbles of liquid light that splattered through the acoustic reverberations as his body joined my body in the water. As his chaos smashed through the neat equation of probability. It was impossible, but he did it anyway. He'd become seven different animals to get here, jumped from a man running, to a dog running, to a bird flying. Just like my angel-devil, who had appeared to me in seven different forms each day as I walked the night streets of Hobart.

In the darkness, near the bottom of the despair pool, my hands were relaxed in the water, limp and reaching out. They seemed languid and surrendered, not tense and trembling as they had been when I last reached for him. Only now, I had gone limp enough to be rescued. A strong, determined hand closed around mine and pulled me towards the surface with all the strength in his body. Pushed and birthed onto the rock like a landed fish, I was hatched out of the jaws of oblivion. I could hear him panting with the effort that it takes to rescue a man from history. With a shiver, I knew that Arthur's full, magical will for my survival had just been pressed back against my will to die. As he lifted and carried me out of the water, I faintly heard him whisper to me, "I've got you."

I frowned as I came fully conscious on the wet rock surface. For a moment, I had forgotten everything. "What are you doing inside my death?"

"We're in Our Game." Hurriedly, he got to his feet and pulled me up as if he meant to lift me. "The Rag and Bone Man came to me; he told me I had to come back and find you!" His breath came as gasps so he could barely speak, yet he scooped me up into his arms, carrying me the way one might carry a woman or child. Arthur had about him a wiry sort of strength at that age, but I hadn't imagined he could lift me with this much ease in everyday reality.

"What are doing?" I struggled down from his arms.

"Hiding you!" he said, tugging on my hand with a jerk as he pulled me into a run. Hadn't I been drowning a minute ago? His glamour was still lacking in internal logic as we ran. *If we were in my glamour, you wouldn't know it wasn't real because you'd suffer the full effects of having nearly drowned with medical precision.*

"From whom?" I shouted at him.

"Death!"

Even though I knew I was inside his dream, I ran with him as if we truly had some chance of outrunning inevitability. I was filled with a sick feeling that, like a cat with a mouse, trying to run just made it more satisfying to Death. It seemed to me that we ran so fast we ran through a patchworked scenery of our lives. We ran through houses great and mean, sassafras forests, along fragments of Hobart's streets, and across Parliament lawn, and through the tunnels under it. Always he had my hand and was dragging me forward; always he was slamming and locking the doors of houses, pubs, and churches behind us. Until I couldn't run anymore. Somewhere in the background, dogs barked in search of us—

dogs like the one the old publican used to change into at night. They knew we were trespassing against the order of things.

"Henry, run!" Arthur yelled at me. "They're coming!"

"Arthur, stop!" I cried, digging in my heels and refusing move. "You have to stop running!" I stopped him before Our Lady's shrine at All Saints, where candles were burning sombrely, and Mary looked with compassion upon the sinners. "I don't want to run anymore. I can't. I have to be who I am!"

"But we have to!" He began to weep. "We have to keep running…"

I smiled gently at him and reached out for his face to dry his tears and comfort him. "No, we don't." There was a strange peace settling into me, and I'm sure when I smiled at him, my face was suffused with light. "God is love. Let's let Love decide; whatever is Her will is what will be done. Not my will, or yours, but Hers." I indicated Our Lady, who for me in this moment was God. "Hers is the third road—the one your story makes in hitting up against my story."

I could tell he searched his mind for some poetic and appropriate answer, but when it didn't come, he dragged me into his arms and kissed me instead. The truth I've discovered after many years of obsessing over the written word is that, sometimes—some rare times—the poetry of life is just better. This time, when our bodies touched, a different kind of wave caught me up. It wasn't the crush wave that holds your face down against the sandy floor until your lungs burn; it was a lifting wave that carries you on its crest with such elegance and precision that you'd not have believed life outside art was capable of it.

There was no question anymore that both of us felt it. His mouth on mine was perfection rewriting itself. It wasn't his perfect, or my perfect; those had both been torn to pieces. This was something new. It was a kind of clean rightness only tasted by those for whom the beloved means more than life itself, and more than that again, more than their idea of perfection… There is nothing greater to surrender for the artist. For this reason, there was an almost unbearable sweetness in the secret touches I had for him that you can never buy with counterfeit coin. Silver is paid for in silver, and gold with gold.

"I don't know if we've got long enough…" he murmured, in between kissing my throat as if he meant to devour me, fumbling to open the buttons on my shirt. His body was pressing mine up against the altar of Our Lady of Mercy, and somehow, I knew in my heart that, if her title was a true one, she couldn't fault us for it. For if there is a God worth believing in, then Their name is Love. "Will there ever long enough?"

OF THE HEART

I smiled with my eyes closed and my cheeks bejewelled in tears of weightless, ageless joy. "Let's find out." I gasped as his hand found its way inside my shirt and, for the first time since childhood, touched my hidden skin.

Epilogue

Ah, Arthur... The fact that you remembered the dream of us didn't change anything in the immediate facts of our situation. You were not able, in your physical form, to cover that space in time to hold my drowning body in your arms or bear me out of the water. Bound still, unlike myself, to the world of space and time, there was no way you could have made it to Strickland Falls to scoop me out of the weir like Taliesin in his sack was pulled from the salmon weir. Yet, when you did so in your dream body, I was spared the death of memory. You pulled me back out of the past tense and into an eternal present tense.

Though you could not drag me through space and time fast enough to outrun Death, you snatched me still from her more fearsome twin, Oblivion. I walked away awake from my own bones, my body taken as it was by the floodwaters. They lie now at the bottom of Sullivan's Cove, bones wreathed in whale and shipwreck bits, old oyster shells and lost dreams. I walked away whistling a sad, reflective tune. Ours was a defeat so utter and bitter that to bring it to ink is to draw out an old black bruise, bone-deep and tracked with internal bleeding. I want to look away. I want to tell some other story. A story where it wasn't my fault, where some other violence or ailment claimed me, and I get to be blameless.

Yet, somewhere in the midst of our defeat, as the flooded rivulet took apart my form with the violence of water and stone, you could hear the long winter coming to an end and the daffodil bulbs giving way. Cracked in the fist of the long frost, my bulb bloods the river with tears, enriched with blood and bone, myself harvested for the fat of the tallow candles, my bones ground down to dust. If you blink, you might miss the first thrill of resurgence. Ours has been a triumph of memory. "For in dreams, there is another life," as Lord Byron said. A life that, even in its sadness, seeds with fertile brine our future springtimes. So, for this reason, we must sit here a while with the pain.

In human life, I was never able to take your body into my arms and kiss away all the beatings, cover all the no's they'd hurt into you with—yes, and more yes... Always yes... To tear away the *thou shalt nots* with my *thou shall!* Oh yes, you shall... In the end, despite the dream (which was neither my dream nor yours, but ours), where I sought with desperate passion to give you solace with my body, I still left you hollow. You and Clara both had ribcages that the wind blew through by the end, nearly as hollow as my own, almost ready for the rag and bone harvest. The problem was that you knew I could come knocking on your door again one of these days, young as the day I left. You never stopped looking for me to come walking up your street with my bone sack, crying: *Bring out your dead! Bring out your living-dead! Bring out the memento mori of you while you were still alive!* Oh my poor, poor, love...

Time passed. Time passes. Even when your heart broke years ago. Time... Time, which is nothing to us faerie people. It weighs heavy on the hearts of the survivors. Like the sin-eaters of old I sit in the shadow of their sorrow, walking beside you during your longest and loneliest nights, saying always: *Beloved, I will carry it with you.* Twenty-years-old forever—you see me that way, yet the eye lies. I ate the bread and salt from your chests, and I sit with it now, ingesting the leaden load. "With you and J. Alfred Prufrock, I grow old, I grow old, I shall wear the bottoms of my trousers rolled."

It was never clear to me what befell my writing. Once I was gone from your world, it was only love that stuck me to time and place. It is only known to me that by the time you accepted that I was gone, it was far too late to be involved with disposing of or preserving my possessions. For I wrote my last fairytale for you well, and you believed my things had to be left where I'd put them for when I came back. Father of course, eventually, did not.

I was there for the grief when you stopped believing you'd find me, and I wept with you. I tried to lay my hand on you in comfort. After a struggle, I thought might end you, and some drinking bouts I was certain would; you began to talk to me for comfort when you were alone. You never stopped doing that throughout your life. I learned that it brought sorrow to your eyes when I reached out to touch you, so I tried to let life be for the living. I was there again when your father died, and everything changed for you.

It was some time later when you peeled Arthur off and, with a look of deep aching nostalgia in your eyes, put him away inside a secret box in your well-ordered collection of curios, folded his skin up for secret use only, straightened your tie, and walked out of your Cedar Court house as Mr. Allport. You could not undo the fact he'd not managed to preserve my writing, but you could preserve other things, collect other things, save things from the ravages of time. I guided your hand when you saved the artwork of a convict man who left us *Gould's Book of*

OF THE HEART

Fish. You used to smile whenever you leafed through its strange marine beauty and pause on the weedy sea dragon.

I wonder what he thinks of the Modernists? I questioned myself as I strolled up the 1920s Elizabeth Street towards your Newbury House, on the day when it was right that I came to get you. I stayed away a lot, you understand? Once a ghost like me hears the sound of children playing from a yard, we only watch you from the other side of the hedge for a while, if we are wise and gentle. I didn't want to bring the chill of death into a house with a rocking cradle in it. Instead, I came whenever I felt your chest ache for the past, or your tears flow. I walked with you as you followed your grown son's coffin after the Scarlet Baron shot him down from the sky, and they brought him home from the Great War in a box.

On the final day, from among the apple trees all in blossom, I stood and watched you for some time without you knowing I was there, on the day I came to get you. I followed you inside your home. Whatever kind of heart a faerie has was swelling inside me, and excitement churned whatever we have where stomachs are. You had invited me to creep up on you, after all, many years ago, and I had never really properly done so until that day when I became Death. It thrilled me to have finally accomplished it on this extra special day.

Watching you, an expression crossed my face, which owed a little to poignancy and a little to desire. God... I'd almost forgotten how fiercely I'd wanted you... No doubt you were closer to seventy than you were to sixty, but if I only had two words to define my time in the world of Man, they would be *you* and *always*, and there's not much more I can say on the matter. Your hair was mostly grey, but earlier, as you stacked the wood you'd been splitting with your axe, I saw that your shoulders were still defiantly strong. Did I really want you indomitable, though, or did I just want you to be mine? Your hands and forearms were more accustomed to working physically than when I'd known you, exposed by your rolled-up sleeves; they proclaimed that, partially grey hair or not, you were still a man in all the ways that matter to a lover. My eyes found no more things to dislike in your older man's body than they had in your younger man's body. The sorrows of your changed face, marked with suffering and with persistent loss, I wanted to kiss and kiss again. Most of all, your mind, filled with decades of knowledge and reading, I wanted to mine in late night conversations that would go on until our tongues turned to dust.

In my imagination, we would go through every part of your collection, which sought to give Hobart the arts culture you'd always wanted for it, to record the things that others might not have understood or valued, and I would ask you to tell me what each piece meant to you. I would ask you what you thought of modernist poetry, electric lightbulbs everywhere, and men flying through the air? Once I heard you say it was our generation who broke the darkness. The profundity of it was lost on all in the room, but I heard you and understood. They probably thought you meant to praise your era. Only I knew that you believed progress had done violence to the night.

Oh beloved, if you could just turn around and see me…

But you didn't turn around ever again.

You sat down and clasped at your chest. Not the way a man with self-concern responds with fear of his mortality, with the kind of irritated resignation of one who cares more about getting their jobs finished, and for whom dying is but an inconvenience to his schedule. I sat by your bedside, invisible; I watched you and listened as your children talked in hushed tones. This was the only time I ever heard you talk about me aloud inside your family home, within the earshot of others. You held my name close to your chest until you sensed you were dying.

"Dad had a sweet little romantic friendship-thing with a boy when he was young, didn't you, Dad?" your daughter Eileen said, sitting on your bed inside your relatively informal Newbury house.

You smiled faintly with your eyes closed, as if it had started to not matter that they were there. Her tone was teasing, maybe even a little trivialising under the circumstances, but you didn't seem to notice or care.

"There's nothing wrong with that," your son Henry defended you. "It was the age of innocence; in truth, I think it would be nicer if male friendship was still like that today."

You shook your head in mild frustration and eventually opened your eyes. A sudden keenness to talk was coming upon you; it was death creeping up your bedspread, that feeling. Your children couldn't see it or feel it yet. Only I felt it with you, walked with you each step of the way towards it. I could tell you weren't hanging back or dawdling. All of a sudden, it didn't matter anymore, what any of them thought of it; you saw with blinding sight. "No… It was more than that," you whispered. Your heart began to pound with the painful excitement of liberation; finally, you could see your way out of the silence-bind, beyond the blocking tumour of the silence-cancer.

You were always an observer of human nature, my dear. So, I know that, along with me, you'd have noticed the faint flinch of discomfort on Henry's face as he realised his father might be about to confess something different to what he'd imagined.

Of the Heart

"Dad!" Eileen exclaimed in disbelief. "You're not trying to tell me you were…"

"Of course he isn't; it was the Victorian Age!"

Eileen patted her father's hand in the way people tend to patronise older people. "Let him talk, Hen!"

"Henry," you managed to whisper.

"Yes?"

You shook your head with a moment of frustration, closing your eyes again with a sudden peace pinkening over you all the way to your fingertips as you clarified; I could see it like a spreading shimmer. "His name was Henry." You blinked a few times, and wetness sanctified your face with gentle tears of release.

Invoked in this manner, I knew I would soon be visible to you. I took a deep breath and slowly released it (because living-dead Schrodinger's cat changelings still need to do that, you know?) and I walked towards you, into view. As I did, I got ready to Be Him for someone. It was daunting, as it always had been, no matter when you're called on to step up and grab someone else's hand when they're reaching out for you. But, you see, I couldn't bear for it to be ungentle… I was part of a legacy of love that I needed to live up to—to become the hand that had been there for me on my day of undoing.

As you perceived it, the pain and tightness passed, and you got back up to your feet. When you glanced up, there was a figure standing in your field of vision. Slowly, the way someone does who knows with every hair on his body— and yet whose brain is too afraid to believe —you looked up at me. Even if I could describe what I saw in your eyes at the moment you recognised me, I'm not sure I would. It's ours. There are some things that can't be explained for a reason. For the extreme edges of joy and agony are so very close to each other.

"Henry?" you whispered, in your new older man's voice.

I smiled. "Hey there," I said, using the new, looser lingo of the era. I lit up a cigarette and began to smoke, mainly because it was what my angel had done when he came for me, and I was still learning. "You ready to blow this place?"

It was exquisitely painful to watch the many-layered ripples of suffering that passed through your eyes as you tried to assimilate my presence. As a human man, I'd have reached out for you and tried to ease the shock with touch. As a faerie, I had a better understanding of timing, tension, and release. Instinctually, I understood that you needed to pass through each part of this process. Only in that way could you unravel Mr. Allport and step back into being Arthur.

"Can it be true?" you whispered in a tone of awe. You blinked several times, like one uncertain of his eyes. "I've waited for you to come home for so many years…" You seemed almost confused, as if a sudden senility had taken hold, and you were no longer certain of your own senses. "Been talking to you for most of them; sometimes, it's hard to tell the difference between imagining you're there, and you being there… They already think I'm a bit cracked."

"I'm real this time." I threw my cigarette away and took a step towards you.

"God, just look at you…" you murmured, reaching out an unsteady hand to cautiously touch my face. You touched me as if you feared I'd turn to dust on first contact. "Just as beautiful as you were on the day I lost you…"

The way his older, deeper voice crackled with wear-and-tear brought human salt to my faerie eyes, and I covered your weathered hand with mine. "As are you."

You looked away from me, looked down, shook your head, refused to meet my eyes. "You don't understand," you muttered. "I've not… I've not lived like we said we would live." Your voice cracked, and tears flowed. They weren't the easy tears of a young man's surface-well; the source of an old man's tears is dredged from fathoms deep and comes up full of grit. Although I had played it well enough, I hadn't truly understood cello until I heard its deep-bellied voice echo in your old man's tears.

Gently, and without haste, I moved into your space by degrees while these harsh sobs wracked you. Finally, I was close enough to whisper into your hair, even though I didn't yet reach out to hold you. I had learned an older man's discipline from walking with you over the years. I had learned to get the tension on the strings—and on the audience—just right before the much-awaited moment when I would lift my bow arm and begin to play.

"Tell me, dearest," I murmured into hair that was partly bleached by time, my voice more of a seductive whisper than a tone of consolation. After all, a true lover of music loves the poignant lower tones of human grief and regret just as much as the higher pitches of driving elation. "For, I can't remember… has your era as of yet translated the work of Jelaluddin Rumi into English?"

"Not that I'm aware of." I enjoyed the touch of irony your voice could carry now, even in conjunction with deep emotion. "Did you come back just to make sure I'm keeping my finger on the literary pulse?" You sighed. "Because I've been remiss of late, though I imagine you'll be much impressed by Yeats… God, Henry…" Here it seemed you would succumb to your emotion, which cracked your throat and hurt its way free from you. "There's barely been a day I didn't betray who we were in some small way…"

I only smiled softly and told you the words you needed. I told Rumi's past-future words into your hair, while touching you with the tenderness and adoration normally only reserved in this undiscerning world for the young and heedless. "Come, come, whoever you are." I stepped back and held my hand out to

OF THE HEART

you. "Wanderer, worshiper, lover of leaving. It doesn't matter," I whispered, still holding your gaze that had seen too much of life, with mine that had seen too little. There was a foreshadowing of rising triumph in my voice because, *this time*, I saw you immediately lift your arm to take the hand I offered you. "Ours is not a caravan of despair! Come!" I urged, pulling you into my space at the moment when your hand clasped mine hard, and whispering the words fiercely into your ear. "Even if you've broken your vows a thousand times. Come, come again!"

**Extract from Rags and Bones:
a Performance Art Piece offered during "The People's Library"
here in Old Hobart Town.**

Words and Vocals: Lee Morgan
Soundscape and Visual Editing: Brett Tait
Original Photography: Rebecca Rose
Text: Referenced from "The Yellow Line" by Justy Phillips

PART III

OF THE HANDS

PART III

OF THE LAWS

THE RECORD-KEEPER'S GRIMOIRE

You work a grimoire when you've been convinced to play a game with the person who wrote it. It is that simple. Whether that person is alive or the ghost of someone from history. This could be as profound as sensing a certain reason to trust them, or because others throughout time have trusted them. Or it could just be an experiment. So, the first rule in Our Game is that you must read the whole grimoire through from beginning to end before attempting any of the Work, so that it can be said that you fully understand the experiment. The thing about the nineteenth century was that experiments of all sorts were very much in vogue. This grimoire—which views itself as an artwork—as well as the instructions within the art itself, adjusts its ear to the tender notes of the romance earlier science occupied in people's minds.

People believed that science was going to change the world, and they weren't wrong... They also believed it would save it. A lot of things that used to lie within the arts became experiments; the only way to make the presence of this power canny is to take the experiment form up in our hands and turn that, too, into a new kind of art. Therefore, this grimoire comes with a list of ingredients, methods, and outcomes. The form will sound exact in parts, but you must interpret it both artistically and creatively. By this, I mean, artistry asks you for velvet, yet the *point* of the velvet is to be found in the sensual experience of velvet. What does the sensory experience of velvet exhibit to your fetch? It is heavy; it is soft and plush against the skin; perhaps it breathes a little but not a lot. For this reason, we may associate it with a sweet, heavy pressure that allows some oxygen, but not as much as you're probably used to. There may be people who can't afford to buy velvet. At this point, they may not yet have decided to put their eggs in their money-earning, sorcerous basket, which is a perfectly respectable decision. They will need to therefore do the following.

Where you do not believe in gathering wealth—or do not have wealth cunning as your current strong suit—consider what sensory experience the velvet is meant to give to the medium, and how could you create this feeling from some other material? Could you do it with a cheaper item and hang weight from it? Until this question can be answered to the satisfaction of your fetch, then truly, the proper velvet must indeed be procured. It is the same with all aspects of ingredients in a grimoire. They may represent a particular power to the spirits, or instead they could be a doorway opener for your fetch; often they are both, as your fetch is also a spirit. You must understand the somatic experience your body—and the body of the spirits—are meant to be having while you use them. If the sensorium of you can be fooled by fakery, then indeed fool it with something cheaper. A candle in a red novena candle can just as easily become a red-light globe.

Ingredients
red glass novena candles
a red velvet interior curtain
a round table where people can sit (optional depending on decisions)
a rocking chair or a stool or cushion where you can rock both forwards and sideways
a pin-struck doll
a clock with a pendulum, or a mesmerist who can hold a pocket watch

Methodology
1. Meeting the Pin-struck Doll Body People
2. Awakening the Hidden Body of the Medium
3. Inviting the Forgotten Ones

1. Meeting the Pin-struck Doll Body People
Take your pin-struck doll. This can be made of any type of material where things can be pushed into it and stay put. It could be clay where the holes are already open for the pins or darts. Or it could be made of a strong material and stuffed. When you make it and when you strike it, keep your mind on something else entirely—something that has nothing to do with other people. Only when it is done can you declare it to be your own body. Meditate on how we are all like St Sebastian; hit many times with arrows. There are pains in parts of our

bodies, aches in others, joyous feelings in others; some of them have a seething range of layered feelings in them.

For the sake of this experiment, each of those feelings is one of your dead ancestors. Begin to consider where in your body you feel the different people to whom you are connected, who have died. Which ones feel like a blocked pathway? Which ones are connected to pleasurable sensations? If you had to give an identity to each feeling in your body, especially the ones that come up out of nowhere, what would they be? Some of them might be Aunt Ethel who you knew as a child and who had arthritis. But most won't. We are looking, after all, for the Forgotten. It's possible that you have semi-forgotten people among your ancestors to whom you are the only one to remember them. In today's English-speaking world, aunts who never had their own children are a prime candidate among the semi-forgotten.

Others are *entirely* forgotten. It can, in fact, be good to give them a completely unreal name, one that stretches their identity in some way. One could be *Archibald Monte Funkistan,* which is probably not his real name, but might give some space to a silent man who in life had to swallow his strangeness and could not speak out. For this experiment, we will take it that the mysterious feelings that arise in your body—the aches, pains, quavers, spasms, flutters—all have a name. They are lodged in your body even if they aren't your blood ancestors. They may have entered you through a story they told you that obsessed you as a child; they might be the suffering of someone you empathised with to the point of fear. They might have entered through having cared for one of your blood kin when they were a child, so much so that they willed their Fat to that child upon their death. There are many ways in which people can get up inside each other. Some of them come from the land we live on—others besides, a kind of haunting.

When you begin to think about the doll as being you, they will start to slowly become you. As we give names and identities to the various pins or darts, we will take them out. If you need to, label them, or keep them in a pattern that resembles a body. You will have storied them as what they are at that moment in your body; no sentimentality is necessary. Name each ache, each pain, just the honest truth about your bodily experience. The pin could even be named after someone who is still alive who nonetheless exists inside your flesh matrix. Make sure that you are honest and impartial in your assessment of your own body. There is no one who is going to see this Work, no one to be impressed or sympathetic towards you because you named your hurts or your pleasures for them. Consider everything—even passing pleasures like eating food and what parts of the body they involve. Who lives within your eating? Who lives within your digesting? Who lives within your menstrual pains? Who suffers in your aching joints? Who is crying out for attention?

Give them easy-to-remember faux names if you need to. Each of these people is someone in your upline who is not fully remembered and still has words to say. When it is time to name your doll, you will need to put something of your body on the doll: maybe saliva, blood, or hair. It will take a little time to think of it as your own body. When you can, begin with the thing on your body that draws your most attention. It might be the greatest pain, or it might be the greatest longing. Don't be too choosy about it; be a bit wild and pick one in a seemingly random way. This will work a lot, like picking cards at "random" does in a divination. Begin by taking up the needle and praying in the name of the person to whom this sensation belongs. Remember that they have been silenced and forgotten, so you may need to listen for them to tell you something or perform an art or music work in their honour. They may want truths told and messages passed on. When I say pray for them, I mean whatever that means to you within your system of belief; think well of them in the presence of the divine.

Imagine them resplendent. This needs to be possible for you, even if you knew them and did not like them in daily life. Visualise them cracking free of their human limitations and stepping into a kind of sainthood or daimon-hood. They are free of their pain, they are heard, they are honoured. When you can do this well, that feeling will enter that part of your body. In some parts— especially in highly charged areas of your body like your genitals and your third eye—this feeling can be rapturous. Work your way through each of these parts of your body until all the blessed shafts of light and blessing have been inserted back into your body filled with radiant possibilities. Remind yourself that it is normal to have the resplendent dead inside our bodies. Perform this whole process first at a waxing moon, again during the full moon (bringing the emotion and exultation to a natural peak during this second attempt), then a third time during the waning while you settle the power in, and a final consolidating time during the dark moon.

By exteriorising your pains in this manner, you have slightly detached your relationship with your own body. This happens in a kind of *both/and* sort of way, in that it is yours, but it is also Other, yet it is also shared. After the four applications of the needles, they must now be stored in a smaller version of the shroud of séance-red, cut from the same cloth. If you can, seat or stand the doll so it is wrapped and covered entirely by the red cloth. You can take the further step of placing it in a wooden, red-lined box and invite others to share this space with you later in the Work. At the moment, this isn't necessary, though. As long as it is kept hidden from the eyes of other humans. The very action of containing what you are working on and not discussing it until it is over is part of what is helping you to gather extra Virtue to your Work. You can take the doll out whenever you wish to work again on particular pins until you feel something shift and change inside yourself.

During this process, you want to remain open and aware of the idea that one spirit will be most active, powerful, and dominant over the others. You may have already known this spirit before you began this Work, or you may not. Make sure that you do this process until you know who this operative spirit is. Giving them an extra offering of some kind—such as pouring water or whiskey, or burning a particular incense for them before the you practice—can help to keep you safe. It is this spirit that you need to build a strong relationship with to keep clear and clean after the Work begins to really develop.

2. Awakening the Hidden Body of the Medium

Now that you have undertaken this process on a smaller version of yourself, you can begin to fashion the red shroud. Ideally, you want to be able to suspend the velvet in a heavy, layered way that hangs down over you, so that your face and body are covered. If this is not possible, you can simply lay the velvet over you in folds. If all goes according to plan, you are able to rock back and forth inside this, and whilst you do, you will feel the fabric touch your face, and your oxygen supply will be slightly diminished.

Here we will learn two different types of rocking motions that will afterwards reveal a third technique:

1. **The Spinning Lady:** This is a back-and-forth, rocking motion that, to my mind, mimics the process of pedalling a spinning wheel, a piano, or moving back and forth on a rocking chair. Each of these images should give you a little something of the ghost of the kindly elder women who watches over you and yours from your upline, sending you her benign feelings. It's best to learn this technique first, because that way, you draw as many of these kinds of foremothers to spin with you as possible. Whilst we will think of her as a singular, kindly old woman, in reality, she becomes a collective ancestor.

2. **The Hangman's Quarry:** This is a side-to-side rocking motion that mimics the motion of a corpse hanging from a noose. To do this, one must still their rocking chair if they are using one. This rocking motion should be practiced second, because that way, you have the aid of the good women of your mother's blood, the ones whose bone marrow went into yours, and whose blood and blood-thread your own veins were filled with at birth. It is this physical nature of the mother—to mother's-mother, to mother's-mother's-mother—that explains why we follow this particular line. What we are after here is the building-up of the substance that would be called "ectoplasm." These women will also protect you, because in a very literal, physical sort of way, you are an expression of their extended body that still blossoms up from the Underworld into this world. The Hangman's Quarry side-to-side rock is about sacrifice, and it will expose you to the powers of the Underworld. During this Work, sometimes less content dead will surface, and you may find yourself having to return to your doll to work with them. Always remember that, if they feel too overwhelming, you can also send them away.

3. **The Crossed Roads:** After you've passed through the forwards path, and then the sideways path, you will need to combine these to bring yourself to the Crossed Roads. This involves a combination of both back-and-forth and side-to-side. To do this, you will need either a clock or a pendulum that swings back-and-forth. A clock is very helpful, because it covers the dual purpose of asserting a back-and-forth motion on the mind, in the manner of a hypnotist's watch. It also serves as a functional *memento mori*, reminding us of the finitude of human existence, and that we will all one day be like the dead. Having a living companion to help you is also efficient, especially if that person has the natural gift of the hypnotist. This skill is often found in those with a confident and persuasive temperament, much like Arthur in Henry's story.

This state is brought out in the medium—a person of a more receptive type—with the following practice. The lights are set to red, and the usual process is passed through, starting with The Spinning Lady. Pass naturally into The Hangman's Quarry, a further assertion that not only will you one day die, but

Of the Hands

by placing yourself here in this state, part of you *already has*. Part of you has already leaped the watery ditch and glimpsed the secrets of the dead. As you do this act, open your mind to the silent parts of history, the forgotten parts—those who were not given voices in the story we call history, especially those who might belong to groups that we may well now feel sympathy towards, such as women, the poor, the indigenous, those of diverse sexuality or gender expression, various races who might have been made enslaved persons, those now classed as neurodiverse, and of course, natural witches and intuitives.

Let this take as long as it needs to. You have no choice really. Because when The Crossroads State descends, you can neither help it nor hurry it. Something will change in the way your body is moving. It will feel like a faintly jagged sensation in your spine at first, then pass into a sense of a crooked wiggle in your spine. You are still moving side-to-side, but the motion has changed; only you would notice. You will feel a shift in your state of being. Whilst this state is difficult to describe, you may find yourself aware of a feeling of being on the edge of a deep hole or a well. This feeling might also extend above you. For The Crossroad State is actually more of a Witch's Footing, as you are standing at a crossroads, but there is also a path above and below you.

When you feel this state open up, you may find it either blissful or disturbing, or a thrilling combination of both. Gently extend your awareness, a bit like reaching out your hand, to your operative spirit. They are the key to the door you are opening, and without them being present, it might not always be safe to engage in this Work. By this stage, you want them to have demonstrated to you that they can answer questions correctly, and that they can bring you information, and clear out unwanted entities that you don't feel comfortable with. Spirits of this sort have been familiars to witches and are also called operative spirits in necromancy. You may wish to go no further than this. If this is the case, take up your pin-struck doll, remove each of the pins one by one, and bless the ancestral dead that live within you, before replacing each shining shaft of light and revelation into the doll.

If you have some prior experience with these arts, you might wish to ask your familiar or operative spirit a simple question, such as: What other spirits are they currently aware of around you? The answers to questions of this sort will give you a sense of what kind of things your spirit will be able to answer for you going forward. You want to ask questions that make it clear how well they perceive others, and what they can tell about those others.

3. Inviting the Forgotten Ones

Here we need to think about the kind of etheric power, Virtue, or richly developed Fat that became known to the Victorians as "bioplasm," and later, "ectoplasm." This word was usually applied to physical-seeming substances that emerged from the bodies of mediums whilst they attempted to allow ghosts of the dead to communicate through their bodies. This makes mediumship a much more physical and visceral art than other forms of necromancy. Whilst the production of ectoplasmic responses might tip a table or even appear to emerge as a slippery mist or mass of some kind, our attitude towards the physical nature of the dead has changed today. People do not usually expect to see ectoplasm, but they might expect some of the side effects of what was once connected with it.

However, there are a great many aspects to the appearance of the dead that benefit from the presence of a strong etheric charge. Changes in the voice of the medium, moving objects, spirits speaking in other languages, and other so-called "proof" of the dead person's presence all require a strong draw on what Western Occultism usually terms the "etheric body of the medium." These forms of proof may still be important to some viewers, even though they might not always matter as much to the witch themselves, who is usually convinced of the veracity of their art, to the extent, perhaps, of identifying with their art. Proving one's Work is usually only necessary when involving other people. So, here we will discuss the good and the bad aspects of involving an audience.

The séance typically involves other people; this was how the medium in the past got paid for their activities. Today, this is less likely to be our motivation in doing this Work to begin with. This all being said, there are still many people in today's world who make an ample living out of selling contact with the dead to the public. Running séances can be another great alternative for the modern witch to reading people's cards. Especially if that contact involves felt touches from the dead, messages that would be hard to fake, and other sensory proof of the truth of visitation. Of course, such a business can be fraught with its own kinds of pressures and emotional content, that must all be considered before exploring this route.

Other advantages involved in inviting others to your parlour can be spoken of. One of them is the free etheric power that these people can contribute. There is a right kind of participant, and often it is these people who are attracted to such events but are unable to get them started themselves. Often, they have the same abilities as a medium but without some of the other characteristics that make someone appropriate for that role. Typically, someone interested in

OF THE HANDS

attending such an event—and pays for the privilege—is what I define as an "intuitive" who is not a practicing witch. They are usually someone who is easily made aroused or even afraid of the supernatural, yet are also deeply curious about it. These people often possess the strongest charge, partially because they are charged in the same way as a witch but don't have the developed control of their faculties. Their presence can be very helpful.

This leads us to the question that we must start with before we begin to put any of this into action. The qualities of an appropriate medium. A perfect medium would be someone a lot like Henry. They would possess an open, imaginative, creative life. The person will do very well if they are already Sighted and sensitive to the energies of the dead. A medium must also have a hidden backbone of steel, something subtle but strong that rises from within their sensitive exterior. This balance between yielding and resilience is a rare enough quality in people, but it can be developed. Most people find one easier than the other. It is important that the potential medium considers themselves as objectively as possible and works to address this balance.

In a séance—which is by its very nature a performance—the medium will be at their peak when working with a team. Three people with a strong natural chemistry is ideal. One will be the medium, someone with a strong tendency towards trance states and a hidden backbone. A mesmerist or hypnotist, a person with a strong personality. Unlike the medium who doesn't like to be watched (as can be seen by the traditional format of hiding the medium behind a curtain or in a cabinet), the mesmerist may like to be watched. There is part of these people that feeds off moments of magical agency and the thrill of control. It's important that, like Arthur, they have a good heart and are dedicated to the safety and success of the medium; otherwise such a power could become too intoxicating.

The third person who keeps records takes Clara's role. This person is a copyist, someone who doesn't hold hands with the participants, nor enters a trance, nor induces one. The copyist is a storyteller; their role is to be utterly truthful in recording how they experienced the situation themselves, and how others reacted to it also. They need to be able to quickly note down all words spoken, down to tones of voice, accents, languages, atmosphere, and to improve on the rough draft later if there comes a chance to speak about the séance with the guests. If further information is gleaned, the record-keeper must note down who provided it. These records cannot be replaced by simply pressing record on a phone or even setting up a video, as there are sensory parts of the experience that will not yield to this form of recording.

For these reasons, the first part of this book was dedicated to the mesmerist, whose swinging hypnotist's watch helped us to open to the bulk of this book, the part that belonged to the medium. This third part, the grimoire, belongs to the record-keeper. Each of these stages has performed a Work inside you, readying you for the creative chaos that is to be found in the act of becoming a visceral witness to the dead and awakening their powers in you. Before you take the final step of including an audience, it is important to experiment thoroughly. This can include or begin with the spirits that already live inside your body. But it can also become far more adventurous than that, including discussions with the beinghood of fictional characters, where you enquire of them how they experience their life and sentience?

When you do decide to include an audience, having a mesmerist can greatly help to prepare the room. A sense of the theatrical is never lost on intuitives, and it is more likely to stir up their etheric substances, as it will cause them to feel things. It is less likely for a seasoned occultist to feel fear in the presence of the dead. So, don't be afraid to help them find their holy-dread in the presence of the partially hidden world of the dead, as the power of fear can be quite delicious to the spirits. Encourage them to think of questions ahead of time, to come with things they want to know. The medium will have practiced this art to the point where they are able to lift off their concern for the thoughts and opinions of the audience as they lower their velvet covering over themselves. It may be necessary for some people to use a helper aid plant or ally to reach this state at first, or maybe in an ongoing capacity. For some mediums, this is just a nip of brandy; for others it can be a flying ointment or a smoked substance. It tends to be preferable, though, if that substance becomes a doorway only used for sacred events.

When the medium decides it is time to draw on the collective etheric power of the audience, they can touch hands with the circle. This is done through everyone placing their hands down on the table with slightly spread fingers and only the little finger touching the little finger of the person next to them. As the little one is the witch-mark finger, this provides a low contact, relatively specific link for the group. The medium can experiment with this ahead of time alongside the mesmerist and the record-keeper. Other roles are also possible during the stage of preparation. For instance, there might be a *seer* as well as a medium; this person might be very good at seeing images but not in bringing through voices. Your seer might also be your copyist. Whatever team you assemble, it is important that you practice around peers before bringing an audience in. This is where the medium will learn how to draw on the collective energy of

OF THE HANDS

the group, how to draw it into their body, and how to expel it, possibly with ectoplasmic results.

In the voice of the record-keeper, I would like to encourage you to use the following pages to record your own records of this Work. This will ground the power of this book by rooting its Fire down into the pages of this book. Describe what you experience with as many senses as you can muster. Tell us about the smell in the air when a spirit rises. Tell us about strange, static sounds. Don't assume anything is unnecessary. If you are part of a team, then this will require some consultation, layering, and artistic cooperation with your fellows. This collaboration is also one where you learn to dance with the spirits that inhabit you and yours. The forgotten have their own stories, their own feelings they need to excrete into the world. It is important that the medium learns how to clear themselves afterwards, as if allowing a great river to flood its banks through their forehead, washing away anything that has got their stuck there— washing it away out to sea.